Ball Nuts

A Mad 1977 Baseball Replay Odyssey

JEFF POLMAN

Grassy Gutter Press
Culver City, CA

Cover photo and design by Jeff Polman
Title page photo of Jim Rice, Unidentified, and the Author, 1978 by John Dillon
Author page photo by Carmen Patti

BEFOREWORDS

It's me again. Back with another fictionalized, full-season Strat-O-Matic baseball replay. This one starts in the recent present, but quickly transports us back to the turf-rampant, funkified ballparks of 1977.

The story was extracted, tightened, and put through the wah-wah pedal from my *Play That Funky Baseball* blog, which ran on the Interweb for a year starting in February of 2010. With that project, I had the good fortune of attracting sixteen talented "absentee managers", baseball writers and bloggers from around the country who provided me with five-man rotations and lefty-righty lineups to conduct my 154-game replay of 1977's best teams with. Knowing there was someone in the "front office" of every club added to the fun, and here they were:

PIRATES: Pat Lackey, of *Where Have You Gone, Andy Van Slyke?*
DODGERS: Larry Granillo, of *Wezen-Ball* and *Baseball Nation*
ASTROS: James Yasko, of *Astros County*
REDS: Amanda Cross, of *Red-Hot Mama*
EXPOS: Jonah Keri, *Grantland,* author of *The Extra Two Percent* and *Up, Up and Away*
PHILLIES: Daniel Rubin, *Philadelphia Inquirer*
CUBS: Scott Simkus, author of *Outsider Baseball*
CARDS: Mike Metzger, of *Stan Musial's Stance*

YANKEES: Joe Sheehan, of *Sports Illustrated*
ROYALS: Rany Jazayerli, of *Grantland* and *Rany on the Royals*
INDIANS: Joe Posnanski, twice-voted Best Sports Columnist in America
RED SOX: Josh Wilker, author of *Cardboard Gods*
TWINS: Howard Sinker, *Minneapolis Star-Tribune*
RANGERS: Ted Leavengood, Washington D.C. baseball author
WHITE SOX: Keith Scherer, contributor to *Baseball Prospectus* and *Hardball Times*
ORIOLES: *The Eutaw Street Hooligans*

(I'd also like to thank Mike Lynch of Seamheads, who invented the Seamus Headley character and penned his introduction when I was on vacation.)

Ball Nuts is a far stranger tale than my well-received first effort in this self-created genre, *1924 and You Are There!,* but no less fun. As with that book, the direction of the plot and character arcs was heavily influenced by the rolls of my tabletop dice, but this time there were far more characters to play with. I've always loved a good challenge, though, and hopefully you will dig how it all came together.

—J.P.,
Culver City, CA

for Carmen

First Things First

So here I was in my Skyline Nomad five-wheeler, just a burp down Route 22 from downtown Squallpocket, Maine, minding my own business with a bottle of Sam summer brew, waiting through the late-night ball scores to see how Jon Lester made out in Anaheim...and someone knocked on my trailer door wicked loud.

Now I've been doing okay since Pam left and took Timmy with her, but I really don't like living alone because you can only watch so much baseball in a day, even with the dish package, and I find myself on the phone with friends more than I'd like to be, and every noise outside gets your hair up. So this knock just about scared my shorts off, and when I opened the door, who was standing there but two guys in dark suits and shades, basically Tommy Lee Jones times two.

"Are you Carlton B. Gip?" asked one of them.

"Uhh...yeah? Except I've gone by C. Buzz Gip since I was nine. Ever since Fisk left us for the White Sox." They nodded at each other and waltzed right in, looked over every inch of the trailer. I asked five times what the hell they were doing and when I finally made them some bad Chock Full of Nuts coffee they sat and told me.

"We represent Timeco Incorporated, a discreet company exploring the power and opportunities of dimensionary travel. We need a committed, volunteer researcher, and our state-of-the-art databases tell us you have an unusual obsession with the year 1977."

"Well, yeah. That was the year Mom and Dad broke up and I went to my first Red Sox game—actually about 38 of them—and I saw them outhomer the Yanks 16-0 one weekend in June, and then Elvis died and then Groucho Marx three days after that and *Star Wars* and *Close Encounters* and the *Saturday Night Fever* album all came out and Son of Sam was doing his murder thing and the Yanks ended up winning the division anyway and Reggie hit those World Series homers and—"

"Good, Mr. Gip. Because we have a special mission for you. One which will earn you the money to pay off your outstanding loan on this trailer."

"What? How the hell did you know about—"

"Your job is to replay the 1977 baseball season with the eight best teams in each league, 154 games per club, the same format they used for sixty years last century, using these Strat-O-Matic cards..." The man lifted two stacks of inky-fresh card packs out of his briefcase and set them on my formica. I'd played that well-known tabletop game before, but not since the week I got thrown out of college.

"...along with these very special items." He took out a small black box, spun a miniature combination dial on the front and lifted out a set of four glowing dice, one with twenty sides.

"These are called 4-D Cubes, a new product we are secretly experimenting with, and they've been programmed to transport you virtually to the 1977 contest of your choice whenever you wish, for a more enriching and reliable experience."

I stared at him, the Sam Adams sloshing through my head. "Are you kidding me? I can actually go back to that amazing year and maybe see my Crunch Bunch win this time? And groove on all those awful uniforms? And not hear the word steroids even once?"

"Yes, Mr. Gip. We expect you to send us reports every Monday, Wednesday and Friday, with occasional Twitter dispatches in between."

"But what about my job? I'm a disc jockey over at WHOA-690, y'know—"

"Employment will be unnecessary. We will also provide your food, and our support team of sixteen crack baseball minds in various parts of the country will issue you the lineups and rotations you'll be using."

"Whoa...Is this an absolute pisser or what? When do I start?"

"Mr. Gip? Take the dice."

OPENING DAY TOMORROW: Expos at Reds (Rogers vs. Seaver) Astros at Cubs (Richard vs. Reuschel) Dodgers at Cards (Hooton vs. Forsch) Pirates at Phillies (Candelaria vs. Carlton)

Red Sox at Orioles (Jenkins vs. Palmer) Yankees at Indians (Guidry vs. Eckersley) Rangers at White Sox (Blyleven vs. Barrios) Twins at Royals (Goltz vs. Leonard)

DR. GROSSINGER'S REPORT: *The subject (Gip, Carlton Bosworth, b. 4/28/72) has shown acute signs of paranoia, melancholia, and schizophrenia over the last few weeks. Today this was replaced with a highly unusual elation, common when a subject creates a new fantasy friend or friends, in this case the "men wearing black" from the obviously fictitious Timeco Incorporated.*

Mr. Gip still firmly believes he is residing in a nearby trailer park, and employed on a part-time basis by WHOA, a radio station that went out of business thirty years ago. These delusions remain harmless, but I will be closely monitoring his "1977 replay" as the days go on to see if his "game results" warrant an increase in medication.

—SHEILA H. GROSSINGER
Chief of Psychiatry
Squallpocket State Hospital

Opening Grippers

April 15, 1977

So I assembled all the cards for Opening Day, picked up the 4-D dice, which felt sort of warm and ticklish in my hand, and threw them on the table. Before I knew it the light inside the trailer began to fade, I started to smell grilled hot dogs, I was drenched in sunshine, and a field of perfectly clean and green Astroturf appeared before me...

Game of the Day

KANSAS CITY—Minnesota's Goltz against Leonard for openers on a weirdly warm spring day, and I can't even count the incredible moments in this one.

First you get Hisle rapping into two DPs in the first four innings, both coming after Carew singles. Then with the game still scoreless in the top of the 8th, Wynegar singles, gets run for by Terrell, Carew walks him to second, Hisle learns from his mistakes and bunts them over—but Adams whiffs and Cubbage pops out.

In the last of the 8th Patek singles, swipes second, gets bunted to third by White and just plain rots there as Poquette and Cowens go out.

In the last of the 9th Cubbage kicks Brett's dribbler into a 2-base error to lead the inning, after which Bostock climbs the wall to rob McRae of a walkoff homer, Porter whiffs and Otis grounds out.

Finally in the bottom of the 10th, Mayberry singles, Wilson pinch-runs and steals second, and Frank White singles him home for the only run of the game. For Leonard, it's nine Ks and one walk in 10 innings of work–but Goltz is just as good.

MIN 000 000 000 0 – 0 7 1
K.C. 000 000 000 1 – 1 6 1
W-Leonard L-Goltz

The Other Openers:

at ORIOLES 1-4-1, RED SOX 0-4-0

In almost a mimeograph copy of the last one, Jim Palmer whiffs eight Bosox in the Memorial Stadium cold. Jenkins is equally brutal but DeCinces tags him for a 7th inning solo shot to decide the thing. Can't believe my boys laid down for this underwear clown.

YANKEES 6-11-0, at INDIANS 5-9-1

The Lake Mistake is filled to capacity, and everything twisted that can happen to the Tribe does. For starters, the first Cleveland batter Ron Pruitt gets hit with a Guidry fastball and goes out with a 10-game injury. Grubb replaces him and goes out later in the game with another injury. And still the Indians almost take the game. Spikes hits a 2-run shot in the 2nd to give them the first lead, but Nettles ties it with a 4th inning blast, and Reggie takes Eckersley way deeper with two aboard in the 5th. Down 6-2 in the 8th, two singles and a walk bring on Tidrow, who gives up a run-scoring single to Bochte. Lowenstein hits for Spikes and misses a 3-run homer by inches. Norris starts the 9th with a double to bring on Lyle, but Sparky gets Kuiper, Fosse and Bell to end the ordeal.

at WHITE SOX 4-6-1, RANGERS 3-8-1
Future Hall of Famer Blyleven has one rough inning, a three-run Chicago 4th, but it's enough to give the Sox a close win and get Comiskey Park singing that annoying Hey Hey Goodbye song.

EXPOS 5-11-0, at REDS 3-8-2 (10 innings)
Runner-up for Game of the Day. Rogers and 'Spos take 3-0 lead with mini-rallies off Tom Terrific. Cincy explodes for three in the 8th on Griffey and Bench doubles and jettison Rogers. Gary Kid Carter bashes 2-run homer in top of the 10th off Sarmiento for the game-winners.

PIRATES 3-7-0, at PHILLIES 0-7-0
The Candy Man cometh: John Candelaria allows zero walks in a CG shutout vs. Carlton. Stennett double, Robinson single produce Buc run in 1st, Gonzalez single, Oliver and Taveras doubles assemble two more in the 7th.

at CUBS 8-11-0, ASTROS 3-11-2
Houston finally wakes up on the late side with a flurry of hits and all three of their runs, but this is a Cubbie onslaught for most of the game. Slim Rick Reuschel puts Ferguson and Cedeno on with a walk and single to start the day, then whiffs Watson, Cruz and Puhl in a row, and four of the next six he faces.

DODGERS 5-12-0, at CARDS 3-9-0
L.A. scratches out 1st inning run on Forsch, Reitz puts Cards ahead with 2-run smash off Hooton and the Dodgers take it from there. The first six Angelenos reach base in the 5th as they score three times. McBride's fro not a factor in the St. Louis loss.

Welcome to the Friendly Confinement

April 16, 1977

I'm damn lucky I got people making food for me. That way I can do all this dice-rolling and reporting and not keel over in the process. The Timeco Incorporated guys even started giving me a special pill every morning that they said would help my virtual transporting to the different ballparks even more. After yesterday's good time I'd be some kind of dipstick not to believe them.

Anyway it was raining cats, dogs and mice here today and I figured that if a giant rogue wave rolled in from Dusker's Bay and swept the trailer park away, I'd probably be sitting in a ballpark far away in my mind and wouldn't even notice. So I took out the dice, shook the hell out of them, threw, and suddenly the bottle of Sam in my free hand lost its neck, turned plastic, and became a frothy cup of Old Style draft...

Game of the Day

WRIGLEY FIELD, CHICAGO—It's a very wiggly matchup of Lemongello against Bonham, and Jose Cruuuuz parks one into the Sheffield bleachers with Ferguson aboard right off the bat. But three Cub singles in the 2nd make it 2-1, and Mitterwald's second RBI in the 4th ties the game.

And then it's a baserunners-in-quicksand fiesta for the next seven innings. Forsch and Sambito relieve a spent Lemongello, but Bonham has plenty of stamina, is getting out of every jam and to keep the sketchy Cub bullpen at bay, Herman Franks keeps him out there until the 12th, when a Metzger single and walk to Sambito bring on Bruce Sutter. But Big Cliff Johnson pinch-hits and raps a single to load the bases, and I can hear Jack Brickhouse yell something guttural in the broadcast booth above me.

Cedeno then smashes a single for two runs, Watson hits a sac fly, Cruz walks and Sutter clearly has nothing. He squirrels out of it, but not before Howe doinks a single for the fourth run of the inning. A Cabell error helps Chicago get one back but the big winning Houston rally, coming mostly against Sutter, could be one of those inspiring ones.

HOU 200 000 000 004 – 6 11 1
CHC 010 100 000 001 – 3 11 1

W-Sambito L-Bonham SV-McLaughlin HR-Cruz GWRBI-Cedeno

DR. GROSSINGER'S REPORT:

Mr. Gip has seemingly stabilized, and spends his every waking moment seated at his little table by the window on the west side of Ward Five, his right hand making a "dice-rolling" motion while his left "keeps score" on a blank legal pad. Other patients on the ward wander over occasionally to see what he's doing,

causing Mr. Gip to bark out a "score," but it's apparent they have only slight interest and then walk away. If anything, Mr. Gip's psychosis is one I have yet to encounter in my studies, and will begin to probe further into his file at the earliest convenience.
—S.H.G.

Strat-O-Madness 101

April 17, 1977

So a lot of you are probably sitting there and thinking, "What the hell is this tabletop game old Buzz Gip is playing, and how does it work?" Actually some of you might not even care, but crap, I'm going to work up a quick tutorial anyway while I'm sitting here outside the trailer park waiting for the Timeco Incorporated shuttle bus to take me to a nearby park for some exercise, because that's the kind of guy I am.

First off, you have a card for every player, and they've all been figured out with some super-extra-special-secret computer formula so that each player performs pretty damn close to the way his non-cardboard one does in real life. It's a very reassuring thing.

For the purpose of this lesson I'll use a couple cards from the '77 Blue Jays and Mariners, two awful teams not in my league because they were undergoing birth pains that year. The hitter is Otto Velez, notorious in my head for lining the single in 1976 with the Yankees that triggered Piniella knocking over Fisk at the plate and the full-scale donnybrook that followed and mashed Bill Lee's shoulder. But I digress. Out on the tabletop hill we have lefty pitcher Tom House, famous for catching Hank Aaron's 715th homer in the bullpen and ending up on the awful Mariners three years later for all the fame that brought him.

Anyway, you take a 6-sided die of one color, two other dice of a different color, and roll the bastards. The one die tells you the column to look at, 1-2-3 meaning batter, or 4-5-6 meaning pitcher. The other two die give you the result inside that column.

Then it all goes hieroglyphic. The hit readings separated by 1-20 numbers require the roll of a fourth, 20-sided die, known in some Strat circles as "the boulder," though for me "the atom bomb" always worked better. The results in capital letters with little Xs after them mean you have to look at the super-advanced fielding chart, which is so huge and detailed that your brains might collapse if I pictured it here. The super-advanced fielding chart takes a little getting used to.

Then there's the cool readings, meaning the fat black diamonds (ballpark/

weather home run chart), the little upside down triangles (ballpark/weather singles chart) upside down horseshoes on the hitter cards (Velez, you don't have any, ya bum ya!) which are the clutch hitting factor, the As, B, and Cs following grounders and flies (runner advancement) and of course, the buffet table of ratings under the batter's name for stealing chances, fielding range, error capacity and throwing arm, and on the pitcher's card for balk, wild pitch, fielding, holding runners and endurance.

Finally, there's the little traps Strat adds to each card designed to do nothing but drive you insane. On the column 1, number 9 reading on the left-side of Velez's card (because he's facing a lefty, a dinky fly out to center is placed smack between walk, hit, and home run chances. That's what you are guaranteed to roll with the bases loaded and two outs in a tie game in the top of the 9th. Which sometimes leads to sudden mutilation of a hitter or pitcher card. In my college years of Strat playing I was known as Buzz the Ripper for committing constant card-murder, most of the time to pitchers, except I did change up the routine after a while to include burning, toilet dunking, smashing a glass coffee table I was playing on to pieces or trying to flatten my atom bomb die with a large hammer.

When people stopped wanting to play with me, I gave up the practice altogether, and now, in the comfort and solitude of my own trailer, an important Strat mission given to me that I can focus on, it's kind of like I can just let what happens happen. Which leads me to...

Game of the Day

COMISKEY PARK, CHICAGO—Down south I go on the el train, get off at 35th and there's the big old white and green beast called Comiskey waiting to take me in. I actually went to the new one in 1996 and have little memory of the place except the seat was twenty dollars, the temperature was 36 in the second week of April but felt like 16, and the A's beat the home team like 10-5 or something in over three frozen hours. So compared to that this is a treat.

The game ain't bad either. Greaseballer Gaylord Perry's on the hill for Texas and Ken Kravec for the Chisox and Eric Soderholm puts the good guys ahead 2-1 with a 3rd inning blast in the bleachers. In the 5th, though, Beniquez singles with one out, Human Rain Delay Hargrove walks, Roberto Alomar's dad Sandy singles in one, a Harrah grounder gets in another, and Willie Horton's double plates a third.

Perry used the wrong hair tonic, though, because Soderholm singles, Gamble doubles and Zisk homers and it's Chicago back on top 5-4. Four 8th inning singles and two more runs finish off Gaylord, and Kravec goes for the

CG. Except Alomar singles, Horton homers, and the dreaded Kurt Bevacqua bats for Claudell Washington with two outs. Dreaded lines out to Bannister though to avoid a fourth lead change and give the South Siders the very close 2-1 series win. Na-na-na-na, etc.

TEX 010 030 002 – 6 11 0
CHI 002 030 02x – 7 13 0
  W-Kravec L-Perry HRS: Horton, Soderholm, Zisk GWRBI-Zisk

Jour la Balle!

April 18, 1977
  I had an uncle who lived way up in northern Vermont and during the late '70s he'd drive up to Montreal in his Volvo 122S pretty often to take in a few strip bars and an Expos game. Once he took me with him (skipping the bar of course) and I never forgot it because after driving on these flat country roads for two hours that may have well been in France, we got to the city and found out that the game had been snowed out. In May.

  So I couldn't wait to whip those 4-Ds across my table this morning, even though Mikey, this really weird neighbor of mine who always smells like grilled onions, was staring at me from his trailer window...

Game of the Day

  MONTREAL, QUEBEC—It's April so it's butt cold and here's all these fashionable dudes on St. Catherine Street walking around in leather jackets that aren't even zipped. The green line Metro station at Place-des-Arts is packed with Expos fans in their nutty red white and blue striped hats, and at every station it gets even more stuffed, because Opening Day at Stade Olympique is always in the 45,000-plus range. The next day's game will be lucky to draw 10,000, and you'll understand why soon.

  The Metro rolls into Pie-IX station and we all get off, walk up a grey, endless ramp to the surface and stadium entrance that's more like approaching an airplane gate than a ballpark. I'm too young to have gone to Jarry Park when the Expos were born in '69, but I have to think the franchise might have never left Montreal if they'd just keep that charming little field and added on to it, because Olympic Stadium is the sorriest place to watch a ballgame I've ever been in.

  For starters, it's not a totally covered stadium, so there's this weird dim light pervading everything, and when the ball is hit on the ground you constantly lose the thing in the Astroturf. The seats make this ungodly spring-release clattering sound that echoes all around the place whenever people stand at the same time. The Expos' mascot is Youppi, a giant fuzzy orange eggplant with eyes who always manages to distract you at a critical moment. My uncle said the only thing that made the place bearable for him was the fabulous Canadian beer and the fact he could climb to a usually empty upper deck section and smoke a joint without being bothered. But that was then.

And this is now: the winless Phillies are here for the opener, and they rough up Jackie Brown for three hits and two runs in the 1st. Randy Lerch says watch me barf that right up, and there go hits by Dawson, Carter and Perez in the last of the 1st and it's 2-2. Throwing any lefty against these 'Spos is begging for punishment, and when it's Lerch he just about locks himself to the rack and throws away the key. A Carter double and Valentine single in the 3rd makes it 3-2. A Cromartie triple and Speier single makes it 4-2. Shockingly, the Phils get sort of mad and re-tie the game in the 5th on a Lerch walk, Maddox triple and Bowa sac fly.

Danny Ozark wises up and yanks Lerch for Ron Reed, who then tosses five no-hit innings. Naturally, the Phillie offense goes into another coma. Their 3-6 spots of Hebner, Schmidt, Luzinski and Johnstone go a robust 2-for-24 on the day, and with Garber now in to throw over five innings of 2-hit shutout relief, the contest slogs deep into extras. A leadoff double from Bowa in the 13th gets Philly nowhere, and finally with two Expos out in the last of the 15th, Andre the Hawk Dawson smokes a line-drive homer into the clattering left field seats to give Youppi orange spasms and thrill the local spectateurs.

PHL 200 020 000 000 000 – 4 10 0
MTL 201 100 000 000 001 – 5 11 0
W-Atkinson L-Garber HR & GWRBI-Dawson

Double-Duty Randolph

April 19, 1977

Mikey's watching me all the time now. I know it. He's jealous because he's home all day every day just like me, but he doesn't have an all-important mission like replaying a baseball season to keep him busy. I don't even know what he does to pass the time. I'm going to have to keep my trailer door locked now because I don't want him barging in here with that onion breath of his and ripping off my 4-D dice...

Game of the Day

NEW YORK—Catfish almost hurled a masterpiece for the Yanks' home opener yesterday, and even though I'd rather have three wisdom teeth pulled than walk into the House That George Renovated, I gotta go where the grooviest action is.

So it's Rudy May against Mike Torrez, and this game, a lot like yesterday's, seems to be played in a 1968 time bubble because the pitching is downright brutal. The Birds tweet out a run in the 4th on a Bumbry walk, Maddox single (filling in for injured Kelly), and a ripped single by Singleton. May is also tough, getting out of a 3rd inning jam when Rivers leads with a double, and another the next inning when Munson triples with one out. The real problem for Baltimore is New York's infield, which turns five double plays in the game, three started by Willie Randolph.

Now in the late 70s I loved the Yankees about as much as I loved the Manson Family, but I never had a problem with Randolph. Matter of fact I actually dug him. How can you not like a scrappy middle infielder who is always on base and never calls attention to himself? He was the opposite of Reggie-Reggie, a class act and the perfect foreshadowing for Jeter.

Bucky Dent's another story, of course, and when he-who-must-never-be-named-again pops a homer into the left field seats leading off the 8th to tie the game, I just shake my head. Murray singles and DeCinces walks with two out in the 9th, but Torrez whiffs Lee May and we end up in extras.

With a man aboard and two outs, none other than Wonderful Willie smacks a HR 1-6 chance to deep left. Back goes Bumbry, back, back...I shake the atom bomb over my head, drop the "3" on the table, and this walkoff win goes to the Yanks before a delirious crowd that has no clue what a walkoff is.

BAL 000 100 000 0 – 1 6 0
NYY 000 000 010 2 – 3 10 1

W-Torrez L-May HRS: Dent, Randolph GWRBI-Randolph

DR. GROSSINGER'S REPORT:

Mr. Gip's anxiety level has undoubtedly increased in the last few days. He does a low-decibel "play-by-play" to himself with every fictional game, and it's apparent the difficult doings of his Boston team are beginning to wear on his faculties. There is also evidence of acute rage with each Minnesota contest. To complicate the issue, the patient from Bed 14 (Spano, Michael, b. 6/13/74, Philadelphia) has been showing undue interest in Mr. Gip's "replay." I will e-mail a well-know colleague of mine at Johns Hopkins in the next few days for further advice.

—S.H.G.

The Power of Dice Compels You!

April 20, 1977

MINNESOTA HIRES CLUBHOUSE EXORCIST

After dropping both ends of a Sunday doubleheader in ghoulish fashion, Twins owner Calvin Griffith announced the team has acquired the services of Father Augustus Rallycappus, the famous spiritual sports consultant, to cast out an apparent demon possessing the bats, balls, and dice at ancient Metropolitan Stadium. Father Rallycappus was last used during a 1955 season replay to alter an 1-11 start by the Yankees, who went on to post the best record in either league and win the World Series against Brooklyn. "I may not be doing the best job," admitted Twins skipper Gene Mauch, "but there are forces at work here even beyond my freakish control." At 0-7, Minnesota will put the priest to work immediately before they fall too far out of the race, rubbing a rag annointed with holy pine tar on Larry Hisle's bat.

Games of the Day

PITTSBURGH—These two scary hitting squads, playing in nearly identical concrete and plastic soup bowls, have mixed it up four times for the National League pennant (once two years from now), and I don't think they like each other. Game One proves it.

Candelaria might've thrown a shutout on Opening Day, but these aren't the noodle-swinging Phils anymore. Geronimo pokes a homer off him to lead the 2nd, and pitcher Billingham doubles. Morgan then cranks one out for a 3-0 lead, and George Foster gets a fastball square in his back. Triggering Buzz Gip's Trusty Brawl Chart, there goes Foster to the mound to throw punches at the Candy Man! George is heaved out of the game, and the incident gets the Buc bats booming.

With the expected help of a Robinson triple and Oliver double, they take the lead with four runs in the 4th. A Reds sac fly ties it back up but Garner singles in Stargell to chase Billingham and put Pittsburgh back up by one. The Reds are a bunch of hot mamas today, though: Ray Knight, taking over for Banished George, belts a homer in the 7th to tie it up again. Candelaria puts Reds on in almost every inning but keeps escaping jams, and after a Garner walk and Taveras bunt in the 10th off Sarmiento, he singles into right to give himself the win.

CIN 003 010 100 0 – 5 12 0
PIT 000 410 000 1 – 6 13 1

W-Candelaria L-Sarmiento HRS: Geronimo, Morgan, Knight GWRBI-Candelaria

Now I know this is just some wacky tabletop game I'm playing, and the players are made out of thin cardboard, but there's been some very super-naturally weird things going on since the season began and I'm not just talking about at Twins games. I'm talking about George Foster getting tossed from the first game, then destroying a Terry Forster pitch in the 1st inning of the nightcap for a mammoth home run. And after Robinson homers and Pops hits a grand slam off Soto to but the Bucs up 6-3, Foster hitting another 2-run homer to make it 6-5. And after Bench homers on the next pitch to tie the game and bring in Grant Jackson, Foster hits a THIRD home run in the top of the 7th for the game-winner. They're alive, I tell you! Alive!!

CIN 200 013 100 – 7 12 0
PIT 015 000 000 – 6 7 1

W-Soto L-Jackson HRS: Foster-3, Morgan, Bench, Robinson, Stargell GWRBI-Foster

American League through Sunday, April 20

Chicago	6	1	.857	—
Kansas City	5	2	.714	1
New York	4	2	.667	1.5
Cleveland	4	3	.571	2
Boston	3	4	.429	3
Texas	3	4	.429	3
Baltimore	2	4	.333	3.5
Minnesota	0	7	.000	6

National league through Sunday, April 20

Pittsburgh	5	2	.714	—
Montreal	3	2	.600	1
Houston	4	3	.571	1
Cincinnati	3	3	.500	1.5
Los Angeles	3	3	.500	1.5
Chicago	3	3	.500	1.5
St. Louis	3	4	.429	2
Philadelphia	1	5	.167	3.5

For This I Got Out of Bed?

April 22, 1977

DR. GROSSINGER'S REPORT:

Flying down to Johns Hopkins to meet with colleague regarding Mr. Gip's un-fortunate incident last night: assaulted in his sleep and knocked unconscious by bed 14 patient Spano. Mr. Spano was apparently out to rob Mr. Gip of his ficti-tious "4-D dice," and has been transferred up to Chronic and Severe for minor electro-shock therapy. Mr. Gip's injuries are not serious, and he should return to the ward in a few days.

* * *

Nice to meet you folks. I'm Sherman from Bed 11. Sherman Wayman from L.A. if you just have to know. Been a Dodger fan since they were in the Coli-seum and could tell you Wally Moon's birthday for crying out loud. It's April 3rd, and did you hear the one about the horse doctor who wouldn't eat his wife's casserole?

Anyway, that Gip character with the baseball league and the crazy one from Philly got into it in the middle of the night and they shipped them out for a few days, so now the rest of us can get some peace and quiet around here, thank God.

But guess what I find under Gip's bed this morning? Would you believe those meshugginah dice of his? I was going to wait till tonight to throw the things, but to hell with that idea. It's an outrage they put me in here in the first place. I've missed 42,444 box scores since they ruined my life, and need to get to a ball game quick before I plotz.

Okay, I laid out all the cards here under my blanket. Not a lot of room for dice-throwing, but here goes nothing...

Game of the Days

BOSTON—I wouldn't watch Arnie Palmer golf in this weather, and it's hard to sit in the stands without Vinny on somebody's radio nearby, but I'll sur-vive. Pudge Fisk is back in the Red Sox lineup, even though Evans is out for this game, but that means nothing because they got Flanagan all fercockt right out of the gate. Fisk got moved down to the 5th spot with Carbo second because of Evans being out, says the four-eyed kid with the scorebook next to me, and he doubles to start a rally that ties the game 1-1 in the 2nd. Then Boomer Scott takes over with a booming tater in the 3rd and it's 2-1 home guys. Don Aase isn't painting any masterpiece either because Singleton dou-bles and Dave Skaggs singles him in to re-tie the game in the 6th.

But Scott re-taters, this one clearing the net above the fence next to the flagpole, and it's 5-2 Sox. Then it's 5-4 after two singles, a scoring double play and a Singleton homer. Then Tommy Helms (Remember him from the Reds? I once saw Drysdale undress him with inside heaters till he was standing up there in his jockstrap.) pinch-hits with the bases fat and singles in two to make it 7-4. Aase then gives up a triple to DeCinces and two singles and Stanley comes on to bail him out with a DP ball.

So Boston's got this guy Bill "Soup" Campbell as their bullpen big-shot, but so far this year he's been throwing nothing but matzo balls. Well, Bumbry whacks his first pitch for a double down in the corner and Elliot Maddox, filling in for injured Pat Kelly, golfs one into the net with his 9-iron and we're all tied 7-7 and chowderheads on all sides of me are calling Campbell a putz and a schmuck and a shmendrick and other words I can't even spell it's so bad. The game drags into extra innings, McGregor and Campbell wearing their arms out, until Rick Wise is forced to take over in the 14th, and —that's all, folks—grooves a homer ball to DeCinces leading off the 15th. Tippy Martinez gives out a two-out Fisk double but Hobson, who collects whiffs like my wife collected bargain bras down at Bullock's, strikes out to end this tragedy of a debacle.

BAL 100 001 212 000 001 – 8 17 0
BOS 011 003 200 000 000 – 7 15 0

W-T. Martinez L-Wise HRS: Singleton, Maddox, DeCinces, Scott-2 GWRBI-DeCinces

Far Out, Brotha
April 23, 1977

Whassapenin, people? Friendly Fred comin' at ya straight from Bed 6 with the far-out dice rolls today, thanks to Old Sherman fallin asleep with the things in his dusty paw last night. I didn't check into this jive hospital joint because of my swipin' skills, more for what I did with them matchbooks, but when a man's too much of a fool to take care of his stash, how can a righteous cat like myself not snap some of that up?

And it is the day for this, brotha, the day. Because the Yanks and My Man Reggie are hittin' that creaky-ass ballpark with the not-so-friendly-to-my-people reputation up in Boston, and I do believe we are gonna make their skid row of a pitching staff spill down a gutter, because that's what the Bombers do to chumps every time, baby.

My grandpa used to see the Yanks in the early 60s when they won every year, and sat way out in the left-center bleachers at the Stadium above the dead Yankee graveyard where even binoculars didn't do shit, and I been catchin' em in the paper here a good ten years and it killed me that I didn't watch em take the muthafuggin Phils last year, it killed me. ('Scuse the language, brothas, but I just don't like to say the real badass version of that word cause it's offensive to my mama and all the other muthafuggin mamas out there.) So backin up, this dice trip oughta be the absolute shizz, if I can just throw these puppies the right way here...

Game of the Day

BOSTON—Damn! There ain't one brotha IN this place! Guess you can't expect fuggin miracles when the first black man you put on the field is named Pumpsie Green. Looks like chubby little Looie Tiant's whippin it for the Sox, but we got The Catfish, who just about perfect-gamed Baltimore his first time out.

And here's My Man Mickey Rivers, smackin one in the bullpen with one out in the 1st! I do see a bunch of New York college fools here, and they're makin more noise than me, but shit—Bernie Carbo hits the Cat's first pitch outta sight and it's tied 1-1.

It stays like this till the 4th, when Thurman bangs a double off the Green Muthafugga and My Man Reggie bombs his third of the year into the bleachers! 3-1 Yanks! Reg flashes me a peace sign going back in the dugout, I know he does!

Nobody tells me it's Home Run Derby De-lite Night, though. 'Cause here's Butch Whiff-Boy Hobson puttin' one in the net in the 5th to make it 3-2, and after Bureson, Doyle and Carbo all get on base, Fisk sticks his fat butt out there, takes a pitch on it, and the score's tied again.

Then it's that ancient dude with the long name I gave up on trying to pronounce a long time ago. Yazzamatazz or whatever creams a Catfish ball high and deep and over the bullpens for a grand slam, brothas, and I'm just a puddle of big-ass hurt sittin here. 7-3 them now.

But just wait a good god second. My Man Mickey singles, My Almost-Man Munson homers and it's 7-5 in the 6th! Tidrow's taken over on the mountain, but Yazzamatazz takes care of him too with another jive missle into the bleachers, and after a Rice walk and Rick Miller triple that's the final crud right there. Chambliss triples to start the 9th, but Looie smokes Piniella, then My Man Willie Randolph, then gets pinch-hitter Alston on a pop out and ain't that a bitch.

Twenty hits in the game, 13 of them extra base ones. It's Torrez against Paxton tomorrow, and I'm puttin these dice-bones somewhere dark and cold tonight, cause I am countin on some tasty revenge. See you on the flip side!

NYY 100 202 000 – 5 9 0
BOS 100 060 20x – 9 11 0
  W-Tiant L-Hunter HRS: Rivers, Jackson, Munson, Carbo, Hobson, Yaz-2
GWRBI-Yaz

April Madness
April 24, 1977

DR. GROSSINGER'S REPORT:

My colleague at Johns Hopkins had little to offer regarding patient Gip, who returned to the ward this morning with a head bandage, but while poring through his file on the plane I did come across a newspaper clipping from the Globe, dated 6/12/77. "Boy Discovered Living Beneath Ballpark." The short article was water damaged and impossible to read, but I will be researching this further over the weekend.—S.H.G.

Nice to be back in my trailer again. I've had a bad feeling about that Mikey Spano since I moved here, and it was a good thing I hid my dice from him. Of course Sherman and Friendly Fred got ahold of them but doesn't look like any harm was done, and at least they're baseball fans. For today's featured tilt let's two-step down to old Arlington Stadium, deep in the heart...

Game of the Day

ARLINGTON, TX—It's only April but I gotta change my shirt three times in the restroom by the third inning due to the humidity. No wonder they play Sunday games at night down here. Problem is that it's Thursday afternoon and my white boy fro's grown about two inches on all sides.

Arlington Stadium always reminds me of a Roman coliseum with its high-sided pit look. Kind of always expected an iron gate in left center to slide up between innings and a pack of lions to run out and maul Tom Grieve or something. Anyway it's Chris Knapp for the White Sox, recently knocked one game out by K.C., and veteran Doyle Alexander, who I assume is crafty, for the Rangers.

This game is like one of those slow, complicated murder mysteries where you're waiting around for the plot to happen and suddenly your pants get pulled over your head in the last ten minutes. Soderholm does hit a solo shot for Chicago in the 4th, but most of the scoring has to do with walks, and I mean freakin bushels of 'em. Knapp hands out four and Doyle tops that with seven, including three in a row to begin the 6th, which boots him into the showers.

Moret comes on, gets Essian on a force at the plate, but Orta singles in two and it's 5-2 Sox with no signs of life in Rangerland. Claudell Washington misses a 1-16 homer roll while Alan Bannister, the worst fielding regular shortstop in either league, turns another in a series of ridiculous double plays to bail Knapp out of the 7th.

Half the crowd is already sitting in exit traffic when Hargrove doubles with two outs in the last of the 9th. Sundberg walks, and here's Harrah, leading the world in RBIs with 16.

Make that 19. Knapp grooves one and Toby don't miss, driving it into the left field bleachers to tie the game! Mike Marshall is still out there for Texas in the 10th, but when Campaneris boots a grounder to start the inning, Adrian Devine is hailed. He walks Zisk, but then starts a 1-6-3 DP on an Essian dribbler. With a guy on third should he walk Orta on purpose? Naw. Jorge says gracias and blisters one into the gap for a triple. Bannister singles and it's 7-5 Chicago.

So here's Larrin LaGrow to finish off the pesky Rangers. And there's Claudell's line drive going into the bleachers. 7-6. May singles, Campaneris walks. Wills lays down a perfect bunt and up steps yesterday's stud against the Twins, Ken Henderson. Three dingers in that game and two singles in four trips today, and the only reason he's in there at all, gosh darned it, is because Beniquez is out with a minor injury. Hargrove's up next, but you can't put Ken Henderson on to face the Human On-Base Factory, or whatever he was called.

So Henderson hits, drives it into right for a 2-run single, any guns in the stands are fired into the air, and the Sox are Texas toast.

CHX 020 102 000 2 – 7 7 0
TEX 001 100 002 3 – 8 11 2

W-Devine L-LaGrow HRS: Soderholm, Harrah, Washington GWRBI-Henderson

From the File of Dr. Grossinger...

BOY DISCOVERED LIVING BENEATH BALLPARK

A five-year-old boy was placed into custody today by authorities after being discovered sleeping in a dark alcove beneath the third base stands of Fenway Park. The youth, who was unable to give his name, actual residence or reason for being there, had been apparently living on ballpark food scraps and sleeping on flattened cardboard for over two weeks. "I thought the place was haunted," admitted maintenance worker Jose Torres, who heard the boy talking in his sleep last Tuesday night with the Red Sox away on a road trip. Anyone with possible knowledge or information about this boy is being asked to contact Suffolk County Social Services.

May the Forsch Be With You
April 26, 1977

Last night I had this screwed-up dream that the two Tommy Lee Jones clones from Timeco Incorporated were in my trailer taking pictures of me and typing words into their little phones. "C'mon!" I yelled, "I'm replaying your damn '77 as fast I can, what more do you want??"

Anyway, I was happy to wake up and just see Sammy, the park's deaf and dumb maintenance guy, sweeping the asphalt with his big broom outside my window. Sammy's around all the time but never bothers anybody, and even if he WAS curious about what I was doing he couldn't even tell anyone. Which is nice not to have to talk about, because I got two days of games to report here, starting with some Astroturf craziness under the old Gateway Arch...

Games of the Day

ST. LOUIS—I'm no fan of phony grass as you know, but the fans are blazin here and nothing's been sweeter so far than these Astro-Card battles. You got two speedy outfits with major gap power and shaky pitching and it's been nip and tuck and nip again from the get-go. Here it's J.R. Richard's third try for his first win, and he's got a 4-0 lead and a two-hit shutout after five. Tom Underwood's been a Houston punching bag and a Howe triple and Ed Herrmann sac fly knock him out in the 6th down 6-0.

Then the 7th rolls around and J.R. gets tired for no special reason. A Hernandez walk, Simmons single, Scott double and single by Tyson fill-in Mike Phillips gets two runs back. Richard bears down, has an easy 8th, but loses it again in the 9th. McBride leads with a single and Reitz whiffs, but Scott walks and Phillips gets hit. In comes Joe Sambito, and up walks dangerous ringer Roger Freed to pinch hit with the bases juiced.

Freed lofts one out to Cruz in right. Cruz drops the ball, two runs race in, it's 6-4 and the 'Stros are seeing red. Then Brock walks to reload the bases. Templeton rips one back to the mound, which Sambito nabs and fires home to get the sliding Phillips. Two outs. Keith Hernandez now, sporting a card with a minefield of clutch. Keith skies out to right and J.R. finally wins one.

HOU 100 032 000 – 6 12 1
STL 000 000 202 – 4 7 1
  W-Richard L-Underwood SV-Sambito GWRBI-Watson

I stick around for yet another beauty on Saturday. Mark Lemongello starts for Houston and gets out of a crapload of jams, but Phillips knocks one in with a 4th inning single. Bob Forsch, brother of Ken in the opposing bullpen, has his light saber out this time, and has given up just three singles through five. Problem is that the fourth one is by Cedeno leading off the 6th, who rips off second right away and scores on a two-out single by Puhl to tie the game.

Now it's the Jelloman's turn. Mark gives up a Simmons single, then gets the next eleven Cards in a row to bring up Scott with two outs in the 9th. Seems like we're going extras. But Scott pings a single. Phillips does too. And here's that man Freed again. Sambito's available but Lemongello is tough on righties and Rogers bashes both kinds of arms. So here's Jello's windup, here's the pitch...

...and it's high and deep and into the upper deck for a 3-run Clydesdale trot-off! Oddly enough, the season series is now tied 3-3.

HOU 000 001 000 – 1 5 1
STL 000 100 003 -4 10 0
  W-B. Forsch L-Lemongello HR-Freed GWRBI-Freed

Phigeddaboutit
April 28, 1977

Think I'm stupid? Think them high-priced mechanics upstairs are gonna hot wire my head a few times and keep me from going after Gip's dice? Every clown with a clipboard around here thinks Buzz is missing springs in his clock, but not me, oh no. Mikey Spano knows the street, knows the alley, and I'll swear on my dead parole officer's grave if I don't know when someone's got a good thing going. Gip was shaking his head over every damn Phillie game a few weeks ago, and now the sons-of-bitches are winning. I know it. And I'm not stayin cooped up in this goofy room one more night without a trip to the Vet. The stadium, I mean.

So here I go pickin' open this lock with my nail clipper. Dr. G's back from her trip, but she went home already and Sweeper Sammy's across the yard doing his broom thing in the girls wing. Smart guy. Mistake I made last time was trying to get the dice by just knocking Gip out. This time I use the brains they made me with, and find all the stuff I need under the bed, stuffed in his slippers. Back to my room now, lock myself in, and I can forget those lousy onions I've been eating cause I can taste them ballpark peppers and the sausage they're in bed with already.

Whoa, these dice babies are cookin', and he's even got one with twenty sides! How'd they do that? Think I've been in this place too long...

Games of the Day

PHILADELPHIA—A Sunday afternoon game, followed by the only Monday one in the bigs, both against those doofy Expos. We beat 'em yesterday even though Lefty didn't get the win, and now we got Christenson going against Rogers, who's like their only starter who doesn't suck. So why are they scoring two runs in the 1st? Think I'm joking here? Yeah! there's a triple by Johnstone and a single by Boonie and we're at it again. The Bull ties it with a sac fly the next inning, then hits the snot out of one in the 5th with two guys on for another triple and we're up 4-2!

Christenson's been useless, though, and falls apart in the 7th and the Molson-heads get three and take the lead back. YO PHILLIES! LIFT YOUR SKIRTS AND INFLICT SOME PAIN!!

And they do. Schmidt walks and the Bull singles and then Rogers throws one past Carter and Johnstone singles and here's some tool named Kerrigan and Boonie and Sizemore single and Bowa hits a sac fly and we got four runs and the game, mama!

MTL 200 000 300 – 5 11 0
PHL 011 020 04x – 8 11 0
W-Reed L-Rogers SV-Brusstar GWRBI-Boone

Same kickass business on Monday. Johnstone and Hebner go back-to-back off twitchy Twitchell and it's 4-0 when Del Unser bombs a 3-run job off Lonborg to make it close. FOR LIKE TEN SECONDS! We're talkin' five singles, a Hal Dues balk and a Davey Johnson pinch-hit prosciutto that's still going, for six runs! How can this lineup not win the goddamn pennant, I ask youz?

Oh, maybe because we haven't gotten a relief job yet that you don't wanna stick in a dumpster. Garber gives up two singles, a homer and triple in the 8th when the game shoulda been over, then Reed chips in with three singles in the 9th to give every one of us a freakin heart attack.

But it's an eight-team race now, guys and skanks. And that's the skinny.

MTL 000 030 031 - 7 17 0
PHL 010 306 01x – 11 13 0
W-Lonborg L-Twitchell SV-Reed
HRS: Unser, Valentine, Johnstone, Hebner, Johnson GWRBI-Bowa

American League through Monday, April 28

Kansas City	10	3	.727	—
Boston	9	6	.600	2
Baltimore	7	6	.538	3
Chicago	6	6	.500	3.5
Texas	6	7	.462	4
New York	6	7	.462	4
Cleveland	6	9	.400	5
Minnesota	3	9	.333	6.5

National League through Monday, April 28

Los Angeles	8	5	.615	—
Cincinnati	7	6	.538	1
Pittsburgh	7	7	.500	1.5
Montreal	6	6	.500	1.5
Houston	7	8	.467	2
St. Louis	7	8	.467	2
Philadelphia	6	7	.462	2
Chicago	6	7	.462	2

The Redemption Game

April 29, 1977

Checked my scorebook this morning and saw that someone had stolen my dice again and played a whole slew of my games. And I know it was that creep Mikey because the pages had an onion and pepper smell and the guy's handwriting looks like a six-year-old's.

So I went over to complain about it to Doctor Sheila in our first aid trailer. She's nice and listens and always makes me feel calm, and even though she asked me more questions about what I remember from the real 1977 for some strange reason, she did promise to keep Mikey away from my rig no matter what. See, I already got Sherman Wayman and Friendly Fred snoopin' around wondering what I'm doing with these cards and dice, plus there's a rumor now that Crazy Amy Gulliver has been asking about me over on the female side of the park, and she's already been arrested once for stalking minor league ballplayers or something. Can't remember exactly what her story was.

Anyway, I closed all my blinds this morning, pulled my cap down real low over my eyes, threw some Herbie Hancock on the turntable and whipped those 4-Ds across the formica—

—and found myself in a box at Three Rivers on a cool April night...

Game of the Day

PITTSBURGH—This is one of those contests you wish you have witnesses for, meaning ones you know, not just the 15,000 or so Burghers who are only virtually here, if that makes any sense. Never mind—you'll understand what I mean when the game's over.

The "western" clubs have traveled east for the first time, and John Denny and Jerry Reuss hand out the goose eggs through the first five. Then Cobra Parker has to go and drop an easy Keith Hernandez fly for a two-base error in the 6th. Simmons cashes him in right away with a single, and the game's perfect symmetry is out the window.

At least that's what I think. A Reuss single and walks to Fregosi and Oliver load the bases with one out, and guess who's up? The talented Mr. Parker, who rips one into left for a two-base single and the Bucs' first lead.

The Cards can't do much from there, but Heity Cruz works a walk with one out in the 9th. Reitz bounces an easy one out to Phil Garner at second, who's filling in for the hurt Stennett for one last day. We're all thinking double play and end of game but the ball clanks off Scrap Iron's mitt to keep things alive. Don Kessinger cashes that one in with a single right away and we're needlessly tied.

Can I get a witness now? With Mad Hungarian Hrabosky in as the fifth Cards pitcher, Gonzalez greets him with a single in the last of the 9th. Robinson and Ott make out, and up steps guess who? Mr. Garner. So how many times do you see a game where two different guys have key redemption at bats? Well, I've never seen it, not even playing Strat, but Garner rolls a 1-9 automatic blast that's out of the park before it even leaves my table. And if that ain't redeeming symmetry, I don't know what is.

STL 000 001 001 – 2 6 0
PGH 000 002 002 – 4 6 2

W-Reuss L-Hrabosky HR: Garner GWRBI-Garner

Kisses for My Catcher

April 30, 1977

Time to show these silly men why it's worthwhile following baseball. I know they've been calling me Crazy Amy over there but that's because they're just scared of a woman who knows what she wants and will do anything to get it.

My real name's Amy Flora Gulliver, named after my great-grandmother Florence, and her heart was bigger and thicker than mine, that's for sure. Why else would she drown herself in a creek over a ballplayer? Ever hear of Alex Gaston? Well, he was one of the New York Giants' backup catchers in the 1920s, and Florence spent a night with him that must have been more romantic than anything because when he ditched her she just didn't want to live anymore.

Then it was Grandma Esther sending about 3,000 love letters in two years to that California boy Harry Danning, the reserve catcher for the Giants in the mid-30s. See, it always makes sense to fall for the backup backstop, because the starting catcher has too many girls on his plate and just won't make time for you. What's the difference, right? They're still catchers and have those cute pudgy butts you wanna bite a chunk out of when they get behind the plate.

My mom was a Johnny Orsino gal, as you might think. She had every one of his baseball cards from the Giants and later the Orioles with pasted-on kisses on each one and didn't want anything to do with Tom Haller which was too bad because he was a lot better but I understand. The backup thing. Anyway, she died of cancer right before I got put here and I KNOW it was because Johnny wouldn't pick up the phone and talk to her when she called him on the road.

So now it's just me and Mike Sadek. He's like 64 now and I have no clue where he lives, but I know I'll track him down when I find him. He's gotta fall for a hot 40-year-old like me. I tried to tell this to every cop who grabbed me outside his place that night but they wouldn't listen. For God's sake I didn't even have the ladder half up.

I heard Buzz Gip had this weird 1977 replay going from Sweeper Sammy, and I'd be damned if I wasn't going to get in on the act, because Mike's on that Giants team and I was going to meet him once and for all. Why settle for some guy in his 60s when I can have the young version with wavy hair and gunslinger moustache? Wouldn't you do the same thing, girls?

But I'm not going to tell you how I sneaked out of the woman's wing, or seduced Buzz into lending me his dice for a night, because that's private information. Some things are meant to stay under a lady's pillow.

So I put on my brightest red lipstick and sexiest hospital gown, and now I'm shaking these dice babies just for you, Mike Sadek. I'll be right behind your behind in no time...

Game of the Day

MONTREAL—What the hell is THIS place? Everyone's talking French! You mean I can't go to any game I want? And what do you mean the Giants aren't even in this league?? They finished with the same record as Montreal!

They don't want me to find Mike, that's it. They don't WANT me to enjoy himself. They don't WANT me to be happy. And now I have to sit and watch the Astros and Expos and I'm not even...Actually...This smoked meat sandwich is pretty darn good...

Bannister against Stanhouse, who I hear through a translating fan next to me hasn't won a game yet. But this time Parrish and Carter go back-to-back in the 3rd, Vaentine smashes a 3-run job in the 5th, and out goes Floyd B. for the day.

Terry Puhl triples back two of the runs in the 6th, and then Stanhouse has all kinds of grief. Cabell and Roger Metzger walk to start the 6th, pinch-hitter Wilbur Howard doubles, and lefty Schatzeder comes in to pitch. Big Cliff Johnson bats for Ferguson and doubles in two more. A Jose Cruz double two outs later unbelievably ties the game and has everyone swearing in French around me, which sounds kind of cute. Meantime McLaughlin and Ken Forsch start pitching great relief for Houston, maybe because they're right-handed.

In the top of the 8th, Metzger bunts over Howe and Cabell but Crawford and Ed Herrmann can't get anyone home. Top of the 9th, though? Different story. Cedeno leads with a double off Kerrigan. Cruz and Puhl walk with one out, and Art Howe skies one out to right, deep enough to score Cedeno easy, and the Astros take the lead.

Parrish singles to begin the Expo 9th, and here's Carter. I knew girls who thought he was dreamy beyond belief, but he always seemed too stuck up for me and besides Barry Foote was six-foot-three and from North Carolina. Anyway, Gary hits into a force, Valentine grounds into a 6-4-3 and the Astros finish off one heroic comeback.

HOU 000 002 401 – 7 10 0
MTL 002 040 000 – 6 11 0

W-Forsch L-Kerrigan HRS: Parrish, Carter, Valentine GWRBI-Howe

The Sweeper

April 30, 1977

The name's Seamus Headley. I'm the maintenance man around here, which is just a fancy term for janitor. Most people in this place call me "Sammy," which makes enough sense, I suppose. A few of the patients call me "dummy," and I'd like to smack them upside their crazy-ass heads but then I'd blow my cover.

I'm supposed to be acting deaf and dumb, and if I hauled off on one of these nutcakes, everyone would know I'm not who I'm pretending to be. But for now, I've got 'em all bamboozled, especially the docs, who nodded their approval when I grabbed a broom on my first day here and started aimlessly sweeping the place up like that big dumb Indian in that movie that came out 35 or so years ago about all the kooks in the kookhouse and that cold-as-ice bitch nurse that the guy from *Easy Rider* almost choked the life out of. It's funny; I can't remember the name of a picture that came out in 1975, but I can remember one from '69. In fact, I don't remember much after '69.

Anyway, I've been sweeping ever since I got here, but I've also been observing. You see, I'm actually an undercover agent working for the Coalition of Men in Black or C.O.M.B. for short. C.O.M.B. sent me here to keep an eye on that lunatic Gip and make sure he's doing what he's told. I'm also supposed to be keeping him out of trouble, what with all these wackos running around trying to steal his shiny dice.

Yep, after the beating he took from Philly Mikey that night, Timeco contracted out C.O.M.B., who put me on the case. I just need to get close enough to keep track of his dice rolls so I can report my findings and make sure everything's on the up and up. It shouldn't be a problem, though; I'll just toss some dirt on the floor by his little table while he's not looking, then wait until he starts throwing the cubes before I mosey on over and start sweeping. He won't even bat an eye; he thinks I'm as crazy as the rest of these loons, and dumb to boot. I just hope nobody tosses a no-no or something or I won't be able to contain myself. Now, if you'll excuse me, one of these yo-yos just yakked all over my spotless floor and I gotta go clean it up. Damn, sometimes I really hate this job—

Wait a second. What's this? Some kind of spiral notebook here sticking out of Gip's mattress. Let's see if I can grab it without waking the sucker up...

Holy Hannah's Ghost. They're his scoresheets! Might be a good idea to keep these for future reference...

And They're Outta Here!

May 1, 1977

DR. GROSSINGER'S REPORT CONCERNING TODAY'S BAFFLING INCIDENT ON WARD 3:
Our initial background information regarding Patient Gip has been errone-

ous; that much is certain. Feeling it was time to comfort Mr. Gip on the matter, I summoned him to my office.

When I first suggested we had evidence he had been abandoned at Boston's Fenway Park in the early months of 1977, most likely by his blood father, he pretended not to hear me.

Yet when I produced the newspaper clipping about the abandoned boy, he went into a highly disturbed state, calling me an "idiot quack" and demanding to know how I ever got this "trailer park nurse job."

It was time to reiterate what he has found impossible to fathom. "I am not a nurse, Mr. Gip," I began, " but a chief of psychiatry. And this is not the Sea Breeze Trailer Park, but Squallpocket State Hospital, and you have been a patient here since 1993." He stared at me in wide-eyed horror, though something seemed to percolate in his brain.

It was at that moment, however, that a loud commotion was heard out in the ward. Through the glass of my office, a handful of patients could be seen fighting over something at Mr. Gip's bed. "My dice!" he yelled, and rushed out to join the fray. I got on the phone, called for orderlies. Hurried after Mr. Gip into the ward. He reached his bed, got his hands on whatever imaginary object(s) they were fighting over—

—and there was a sudden blinding flash. I staggered, rubbed my eyes. Looked again.

Every one of the fighting patients had disappeared.

"Damn it!" yelled Seamus Headley, our allegedly deaf and dumb ward sweeper who had also just burst into the room. I looked at him in shock.

"Yeah, yeah, I know. Show's over, doc. I can talk and sing and everything. But now we got a bigger problem."

"You know about this? Where did they go??"

He extracted some kind of radio transmitter from a tiny compartment atop his broom. "Headley here," he spoke into it, "We have Condition X. Gip plus five."

I shook him violently. "What's happening??"

"What's happening is we lost 'em. Gip, Mikey Spano, Sherman Wayman, Friendly Fred, Crazy Amy, even Lester, this schizo farmboy of yours from the midwest I've been eyeing since yesterday. They all just got themselves stuck back in 1977."

Back to the Future Past

May 2, 1977

I'm flat on my back on a cold, concrete surface when my eyes open. Rain sprinkles hit my face. The hum of distant traffic tells me I'm in a city. I sit up, look around.

I seem to be at the top of a long, wide flight of steps, but all of us are here, "waking up" at the same time. Mikey and Sherman and Fred and Crazy Amy—even this chirpy-faced kid in his twenties wearing a flannel shirt I've never seen before. The 4-D dice are lying right there next to me so I grab and stuff them in my pants pocket.

"Yo Gip!' yells Friendly Fred, "What did you do to us, bro?" I didn't do anything except try and keep them from stealing my dice. but maybe they fell out of all of our hands at the same time or something. All I know is that something very weird and wrong has just happened. Only one person at a time is supposed to go back to '77, and straight to a ball park. Where the hell are we?

The direction we're facing is too foggy to see anything, but when we turn, we're looking up at tall sandstone-colored columns, like you'd see in front of a national monument. "We better not be in D.C," yells Crazy Amy, "The Senators weren't even there anymore and my Giants already got screwed out of a spot."

"Let your fushlooginah Giants go already," says Sherman, pulling off his glasses to rub a cataract, "inferior organization."

"Compared to who, old man? Your dorky Dodgers?" Sherman turns red and I start to get between them, but at that moment two yellow buses pull up at the foot of the steps and a flood of high school kids pour out. The boys have long or bushy hair and wear gaudy, tight-fitting clothes, while most of the girls have exploding shags and wear either platform shoes or hip-huggers. They bound up the steps toward us, screaming and hooting, reach the top, turn and raise both of their fists in signature victory poses.

"We're on the Rocky steps!" shouts Mikey, jumping up for joy and striking the same pose, "We're in freakin' Philly!"

"Right on," says Fred, "but explain to me what we are not doin' at the ball park?"

"Maybe I can shed light," says the chirpy-faced newcomer, who suddenly stands there holding the sports page of a local paper. "I found this on that bench over there. We are clearly in 1977."

I grab it from him, stare at the lead sports story: CRUZ BLAST SINKS CARLTON, PHILS, 2-1. "That's impossible," I say.

"What's impossible?" asks Sherman.

"I reported that game yesterday, but it was played with the dice. It didn't really happen, right? Wait a sec..." I quickly find the standings. Yup, only eight listed teams in each league.

"Something just fell out of your pants," says Crazy Amy, "your back pocket, I mean." I look down, pick up a miniature version of the spiral score book I left behind. The words MAY TO OCTOBER GAMES stamped on the front. "Um, guys? I have a funny feeling we have to follow the rest of the season or we're never getting back."

"Good!" says Mikey, "who the hell wants to go back to that nuthouse? Besides, the Phils can actually get in the Series this time and WIN it!"

Fred isn't pleased. "Better not let my man Reggie hear that or he will whup your ass—"

And the fighting starts all over again. I break it up with a loud whistle. "Cool it, people! We all got stuck here together, remember? Together! Now my guess is we ended up in Philly because tonight's game..." I glance in the paper. "Lemongello against Christenson...is going to be something else."

"Leomongello only pitched four years, you know," says the chirpy boy out of nowhere, "His 4.06 career E.R.A. is acceptable, but he did give up 56 home runs and his 1.346 career WHIP is nothing to write home about." We gaze at him, until he says, "I'm Lester, from Lazy Creek. If you ever need a stat, please ask. I created my first fielding efficiency database when I was seven."

"Who do you root for, Lester?" asks Crazy Amy, with an icy glare to match.

"The Cards. Or the Cubs. Or the Twins. Or the Royals. Depending on whoever I am that day."

While we continue to stare at him, Mikey says he knows someone that can lend us ten grand or so to get us through the season, as long as we pay it back soon with 40% interest. I don't care. Dr. S. got me thinking all new about myself when she showed me that news clipping, and now I got a few other missions on my mind, along with following the pennant races around the country, of course.

The first is to find the man who abandoned me at Fenway Park.

Game of the Day

PHILADELPHIA—So Lemongello and Christenson both stink up the Vet. It's 2-0 Phils when Watson belts a 3-run bomb in the 3rd. Phils tie it at three but 'Stros get two more in the 4th. Solo homers from Bull Luzinski and Bob Boone tie it 5-5 in the 5th. Christenson homers in the 6th. Doubles by Puhl and Cabell in the 8th tie it 6-6, before a Cruz single off Garber and butchered fly by Luzinski put three on the board for Houston. Sambito's in for the save, but Schmidt walks and Sizemore singles with one out. Mikey's ripping off his shirt next to me, making more noise than the 30,000-plus combined. Boone walks to fill the bases and Maddox rips one to deep left center that drops just over the wall for a game-winning grand slam! In-freaking-credible.

HTN 003 200 013 – 9 12 1
PHL 201 021 004 – 10 13 2

W-Reed L-Sambito HRS: Watson, Luzinski, Boone, Christenson, Maddox GWRBI-Maddox

Dutch Treat
May 3, 1977

Mikey burps in my ear to wake me up, teed off already. "Yo Gip! How come we're not in Philly?"

I seem to remember passing out last night on the floor of some wicked gross apartment off South Street, but as I get to my feet I hear sloshing water and it seems like we're in some kind of boathouse. I step out the door.

Try a Harvard rowing club, on the banks of Boston's Charles River. Lucky for me, because as I was saying, I got business to take care of at Fenway.

"We still got one more at the Vet with the Astros today," Mikey continues, spitting as he talks, "What the Christ!" I remind him that we seem to be appearing wherever the best game is going to be, and that I have no control over any of this.

The rest of the bunch is grumpy for other reasons, so we find a good breakfast in Kenmore Square to put our brains back in order. Crazy Amy is still whining about her "missing" Giants, but when Mikey threatens to take her shopping cash away, she gives in and agrees to root for the Reds and Indians for now. "My dad was a union guy who coughed himself to death when I was 12, so I guess I can relate to people in Ohio. And that sexy Bill Plummer and Ron Pruitt being the state's backup catchers sure doesn't hurt."

The Rangers and Red Sox are playing their rubber game, and after we buy a few bleacher tickets from a guy on Brookline Avenue, I go looking for Jose Torres, the maintenance guy who found me living under the stands back in June that—

Wait a second. It's only May, right? Even if I find him it's still a month away from this abandonment thing happening! I guess I'll have to come back on a later homestand, if we haven't driven each other even more crazy by then. Sherman wants to see the Dodgers play badly, and Friendly Fred has plans for a Yankee Stadium visit. The good thing is that we're just about certain to end up at a good game every day. I mean, when is there not one good baseball game on a given day?

Game of the Day

BOSTON—One thing I do a lot back in the trailer par—I mean, the hospital, is keep up with baseball articles, and this young guy out there for Texas, Bert Blyleven, is getting some kind of big push for the Hall of Fame up in the future present. He's had nothing but rotten luck so far in '77, though, with an 0-3 record in spite of a decent 3.60 ERA. He's got his killer kurve going today, though, as he only gives up a Rice double through four innings.

And Toby Harrah is at it again, bashing two solo homers off Reggie Cleveland to give him ten for the year, tops in the bigs. It's 4-zip Texans when Carbo gets ahold of one of them curves and drops it right in front of us in the bleachers to slice the lead in half.

But Bert bears down and the Boston offense dies all over again. The crowd around us may as well be at a wake, afraid of dropping another game behind the nuclear Royals. "Can't beat no Dutchman today, bro," says Friendly Fred for what must be the fifth time, and I've even stopped reacting. What the hell is so damn special about this game?

But I know something's coming, and sure enough, Evans leads off the Boston 9th with a walk. Lynn does the same thing. Hobson drops down a bunt which Harrah can't field in time and beats it out for a hit! Blyleven's out of gas and Len Barker comes on, but Burleson rips a single to make it 4-3. Tommy Helms, who went to second when Scott batted for Doyle before, works another walk and we're tied!

Roger Moret comes on to face Carbo. The fans give Roger a nice hand, remembering his work for the '75 pennant winners, but seconds later they want blood. Carbo whiffs. Here's Fisk, though, needing only a fly ball. Moret throws—

—and the ball squibs off Sundberg's mitt, rolls behind him! Here comes Hobson with the game-winner and we've shut Fred up for the rest of the night!

Bert? Sorry, future Hall of Fame Dutchman, but you're 0-4.

TEX 012 010 000 – 4 12 0
BOS 000 020 003 – 5 8 1

W-Cleveland L-Blyleven HRS: Harrah-2, Horton, Carbo

Dodger Visit is the Pitts

May 4, 1977

This time we wake up freezing our butts off on top of some mountain. Except it isn't a mountain at all, but some big-ass hill overlooking what I'm pretty sure is the skyline of Pittsburgh. Well, why not? The first place Dodgers are in town for a two-game series, just a half game in front of the Bucs. No matter how bad the game is, it'll still be the biggest one of the day.

Mikey isn't thrilled, of course, even when I tell him we're at least in his home state. "You kiddin' me??" he blusters, "Pollutionopolis here is too far west to even think about, and the middle of the state might as well be Alabama." Crazy Amy laughs, and I notice she's been staring at him a lot and asking him what position he played in Little League. It's a good thing, because it helps me get away from Mikey for a while and spend the Sunday afternoon with Sherman. He's been wicked excited over L.A.'s great start, and as we take this wacky vertical railroad car down to the bottom, he even ropes Fred into a friendly discussion about how Smith is a better Reggie than Jackson.

Three Rivers Stadium is still there, in all its circular concrete glory, and a pretty healthy crowd is showing up. I check my score pad as we cross a parking lot, though, and see that we're scheduled for both games, meaning we'll actually be in a town overnight. "Wherever we stay needs to have wi-fi," announces Lester, causing the rest of us to just stop and look at him. "Oh. My mistake. I just thought, it being the beginning of May, it might be nice to compile some statistics. I checked the local newspaper and they don't even have OPS in the box scores yet, let alone DARF or PECORP." I want to ask him what those mean, but we only have a half hour before the game starts.

Games of the Days

PITTSBURGH—Two tough lefties are on the hill, Tommy John and Jerry Reuss. The crowd groans and Sherman cheers when Reuss appears to have nothing in the 1st. After Russell doubles, Better Reggie doubles him home. Cey walks, Garvey rips a single into center but Al Oliver nails Smith at the plate when Duffy Dyer blocks the plate like a champ. Baker then singles in Cey, and it's 2-0 Dodgers out of the gate.

Cobra Parker, as hot as Smith lately, bams a double off the wall to start the Pittsburgh 4th, and Robinson singles him in. After a flyout, Oliver picks out a sloppy John curve and golfs it high over the fence in right! 3-2 Bucs and the place is a bigger nuthouse than ours.

Buc fielding gets shaky at this point. A Robinson boot at first after a lead single by that man Smith in the 5th produces loaded bases with one out, but Reuss gets Burke to ground into an inning-ending DP. Then Fernando Gonzalez, playing left vs. southpaws, drops an easy fly hit by John in the 6th for a two-base error. A Russell single gets the man to third, and a passed ball by Dyer gets him in to tie the game.

Sherman yelps with glee, buys Isaly's ice cream bars for everyone, and we move into the even tenser late innings. Stennett plasters a triple off the wall between Baker and Burke to start the 8th, but is tagged in a rundown after Garner hits one right back to John. Parker singles Garner to third, but Tommy whiffs Robinson and gets Gonzalez on a 4-3 grounder and that's that.

It's a treat to see skinny Kent Tekulve out there tossing his famous submarine worm-killers in relief. And the right-handed Dodger lineup can't touch him, going three and two-thirds innings without a hit.

Bottom of the 10th now, John still in there. Stennett grounds out to Garvey and here's Scrap Iron Garner, who's done nothing but hit big homers so far. Guess what, folks? High and deep to left it goes, Baker's back to the fence looking up, the Bucs are in first and Sherman weeps!

L.A. 200 001 000 0 – 3 8 1
PIT 000 300 000 1 – 4 11 2
W-Tekulve L-John HRS: Oliver, Garner GWRBI-Garner

Mikey tries to talk us into looking for a disco later, but has no clue which neighborhood to look in and gives up calling directory assistance when he sees five people waiting to use one of those old-fashioned pay phones outside the park. So we end up in a slummy pair of hotel rooms, wander aimlessly around downtown for most of Monday and make it back to Three Rivers for the Rau vs. Kison finale.

This time L.A. barely shows up. Kison doesn't allow a hit until a Lopes leadoff single in the 6th, and the Pirates have been busy doing everything right. Parker takes a Lopes homer away with a wall-leap in the 1st. Stennett doubles home two after a huge two-base error by suddenly not-as-good Reggie in the 2nd. Oh yeah, and Scrap Iron Garner belts another homer with Stennett aboard in the 5th.

Up 4-1, Kison tires in the 7th and the the Dodgers load the bases with two outs. But Grant Jackson comes on, gets Russell to ground out, and tosses a scoreless 8th. When Mota bats for Monday to start the 9th, Goose Gossage is called in, and Friendly Fred jumps up and goes bonkers. "My Man Goose!!" he yells from our grandstand spot, nearly loud enough for Gossage to hear, "You're on the Yanks next year, bro!!"

I grab his shirt and pull him down. "Quiet, dummy! He ain't supposed to know that yet! You trying to screw up history?"

"Why the hell not?" says Mikey, and I stare at him, because it occurs to me right then, as Mota whiffs, Baker walks, and Oates raps into the 3-6-3 DP that ends the game and puts the Bucs a game and a half up, that we actually CAN change some history here. Not just baseball's, either. All sorts of things...

L.A. 000 001 000 – 1 4 1
PIT 020 020 00x – 4 5 1
W-Kison L-Rau SV-Gossage HR-Garner GWRBI-Stennett

American League through Monday, May 5

Kansas City	16	4	.800	—
Baltimore	12	9	.571	4.5
Boston	12	10	.545	5
Texas	10	11	.476	6.5
Chicago	9	10	.474	6.5
New York	8	12	.400	8
Minnesota	7	12	.368	8.5
Cleveland	8	14	.364	9

National League through Monday, May 5

Pittsburgh	14	7	.667	—
Los Angeles	12	8	.600	1.5
Cincinnati	10	10	.500	3.5
Philadelphia	10	10	.500	3.5
Houston	10	12	.455	4.5
Chicago	9	11	.450	4.5
Montreal	8	11	.421	5
St. Louis	9	13	.409	5.5

The Baltimore Minimalists

May 6, 1977

DR. GROSSINGER'S REPORT:

I was forced to meet with Seamus Headley last night in a nondescript parking lot adjacent to a nondescript warehouse in the old industrial section of North Squallpocket. As yet, no one else at the hospital is aware that our six patients have mysteriously disappeared, thinking they either escaped out an unlocked window, or are off receiving shock treatments in a far chamber of the facility.

Mr. Headley is as mystified as I am about this incident, but seems to believe that a defect in one of these "4-D dice" apparently caused all the patients to experience the same "backward time surge" when they were thrown en masse. "Cheap-ass Timeco Incorporated clowns have all their stuff made in Taiwan," he explained, "What can I say?"

I told him emphatically it is his responsibility to contact or arrange a meeting with me at Timeco Incorporated to find a way to retrieve my subjects from 1977, and he promised to comply. Two weeks ago I placed no value on Mr. Gip's

purported delusions about these dice and the existence of this secret organiza-
tion Mr. Headley is apparently working for, but it is hard to reject evidence seen
with one's eyes. As long as it is my job to watch over the patients here, I will not
abandon them to an uncertain fate in a shallow and unstable age.
—S.H.G.

Game of the Day

BALTIMORE—So I'm perched in the upper rafters here with a bunch of crabcakes, and I'm not talking food. Sherman is still bummed from seeing his Dodgers lose twice, Mikey's pissed because he woke up in Baltimore without the nudie dancer he went to sleep with in Pittsburgh, Crazy Amy thinks Rick Dempsey's the least sexiest backup catcher around and he's starting tonight with Dave Skaggs out, and Fred just wants nothing to do with the state of Maryland because his dad was arrested here once.

So I share a row with good old Lester and his program scorecard, which he's turned into a number-filled coloring book with a handful of special markers. Kravec's going for Chicago against Jim Palmer, and Lester does make the quiet game a lot more interesting. He points out, for instance, that the Orioles have weaker hitting numbers than any other team, but are in second place because they've managed to score high on his Run Efficiency Per Out Margin Ability Number (REPOMAN). In other words, they get hits when they count.

But for a long time in this one, Palmer doesn't seem like he's getting anything. He's got the Chisox hitless through five, but Bannister leads the 6th with a line single, Spencer walks, and Ralph Garr sizzles a triple down the right field line for two runs. The Birds just have three singles and three walks through six, but a Dauer triple and Dempsey run-scoring grounder (dedicated to you, Amy!) cut it to 2-1.

On the scoreboard, the Royals and Red Sox are having a smashfest in Boston, and Baltimore really needs this game. Meaning it's time for classic Earl Weaver ball. Maddox walks to start the 8th, Singleton does the same an out later, then Doug DeCinces launches a fly deep to left. Garr runs back and it drops over the wall for a 3-run homer—on one hit. Dal Canton relieves Kravec, but Chicago is shellshocked. Palmer teases them by giving Soderholm a lead double in the 9th, then sticks Gamble, Zisk, and Essian in his jockey shorts and that's that.

"Where the hell are we waking up tomorrow?" asks Mikey as we exit the stadium, obviously tired of the weird routine. "What's the matter?" I say, "Don't you like surprises?" He just about shoves me up against a brick wall. "Surprises are for two-year-olds and weenies," he says. "I like to know what

I'm gonna eat, and drink, what people are gonna say to me, and what air I'm supposed to breathe. Now we better be headin' back to a Phillies game soon, or I just might get mad."

"Like I said yesterday, Mikey...we lost the dice." He frowns, belches out an onion cloud and lets go of me, and I feel four little lumps burning a hole in my back pocket.

CHI 000 002 000 – 2 3 0
BAL 000 000 13x – 4 5 1
W-Palmer L-Kravec HR: DeCinces GWRBI-DeCinces

Lost in Wahooland

May 7, 1977

I could've seen this one coming. On our crazy '77 road trip we haven't been ending up anywhere we thought we would, so Cleveland seems like the perfect icing on the cake—er, lake.

From the moment we appear on these frigid benches in Edgewater Park and Mikey sees Lake Erie and yells out, "Jersey shore!" the day is just plain weird. We find a neighborhood called Slavic Village and have a fat-tastic late breakfast at this corner market/cafe with old ladies making pierogies in the back room. Then we have one argument after another with Mikey because he wants to either go to the Rock 'n' Roll Hall of Fame (which doesn't open for another 18 years) or see the Raspberries play at the Agora Ballroom, even though the band broke up two years ago.

It takes at least an hour to convince everyone that there's an actual good game going on at Municipal Stadium against the Rangers later, and at least Crazy Amy is stoked about that because it involves one of her two adopted Ohio teams. The problem is the butt-cold spring weather we're about to experience in that giant drafty ballpark cavern, so we spend at least two more hours digging in thrift stores for sweaters and jackets to pile on.

It doesn't help. There's about 15,000 people on hand for the game, but because they're scattered all over the place and the place seats about four times that many, it still looks like Wembley Stadium with a bunch of crows inside. Mikey and Friendly Fred decide to tour the park instead of watch the action, and they drift off in the 1st inning and we never see them again. I'm stuck with Sherman and scoring-mad Lester and Crazy Amy in the upper deck over home plate, the perfect spot for howling winds to blow off the lake and cut through us like razors through jello.

"We r-r-really n-need to find D-d-dodger S-s-stadium soon!" says Sherman, trying to drink a paper cup of coffee with mittens and spilling half of it. As for Amy, she didn't even want to walk in the park when she saw the "politically sickening" Chief Wahoo sign outside, but changed her mind when I told her maybe cute Fred Kendall would catch for the Indians, even though I have no idea what Jason's dad looks like.

Game of the Day

The Rangers and Indians are packed near the bottom of the American League along with Chicago, the Twins, and the Yanks, and with K.C. having trouble in Boston again tonight, both of these clubs have a chance to pick up a huge game in the loss column. So Kurt Bevacqua, filling in for injured Horton in the Texas cleanup hole, bombs one over the fence in left after a Harrah single in the 1st, and the stadium gets so quiet you can hear the ball knocking and clanging off the empty seats out there.

But after Jim Norris takes Nelson Briles out to start the Tribe 1st, we begin to hear something else. BUM-bum-bum-bum-BUM-bum-bum-bum-BUM-bum-bum-bum. It's the bass drum of John Adams, the guy who started pounding the thing in the center field bleachers in 1973, meaning he's only in his fourth year tonight. "Someone should go tell him he may as well bring his whole apartment out there," says Amy in a rare moment of caring about someone, "'cause his team isn't winning the Series anytime soon."

The drumming does get the few fans around us clapping, and it gets the other Indians hitting. Bochte walks, Bell doubles, Thornton singles, Grubb hits a sac fly, and it's 3-2 for the home boys in a hurry. On the hill for Cleveland is dashing Dennis Eckersley, 0-3 so far, but Amy has no interest in him. "Why's Fosse playing?" she asks, "What do they got against Kendall?" Three singles and a Bochte walk make it 4-2, before a horrible Larvell Blanks error in the 3rd scores Bump Wills to make it 4-3.

Eckersley makes a bad throw himself on a dribbler to start a Texas rally in the 4th that ties it up, and the Dashing One is as erratic as ever. "WHERE'S KENDALL, GODDAMNIT??" yells Amy, and Sherman and Lester pick up and move a whole half-empty section away from her. I walk over to join them, and when I turn back, the woman has also disappeared. I wonder how I'm ever going to find everyone after the game, but the good about us being here is that I could probably stand, yell each of their names and they'd hear me.

The drum starts up again for the Indian 5th, and Bochte answers by slamming one over the boards down in right. Briles whiffs Bell and Thornton, but three straight singles and two walks make it 7-4 and bring Lindblad in from the Texas pen. Eckersley gets the first two guys in the 6th, then does his Briles act, giving up a Beniquez single, Hargrove double and walks to Wills and Harrah and it's 7-5.

A Campaneris boot adds another Tribe run in the 8th and Sherman just shakes his head. "Bunch of schmendricks we got here," he says, "All of 'em!" Still, they leave Eck in for the 9th, even after Toby Harrah leads off by smashing homer no. 12 off him. Washington singles with one out, but Sundberg whiffs, Dave May skies out, and Eckersley has his first win.

The second the game ends, though, we see a commotion down by the Cleveland dugout, where Crazy Amy is trying to climb over the box seat rail, yelling "Kendall! Where are you, Kendall??" and security guards drag her off. Mikey and Friendly Fred track us down in the parking lot, their ears ringing from sitting too close to the drum man, and we're able to pry Amy out of a security guard house after listening to them lecture her.

"Aw, what the hell," she says, "Plummer's a better catch anyway. And at least the Indians won."

"Correct, and they're in front of the Yankees now," pipes in Lester. "By .08 percentage points." And that is the perfect capper to this wicked crackpot day.

TEX 201 101 001 – 6 8 1

CLE 310 030 01x – 8 13 3

W-Eckersley L-Briles HRS: Bevqcqua, Harrah, Norris, Bochte GWRBI-Bochte

LaGrowing Pains

May 8-9, 1977

"Baltimore? How the hell can we be back in Baltimore??"

It's Mikey's big mouth again, and this time I shove him against a brick wall. "These are my 4-D dice, Mikey, and if I say the best games the next two days are gonna be White Sox ones, first in Birdville and then in Chicago, then that's where the hell we're gonna be. So shut your Philly hole and enjoy yourself."

"Right on!" says Friendly Fred.

"Kick his ass, Gipper!" says Crazy Amy.

"The chances of two straight White Sox games—and three out of four, I should add—are less than ten percent," adds Lester, "and because I'm a big fan of theirs, you should let me report the action."

I tell him I thought he was a Cubs, Cards, Royals and Twins fan, and he gives me a very creepy look. "Oh no, I've always been a White Sox fan...Carlton." I turn away and see we're two blocks from Memorial Stadium.

"Good, Lester. Then knock yourself out."

Game of the First Day

BALTIMORE—Grimsley hits Downing in the head with the first pitch of the game and knocks our catcher out for two weeks. I do not like Grimsley. But my boys respond as they should, as Lemon singles, Soderholm homers, and after a shabby two-out error by DeCinces, doubles by Nordhagen and Bannister increase our lead to 5-0.

With two singles, two walks and an Orta double in the 3rd, it's 8-1. Wilbur Wood is putting Orioles aboard left and right, but their Baserunner Efficiency Index is not helping them, because they can't break through. Ha ha ha.

But then the 6th inning happens, and I don't feel good about it. No, not at all. A single, then a walk, then a Soderholm error, then another single finish off Wood and bring in Dal Canton. Lefty Billy Smith bats for Mora and walks in a run. For goodness sake. A Murray single on a 1-2 roll, then walks to Dempsey and Dauer close the advantage to 8-6!

Grimsley makes it to the 8th before Tippy Martinez tries to stop a rally and just can't. Ha ha. Singles by Johnson, Garr, and Nordhagen make it 10-6. La-Grow relieves Dal Canton but Kelly greets him with a 350.25-foot homer. It is 10-7.

LaGrow starts the last of the 9th, as wobbly as any reliever around. I have the stats around here some...oh, never mind. May pinch-hits a walk with one out. Maddox and DeCinces walk to fill the bases. I do not like this. And there's a Singleton double for two runs! Smith up again, and a wild pitch ties the score! Mora walks, Kelly whiffs, and here's Eddie Murray. He places a single in right and I have no words left in my pocket. Chicago has tossed an 8-1 6th inning lead in the trash, walking 14 Birds in the process, and completely deserves my wrath.

CHI 503 000 020 – 10 13 1
BAL 010 005 014 – 11 11 1
W-T. Martinez L-LaGrow HRS: Soderholm, Kelly GWRBI-Murray

Game of the Second Day

CHICAGO—Yes, it's good to be home again in old dark green Comiskey. My traveling friends seem a little tired, so I hope this game against my first place Royals is a quick one.

If anything, I now understand why Kansas City is leading the American league pack. C. Buzz Gip calls it "the Thang," but I opt for the more descriptive and reliable Derivative of Undulating Coefficiency Habitual Effect, or DOUCHE. Orta is thrown out at the plate on a 1-15 (75%) DOUCHE chance in the 1st to set the game's early tone. A Cowens sacrifice fly in the 3rd puts them up on Barrios, but this is by far ace Dennis Leonard's weakest outing for the Royals, and Zisk ties the game with a solo belt in the 4th.

It stays 1-1 till the 8th, when Orta doubles with two outs, Soderholm singles and Chicago's in the lead 2-1. True to form, though, K.C. fights back instantly. McRae leads the 9th with a triple on a 1-8 (40%) DOUCHE roll. Lefty Hamilton is called to face lefty Porter, and gets him on a liner. LaGrow, fresh off his nervous breakdown in the last game, enters to face Otis but Amos skies another sac fly to tie this one up.

The Royals bullpen is overused, and Littell is forced to come on for extra innings, while LaGrow does the same for Chicago. But real crazy stuff occurs as a result. While LaGrow shocks even me by throwing six and two-thirds of hitless relief, Littell allows eleven baserunners in his first five innings but the White Sox fail to score again and again and I HATE THEM for that. Oscar Gamble and his goofy clown hair goes 0-for-7 on the day in the cleanup hole, whiffing four times despite a clear platoon advantage over the K.C. righties.

It takes a Zisk single, wild pitch, and winning single from Jim Spencer to finally give the Sox the big win in the 15th, but all of us are virtually asleep by then. Littell and LaGrow are gone for days, meaning the next few late innings between these clubs should be some kind of hootenanny.

K.C. 001 000 001 000 000 – 2 5 0
CHI 000 100 010 000 001 – 3 14 1
W-LaGrow L-Littell HR-Zisk GWRBI-Spencer

Notes on the Nice Rivalry

May 10, 1977

ST. LOUIS—Lester reporting again, with Buzz Gip and the others somewhere in the stands. Seeing that two out of my five and maybe six favorite teams are starting a series today, I figured I might take the time to offer up a little numerology about my Cubs and my Cards.

They've been calling this one of the great baseball rivalries for some time, but from what I've seen, it isn't much more than two neighbors complaining about each other's barbeque smoke. The Red Sox and Yanks, the Giants and Dodgers, now those are flat-out death matches, with tidal waves of history to drown themselves in. But Cubs and Cards? Heck, Cincinnati and Pittsburgh are closer cities distance-wise than those two, and they even met for the league championship four times, so how come that isn't a big rivalry?

Thank god I have my PDBR with me. The Pocket Digital Baseball Reference can access historical facts in seconds, and here's a few to munch on:

—Through 2009, the Cards have won 1,038 meetings, the Cubs 1,082, but they're separated by a mere 53 runs, 9,291-9,238 in favor of St. Louis.

—When the Cards finished first and the Cubs seven and a half behind in 2009, it was only the fourth time the two teams finished 1 and 2 in the standings, and the first time since 1945.

Still not a lot of evidence supporting any kind of heated rivalry. But then I find the series results from 1903-1913, the first eleven years the Cubs were actually called the Cubs. It is astonishing:

'03-Cubs win series 16-4 '04-Cubs win series 15-7 '05-Cubs win series 17-5 '06-Cubs win series 15-6 '07-Cubs win series 16-6 '08-Cubs win series 19-3 '09-Cubs win series 15-7 '10-Cubs win series 15-7 '11-Cubs win series 16-6 '12-Cubs win series 15-7 '13-Cubs win series 16-6

That's a 175-64 record for the Cubs against the Cards, a .732 winning percentage over eleven years. My hunch could be wrong, but do you think this may have made these players and fans a little testy with each other?

Oh darn. The Cards take the field in front of me, John Denny stalking to the mound, and I'm not really sure who to root for yet...

Game of the Day

The Cards have been a speedy and scrappy bunch, usually done in by their pitching, but lucky for them my punchless Cubs are on hand to make it easier.

Oh, is that all we are? Speedy and scrappy? How about the homers Simmons and McBride have been hitting, and the eight triples already by Templeton?

You get a single, stolen base and run-scoring single for a 1-0 lead in the 1st, so zip it, Mr. Scrappy. A Buckner double and Biitner single tie it in the 4th, and Krukow is getting out of one jam after another—

And we take the lead again in the 6th on a single, ground out, balk, and another single...which I guess you can call scrappy, but hell, I'll take it!

Yeah? Take this. Mitterwald singles in the 7th, pinch-hitter Joe Wallis doubles, and when lefty Buddy Schultz comes on—

He's been confused...

He's been awful! Morales pinch-hits a single and we're tied again. And here's Willie Hernandez...

He's as bad as Schultz, you know. What's the matter, afraid to use Sutter?

Can't overuse him. It wouldn't be fair—

What do you know about fair?

I said zip it. And here's Buckner with a leadoff single in the 8th. Murcer steps in and bombs one! Deep to right...

NOOO!!!

And it's gone! Sorry Buddy, and hit the showers please.

4-2 , last of the 9th. Sutter's in but his forkball ain't dirty enough. Freed pinch-hits a single and Brock gets hit, knocked out for eight games! Why I oughta...

Screw you! Hernandez tripped Buckner when he crossed the first base bag in the last inning, and he's out for a week himself!

Templeton singles! It's 4-3, Cards on first and third–

Like we're scared? Sit back and watch Mr. Sutter as he WHIFFS Hernandez...WHIFFS Simmons...and WHIFFS Cruz for the BALLGAME!!

Oh...Buzz is here. Guess we have to go. Ha ha. That was exciting.

CHI 000 100 120 – 4 11 1

STL 100 001 001 – 3 10 0

W-Hernandez L-Schultz SV-Sutter HR: Murcer GWRBI: Murcer

The Mother of All Sundays

May 11, 1977

DR. GROSSINGER'S REPORT:

Seamus Headley finally confirmed a meeting for us at Timeco Incorporated next Wednesday morning, which I'm pleased about because it has become nearly impossible to keep the fact we have six missing patients a secret. Lester's mother appeared today to pay her son a visit, as she always does on Mother's Day, coming all the way from New Mexico, and was rightfully distressed when I informed her that Lester was off on a "special outing" to Washington, D.C. with the others. She announced she would check into a local hotel until he returned, and there was little I could say to dissuade her.

After she left, I drank my coffee and sat at my computer to think about my own mother. She was a methodical, emotionally distant individual, but there are still times when I drive by Bunny's Bakery here in town, and smell fresh walnut bread coming out of the oven and think of her regardless. —S.H.G.

Game of the Day

LOS ANGELES— "So? What's your mother doing today, Buzz?"

I really don't want to go into any mother stuff with Sherman, and the fact I hardly remember her makes it easy. If Sherman still has a mother she's gotta be around 110 by now, but it's pretty obvious he still thinks about her a lot because during the game here at Dodger Stadium he has nice things to say about every mom he sees in the stands. Unless he's just horny.

Anyway, we finally woke up in a place with warm weather, and the rest of the gang can't be happier. Amy's in the top deck somewhere, getting a sun bath in her new groovy yellow shades she bought in the parking lot and probably dreaming about Johnny Oates. Fred and Mikey are out in the bleachers giving Dusty Baker the business for no special reason and I have to remind them not to yell anything about him becoming a manager someday soon. And Lester? Three rows below us, staring at the Cubs-Cards updates on the scoreboard and arguing with himselves.

Famous head case Joaquin Andujar is on the hill for the visiting Astros, and he's anything but one of those today. A Lopes double, Garvey single and Cey sac fly make it 1-0 Dodgers in the 1st, but for the next nine innings the Dodgers get nothing but three hits by Lee Lacy, who's filling in for injured Reggie Smith. But Tommy John is just as awesome, and holds a 4-hit shutout going into the top of the 9th. Cabell and Ferguson go out, and it's up to Art Howe.

Howe walks. Gardner hits for Sambito and singles him to third. Jose Cruz takes his licks, and rips a single into right to tie the game! Charlie Hough comes on, but Cedeno bounces out to end the inning.

Ken Forsch takes over for Houston, and gets L.A. 1-2-3 to send it into extras. Sherman's ulcer acts up. With one out in the top of the 10th, Bob Watson doubles, and weak-hitting Roger Metzger steps up. Metz took over at short on a double switch with Cliff Johnson earlier, and smokes a Hough knuckler down the line for another double and 2-1 lead! Sherman's ulcer explodes.

The more amazing news is that the Pirates lost their first game in Montreal, have fallen behind in the second one, meaning whoever wins this could pick up a game and a half. All Forsch has to do is get the bottom of the Dodger lineup.

But he hits Yeager to start the inning. Glenn Burke runs, Many Mota pinch-hits a walk, and Forsch is in wicked trouble. Lopes blows a bunt try and pops out, but Russell singles up the middle to tie it again! Garvey walks, loading the bases, and Bo McLaughlin is hailed to replace Foolish Forsch. The infield comes in, but Ron Cey raps into a 6-2-3 double play to take it to the 11th.

"I'm done," says Sherman, "Spent. Do me a favor and cremate me now before they screw up another rally." McLaughlin and someone named Stan Wall go another two innings, and Bo whiffs the first two guys in the last of the 12th.

Then Russell doubles, and here's Garvey. And there goes one of the best two-out clutch hitters in the league walking to first on an intentional walk. Much better idea to pitch to the Penguin, who is more prone to walk or whiff than—

—hit the waddle-off 3-run shot into the bleachers that he now hits. "Happy Penguin's Day!" yells Sherman, and hugs me like a grandpa.

HOU 000 000 001 100 – 2 10 0
L. A. 100 000 000 103 – 5 9 0
W-Wall L-McLaughlin HR: Cey GWRBI-Cey

American League through Sunday, May 11

Kansas City	18	9	.667	—
Baltimore	18	10	.643	0.5
Boston	16	12	.571	2.5
Texas	14	14	.500	4.5
Chicago	12	14	.462	5.5
Minnesota	10	16	.385	7.5
New York	10	16	.385	7.5
Cleveland	11	18	.379	8

National League through Sunday, May 11

Pittsburgh	19	9	.679	—
Los Angeles	15	10	.600	2.5
Cincinnati	14	11	.560	3.5
Philadelphia	13	13	.500	5
St. Louis	13	15	.464	6
Montreal	11	15	.423	7
Houston	11	17	.393	8
Chicago	10	16	.385	8

A Tale of Two Karmas

May 12, 1977

LOS ANGELES—Yeah, we're still out here for tonight's second straight Dodger Stadium Game of the Day, and Mikey is one happy hoagie because his Phillies are involved, but as far as I'm concerned it's been two days too many in L.A. I got a wicked smog headache, and I'm sick of eating pita sandwiches with sprouts sticking out of the pitas. Crazy Amy's idea of fun is dragging us up a canyon road to see the house where Charlie Manson's creeps killed Sharon Tate and her friends. Worst of all, it sucks to see the ocean and not smell salt in the air.

So I figure it's as good a time as any to talk about the weirdness surrounding the Orioles and Yankees so far. I've watched a lot of ball and played quite a bit of Strat in my time and I've never seen such a perfect mirror image of good and bad luck going on. It's like an evil dice professor is offering them up as examples A and B in some kind of wacked karma science project.

Baltimore is hitting .248 as a team and New York .247. The Yanks have hit 11 more homers, one more double and 7 more triples, Munson with six himself. But they've scored 16 less runs than the Birds and are dead last in the league. The fact they've walked 14 less times and been hit by seven less pitches may have something to do with it, and Baltimore's pitching is a full run better, but there's more to it than even that.

When the Orioles put men on base, they are usually scoring them with key hits from a huge number of players. When the Yankees get on, the runners fester and rot. Mickey Rivers, despite his .326 card, is at .255 with just three RBIs. Piniella is hitting .243. Nettles has nine homers and an .896 OPS but is batting .205. And as you'll see below in their first game in Minnesota, when their fielders make errors—Nettles has four already—they pay the price almost every time.

What this also means, from my dice rolling experience, is that the winds of karma are gonna be a-changing. There is no way New York is this bad, and even though Baltimore's pitching may hold up, I don't expect the Orioles' incredible collection of clutchalia to last forever. Then again...that's why we roll the dice.

Game of the Day

I almost toss Mikey out of the upper deck during this one. He's screaming so loud and so often it drowns out most of the Vin Scully broadcasts blaring out of fans' transistor radios around us. Are ya ready, folks? Hang on:

Luzinski is plunked in the 1st, knocked out for two games. Reggie Smith announces return from injury by belting Christenson pitch into the bleachers in the 1st. Boone and Christenson doubles in the 2nd tie it at 1-1. Three Phillie singles off Rhoden and a Johnstone grand slam make it 5-1 in 4th. Rhoden isn't finished crapping the bed, though, gives up Maddox triple, Downtown Ollie Brown double, wild pitch and Schmidt double before being ejected from premises. Two singles, two walks and Garvey single bring Dodgers right back at 7-4. Phillies meanwhile drop dead at feet of Mike Garman, Stan Wall, and Charlie Hough.Reed relieves Christenson but when McGraw relieves Reed, Garvey says thanks and smacks 2-run homer to make it 7-6. Garber on for 9th and walks Cey right away. Hebner boots Garvey grounder. Baker walks to load bases with one out. Jerry Grote, only L.A. catcher not ailing, whiffs. Two outs. Vic Davalillo bats for Hough, hits one out to Johnstone to end the game—

—and Jay drops it. Make that a tie game. Sosa takes the Dodger hill, grooves one to Maddox leading off the 10th and it's lined into deep left stands for go-ahead run. Mikey drops shorts, moons Dodger crowd under full moon. Garber walks Cey with two gone, last of the 10th, whiffs Garvey swinging for huge Philly win.

Incredible game, but can we go somewhere else now?

PHL 010 600 000 1 – 8 17 2

L.A. 100 030 201 0 – 7 8 0

W-Garber L-Sosa HRS: Johnstone, Maddox, Smith, Garvey GWRBI-Maddox

Can't Get There From Here
May 14, 1977

Seamus Headley back with ya. It's been a rough couple weeks stalling Doc Sheila on the all-important meeting at Timeco Incorporated which we finally had today, mainly because I had no freaking idea why Gip and his cracker patch vanished from our funny farm in the first place, and wasn't sure how to even bring the subject up with the Big Boys, let alone the tools at C.O.M.B. I told you about the last time. The nice thing is I got to spend some quality hours with Doc Sheila, who in spite of her glasses and starchy outfits has kind of a bottled-up sexy thing going on.

I hadn't been to Timeco myself, and to get there we had to drive her Saab about 100 miles north into the Maine woods to a little general store/gas station/post office called The Gus Stop. Gus must've been tied up in a back room because there were two guys in black suits and shades behind the counter waiting for us, and the next thing we knew we were blindfolded, driven another five miles in the back of a big cushy car, and by the time this elevator went down about ten flights into the ground, we found ourselves in a giant boardroom with only two chairs at our end of a massively long table.

"You are here to discuss the problem with Mr. Gip?" said a spooky, metallic voice through a speaker phone in front of us. So I explained what happened, how the 4-D dice malfunctioned when the group threw them together and now won't let them come back, and then Doc Sheila filled the voice in on the diagnosis of every missing patient, until she was suddenly interrupted.

"You do realize the magnitude of this unfortunate error, don't you?" The doc and I looked at each other. If we didn't realize it, we were sure about to.

"We cannot have Mr Gip and his disturbed cohorts running amok in some past decade. If they alter even one event, it can have drastic consequences for the present. Consequences we can barely fathom. Would you like something like this on your heads for eternity?"

We said not really, and the next step was laid out. Timeco will supply us with a prototype of their new invention, called 5-D Dice, which will enable

Sheila and I to travel to 1977 together and use them to return with the whole group.

Except the dice won't be ready for another month. "In the meantime, pray one of your mental defectives doesn't drool on a wall socket at Bill Gates' house and short out the computer system he's building in his garage—or something like that."

The light on the phone disappeared, and in seconds our blindfolds were back on.

Game of the Day

BLOOMINGTON, MN—Buzz reporting. It's a beautiful spring night in Minnesota, and as we sit in the upper left field deck and look up at winking stars between innings it seems amazing that the Twins are going to move into an ugly dome in five years. Maybe I can find some important people in town before we leave and talk them out of it.

Anyway, the Yanks are here so the park is stuffed, but Dave Goltz has nothing in the 1st inning. Rivers, Munson and Reggie all single, and after Nettles whiffs, Piniella rips a shot into the stands right below us, and it's 4-0 just like that. A Munson RBI single the next inning makes it 5-0 New York, and people grumble in the seats around us, but I know better. The Yanks are in last place for a reason, and they've been making a habit out of losing games like this.

Sure enough, Gullett is as shaky as Guidry has been lately, and five double play grounders are the only things that keep him in the game. Minnesota still attacks over and over like barracudas. Down 5-1 in the 6th with two outs and no one aboard after the third double play, two walks and three singles cut the deficit to 5-3.

Meanwhile the New York offense has dropped into a sewer. After getting out of a mini-jam in the 3rd, Goltz mows them down the next three innings. In the 7th, a Carew walk and Bob Randall single finish off Gullett and bring in the worst reliever in the league but believe it or not the best the Yankees have, Sparky Lyle. Nothing has been going right when this guy appears, so it's a big shock when Bostock grounds out and Hisle whiffs for the first two outs.

Then Ford scratches out a single. A wild pitch ties the game. Borgmann walks. A second wild pitch moves the runners up. A Kusick grounder to Dent ends up in the seats and both runs score. The upper deck shakes as a 4 goes up on the board and the latest Sparky nightmare is over. All that's left is for the Yanks to strand four more runners the last two innings and the Twins have beaten them for the third time in four tries.

I gotta admit I'm not real happy about the Yankees being in last. Yeah, I'm from New England, but how can you not feel sorry for a winning team play-ing this bad, no matter who it is? I mean, not having the Yanks duking it out with us is like a western without a bad guy, or a World War II movie with no one to fight but Mussolini's palace guards.

And I really feel bad for Friendly Fred, who doesn't say a word the entire game, then gets plastered on five bottles of Schell's Bock afterwards so he can just pass out ahead of time and wake somewhere else.

NYY 410 000 000 – 5 10 1
MIN 001 002 40x – 7 11 0
W-Goltz L-Lyle HR: Piniella

Field of Rutabagas

May 15, 1977

Here we are, hiking up from a lower parking lot to the Dodger Stadium gates, and Mikey picks the wrong time to push every one of my buttons.

"Give me a good reason why we're not in St. Louis."

"Because the first place Pirates are here, and none of us want to see your damn Phillies, so shut your hole before I—"

BAM! His fist hits my right cheek, I bounce off a teenage Dodger fan with a big foam finger, tumble onto my back—and the 4-D dice I've had in my back pocket clatter across the warm asphalt.

"Are you kiddin' me?" he yells, "You had those the whole time??" The rest of the group is staring at me too as I sit up, feel my chin for a pulse.

"'Course I did...Why do you think we're still showing up at the best games every damn day—"

"You freakin' doofus!" He raises his foot. I grab the three smaller dice but Mikey's shoe-boot slams down on the 20-sider. The parking lot flashes twice around us, vanishes—

—and we're suddenly lying in warm piles of dirt and roots and green leaves.

Somehow we've ended up in a vast farmer's field, surrounded by acres and rows of rutabaga plants. In the distance a group of migrant workers toil away.

"Nice going, Mikey, you wombat," says Amy.

"I got a mind to set fire to your curly-head ass right here," says Fred.

"Where the heck are we?" asks Lester.

I look around, spot some snow-draped peaks through the hazy evening air. "Still looks like California...Come on."

We trudge across the field toward the workers and what looks like a road. Sherman asks the workers in perfect Spanish what town we're in, we're told something called Poplar, and the next thing you know we're heading down the road with thumbs out, and me checking the 20-sided die with my face still red.

"You chipped off a piece, I can't believe it. Not only are we stuck in '77 now, we can't even get zapped around to the best games."

Mikey says he's sorry even though I know he isn't, but all of our spirits perk when we spot a roadside bar up ahead with about twelve pickup trucks parked out front. A wind-swung sign over the door says LUPE'S LOUNGE.

"Think they got the game on?" I ask.

"Well," says Sherman, "It should be if they have a television. Because the L.A. Rams sure aren't playing."

Turns out we're half wrong. A crappy-looking TV near some wobbly tables has the Dodgers on, while the bigger and sharper one over the bar is showing a Lakers playoff game up in Portland. And most of the Latino migrant workers and half of the farmers are glued to the basketball. "Good, because I got no stake in them Dodger fools," announces Fred, and heads for a spot at the bar. The rest of us find a table next to two old-timers in overalls to stare at the fuzzy images from Chavez Ravine, for what they're worth...

Game of the Day

With the Pirates enjoying a three-game lead, Reuss and Sutton have at each other, but neither pitcher is on the beam tonight. Lopes singles, steals, goes to third on Ott's bad throw and scores on a dinky single by Cey for a quick 1-0 Dodger lead, and the old-timers clap and clink their long-neck Buds. Sutton meanwhile gets the first six Bucs, but Ken Macha, filling in at third while Garner takes second for Stennett, singles to start the 3rd. A Taveras grounder moves Macha up, a Reuss single gets him to third and an Oliver single ties the game.

The Lakers and Blazers must be in a heated battle because everyone at the bar is yelling or swearing in Spanish, and Fred runs over at one point cracking up. "Dig this. The players all got righteous 'fros and whacked little shorts, so I look at the tube and yell 'How come there's no 3-point shot?' and next thing I know the bar man's passin' me the biggest snort of Tequila I ever seen!" He runs back to the bar just in time for me to see Bill Robinson double with two outs in the 4th and Ott single him in. 2-1 Pirates.

Dusty Baker bombs a bleacher homer to tie the game again, but Sutton can't close a darn inning out. In the 4th with two outs Parker singles, Stargell gets hit with a pitch and Robinson hits a second double and the Bucs are in front again! Sherman makes a raspberry sound and disappears for a five-minute pee. Mikey says "screw this noise" and goes off to a Pong machine in the corner, and I'm left with bored Amy and Lester, who naturally is scoring the game on a stack of bar napkins.

Reuss has used three DPs to get out of three other jams, but in the 6th he boots a dribbler to put two aboard, Sutton bunts them over, Lopes walks to fill the bases, and Russell floats a single into the left gap to score two and put L.A. in the lead. The old-timers try to clink bottles again but they're too sleepy and drunk and miss. It's too early for Gossage, so Tekulve enters and walks Reggie Smith, but Cey pops out to end the inning.

A Garvey double and Taveras error bring home an insurance run in the 7th, and after Goose finally enters in the 8th, the Penguin plucks him for a 2-run shot and a 7-3 lead. Across the room the Lakers get swept by Bill Walton's Blazers and three-fourths of the place files out. Hough had come in to bail Sutton out of a bases loaded jam in the 8th, but Cobra Parker launches a laser into the bleachers to start the 9th. 7-4 now. Stargell lifts one out to Monday, who drops it for a 2-base error. Robinson walks. Sherman forces himself to take another leak. Ott grounds into a force, but Macha 4-for-4 with a walk on the night, singles again and it's 7-5!

Mikey has started yelling with somebody at the Pong machine. Taveras grounds into another force and here's the original Jerry Hairston to hit for Gossage with the go-ahead run in his bat. Hough knuckles one in and Hairston skies it to left, where Baker puts it away and the Dodgers are two behind.

A great sloppy game, and while Lester is reading me the totals, the runners left on base, the balls in play and the strikes and ball readings for every pitcher, I hear a glass smash and turn to see Mikey rolling on the floor with a mutton-chopped farmhand twice his size. We run over, pry them loose, and race out into the night.

Unfortunately we have no car and no direction to go in, but Amy is suddenly pointing at my pocket. "Look Buzz, it's glowing!" I reach in, pull out the four dice as a gang of Mr Mutton Chop's friends pile out of the bar. "These things got us here, right? So we gotta end up somewhere! What time is it?"

"Six and a half seconds to midnight!" yells Lester, and as the first empty bottle whizzes past our heads we break into a run. A second bottle flies right at my face and we—

PIT 001 110 002 – 5 12 4
L.A. 100 102 12x – 7 12 1
    W-Sutton L-Reuss SV-Hough HRS: Parker, Baker, Cey GWRBI-Russell

Flash Flooded
May 16, 1977

KANSAS CITY—Floating in water isn't the best way to wake up, but even less so on a cool spring night when the icy stuff is down your pants and there's other people around you bumping and splashing as they wake up.

The problem was that Mikey wasn't. He was face down in the Royals Stadium fountain an hour or so before game time, and not moving. Friendly Fred called his name, shook him. Rolled him over. His face was blue, and there was a gash on his head where one of the bottles from that bar in the San Joaquin Valley must've hit him the second before we disappeared last night.

"We gotta get out of here before the stadium cops see us," said Amy, wading to the back edge of the thing.

Fred went nuts. "Say what?? And leave him here??"

"We don't have a choice," I told him, "He's gone and we can't exactly lug a wet body around."

The timed fountain shot into the air just then, missing Lester's head by inches and scaring the crap out of us. I clamped onto Fred's arm, pulled him away. Luckily no one had seen us yet, and we probably had a few minutes before anyone would spot floating Mikey. Amy grabbed a bag of heavy batting donuts from an open equipment shed to sink him with, we found restrooms behind the outfield to dry off, bought a bunch of Royals jerseys and sweatpants, and snagged some empty seats in the back row of bleachers.

"I don't need this aggravation," said Sherman, sneezing into his sleeve for the first two innings, but none of us were happy about Mikey and Fred couldn't even talk. Mikey was a dumb, violent jerk but he loved the Phillies more than I love clam chowder, and Fred and him had really hit it off since we left the hospital. They were even talking about getting a place on the Jersey shore together and opening a guido/soul brother dating service.

On the other hand, he did break one of the 4-D dice, which screwed up our daily soft landings, which is how he ended up drowning in the Royals Stadium fountain. Pretty strange, too, because three years from now his team will beat the Royals in K.C.'s first World Series in six games, making this some kind of reverse-time warp irony.

I just hope Mikey wasn't going to get out of the hospital in the future, get his act together and end up becoming President or something.

Naahhh...

Game of the Day
Jim Bibby takes the ball for Cleveland, and he just died too I heard, which

makes this game kind of double-reverse ironic. The Tribe dropped all three to the Royals at the Lake, so they're out for revenge, and Paul Splittorff helps out by giving up six hits and three runs in the first two innings, helped by an awful two-base error by Mayberry, when he throws a double play grounder past Patek at short with the bases loaded.

And Bibby is ON. He mows down the first eight, whiffing four of them, before a hit batter, Brett single, and scoring force-out by McRae makes it 3-1 in the 4th. Splittorff meanwhile calms down, and two-hits the Indians for the next five innings. Brett raps into a DP but Poquette scores in the 6th, and it's 3-2.

After Rico Carty doubles to begin the 8th, Manning runs for him, goes to third on a Thornton grounder and gets passed balled home. Think 4-2 is enough? Nope, we're talking first-place Royals here. Patek doubles right away, and with two outs, one of the best clutchmeisters around Al Cowens smokes one in the gap to cut it to 4-3.

Bottom of the 9th now. Bleacherites around us are rabid, used to miracle comebacks, and it's hard to believe Royals fans will ever have anything but a winning tradition. With one out Porter singles. Willie Wilson runs for him, steals second on the barely-holding Bibby. But Otis whiffs, and here's Mayberry with the game on the line. John's going to make up for that huge error he made, we know it, 38,000 other people know it.

And the ball sizzles into right to score Wilson. Bibby is cooked for the game, but hangs in to whiff Patek and put us into extras. Splittorff gets out of the 10th, then gets Pruitt to line out and end the 11th after Kuiper's third single of the game, and the typical writing is on the wall.

Jim Kern pitched a scoreless 10th for Cleveland, but now he's got Brett leading off. George spits out some juice from the tobacco tank in his cheek, leans on his back foot and crushes the first pitch deep to center. Manning takes two steps, turns, and watches it spash into the fountain, 420 feet from home plate, and splash the crowd into a frenzy.

Oh shit. The fountain.

We never got out of a ballpark faster than this one.

CLE 120 000 010 00 – 4 10 1
K.C. 000 101 011 01 – 5 9 1

The Antidote to Anything

May 17, 1977

Game of the Day

CHICAGO—Lester reporting again, and happy to be doing so. It was a trying time in Kansas City yesterday, even with my Royals taking another dramatic one, and Buzz and Amy and Sherman are off somewhere consoling Fred about his deceased friend right now.

But Wrigley Field is bright and warm, the humidity no higher than 45 percent, a perfect day to watch my Cubbies face off against the Expos, both teams tied for last at 12-18. I have an excellent seat near the Cubs dugout, a kosher frankfurter in hand and my scorebook and #2 pencil ready for use. Name a better place I can be at this moment and I will convince you otherwise.

Fitting for the occasion, each team has its worst starter going, Bahnsen for the Expos and Renko for the Cubs. Renko fails first. A DeJesus error to begin the game, followed by an Unser double and Carter homer and it's 3-0 Montreal. Raise that to 5-0 by the 3rd, when Perez doubles and Unser homers, but then it's Bahnsen's turn to combust. Four straight two-out hits in the 4th begun by a Biitner triple cuts it to 5-2. A Murcer double and two singles in the 6th whittles it to 5-4.

The Expos get one back in the 7th, but after Atkinson takes the hill, a walk and three more Cub singles ties the game 6-6. With Sutter unavailable, Willie Hernandez gets the relief ball and Larry Parrish bombs one in the top of the 11th.

I'm not ready for this game to be over, though, and the Cubs feel the same. Dave Rosello bats for Hernandez and singles. Joe Wallis gets him to third with another single and DeJesus brings him in with a deep fly. To the 12th!

To Lake Michigan! says Tony Perez, who sends the first pitch he sees from Pete Broberg in that general direction, off by just a few degrees. With Kerrigan in for Montreal, Speier boots a Murcer grounder to start the last of the 12th. The stands are screeching, But Buckner flies to center, Trillo and Mitterwald roll out, and the Cubs have last place to themselves. Their new-look lineup has given them one win and kept them in another to the bitter end, and they have not hit into a double play for two days, their biggest bugaboo.

I will find my companions soon, but I'm in no hurry. Take the two bottom teams in the league, toss them into Wrigley, add a pinch of fine weather, hours of dramatic sauce, and all I can be is satiated.

MON 302 000 100 011 – 8 12 1
CHC 000 202 200 010 – 7 13 2

W-Kerrigan L-Broberg HRS: Carter, Unser, Perez GWRBI-Perez

DR. GROSSINGER'S REPORT:

Something peculiar has happened, in addition to Seamus Headley and I being on schedule to receive something called "5-D Dice." When I looked through my

file cabinet last night to collect more information on the patients in question, all
records for Michael Spano had disappeared. I went into the hospital database
and was met wth a message even more cryptic: no such name found in system.
How could this be?...   —S.H.G.

Yippee-Ki-Yay
May 18, 1977

HOUSTON—I'm not gonna say it's a good thing Mikey died, but he sure wouldn't have cared for this swampy patch of golf course rough we woke up in here, because the mosquitoes hadn't had breakfast yet and treated us like an iHop buffet, and I would've had a headache from all his whining before I even found coffee.

We ended up walking behind backed-up Astrodome traffic down Almeda Rd., and got into the stadium just a few minutes before Houston took the field against the Phillies for the second of three games. They beat Carlton yesterday and J.R. Richard was going today, and another Astro win would mean six in a row, which is amazing seeing where the team was at a week ago. There were doubleheaders all over the map on this sweat-dripping Sunday, but the 4-Ds sent us to a singleheader with the hottest team—one of 'em, anyway.

Game of the Day

It's hard to get used to watching an indoor game, but at least the turf is a darker green here and doesn't make the ball vanish like it does in Montreal. Richard and Christenson for the Phils both put two guys on in the 1st but escape their jams, and then Tom Hutton, boinks one that lands in the right bleachers just to the left of the right foul pole. Christenson has his wicked stuff, and it stays 1-0 Brotherly Lovers until one out in the 6th, when Jose Cruuuz doubles and one out later Art Howe (can't do anything fun with his name) doubles him in to tie the game.

Richard throws a 1-2-3 7th, and Christenson gets the first two Astros in the bottom half. Then Ferguson raps a single. Cedeno singles him to third. Bob Watson picks out a curve and rakes it high and deep and into the left field seats and snorting cartoon bulls charge across the scoreboard!! Real Bull Luzinski doubles to lead the 8th and Schmidt walks, but J.R. bears down to get Hebner and Boone on liners and whiffs Maddox. McCarver pinch-hits a single with one out in the 9th, and here comes Sambito to face tough pinch-hitters Davey Johnson and Sizemore. Not tough enough for the Samb Man.

Zip-zip, and the 'Stros have six in a row!

PHL 001 000 000 – 1 5 2

HOU 000 001 30x – 4 11 0

W-Richard L-Christenson SV-Sambito HRS: Hutton, Watson
GWRBI-Watson

American League through Sunday, May 18

Kansas City	23	11	.676	—
Baltimore	21	14	.600	2.5
Boston	20	14	.588	3
Texas	17	18	.486	6.5
Chicago	15	17	.469	7
New York	14	19	.424	8.5
Minnesota	13	20	.394	9.5
Cleveland	13	23	.361	11

National League through Sunday, May 18

Pittsburgh	22	13	.629	—
Los Angeles	19	13	.594	1.5
St. Louis	19	16	.543	3
Houston	17	18	.486	5
Cincinnati	15	17	.469	5.5
Philadelphia	15	17	.469	5.5
Montreal	14	18	.432	6.5
Chicago	12	21	.364	9

A Mother for Ya

May 20, 1977

KANSAS CITY—Friendly Fred back at ya. Been a while, huh? Last time we rapped it was end of April up in the Fenway hood, and my Yanks were takin' it hard from them Bostons, but don't let me remind myself of that shizz right now. I've been busy tryin' to get over what happened to my honorary soul friend Mikey, and when we pop back in K.C. today, last thing I wanna do is go that stadium again, but my righteous Bombers are can-opening a series here and they have definitely been on the upswing these days.

To help grease my mind, Buzz takes us to this bitchin' barbeque joint at

Brooklyn and 18th called Arthur Bryant's. Now I've had ribs before but nothin' close to this good, and it doesn't even graze me when I hear that Royal bad boy George Brett himself eats in the place. Buzz sits next to me in the booth and tells me how he lost his dog back when he was just a nipper, and how all it did was make him tougher, and that I should do the same about Mikey. Not sure it's him or the Sweet Heat sauce that makes me feel better, but I do decide this Buzz Gip is good people, even for a Red Sox chump.

Headin' over to the ball park after, to find seats as far from those ghost fountains as we can, I share with the Buzz-man how tough it really is bein' a Yankees fan. Every day you gotta deal with the rest of the country piling the hate on, and even though the Sox took a boatload of shit for bein' the last to integrate, the Yanks weren't too far ahead. 'Course we were smarter and picked Elston Howard instead of Pumpsie Green, and he was my grandpa's favorite player for years and years. It just about killed him when he went and helped the Sox win the pennant in '67, but he had a bunch of great years for us so you can't diss the guy.

I get the shivers seein' those fountains again when we hit the stadium parking lot. What kind of field is this anyway, in the middle of rollin' green nowhere? Yankee Stadium is a real ballpark, stuck in the Bronx across the river from Harlem like it was meant to be. Makes me wanna just burn this place right to the everlovin' groun—

I know, Buzz, I know. Ain't cool.

Game of the Days

Like I said, the Yanks have been burning up. Hell, they just took two down in Texasland, against some Ranger fools who took them twice in New York. And they got Gullett on the hill tonight against Pattin, and he ain't no damn general.

Joe Zdeb drops a ball with one out in the 1st for a two-base fail, and My Man Thurman bombs one out on the next pitch. 2-0 Us! The Munsonizer's at it again in the 3rd, hittin' a two-out double, scorin' on a Reggie single and then Reggie crankin' the wheels around on a double by my new man George Zeber.

Otis gets a K.C. digit back with a single, but then it's Piniella Time, as he spanks one out the opposite way and the Yanks are up 5-1! 'Course I gotta be crazy in the head to think this game's gonna be easy. Nothin' is in the Land of Freaky Mojo they call K.C. Brett, McRae and Wathan open their 4th with singles, Zdeb and Mayberry walk, after two outs Otis scratches a single and Cowens walks and guess the shit what? Game's tied.

Then it's four innings of leave-on-base scorelessness, and I got my hood over my head 'cause it's too hard to watch. After Piniella walks with one gone in the 9th, though, Pattin hits Chambliss on the knee with a pitch and he's gotta leave. Did I just see that? Not only is it just the second time a Yank's been hit all year, but it's our first injury! It ain't bad, it's a GOOD sign! Things could be normalizing out! Sure enough, My Man Roy White whacks one high and deep to right, where it bounces off the fence just over Cowens' glove for a double. My Man Mickey Who Never Does a Thing Rivers then slaps a single the other way, and we're up 7-5!

Frank White singles to start the last of the 9th, and my gut starts doin' its cement mixer thing. I know Billy is itchin' to bring Sparky in, but we can't let that happen. Lyle's been downtown crud. So Gullett's left in, and whiffs Otis, gets Cowens on the fly, and just has to beat BBQ Brett for the game. He whiffs his ass! Chambliss has to sit out two games, but who cares! We got it back, brothas, and look out you first divisioners! See y'all on the flip side.

NYY 202 100 002 – 7 10 0
K.C. 001 400 000 – 5 7 1
    W-Gullett L-Pattin HRS: Munson, Piniella GWRBI-White

Games Peoples Play
May 21, 1977

CHICAGO and MINNEAPOLIS—I was afraid this might happen. It's Lester again, and because I'm a lifelong fan of the Cubs and Cards and Royals and White Sox and Twins and maybe the Astros soon, and because it was my turn to toss the 4-D dice, we were zapped back and forth between two incredible games on the same day, played 350 miles apart. Normally I'd enjoy a thing like that, but the games were long and strange and my glasses fogged up and I started to forget who was playing in which game. Thank the Lord I had two facing blank scoresheets in my pad...

WRIGLEY INNINGS 1-3

I'm starting to lose faith in my Cubbies, purely for pitching reasons. Rick Reuschel and Steve Renko are a combined 7-2, but Bonham, Burris and Krukow are 0-14, and it's Krukow's turn to not shine today. He gets Hutton and Hebner to begin the game, then Luzinski walks, Johnstone doubles, Schmidt homers, Boone singles, Maddox singles, Bowa singles, Bowa steals, Jim Kaat singles, Hutton singles and Hebner singles and it's 7-0 Phillies before half the bleacher bums are even drunk.

But the wind is blowing toward the Lake, Kaat is in the twilight of his career, and Chicago scores single runs in the 1st, 2nd and 3rd to give me hope...

MET STADIUM INNINGS 1-3

Rick Wise and Paul Thormodsgard on a warm night? No pitching duel here seems possible, either. Boston gets a a run in the 1st on a Rice sac fly, and then the crowd starts buzzing two batters before Carew even walks up. Wynegar singles with one out, and then Rodney flicks one into the left gap to get Butch to third, push his magical hit streak up to 35 games and stop everyone from thinking about it the rest of the night. A Hisle double and Adams single and it's 3-1 Twins out of the gate.

A DP grounder off Tommy Helms' bat with the sacks full makes it 3-2 in the 2nd, and when Hisle muffs Carbo's fly, it's tied up. And then Rice is at it again, flatlining a pitch into the bleachers to put Boston up 4-3 as Wise has settled in...

WRIGLEY INNINGS 4-6

Kaat and Krukow kontinue to have nothing but krap. 9-3 Phils in the 4th, then 9-4. Then 10-4. Then 10-6 after five. Then after reliever Willie Hernandez singles to start the Cub 6th, Tug McGraw is summoned, and all he does is hit Morales, walk Gross and serve up a Murcer Meatball for a grand slam and a 10-10 tie! There's no doubt about it, we're headed for a carbon copy of this famous game I researched and read about once which will take place here about two years from now but I'm not supposed to talk about...

MET STADIUM INNINGS 4-6

Come on, Twins, darn it all! They just don't get the luck at home that they do on the road for some reason. Carbo leaps at the fence to rob Hisle of a homer in the 4th. Bostock singles to lead the 5th and Wynegar bunts him over but he gets stranded there. Finally Adams gets his third straight single to begin our 6th, Ford gets plunked, and Cubbage pounds the gap between Lynn and Carbo, who kicks the ball away for a double and error and puts us ahead! Smalley greets Jim Willoughby with another single, and it's 6-4 Twins. Somehow I don't think this will be the final score...

WRIGLEY INNINGS 7-9

Between McGraw and Garber for Philly and Hernandez for the Cubs, it's three innings of torture. Gross and Murcer single to start our 8th, get bunted over, but Buckner and Trillo ground out. DeJesus triples with two gone in the 9th, Clines walks but Gross flies out and we're heading for a darkness curfew...

MET STADIUM INNINGS 4-6

After a Helms triple starts the Boston 7th, Butler comes on to get Scott, Fisk and Yaz. But Evans tags him for a mammoth blast with one out in the 8th, and Lynn walks. Tom Johnson is on, and Hobson doubles to tie the game. Top of the 9th the Boomer walks, Fisk doubles and a sac fly by Rice

(RBI no. 3) puts Boston up 8-7. With K.C. losing again on the scoreboard, this could be a huge win.

But Soup Campbell is rancid once more. Wynegar doubles, Carew doubles to tie, and after one out, Adams rips his fourth single for the ball game! We're up to 5-13 at home!

WRIGLEY INNINGS 10-11

Hebner has been knocked out for five games, while the Cubs have lost Morales, Ontiveros and Swisher. The grass is bloody, and after scoring the first six innings, the Cubs attack has evaporated. Not the Phils', though. Into his sixth inning of relief with Sutter unavailable, Hernandez is finally touched, or I should say manhandled. Johnstone singles, Schmidt bombs his second homer and only his fifth on the year, four more singles bring in two more, and the latest Cubbie debacle is complete. They are 5-16 in the month of May. And I could use two comfy beds to collapse in.

PHL 700 210 000 04 – 14 20 1

CHI 111 124 000 00 – 10 14 1

W-Garber L-Hernandez HRS: Schmidt-2, Morales, Murcer GWRBI-Schmidt

BOS 121 000 021 – 7 10 1

MIN 300 003 002 – 8 17 1

W-T. Johnson L-Campbell HRS: Rice, Evans GWRBI-Adams

Hospital Mum on Patient "Disappearances"

By Buster Finch
Maine Life Section Editor
Portland Press-Herald

SQUALLPOCKET—Local authorities in Beavertail County are investigating rumors of a recent disturbance at the State Hospital in which five patients may have escaped from the premises. The patients, whose names are being withheld, were involved in an apparent fight on one of the wards two weeks ago, and were not in their beds or on the hospital grounds the following morning

"We're doing all that we can to locate them," said Chief of Psychiatry Sheila Grossinger, "We have a large facility here and it's possible they could be hiding in one of the storage rooms or service tunnels. Family members have been contacted and reassured that there is no cause for alarm."

A hospital custodian, Seamus M. Headley, was reported to have more detailed knowledge of the ward disturbance, but attempts to interview the verbally impaired worker were unsuccessful.

Arch Nemesis
May 22, 1977

I had my first dream since forever. I was at Squallpocket Beach with Pam and Timmy, and we were building this beast of a sand castle, and Timmy had potato chip crumbs stuck in the peanut butter around his mouth, and a Go-Gos song was playing on a boom box nearby, but waves were rolling in and the water was flat-out boiling, and Pam screamed and tried to grab Timmy's arm and then the water was crashing over us and —

Crazy Amy's pale, once-pretty face was next to mine as my eyes opened. We were in some kind of narrow room with a hump-shaped floor, and morning light was slicing in through these weird slit windows on both sides. Fred was already up, peering through one of them.

"We're in that big funky-ass St. Louis Arch, can you believe it?"

I coughed and Amy woke up, gave me a curious look. "You okay?"

"I guess....Just had a freaky dream, that's all. About my wife and kid."

Her eyes popped. "You're married?"

"Was, at least. Another Buzz ago."

"Geez! The hell with this guy who left you at Fenway! How come you aren't beatin' the streets lookin' for your squeeze?"

She was right, of course. But I didn't need any more of that craziness. "How about we talk about something else?" I said, "Dave Rader's the backup catcher here for Ted Simmons, y'know."

Amy just stared at me, the first time I'd ever seen her close to being caring.

"Never mind him...Say, what position did you play in Little League?"

Game of the Day

ST. LOUIS—The Clydesdale clumps have been cleaned off the turf, and it's a gorgeous weekday matinee at second generation Busch Stadium. Picked to derail the Cardinal express is veteran Stan Bahnsen, but John Denny has the Expos without a hit through four. McBride slaps one into left though with one out in the Cards' 4th, a wild pitch gets him to second, and Brock plates him with a clean single.

Denny then picks a bad time to lose his stuff. Carter opens the 5th with a double, Valentine singles him in, and after Denny balks, Cash doubles and Montreal skips in front. Cue the next Templeton triple, number 12 in fact, and he's on a pace to hit 48 of them. With two out, it's Bahnsen's turn to throw a wide one, and Garry runs in for the tie game.

Denny gets out of jams in the 6th and 7th, and after a one-out single by Perez in the 8th, Butch Metzger takes over. The Cardinal pitching up and down has been phenomenal, and Metz gets Unser on a fly and whiffs Carter to escape.

Jerry Mumphrey then gets the house rockin' with a one-out triple of his own. Hernandez and Simmons follow with doubles, lefty Schatzeder replaces the Bahnsen burnout, but McBride singles anyway to make it a 4-2 lead. Metzger rolls the 'Spos in the 9th, and St. Louis has won eight straight and now is the proud owner of second place!

And Lester is hopelessly confused because his Cards are going to Wrigley for a weekend series with his last-place Cubs, and he has no clue who to root for. I swear, the guy's nuts.

MTL 000 020 000 – 2 6 0
STL 000 110 02x – 4 10 0
W-Metzger L-Bahnsen GWRBI-Hernandez

Darth Foster, the Red Menace
May 24, 1977

CINCINNATI—So I grab a morning paper as soon as we make a dry landing in Fountain Square, and happen to see an ad for the Southern Ohio premiere of a new "science fiction spectacular" called *Star Wars*. And suddenly the Reds-Phillies game tonight means nothing.

"How can we not go to this movie?" I ask everyone, "I mean, do we evaporate or something if we skip the baseball game?"

"That movie's lame," says Amy, "and haven't you seen it 65 times by now?"

"No, only 47, but who cares? We're here on the day it's opening nationwide! Is that wicked cool, or what?"

"I don't like spaceship chases," says Sherman, "They give me vertigo. And the Reds just beat up my Dodgers and I'd rather go watch them lose."

"Zip it, old man," barks Amy, "They're my team now, and when Bill Plummer bats for Bench and wins it with a homer, you'll be sorry.

"If Bill Plummer even picks up a bat I'll eat my dentures—"

"Okay, enough! Far as I'm concerned, as long as we're in 1977 we might as well dig on some of the culture, right? I'm up for a cool concert, too, if we run across the right one."

Amy raises her eyebrows. "Cat Stevens?"

"Cripes, no. I'm thinking more like Talking Heads, or a great punk band."

They look at me like I have a faucet on my head. "Okay, forget it. I'll go myself, and we'll meet here after the game. Lester can score again."

* * *

The Skywalk Cinemas are right downtown, but when I round the corner I'm shocked to see only about twelve people in line. I side up to a guy in a pink-striped shirt and green pants who kind of looks like he wants to be here. Without saying too much I try and tell him I think this movie will be a gigantic success and there "might even" be sequels down the road.

"Well, I'm just here because the same guy did *American Graffiti*," he says, "Do you know if Candy Clark is in this?"

Other people in line are complaining about the ticket prices being hiked to $2.50, and after getting a bucket of popcorn I pick out a seat in an empty row behind two teenage boys.

The movie is fantastic even for the 48th time, but it's even more fun to listen to the oohs and aahs from the two kids, and on the way out later one says to the other "Darth Vader was the best villain EVER!" I pipe in "Yeah, and it's amazing he turns out to be Luke's dad!" before realizing I screwed up. I bolt from the place before I say something dumber, and head back to Fountain Square. I don't care what happened in that Reds game, there's no way it beats this.

Game of the Days

Amy here. Sherman's right, my guy Bill Plummer doesn't even get his jock on, but who the fig cares? George Foster belts a two-run homer in the 1st, a two-run homer in the 3rd, a solo shot leading off the 5th, and a three-run ICBM missle in the 6th, for FOUR HOME RUNS and nine RBIs off Larry Christenson! Brusstar tries his luck in the 8th but George rolls out shooting for Number Five with Rose on third.

Too bad Buzz, hope you were happy watching Darth Doofus.

PHL 100 020 010 – 4 8 2
CIN 204 013 21X – 13 14 1

W-Norman L-Christenson HRS: Foster-4 (ties Bench and Carter for NL lead with 13) GWRBI-Foster

Nightmare on Landsdowne Street
May 25, 1977

BOSTON—Friendly Fred was anything but. Not after the Bosox had ambushed his Yanks 8-4 in the first game yesterday. Not when his Yanks were 0-3 at Fenway and people on every corner outside the park were selling "NETTLES SUCKS" and CRY ME A RIVERS" and "CERTIFIED YANKEE HATER" T-shirts by the gross.

"Ain't no way! I don't care a good goddamn if Guidry's on the mound. Hell, I don't care if Whitey Red Ruffing Gomez Ford Downing is throwin,' you Boston bitches got our number so far and I'm no fool. I got better scenes to make than sittin' with you and all the white cats in those seats built for midgets watchin' our butts get whacked by Rice and Fisk and Yasmeltski or whatever his name is. HELL no! I'm gonna find me a righteous record store somewhere to occupy for at least an hour, tnen mosey back up here for a cold, tasty one at the Cask 'n Flagon till the game's done, which is where you can find my relaxed, not-caring-one-bit ass." he explained.

Game of the Day

Fred must also be nuts or something, because the Yanks just swept K.C. on their Turf, have Guidry going after his first great outing in a while, and I don't care who you're rooting for, how can you pass up a game on a sunny Sunday with Reggie and Mickey and Graig and Thurman doing battle with Lynn and Rice and Pudge and Yaz and Dewey and Boomer on the same field?

Too bad Fred's hiding out in Strawberries browsing funky vinyl because he misses His Man Mickey hooking Don Aase's first pitch of the game around the Pesky Pole. Stanley walks, Munson singles, Reggie gets a run-scoring grounder and the Yanks are up 2-0. A Roy White single and Stanley double in the 2nd makes it 3-0. Thurman then rips another single, but this time Jackson whiffs and leaves two on. It ain't a good omen.

Guidry meanwhile throws three scoreless innings to start his day but Scott booms one onto Landsdowne to lead off the home 4th. Aase, with a 5-0 record coming in, is shaky from the get-go, but one of the story lines in this one is the wasted base runners by New York. After leaving four aboard in the first two innings Zeber and Nettles reach to start the 3rd and stay there. Stanley singles with one out in the 4th but Munson and Reggie do nothing. Zeber walks to start the 5th but gets stuck in cement. Randolph singles to start the 6th, gets doubled up by Rivers before Stanley and Munson get left on when Reggie whiffs.

* * *

Between innings I go for a soda and bump into a maintenance guy with a mop. He's Latino, gives me a weird stare and I flash on a name tag pinned to his shirt pocket: Jose Torres.

Holy crap. It's the guy who's going to find my 5-year butt next month living under the park! Dr. Sheila showed me the article before we disappeared but I still can hardly believe it. Anyway, I stand in front of him with my tongue all tied for a good fifteen seconds, he asks me if I need something and I say no and just hurry away. Why freak someone out by telling them they're going to meet a younger version of yourself? There's enough weirdness already going on with this game and I want to get back to it.

* * *

And it's right where I left it. Zeber and Chambliss single with one out in the 7th and go nowhere after Bob Stanley comes on for Aase. Stanley and Munson single in the 8th with one out but Reggie finishes his 0-for-5 afternoon by flying out to deep center, before Zeber grounds out.

Guidry zaps the Sox 1-2-3 in the 7th and retires the first two in the 8th, but then Scott gets hit. Rice lines a single. Hobson skies one out to right, Reggie backpedals and the ball clanks off his glove for a two-base error and a 3-2 game. The infield comes in. Yaz rips one past Randolph's dive for a 2-run single and the shocking Boston lead!

I'm stoked for my team, of course, but groaning inside for Friendly Fred, who we pray isn't watching this travesty at the Cask 'n Flagon. Soup Campbell comes on, gives the Yanks their first and only 1-2-3 inning of the game, and Boston moves into first by half a game.

The recent sweep in Kansas City brought New York in here flying, but this is their dumbest, most crushing loss of the season. They outhit Boston 13-9 but leave 16 people on base, half of them by Reggie, who personally hands over the game with his bonehead outfield play. From our standing room location we see Billy Martin in the dugout pacing and ranting, and we figure he's probably going at it with Reggie after the last out but Amy is already pulling us down the exit ramp.

"We gotta find Fred!" she says, and she's right. It takes us a good fifteen minutes to get around the park and squeeze our way into the saloon, but by that time Fred is nowhere. We wait almost an hour with loud, sweaty, drunken Sox fans and finally give Fred's description to the bouncer at the door. He remembers seeing Fred exit the place after Reggie's dropped fly and head down Landsdowne Street with some shady characters, and just like that we're heading in the same direction.

We find him at a wire fence, watching cars whizz by below on the Mass Pike, swaying and his head bobbing to some tune only he can hear as he I nudge him from behind. "Fred?"

He turns, wearing star-shaped dark glasses with the price tag still on and an insane grin even for him. "We pulled it out, brother! Didja catch it?" The rest of look at each other.

"Pull what out?" asks Lester, "The Yankees lost. I can show you the score—"

"Oh no, we won!! My Man Roy tied the game in the 9th with a home run that tripped the light tower fantastic, and the ball bounced on the sidewalk right in front of me, and then it all came back around to Reggie, and this time he killed one for all of us, brothers, for all of us and it was beee-yoo-tifull..."

It's pretty clear that Fred got too friendly with someone selling psychedelics, and now he might never shut up. On the plus side, though, if he continues to believe the Yankees won, maybe he won't light anything on fire.

NYY 210 000 000 – 3 13 1
BOS 000 100 03x – 4 9 1

W-Stanley L-Guidry SV-Campbell HRS: Rivers, Scott GWRBI-Yaz

American League through Sunday, May 25

Boston	24	15	.615	—
Kansas City	24	16	.600	0.5
Baltimore	22	18	.550	2.5
Texas	22	20	.524	3.5
New York	17	21	.447	6.5
Chicago	17	21	.447	6.5
Cleveland	17	23	.425	7.5
Minnesota	15	24	.385	9

National League through Sunday, May 25

Pittsburgh	26	16	.619	—
St. Louis	25	16	.610	0.5
Philadelphia	21	19	.525	4
Los Angeles	20	19	.513	4.5
Houston	21	21	.500	5
Cincinnati	19	20	.487	5.5
Montreal	16	23	.410	8.5
Chicago	13	27	.325	12

Hot Time Deep in the Heart

May 26, 1977

By Ed "Peachy" Calhoun
Jewett Babbler Sports Columnist

Here I was kicking back on the porch with a Marlboro, halfway through my third bottle of Shiner's Bock, when all of a sudden there was a rogue lightning flash and these five runaway baseball freaks just appeared in my back yard.

Think I'm kidding? You readers all know my stuff. You know it's against my newspaper religion to make something up. Yet here's this white guy with an afro haircut calling himself Buzz claiming that he and his weirdo friends are here from the future and they need to get to either the Astros or Rangers game because something "amazing and far-out is gonna happen," like one of them life-and-death matters you always see on TV.

Well, I told them that little old Jewett, Texas happens to be smack dab between both of them towns, which got the scary-looking girl all worked up. "That means we have to go to both games!" she honked, so I told her my Chevy 4X4 doesn't work all that well when you cut it in half. What I didn't tell her was that I'd rather watch a Leon High wrestling practice than get in my car and drive to some crowded, overcooked sport event, but their desperate faces and overall bizarre patheticness was working on me. To make a short story long, it was decided we'd shoot up to the Rangers game because I used to drink shots with their press box guy in college, not to mention there's a Rusty's Pulled Pork Palace to sell your soul and half your stomach to on the way up.

Game of the Day

ARLINGTON—My former good buddy sticks us down the left field line, which isn't too bad a view here as long as you can swat the bugs away with your program. Lester the four-eyed future person is making noise like he wished we were at the Astrodome seeing his Cardinals shoot for 12 straight wins, but watching a game in that place is sort of like doing a two-step in a coffin, and I'll take a nice 85-degree night anytime.

It's Marty Pattin for the Royals, suddenly a half game out, against Dock Ellis for the Ranger boys, and after Harrah and Hargrove walk in the 1st, Claudell Washington ropes a double down the line. Toby scores easy but Hargrove gets his rump roasted at the plate by an Amos Otis chuck.

The 1-0 lead is tacked to the wall and for the next six innings and never falls off. Marty and Dock buzz through the lineups, with the Yanks beating up on the Bosox on the out-of-town board, and everyone in the place knows that if Texas wins, they can be two and a half out of first.

Think George Brett gives a crap? Nope. With one gone in the 8th, he does what he does, sling-shotting a triple into the gap. McRae gets him in right quick with a deep fly to center, and it's 1-1.

I spring for chile dogs for my stowaways, because it looks like we got a long one coming. Except Joe Zdeb, who went in for defense for K.C., singles to start the 10th. Brett doubles him to third with one out, and Barker's in to face McRae. Hal insults us with a Texas leaguer, but Zdeb is holding up and doesn't score! Barker then whiffs Porter, but throws one past Sundberg and the Royals go up 2-1.

But this Toby Harrah, I can't get enough of the man, and I only read about him when the *Babbler* sports desk remembers to publish the box scores every other day. Littell, who whiffs the first three Rangers he sees, hangs one a little too high and Toby pops it into the bleachers for dinger no. 17 and another tie game!

The 11th and 12th are scoreless knuckle-chewers, Barker and Littell settin' up the pins and knockin' 'em down. Singles by Otis and Patek in the 13th, though, put Royals at first and third, two outs, with Tom Poquette up. Barker stretches, throws, and the ball bounces past Sundberg for another wild pitch and a 3-2 K.C. lead!

It ain't over till the fat peanut vendor runs out of bags, though. With Mingori now in, Patek hurls an easy Bevacqua grounder into the seats to start the Ranger 13th. Beniquez flies out and Horton is walked on purpose. Campaneris grounds into a force and it's backup catcher John Ellis for the last call. Amy the weirdo-girl stands and begins screaming Ellis' first name for some reason, but John grounds out to second, and the Royals somehow are back in first place. They had fireworks scheduled and blow them off anyway, and this Fred guy that's with them stares up at the explosions with his sunglasses still on and starts saying a bunch of poetry nonsense and I can't wait to get back to my truck.

* * *

We zoomed back down the road, thankful the Pulled Pork Palace closed at midnight because my new friends wouldn't have let me stop, but then the dangest thing happened. First light we hit, I looked over at old Buzz who was sitting up front with me and was suddenly *not there*, and his friends who were bouncing around in the way-back were gone with him! I guess you can chalk this up as my very own UFO abduction story, except with nutty baseball fans from the future instead of aliens. Or maybe I just drank one too many Shiner's. I've been known to do that.

K.C. 000 000 010 100 1 – 3 10 2
TEX 100 000 000 100 0 – 2 11 3
  W-Mingori L-Barker HR: Harrah

Lone Star Encore
May 27, 1977

Let's keep it right down here one more day, y'all. I wasn't too thrilled about missing Houston ditching the Cardinal win streak last night, so tonight I'm cranking up the old tuner, making myself a mile-high beef sandwich and en-joying the action courtesy of our new announcer Dewayne Staats. We were lucky to get Bob Prince for a year after the Pirates booted him out of their radio booth, but I kind of like this Staats guy. He's got one of them long sum-mer voices that just wraps around every play, and if you're a baseball fan how do you beat his name?

Guess I should mention I've been an Astros fan ever since they were born down here in '62 as the Colt 45s. Yup, used to get pointed to my seat by one of them fetching Triggerettes, and I have to say I preferred buggy-muggy Colt Stadium to the Astrodome any day, but that's just me and a bunch of spilled milk at this point.

Game of the Days

Beat those Cards again and we're two and a half out! Denny's going against Pentz, neither of them all that good, and they prove it right quick when the first four Cards get hits for three St. Louis runs. Denny then gives us a run back on a single and three walks, and after two singles, a walk and a Cruuuz triple put us up 4-3, a yell so loud I scare my dog. Dewayne says we're in for a long night, so I get some more beer from out back and miss the Cards going up 5-4 on a ball through the wickets of Enos Cabell with Cards on second and third.

Then McBride swats one off the foul pole, McLaughlin takes over for Pentz and I can hear the distraughtness in Dewayne's voice. Down 6-4, last of the 8th, Art Howe leads with a single. Cabell, who missed a chance to redeem himself last time up when Howe was cut down at the plate on his double, hits into a force now. But Metzger singles to put the tying runs on. Schultz comes on to face Cedeno, who whiffs. Up steps Puhl, last night's hero, and this time he rips a triple! Both runs score and it's 6-6! Cliff Johnson pinch hits and whiffs and Schultz is out of the pickle.

Around the time I run out of beer, the Astros run out of luck. Howe leads the last of the 10th with a double but they can't bring him home off Metzger. Sambito bats for himself and doubles with one out in the 11th but Watson and Cruz can't bring *him* home. After Sambito gives up three singles in the 12th with two outs but gets Reitz to end the inning, Howe doubles for his 4th hit with one out but is hung out to dry.

Two more singles start the Cardinal 13th and Forsch is in to face Heity Cruz, who walks. Templeton singles home the go-ahead, Mumphrey adds a sac fly, and it's 8-6 St. Loo. There's also something else, because the Bucs have dropped another to the Reds, and when Al Hrabosky gets us 1-2-3 to end the thing and send me to bed, the Cards are in first place by their lonesomes for

the first time this year. Dang.
STL 300 201 000 000 2 – 8 17 0
HTN 130 000 020 000 0 – 6 13 1
  W-Metzger L-Sambito SV-Hrabosky HR: McBride GWRBI-Templeton

Ruth, Gehrig, DiMaggio, Mantle and Zeber
May 29, 1977

NORWALK, CT—It's been a long, wiggy week. After two days in Texas old Buzz here needed to get his bearings back and work on his life a little.

Ready for this? I actually thought there was a way I could keep Pam from leaving me in twenty years, or whenever the hell it's going to be. So when we showed up on the east end of the GW Bridge this morning I sent Fred and the gang on to Yankee Stadium for the game with the Indians while I took a bus up the coast to Pam's home town.

The problem, which I didn't even think of till I was halfway here, was that Pam is like six years old, meaning there was no way I could look her up for a serious conversation without getting reported for suspicious perversion.

So instead I looked up her parents, who were much younger and thinner than I remember and worked side by side at Girkich Hardware on West Avenue, just like she said they did. I told them I was building a wooden doll house for "my little girl", and steered the talk around to what it's like to have a little girl, and then they started going on about their Pam. I guess I got too interested all of a sudden and began asking too many questions, because they wrapped up the sale on that bag of screws wicked fast and moved on to other customers.

Boarding the train back into New York, all I could think about was how idiotic my idea had been. Okay, so what if I had actually gotten lucky enough to meet Pam as a six-year-old? One little wrong sentence or pat on the head to make her miss a ride or a nap or an important TV show and who knows? I could've screwed up any chance of meeting her in the future. And would Timmy ever be born? I'll tell ya, this past-traveling business creates all kinds of headaches.

Game of the Day
NEW YORK—First a Star Wars premiere and now a punk-ass trolley ride up to rich white people land? Damn! My Man Buzz sure knows how to miss the good ones. Anyways, took me at least a day to come down from that nasty junk someone put on my tongue up in Boston, but now I'm bouncin' like a

baby boy again, and the Yanks are gonna put these Indian boys in diapers.

Waits takes the floor against the Catfish, and it's zero hour for the first four innings. Until that fool called Larvell Blanks pops a 99-cent homer around the left pole, and it's 2-0 Native Americans. Don't know why or how but my Yanks are all asleep again at the plate, and get only two singles and a double the first eight innings. Buddy Bell hits another homer in the 8th, so we're down 3-0 and the worst fans are already makin' beelines for the exits.

My Man Mickey Rivers works a walk to start things, and M. M. Munson singles him over to third. We call this Hope. Reggie grounds into a force but a run scores, and then Waits falls apart like one of those jive falafel sandwiches. White raps one to the mound and he drops it for an error. Nettles singles to load the bases. Chambliss pings one into left-center, two runs score and we're tied!

Jim Kern tries his luck with the ball, and here comes My New Man George Zeber to hit for Paul Blair. Now Zeber just had 71 at bats this year and next year for the Yanks, but with Piniella out he's been filling in lately and spankin' the ball like a crazy person. Kern stretches and throws and George belts it high, and deep, and the hell out of here for a 3-run winner and put THAT in your peace pipes and smoke it!

CLE 000 020 010 – 3 7 1
NYY 000 000 006 – 6 7 0
   W-Hunter L-Waits HRS: Blanks, Bell, Zeber GWRBI-Zeber

Meet De Boys on the Battlefront
May 30, 1977

BOSTON and MINNESOTA—The dice split us up today, dropping us outside two ballparks, which was bound to happen with eight holiday doubleheaders being played. Me and Amy and Fred took the Orioles at Fenway, while Lester and Sherman got the Royals at Twins. I was actually going to let Fred report for me, but he's a little burned out from that latest Yankee miracle, and it being Memorial Day and all, he's also too busy remembering someone very close to him.

Seems that Fred's older brother Lucius went off to fight in Vietnam around 1971 and got shot at An Loc around this time a year later. They swapped some letters and had a long distance talk or two while he was in the vet hospital, but Lucius lost his fight with a serious stomach wound infection soon after that. "Didn't even get to give him the Sly album I bought him for Christmas," Fred said to me today while we watched the Sox and Birds warm up. "I was only eight or something but we were pretty damn tight. Think I set my first mailbox on fire soon after." I teared up a little myself, put my arm around his shoulder and gave it a good pat as Fergie Jenkins walked out to the mound in front of us. Thankfully we had at least six hours of ball to lose ourselves in, and good god, did we ever get lost.

Games of the Longest Day

FENWAY GAME ONE—Palmer coming off his worst outing of the year, falls behind right away on a Carbo walk and Fisk homer, followed in the 3rd by a Fisk single, Rice double and Evans homer...Birds obviously paying for 10-0 bashing of Sox yesterday...But they're coming back! Two-run Kelly homer in the 4th, three-run DeCinces blast in the 5th, and it's 5-5. Two walks, a single and Kiko Garcia error makes it 7-5 Sox...7-6 after Lee May single in 6th...Belanger in for D, makes error to score Evans and it's 8-6...Palmer has crap, but stays out there because he isn't tired and the Baltimore pen is thinner than a fly wing...Stanley pitches two innings of tough long relief, gives up single and double in 9th and Soup pours in. Murray singles, Scott boots one, Skaggs and May single and the O's have four runs and 10-8 lead!...Palmer back out to finish his horrible CG and DeCinces boots one. Scott fans but Fisk, Yaz and Rice all double for three runs and the ridiculous comeback win, their 14th of the year!

BAL 000 231 004 – 10 17 4
BOS 203 201 003 – 11 14 1
W-Campbell L-Palmer HRS: Kelly, DeCinces, Fisk, Evans GWRBI-Rice

METROPOLITAN STADIUM GAME ONE—Colborn is clubbed for six Twins runs and a Rod Carew single for 43 straight games, and K.C. is behind 6-0 after four innings. Except this is the non-Goltz portion of the Minnesota rotation, in all its ineptness, and Pete Redfern, still without a win, hands the Royals five runs in the 5th to put them back in the game. Gary Serum does little better, serving up a 3-run Cowens blast in the 6th for a 9-7 K.C. lead. Jeff Holly gives it a shot and Mayberry hits one, as the Twins stay winless against their nemesis and get outscored 11-1 after the 4th.

K.C. 000 054 200 – 11 12 2
MIN 105 010 000 – 7 13 3
W-Colborn L-Serum HRS: Cowens, Mayberry GWRBI-Cowens

FENWAY GAME TWO—Can we see anything weirder than the first game? Why not?...Orioles score five for McGregor off Paxton in the 3rd, capped by Lee May 3-run Turnpike shot (he went 4-for-5 in Game One), but Boston chips away the rest of the game, finally ties it in the 8th on two-out singles by Montgomery, Dillard and Burleson...Against Paxton, Willoughby and Campbell, Birds have people on base the final eight innings of the game and can't get one big hit, stranding 17 for the game. and we know what that means... Bottom of the 11th, Tippy Martinez in, Fisk walks, Scott walks, Rice singles to load the bases and Tippy BALKS in the winner. Earl Weaver tries to put his lit cigarette in the second base umpire's eye but is pulled away by Al Bumbry... Orioles still lead the season series but these are two brutal losses.

BAL 005 000 000 00 – 5 12 1
BOS 002 010 020 01 – 6 16 0
   W-Campbell L-T. Martinez HR: L. May

METROPOLITAN STADIUM GAME TWO—Sherman has to move into shade to avoid heatstroke, and it's a good thing I joined him because this one might have put us both under...Carew opens Twins' 1st with single to make it 44 straight games, gets standing ovation and team responds with six runs off Gura and another big early lead. Except this is still the non-Goltz portion of the Minnesota rotation, in all its ineptness. Butler gives the Royals five runs immediately on a McRae solo blast and a White grand one, Cowens ties it with a homer in the 4th, Twins untie it with three in the 4th to bring on Doug Bird...Bird shuts Twins down for four innings while K.C. feasts on Dave Johnson, Serum and Tom Johnson for the next seven runs of the game...Only pitcher left is Burgmeier, and he lets Royals tack on two more in the 9th. 15-9 should be a safe lead, I imagine. Minnesota never stops dreaming, though. Hisle, Adams and Kusick open with hits. Gomez and Cubbage walk with one out. Carew singles and here's Littell, the score suddenly 15-12. Wynegar singles, it's 15-13. Bostock steps up, creams a grand slam out of the ballpark and if Met Stadium had a roof it would blow off. The Memorial Day Miracle marks the Twins' first win vs. the Royals in six tries. For K.C., five homers and 22 hits still isn't enough, and now they head back to Fenway Park.

K.C. 050 132 202 – 15 22 1
MIN 600 300 008 – 17 17 0
   W-Burgmeier L-Littell HRS: McRae, White, Cowens, Otis, Brett, Bostock GWRBI-Bostock

DR. GROSSINGER'S REPORT
Seamus Headley was waiting for me in my office this morning, a decided smirk on his face. "Those 5-D dice they're making for us? Ready in two days." I asked him how he knew they would even work, and how we would know which 1977 "game" to find Patient Gip and the others at. His manner became abrupt,

his smirk vanished, and he merely said. "Trust me, Doc."
   If I only felt confident doing that.
   —S.H.G.

My Dear Duffy Letter
May 31, 1977

PITTSBURGH—*Amy here. I wrote a special letter to Duffy Dyer today after his absolute dashingness against the Astros. Not sure if we'll be back for tomorrow's doubleheader, but in case not, at least that backstopping hunk will know I'm following him.*

Dear Duff (is it OK to call you that?):
First of all, I can't believe you're from Dayton, Ohio and your birthday is August 15th. I actually drove through Dayton once and my birthday is August 19th! I'm sorry it's taken me this long to write, but because you've been backing up Ed Ott I figured you don't get as many fan letters as he does and mine would still stand out. Your Pirates have been at the top or in the thick of the race for the first two months, and it's amazing how many big hits you've had playing maybe a third of the time. Well, from now on you can dedicate them all to me if you want.
   I was so happy I got sent to today's game, or at least picked it out. Houston has barely been able to beat you all year, so even after Cruz doubled in that run in the 1st off Kison, I wasn't worried. Oliver's double in the 3rd off Niekro tied it, of course, and then Joe sac flied in their go-ahead run, but I could see you squeezing your bat while you sat on the bench, just waiting for your gallant moment to shine.
   From what I've seen of the Pirates, they just never say roll over, and the 9th inning proved it again. Niekro got Oliver on a fly, but Parker walked and Pops singled him to second. Robinson then singled in Parker for the tie, and Sambito came on to face Ott, the happiest thing that could have happened to both of us.
   Out you came, sweat on your perfect moustache glistening in the late afternoon sun. Sambito had no chance. I'm not sure if you could hear me with all the other fans screaming, but I was the one going "Please, Duffy, do it!!" over and over.
   And then you did it! Spanked that ball silly, right over Puhl's leap at the fence, and I was jumping up and down so much I almost peed myself. I guess they don't do giant home plate celebrations yet because you only got a bunch

of hand-shaking and head-patting and butt-slapping, but I'm glad about that too because a player can get hurt jumping onto a dog pile.

Anyway, I've been traveling a lot around the country with my friends, but they're all starting to get on my nerves in different ways, so I was wondering if we could meet for a beer or dinner at your favorite place before midnight tonight. Whaddya think? I'll be just outside the players parking lot wearing a bright yellow midriff top. You won't miss me.

–Love & kisses from the grandstand, Amy Gulliver

HOU 100 000 100 – 2 6 0
PGH 001 000 004 – 5 8 1
W-Gossage L-Niekro HR: Dyer GWRBI-Dyer

There Goes the Party

June 1, 1977

CLEVELAND—So here we are, standing in line for grandstand tickets against the Rangers, trying as usual to not tell local fans they're about to see an awesome game, when there's this weird flash and clap of thunder.

But the sky is sunny and clear.

We swap curious looks for a second, then hear two things land with loud thuds, just around the corner. "Hold this please," says Lester, handing me his scorebook, and walks off to investigate. I pay for the tickets, pass them out to Amy, Fred, and Sherman, then suddenly hear Lester yell, "Get away from me!" We turn, and see him running across the parking lot in the general direction of Indiana.

"Oh no...oh no..." says Amy, her pale face even whiter. She nudges Sherman and Fred, and suddenly they're each taking off in a different direction.

Standing five feet away, her hair bun off-kilter, white coat wrinkled and stained with mustard, and glasses crooked on her face, is Dr. Sheila. Before I have a chance to split, she's grabbed my arm.

"Not you, Mr. Gip. You're staying with me."

"How the hell did you—"

She opens her hand. Shows me a set of glowing dice, larger and more blinding than the ones that Timeco Incorporated gave to me.

"5-Ds. But I'm afraid we have a problem."

She pulls me around the corner to the dumpster, where none other than Seamus the Sweeper Headley is lying unconscious inside a trash dumpster.

"He's alive but he's hurt. We have to get him to a hospital."

"Screw that, I'll miss the game!"

She gives me that calm, fake smile she's always good at. "No more games, Carlton. We've been trying to get these new dice made for weeks so we could find you. And now we have, so I think the first thing we need to do is get you back to the ward for a little rest."

"But what about my friends? You can't just leave 'em—"

"Exactly. Which is why I'll be coming back."

I try to slip free but she keeps a grip on my arm, tosses the dice against the wall—

And nothing happens.

"Gee," I said, "Bummer." She grabs them again, tries another roll. Dead. Looks at me with panicked eyes.

"Where's *your* dice? Still have them?"

I glance around, take two steps backward and drop them into a storm drain. She gapes at me.

"They didn't work that good, either."

"That's great, Carlton. That's just wonderful. Now what do we do?"

"Well, Doc...Guess we'll just have to take in a ballgame."

Game of the Day

Dr. Sheila doesn't let me out of her sight for the whole game, but I don't mind, because I always thought she was nice and not too bad to look at for an uptight doctor, and I believed that even when I thought the hospital was a trailer park.

As the game goes on she starts to forget that Seamus was sent to a local hospital, and that we have no "magic" dice left to transport us around to games, meaning for the most part we're stuck on the ground here in 1977 until the season ends. I can think of worse punishments.

I mean, Dock Ellis against Dennis Eckersley on a warm Ohio afternoon? How do you beat that? The Indians haven't been hitting spit lately, and it's 3-1 when Larvell Blanks gets them on the board with a long homer to left that bonks around some empty seats. It's only the fourth hit Dock's given up, and he tosses out a few more harmless ones until Paul Dade walks to start the Tribe 9th. Barker comes on to face homer threat Charlie Spikes, and he walks too. Fosse bunts them over, bringing up Kuiper.

Little Duane narrowly missed a homer in the 7th, and this time pounds a double down the right field line, scoring two and knotting the game! A wild pitch gets him to third and Moret is called in to get pinch-hitter Pruitt to line out.

The Eck had settled down after a rough first few innings, but loses it quick in the 11th. Washington and May open with doubles. Beniquez bunts May over, Horton singles, and after Monge gets the nod to face Wills, John Ellis pinch-hits and crushes one out of the yard for four Texas runs. Moret gets Cleveland in order, and the Rangers have pulled out another one. No team in the AL is playing as good as them right now, and with a rotation of Blyleven, Ellis, Perry and Alexander and with the Hargrove and Harrah .OPS twins, they have to be a strong pennant candidate.

Dr. Sheila was all anxious as we left the park. Seamus was drugged up at the hospital, and now she had to think about how to get the other patients back and earn their trust. I said I'd help her, but it would take a lot of traveling and ballgame-watching to get it done.

"And I'm sure you brought a bunch of money along," I said.

All she did was stare at me.

TEX 200 100 000 04 – 7 11 1

CLE 000 010 002 00 – 3 8 1

W-Moret L-Eckersley HRS: Ellis, Blanks GWRBI-May

American League through Sunday, June 1

Kansas City	28	19	.596	—
Boston	26	20	.565	1.5
Texas	27	22	.551	2
Baltimore	25	22	.532	3
New York	23	22	.511	4
Minnesota	20	26	.435	7.5
Chicago	19	26	.422	8
Cleveland	18	29	.383	10

National League through Sunday, June 1

Pittsburgh	31	20	.608	—
St. Louis	27	21	.563	2.5
Philadelphia	25	22	.532	4
Los Angeles	23	23	.500	5.5
Cincinnati	24	24	.500	5.5
Houston	24	26	.480	6.5
Montreal	20	26	.435	8.5
Chicago	18	30	.375	11.5

And on the 47th Day, He Rested

June 2, 1977

ERIE, PA—Funny how you learn things about people. Like Dr. Sheila having a dentist uncle named Sid Grossinger who lived in Erie, Pennsylvania in 1977. When she was a teenager she went out to visit him and her Aunt Flo a couple times, and remembered a cigar box on a shelf in the garage that he kept a spare money clip in.

Dr. Sheila wasn't too keen on my idea of taking a bus to Erie from Cleveland, sneaking into the garage and "borrowing" the money, mainly because once she got back to the present there'd be no way to pay Sid back in the past, but what else could we do? We needed fundage to follow the rest of the baseball season, to keep tabs on poor Seamus until he got his senses back in the hospital, and to track down Lester and Fred and Sherman and Amy before they did something idiotic and messed up the future.

Sid and Flo lived on a serious suburban street. Flo was pruning bushes in the backyard and Sid was off filling cavities somewhere, so we snuck in the garage through an unlocked side door, found the cigar box, grabbed the dough, and beat it down the street, Dr. Sheila saying she was going to hell about five times.

We didn't get to hell but did end up in a used car lot, buying a six-year-old Dodge Coronet with dents on both sides. And by the time we camped out in a chain motel outside of town to plan our next move, I was happy to turn on a clock radio and find the Twins-Yankees game on a Buffalo, NY station. One "Holy cow!" from Phil Rizzuto and the day's craziness melted away. I tried to help Sheila melt hers by filling her on the great Rod Carew hitting streak, at 46 games going in, but she just sat with a pad across the room and scribbled things during the game—and you can bet they weren't lineups.

Game of the Day

Joltin' Joe himself is in the owner's box for this one, and Rizzuto says it so I got no reason to doubt. Figueroa's going for the Yanks, and he's not only been their best pitcher so far but is tough on lefties. New York should beat up Thormodsgard pretty good, but with Carew making outs his first two times up, no one scores at all.

In the 4th, Bostock gets hit, Hisle singles him to third, and with the corners in, Adams scores Bostock on a deep grounder. What nobody counts on is Thormodsgard mowing down the Yankees, let alone anybody. After Jackson's single in the 1st, he retires the next 16 in a row. The Twins get three singles to load the bases in the 6th, none by the 0-for-3 Carew, but Cubbage leaves them there with a line out.

In the top of the 7th, Carew comes up for the fourth time. Rizzuto and Frank Messer set the stage beautifully, DiMaggio leaning out of his seat, but Carew slaps a grounder to Randolph and gets thrown out. He's 0-for-4, but will he come up again? His spot in the order is two batters away when Randall makes the last out in the 9th, the score still 1-0. Thormodsgard has a 3-hit shutout going, but Rivers, Munson and Jackson are coming up, all home run threats to tie the game and get Carew another at bat.

Rivers grounds to third, though, and Munson to second. It's up to Reggie, Mr. Drama himself. Thormodsgard winds, and the ball is cracked out to left-center. Hisle and Bostock converge, Lyman makes the catch for the only good game Thormodsgard's thrown all year and the end of Carew's hit streak, ten games shy of the Yankee Clipper.

The losing home crowd gives him an ovation anyway, and Rodney will head up to Boston to start his next streak. In that park against that pitching, he should have no problem. I'd sure like to be there of course—but first we have a Lester to find.

MIN 000 100 000 – 1 6 0
NYY 000 000 000 – 0 3 0
W-Thormodsgard L-Figueroa GWRBI-Adams

It's All About the 8-Track
June 3-4, 1977

Dr. Sheila sort of had a lead about where to find Lester. He grew up all over the midwest, but according to her notes he was the happiest on his dad's farm outside of Elk Horn, Iowa. So that would be our first far destination.

Lucky for us, the Dodge Coronet had an actual 8-track player mounted on the dash, and a box of 8-track cartridges the last owner had left in the trunk.

Unfortunately for Dr. Sheila, there were no Mozart ones.

"Deep Purple? How can you listen to this?"

"Because they're better than Renaissance, that's how."

"It's a long drive to Iowa, Mr. Gip. Can't we just talk?"

"That's all we do is talk. I need killer tunes if I'm driving. And you can just call me Buzz from now on, okay?

She straightened her glasses and sighed. It was pretty weird sharing a motel room with her last night, even with separate beds. She tossed and snored too much, probably worried about a supposedly nuts person like me attacking her, but smart, snooty doctors have never been my type so she didn't have to worry .

Anyway, we finally settled on an 8-track of Aretha's greatest hits, but the tape started gurgling and crunching and strangling inside the cartridge half-way across Indiana, and I had to pull off the road to dig the whole thing out of the dashboard with her eyebrow plucker.

Which was actually just fine, because it forced me to try the AM radio, and I found the White Sox-Indians game on WMAQ Chicago, complete with Harry Caray and Jimmy Piersall calling the action, and was I ever in heaven! Dr. Sheila could whine all she wanted to now, because I wasn't going to hear a word.

Game of the Days

Not only is Caray the second different radio guy in two days to yell "Holy cow!", but I forgot what an absolute fun announcer he is. I don't give a crap how much he roots for the home team, listening to him is like sitting in a bleacher seat with your drunk buddy, and he calls every game like a September battle for the pennant.

For now, neither of these outfits have a pennant to worry about. The Tribe's been scuffling for a while, but the White Sox took a long, unexpected dive after the opening week thanks to splotchy pitching and even splotchier fielding, and now battle the Indians daily to stay out of last place.

Today sounds different, though. Soderholm gets them going with a 3-run blast off Bibby, and after a Bannister error helps the Tribe get two back right away, a Gamble single, Zisk triple, Essian double and wild pitch give the Sox three more in the 5th. Gamble powers one out of the park in the 7th and it's 7-2 and game over, right?

It would be if Kravec were pitching, Chicago's only reliable starter so far. Instead it's the knuckleballing flutterations of Wilbur Wood, and Cleveland starts their 7th with three straight singles to knock him out. A Dade sac fly cuts it to 7-4, but Fromaster Gamble slams another homer in the 9th and it's 8-4 going to the last of the 9th.

I hardly notice as Bell works a walk off Dal Canton to begin things. Norris bats for Rico Carty but Hamilton comes on to bring up Fosse instead. Who singles. Dade singles off closer LaGrow and as Harry says, from one who knows, "the bases are drunk!" John Lowenstein, owner of many clutch hits so far, buys himself a special one and spanks a grand slam to tie the game! Holy cow, it's another LaGrow meltdown!

Three innings of impending Cleveland victory follows. Pruitt doubles but Garr throws Bochte out at the plate to end the 10th. Lowenstein does it again with a triple to lead off the 11th but LaGrow gets out of that one. Finally in the 13th (isn't it always the 13th?) Lowenstein singles with one out, gets moved along, and Bochte rips a single for the win. Bibby goes all 13 innings because believe it or not, pitchers were sometimes allowed to do that. As it turns out, all four AL games on this first day of action are 1-run thrillers, but the only one without contenders is the best of the bunch.

"Did you hear that game, Doctor?" I ask my passenger. She's half asleep, gazing out at the passing trees, mumbles "You can call me Sheila..." and falls back asleep.

CHX 300 030 101 000 0 – 8 14 2
CLE 200 000 204 000 1 – 9 16 1

W-Bibby L-LaGrow HRS: Soderholm, Gamble-2, Lowenstein GWRBI-Bochte

Expert Surgery by Dr. John
June 5, 1977

PITTSBURGH—Sherman Wayman here, remember me? It's been a century and a half, I know, but don't think I've lost interest in this baseball season, even though my Dodger boys have been giving me conniption fits these days. I mean, c'mon, my dead Bubbie could've hit better than they have lately with a hot towel on both her ankles, and now I've taken Greyhounds all the way back here to Three Rivers just to watch Tommy John battle future Dodger Jerry Reuss for the afternoon rubber game in this gotten-to-be desperate three-game series.

I wish I didn't have to run away from my friends in Cleveland the way I did, but I really don't need Dr. Grossinger in my life anymore, thank you very much. This old sponge knows who he is and where he's going now. If I can just keep these damn shoes of mine tied...Hold it a second...

Game of the Day
Of course you have to understand that Reggie Smith's been sitting on his *tuches* this whole series with some kind of bruise nonsense, but Pops Stargell has also been out, which is like comparing pastrami to corned beef in my book.

There's a fair amount of folks here for this Thursday matinee, or maybe just a lot of unemployed steel people. Either way they're making a racket and L.A. puts a cork in 'em in the 1st when Baker singles with one out, Teddy Martinez, playing short for Russell to get us some more offense against the lefty, singles Dusty to third. Cey, in a road trip slump I can't even begin to tell you about, works a walk, and Reggie replacement Lee Lacy slaps a single to left for two quick runs. Garvey, also swinging like a big chiseled pansy, beats out a possible DP grounder to score the third run.

And then it's Tommy Time. Dr. John hasn't been getting anyone out for a while, but today he's got his sinking fastball freezing Pirate kneecaps. Parker touches him for a double and single in the first six innings but John walks no one and gets practically everyone else. A 2-base error by Taveras and Yeager pop homer makes it 5-0 Dodgers, then 6-0 when Forster relieves Reuss and L.A. piles a two-out walk and singles by Garvey and Burke into another run.

But I wasn't born yesterday, or even the day before that. I know what these Bucs can do. Seen it all year. And there goes a Bill Robinson homer in the 7th to get them on the board. Parker leads the 9th with a single, Robinson walks, and they're at it all over again. When Oliver singles one out later, the bases are stuffed and Charlie Hough comes on for the second straight day to save our skins.

Except Taveras singles and it's 6-2! Duffy Dyer with his ton of on-base business somehow whiffs on a knuckleball, and Ed Ott hits for Tekulve. All steel-people on their feet! One Dodger fan afraid to look! Ott swings, lines it into Lopes' glove, and L.A. takes two out of three!

Thank God for this, but now I'm exhausted and have no idea where to go. Guess I could stick around to watch the Cubs here this weekend, but we know how that one probably turns out. Should I follow the Dodgers to Cincinnati? Amy rode with me on the first bus and got off somewhere in Ohio when I was taking my nap, so otherwise I'd be asking her. Hate to say this, but…I miss my poor sweet Hannah more than ever right now.

L.A 300 200 100 – 6 10 0

PIT 000 000 101 -2 10 1

W-John L-Reuss SV-Hough HRS: Yeager, Robinson GWRBI-Lacy

DR. GROSSINGER'S REPORT

It seems that Mr. Gip—or "Buzz," as he prefers to call himself—has been making ample time in our unsightly Coronet as we drive to Iowa in search of patient Lester Creech. It pained me somewhat to leave Mr. Headley in the Cleveland hospital, but the staff there seemed well-trained, and willing to supply him with the appropriate drugs and therapy to speed his recovery.

"Buzz" seems quiet in control of himself lately, if anything, taking aggressive charge of a difficult situation in a way that didn't seem possible in our sessions one month ago. I will make a point of being as open and accommodating as I can with him, even going so far as to tolerate his obsessive-compulsive relationship with baseball, which will helpfully draw him out further. I did read a recent

study citing road travel as a possible method of behavior relaxation, and I must admit it in the first few days, despite being cast away in a decade I have never had much fondness for, it has helped me considerably. —S.H.G.

Completely Schizo-ball

June 6, 1977

Well, Sheila and I made it out to Lester's family farm in this blink of a town called Elk Horn, Iowa, but there was no one around, certainly no one who could tell us anything more. The front door was unlocked which is typical out here I suppose, and we walked in saying hello about three or four times, but the only thing we heard was a weird clanking from out back.

An old fat guy in suspenders was repairing a tractor engine, but he was pretty hard of hearing, and every time we brought up Lester's name he said he didn't know who we were talking about. Of course THAT made sense because we were at Lester's farm about ten years before Lester was even born. Top of that, his parents had already split up, his dad was off at a pig feed convention in Wichita and his mom had moved down to Oklahoma six months ago. But at least we got her address for our troubles.

Funny, but when we were walking back through the house on our way out I still felt like Lester was around. Maybe the place just had his pre-born vibe or something.

LESTER (hiding in fruit cellar):

It's sad...when a son has to speak the words that condemn his own parents... but I couldn't allow anyone to believe that I was following five baseball teams at once...If they find me they'll put me away again...as I should have...years ago. He was always...confused. And in the end, he intended to tell them that I wore that White Sox hat...and carried a Cubs flag. As if I could do anything except just sit and write in my scorebook...like one of those stuffed nerds.

They're probably up there listening for me. Well, let them.. Let them find out what a harmless baseball fan I am...I hope they ARE listening. They'll see... they'll see...and they'll know...and they'll say... "why, he couldn't even catch a fly..."

Games of the Day

BOSTON—Steve Stone? Okay, so he's 0-8 with an Apollo mission of an ERA, who cares? Probably just a lot of bad luck.

For his two and a third innings of work today: nine hits, four walks, two homers, ten runs. Tiant gives up 16 hits and ten runs and wins. I give up.

CHX 033 001 312 – 13 23 1
BOS 171 140 00x – 14 18 1
　W-Tiant L-Stoned SV-Willoughby, HRS: Spencer, Orta, Gamble, Lynn, Evans (again!), Yaz GWRBI-Yaz

　NEW YORK—Hard to believe these four teams are playing the same sport. Sssssh.... .
TEX 000 000 000 0 – 0 7 0
NYY 000 000 000 1 – 1 3 1
　W-Gullett (CG) L-Ellis GWRBI-Piniella

National Massacre Day
June 7, 1977

　HARLEM—Friendly Fred back with ya, after hitchin' about 17 rides from Ohio to the Big Wormy Apple. Thought my grandma would freak when she saw me show up on her stoop all growed up, but her mind was gone like I remembered, and she thought I was her cousin George from Atlanta so I played along. She put me up on her couch, said she'd feed me soup for as long as I can stand it. That's good news, because the Yanks still got this home stand to finish out and I'd like to catch me most every game even if I'm stuck out in the bleachers.

　Dr. G. showin' up in Cleveland the way she did was pure jive, and there is no way I am goin' back to her loony house any time soon. Figure all I gotta do is lay low at the Stadium or here at Grandma's. Matter of fact today I just caught the Yanks on her fuzzy Sylvania with a Coke and big bag of cheese twists and was happy as a newborn. The game was a cool breeze for us, so I'll brake on the details this time, but there was some kind of evil in the air today 'cause almost every park around had a bloodbath to deal with. Check it:

　CARDS 11-14-1, at EXPOS 1-6-1 When the lefty-clubbing Expos can't score against Tom Underwood, they got problems. Simmons and Templeton with three hits apiece, while Cards' long relief man Butch Metzger has now given up one stinkin' earned run in almost 35 innings pitched.

　ASTROS 12-16-1, at PHILLIES 2-10-1 Worst starter in the league Larry Christenson is torched for a Cliff Johnson 2-run blast and Watson grand slam in the first three innings before he's sent to bed. I swear, if Larry was pitching and Mike Schmidt was hitting, the Phils might be in first place by now. Three whiffs and a double play at the plate for Big Mike today, and yet another error in the field.

AT PIRATES 6-11-0, CUBS 0-4-1 The narrow Cub victory yesterday turns out to be a mirage. Bad Luck Bill Bonham gives up the game on five Buc runs in the 2nd, without one hit roll landing on his card. That's tough to do.

DODGERS 5-11-0, at REDS 2-9-1 Gritty Hooton outing puts L.A. back on track. Garvey's in a major slump, though(.074 with two RBIs in June, and 5 for his last 46) which he better shake out of soon.

at RED SOX 25-25-0, WHITE SOX 8-14-3 I guess you can say Boston is hot. That's 67 runs scored and 16 homers in their last six games. Remember when Jim Rice didn't have an RBI for the first two weeks of the season? Well, he now has 50. Chicago actually scores four runs in the 1st in this one before they get disemboweled.

at YANKEES 6-6-3, RANGERS 0-3-0 Figueroa and Perry duel it off and are now both 7-2. Reggie with a bases-clearing triple to ice the proceedings.

ROYALS 12-19-0, at ORIOLES 0-3-0 Rudy May is drawn and quartered in front of the home folks. Over half the K.C. hits are for extra bases, as they keep pace with the Red Sox. Highlight of the game is when Drago hits Mayberry with a pitch after the brother hits two straight homers and Big John charges the mound, decks him, and gets suspended for three games.

TWINS 6-10-0, at INDIANS 1-9-1 New Carew streak up to four, Gary Serum relieves and actually doesn't suck, and poor Jim Bibby is smacked silly as the Tribe home record drops to 9-20.

Time-Warped

June 8, 1977

I've always said there's two easy rules to make any man-woman relationship work: He lets her freak out once in a while, and she lets him watch the game. Of course, my wife walked out on me years back because I watched too many games so maybe I'm not one to talk, but there's no harm in starting over with Sheila, right? I know she's just my doctor and we haven't even sniffed at anything romantic, but if I'm going to be driving around the country with her all damn season, might as well learn how to get along, right?

Her opening freak-out was today, somewhere between Iowa and Oklahoma, when she dug into her purse for a pen and saw that her expensive Papermate ballpoint had for some reason turned into a 19-cent Bic. Next came her small jar of skin moisturizer, which had been magically replaced with a tube of frosted lipstick. She looked at me in shock and dumped the entire purse contents in her lap.

Her cell phone, unusable since she landed here in 1977, had sprung three miniature woofer speakers and was now suddenly called a SuperPhone.

"What the hell is this??"

"I don't know, but I think we should turn it on." She stared at the thing for too long so I grabbed it away, pulled off the road and found a button on its back. It whirred to life like a small fan, beeped and booped and a couple buttons flashed red and blue.

"Can I get my e-mails??" Sheila barked.

"I don't know. The screen still hasn't lit up. Wait—there it is."

There was no screensaver photo, just three options: GAMES...SONGS...SCORES. The games were Pong and something called Super Chess, with a board that looked more like a miniature waffle. The two songs on the phone were "You Light Up My Life" by Debby Boone and "Rich Girl" by Hall & Oates. But the scores—baseball only—were something else, complete with box scores, play-by-play and a goofy little diamond with stick figure players racing around. Yup, the time warp phone was gonna taking care of Old Buzz just fine.

"What can it do??"

"Oh, nothing you'd be interested in. Feel like driving?"

Games of the Day

CINCINNATI—Not sure where the hell Sherman disappeared to, but if he's back in California he missed out on his team getting back in the race big time. Cincy gets to Sutton for two runs to open Game One, but a Reggie Smith triple and Cey sac fly ties it in the 3rd. Then Oates, starting at catcher to get another lefty in against lefty-challenged Moskau, parks one in the 4th to start a 3-run rally topped by a Penguin double. Baker gets plunked on the wrist to open the Dodger 5th and gets knocked out for five games, but L.A. doesn't even flinch, scoring three more times to go up 8-2. Sutton then loses his stuff, Driessen homers, and four Red runs fly across in the 6th. But Don bears down, 1-hits the home team the rest of the way and goes the distance.

Game Two is just a big shock. Rick Rhoden, he of the 1-6 record and not one good start all year, fires a 3-hit shutout, Garvey wakes from his coma to smack a 2-run homer, and the Dodgers roll the table. Cincy's great everyday lineup and fielding gets nullified all the time by their weak bench and outside of Seaver, sub-mediocre pitching. It's no wonder they're back at .500.

L.A. 002 330 000 – 8 9 1

CIN 200 004 000 – 6 10 1

W-Sutton L-Moskau HRS: Oates, Driessen GWRBI-Oates

L.A. 000 112 022 – 8 9 0

CIN 000 000 000 – 0 3 1

W-Rhoden L-Soto HR: Garvey

American League through Sunday, June 8

Boston	34	20	.630	—
Kansas City	30	24	.556	4
Baltimore	29	24	.547	4.5
New York	29	24	.547	4.5
Texas	28	28	.500	7
Minnesota	25	29	.463	9
Chicago	21	32	.396	12.5
Cleveland	20	35	.364	14.5

National League through Sunday, June 8

Pittsburgh	34	23	.596	—
St. Louis	32	23	.582	1
Philadelphia	29	25	.537	3.5
Los Angeles	29	25	.537	3.5
Cincinnati	28	28	.500	5.5
Houston	26	30	.464	7.5
Montreal	21	32	.396	11
Chicago	21	34	.382	12

Early Nervous Time

June 9, 1977

I would have been just fine living in our old storm cellar out here in Iowa, but the Cards were opening a four-game series in Pittsburgh, and I needed to listen, so when Cal finished his two days of fixing the tractor I came up, made myself a giant roast beef sandwich and got Dad's old Panasonic radio tuned in to KMOX St. Louis. Some days—matter of fact most of them—I don't have a clue which of my teams to root for, but the second I hear old Jack Buck things get rather clear in a hurry.

Game of the Day

It's been amazing how St. Louis has come on, 25-13 since the beginning of May, especially with mostly ineffective starting pitching outside of Forsch. Bob is going today against tough Jerry Reuss, but the Pirates come to play in the 1st when Stennett and Oliver lead with singles, Parker plates one run with a force, Stargell walks, Robinson and Ott single and it's 3-0 in a jiffy.

McBride is off to Philadelphia, but he wouldn't have been starting this one against lefty Reuss anyway, and Mr. Heity Cruz has been doing just fine, thank you. With one out in the 3rd, Hernandez singles. With one out later, Cruz, Scott and Reitz weed-whack nearly matching doubles down the line and the game is tied.

The Pittsburgh crowd is nervous; I can hear the tension right through the radio. And it all gets tighter and quieter two innings later, when Cruz triples, Scott singles, and we take a 4-3 lead. You don't hear too many games where the 5-7 spots in a lineup do all the damage (9.7% of the time, maybe?), but that is exactly what happens here.

Meanwhile Forsch settles down wonderfully, and Reuss falls apart in the 7th. Simmons, Cruz and Scott single with one out. Tekulve and his one earned run allowed all season comes on to face Reitz, and little Ken bombs a 3-run homer on the first pitch to basically file the game away. The Bucs make their usual 9th inning noise, but they're too far back and Forsch has zeroed in for the kill.

I shut off the radio, go out on the front porch and watch some distant thunderheads roll across the plains. St. Louis has moved into first by percentage points, which is pretty amazing...Except it shouldn't make Cubs and Astros fans too happy.

No. Not happy at all.

Dumb stupid Cardinals, I HATE THEM.

—*Lester*

STL 003 010 402 – 10 17 0
PIT 300 000 002 – 5 10 0
W-Forsch L-Reuss HR: Reitz GWRBI-Scott

The Agony and the Eckersley

June 10, 1977

CLEVELAND—Amy here. So I've been hiding out deep in Ohio, digging on the cheesy shags, sideburns and slacks every guy seems to have around here, when I'm suddenly itching to see another ball game. Here's my choice: the no-doubt Plummerless Reds against the last-place Cubs, or the Indians home against the K.C. Royals, who've beaten them all five times this year. Riverfront seems like the best ticket, until I check the pitching matchups in the *Beacon-Journal* and see Dennis Eckersley's going for the Tribe. Needless to say, this hot-blooded lady has made her decision.

I have to be extra careful, of course, because Dr. Grossinger might still be snooping around up here, not to mention that creepy Seamus Headley, but I figure the risk is worth it to watch Eck the Dashing Gunslinger for a night. Little do I know I'm about to see the most amazing game of our rehashed '77.

Now Dennis is 2-6 so far but I can tell you that he's had less support than a highway ramp built with Legos. And he is ON once again. From my third base box seat which was damn easy to sneak into with about 19 people here, he's got that buggywhip arm freezing and melting Royal bats from the start. I've been following the Reds more than the Indians so far so I don't know the details of this supposed Curse of Colavito they got going on, but even in a league like this that few thought they'd win, it sure seems like they get more haunted stuff than they need.

And this one's a slasher movie/gothic novel/real-life possession all in one. While Cleveland's busy stranding one runner in the 1st, one runner in the 2nd, three in the 3rd, one in the 4th and two in the 5th against Splittorff, Wyatt Eck guns down the first twenty Royals in a row. Not even a scent of a baserunner. Top of the 7th, Brett works him for a two-out walk, but McRae fans for the third time and that's that.

Thornton singles with two gone in the 8th but Dade fouls out and we go the 9th, K.C. still hitless but the game scoreless. Patek grounds out. White whiffs. Pete LaCock, filling in for Mayberry at first today, bounces out to Kuiper and Dennis has a no-hitter through nine! I want to run out on the field and kiss him, but also don't want to miss history by sitting in a room in handcuffs. Win the damn game, Indians!!

They try at least. Grubb gets hit to lead off the Tribe 9th and gets sent to first. Charlie Spikes just about throws himself in front of Splittorff's next pitch, and before you know it him and Darrell Porter are duking it out on top of home plate! Both of them get kicked out of the game, Manning runs for Spikes, and Duffy bunts them both over. One out, Kuiper at the plate, Grubb

90 feet away from an Eck no-no, and Duane weakly grounds out to a drawn-in Frank White. Two outs. Pruitt skies out to right, and we're going to extras!

Where Cowens whiffs on a freaky curve. Brett bounces out, and McRae gets smoked for the sombrero. TEN innings of no-hit ball! How could this happen? I just want to hug Dennis now, hold him in my arms and—

Okay Amy, calm down. He can still win this. And here's a line drive double by Rico Carty with one out! Lowenstein runs for him but Thornton and Dade both fly out to left, and all 19 nervous breakdowns break out.

Eck back to the hill. Leading off the 11th is Wathan, who replaced Porter behind the dish. John's hitting .369 part-time and we got a bad feeling about this. WHACK—line drive into center for the end of the not-hitter, the shutout and most likely the game. Dennis gets Poquette but Otis then rifles a double into the corner and Patek grounds out.

White is pulled for lefty bench bat Joe LaHoud, who promptly doubles into the right gap for two runs and I'm walking up the aisle in tears. Yup, some days there IS crying in baseball, and plenty of it, because some days there just isn't any justice. Splittorff gets the Tribe 1-2-3 in the 11th like I knew he would, and Eckersley drops to 2-7 for no good reason, while the team loses their seventh straight and is now 9-23 in their home park.

All I know is this girl needs a six-pack of Falls City right quick to drown her tearjerking heart in.

K.C. 000 000 000 02 -2 3 0
CLE 000 000 000 00 – 0 7 0
W-Splittorff L-Eckersley GWRBI-LaHoud

Fooey on Looey!
June 11, 1977

By Ed "Peachy" Calhoun
Jewett Babbler Sports Columnist
Had to drive Cooper all the way up to a vet I know in Corsicana because he got stung by a yellowjacket and his paw swelled up like a water balloon. Don't ya hate that?

The good news is that between the long haul and the time I spent waiting for Cooper to get his shots, I got to listen to the whole four-hour Rangers game in Boston. I don't know what the hell happened to my boys. Seems like a week ago we were two or so games out, but that was before them New Englanders ate their atomic beans. Anyway, you know I wouldn't be filling you in like this unless the game was more than special.

Game of the Day

BOSTON—Us Ranger fans can't exactly relate to where they're coming from up there. The Red Sox have been closing their eyes, swinging with one hand and putting half the balls on the turnpike. For nine straight days. Yesterday they even gave Blyleven a big what-for.

This time it's a couple of real characters having at it, Dock Ellis and Luis Tiant, and Dock seems to need some of that hippie medicine he took a few years back when he threw that no-hitter. He walks Carbo, Fisk and Yaz to start the Boston 1st, before Rice hits into a double dealer and Evans whiffs.

Tiant's got his full goofy act down, whirling and dervishing and looking up at the half-moon and Dave May takes him out of the park anyway after a Claudell single to put us up 2-1 in the 2nd. Not for long, of course. With two outs in Boston's 2nd, Burleson singles and Doyle doubles and Carbo walks and Fisk gets bonked and the Polish fella singles and we're down again 3-2.

Looey looks even worse than Dock, though. Two doubles two singles, a walk and a sacf fly in the 4th and we're back up 5-3. What? You think we're not gonna hold that? You'd be right, podner. Polish Fella hits his 13th homer in the 4th, Evans hits his 16th and eighth in his last seven games in the 6th and we're losing again 6-5.

But here's where Boston gets all cocky, because in most cases they'd have their danger-zone bullpen in the game for the late innings. Instead, Tiant stays out there, not being tired I suppose. Well, May rips another tater off him to tie the game in the 8th, and a Hargrove double and Bevacqua triple puts us ahead in the 9th!

Cue Butch Hobson, schooled once by Bear Bryant himself, and as hot as everyone else in the lineup. Butchie pops Len Barker's first 9th inning pitch into the net to tie the game and this Red Sox streak might never end.

But Tiant won't leave the game, because everything Boston spits out somehow turns into gold nuggets, but after Beniquez singles in the 10th, Bump Wills rides a Tiante dipsy-doodle curveball straight into the bullpen. Barker gets Rice to ground into his second DP to end the nine-game win streak, and this old boy and the American League rejoice. Boston hits the road for a western big ballpark tour after tomorrow's finale, so I'd look for them to get sort of human again.

TEX 020 300 011 2 – 9 17 0
BOS 120 102 001 0 – 7 14 0

W-Barker L-Cocky Tiant HRS: D, May-2, Wills, Yaz, Evans, Hobson GWRBI-Wills

Fly Me to the Fens

June 13, 1977

So me and Dr. Sheila finally get to Oklahoma City where Lester's Mom lives, track down the beauty parlor where she works and find out she's on a long lunch break. Great. We decide to sit around and wait, and I'm leafing through a stack of *Ms.* Magazines when I realize it's June 12th–the day my five-year-old self is due to be found at Fenway Park! Damn...

I can't imagine Sheila is going to want to leave this Lester goose chase for one of mine, so while she's in the rest room I leave her a note, saying I'll meet her back here in 24 hours. Grab a whole wad of cash out of her purse and run out to hail a cab to the airport.

I haven't been on a plane since I won a trip to Disney World with Pam and Timmy in the early 90s, but I can't remember if those flights were this awesome. The TWA stewardesses are young and sexy for one thing, wearing these cute little hot pants and boots, and the one named Lori flirts with me non-stop after she notices my dirty jeans and mistakes me for an oil driller. They serve an incredible meal of roast chicken breast with rice and vegetables, give me a pillow so I can stretch out my legs and watch the entire movie *Silver Streak* before we land in Boston five minutes early. I can only imagine how amazing flying must be now.

Unfortunately, I dumbly didn't check the game time, and as soon as I get in my Boston taxi late in the afternoon and ask to be taken to Fenway, the cabbie says the Rangers already beat them. He takes me there anyway, and I find a way to sneak in and nab an aisle sweeper's uniform and broom. It takes a few hours to clean up the park, and it's almost dark when I see Jose Torres arrive for his night maintenance shift.

I follow him on his rounds, staying in the ballpark shadows. Around ten he hears the same noise that I do—a kid talking in his sleep—and I follow him to a hidden alcove under the third base stands.

There I am, five-year-old Buzz himself—laying on a flattened cardboard box. I get the chills something fierce. He wakes with a start, gives the two of us a terrified look. Then Jose turns and sees me.

"Who the hell are you, man?" he asks.

"I lost Buzz during the game," I say, off the top of my head. "Don't worry, I'll take care of him from here."

Games of the Days

RANGERS 9-16-1, at RED SOX 7-12-0 (11 innings) I would've let the cabbie explain this one, but I could barely follow anything he said so I just checked the box score in the *Boston Herald* later. Basically, it's the same score as yesterday and almost the same game. Perry has a 3-2 lead into the 4th when Yaz smacks a grand slam, but Aase can't even hold his jock, and Texas finally ties it in the 7th on a 2-run Claudell Washington homer. Perry, Moret and Barker hold the Sox scoreless for the last six innings until Claudell does it again, a 2-run double in extras that tightens up the A.L. even more. Boston heads off to K.C. for three, with no friendly home run wall in sight.

W-Barker L-Aase HRS: Washington, Yaz GWRBI-Washington

Boy Oh Boy
June 14, 1977

Little Me had never been on a plane, and certainly never out of New England, but it was too late: I was going all the way with this history-changing business. Of course I couldn't exactly tell little Carlton that I was really him, and when he asked why we looked so much the same I just said I was his distant Uncle Buzz, knowing he wouldn't be called Buzz for another four years or so. He wouldn't say a word about who left him at Fenway Park, so I took him back to Oklahoma City on another plane, only to find Dr. Sheila just about waiting with state police.

She did finally talk to Lester's Mom, who wasn't much help like I figured, but now there was a new project for her. The first second she looked at Little Me she just about melted. Carlton said he was a huge baseball fan and the next thing you knew all Sheila's maternal stuff was pouring out and she was sitting in the back seat with him, a cold milk shake in his hand as we hightailed it down to the Astrodome for the game with the Pirates. As usual, fine by me.

Game of the Day

HOUSTON–I can't tell you how weird it was watching a game with myself, but then again, the Dome kind of makes you feel weird anyway. It's Reuss vs. Lemongello and after a crappy road trip the Astros have never been so happy to get back home. Stennett pops a solo homer in the 3rd, but Houston comes back pronto on two walks, a Puhl single, Watson double and sac fly from Cliff Johnson, who's about to go to the Yankees.

As usual, the Bucs battle back right away, getting an Oliver RBI single in the 5th and three more in the 6th to take the lead, with the help of the daily Julio Gonzalez error. Then Bill Robinson drops one in left, and a Cabell sac fly cuts Pittsburgh's lead to 5-4. Now the Astros are a pathetic 1-8 with the Bucs, losing many heartbreaking games, but I just have a good feeling about this one.

Sheila has a different kind of feeling, because when she isn't buying Little Me snacks and asking him every question she can think of and jotting his answers in her open program, she seems to be pulling for the Pirates for some reason.

Reuss is still in there for them when the bottom of the 9th starts, and the hardly-ever-used Art Gardner pinch-hits for Gonzalez and raps a single. Jose Cruz hits for McLaughlin and works a walk. In comes Kent Tekulve, with his gangly, bumblebee top and opium dealer glasses, still having given up only two runs all season. But here's Cedeno lining a single, and Gardner's scores the tying run! Puhl is next up, the Astrodomers on their feet screaming, and Little Me covering his ears, and Tekulve wriggles one to the plate—

—and it gets past Ed Ott! Cruz runs home with the win, and Houston has beaten the Bucs with a shocking ambush of their own.

PGH 001 013 000 – 5 10 1
HOU 003 001 002 – 6 7 1
  W-McLaughlin L-Reuss HR: Stennett

DR. GROSSINGER'S REPORT:
Meeting and spending time with young Master Gip has opened a part of me I had not been aware of. I've often thought of bearing children some day, or at the least, treating them, so I would be foolish to not collect valuable research from this unusual opportunity. If I can learn who abandoned Mr. Gip and why before we find our way back to the present—and secure a proper upbringing for his 5-year-old self, perhaps stabilizing his later emotional future—then these grueling daily travels will have been well worth it.
  —S.H.G.

Can't Beat Suffering at the Old Ballpark
June 15, 1977

CHICAGO—Lester reporting once again, happy as a peach pie to be out of my sad and clammy Iowa basement. Neither Mother nor Father was coming home anytime soon, and handyman Cal never had a clue who I was. So what better place to feel good again but a Sunday doubleheader at Wrigley Field with my beloved Cubs taking on the Phils?

I got off my Greyhound Bus downtown, hopped on the red El line and waited for Wrigley to roll into view at Addison. The good seats were all sold out, but it was gorgeous out and I was more than comfortable in the packed bleachers, even if a few too many white men with afros and girls in halter tops were staring at the calculator sticking out of my shirt pocket.

Games of the Day

Philly has been the tortoise to everyone in the league's hare, slow and steady, slow and steady, and suddenly within a hot streak of the top. Lefty Carlton is on the hill for them, scorching now after a cold start, but we stitch together two runs in the 1st off him on two walks and singles by Clines and Ontiveros. The shirtless fellows around me cheer and spray a bit of beer from their plastic cups, but I'm very reserved as I make the notations in my scorebook. No pitcher has been safe for the Cubs lately, and Steve Renko is not exactly their ace.

A Hebner double and Boone single bring in the first Phillie run an inning later, before a Schmidt double and 2-run Luzinski bomb nearly into my lap puts them ahead in the 3rd. Sudden silence washes over the bleachers, as Carlton goes to work and has his way with us. The Cubs get a DeJesus double and four scattered singles for the rest of the game and score nothing, while Philly adds three more runs off Renko and Paul Reuschel, Rick's bad brother, and that is that.

No one imagined the Cubs winning the pennant, but they sure weren't expected to be the league doormats. At this writing, Bonham, Burris and Krukow are a combined 2-24, and their offense has produced the fewest homers and grounded into the most double plays. Still, in the twenty minutes between games, the fans drink more Old Style, flirt with each other, spin off loud trivia contests (two which I manage to win) and manage to have a fine time anyway. I realize it is a godsend that Cub fans have Wrigley Field, because in a dismal, cavernous pit like Olympic Stadium, their play would be lucky to draw 10,000 a game.

Note to self: create new stat for measuring ratio of attendance to poor team performance. Possible acronym—BFD (Broberg Factor Differential)

Game One:

PHL 012 002 100 – 6 12 0

CHI 2000 000 000 – 2 7 1

W-Carlton L-Renko HR: Luzinski GWRBI-Luzinski

With Dennis Lamp being the only sixth starter available to spot start the nightcap for the Cubs, I'm afraid Dennis Lamp starts Game Two for the Cubs. You would think with his Wild Bill Hickock moustache and imposing frame, the Phillie hitters would quake in their maroon shoes.

Not quite. Once again we take a 2-0 lead out of the gate when the only pitcher maybe worse than Lamp, Randy Lerch, allows a DeJesus double, two wild pitches and a Morales homer to start his afternoon, and is extracted from the premises for Warren Brusstar. Burning his pen is a risk Danny Ozark is willing to take, for he knows the wind is blowing out here and how suspect the Chicago staff is.

Nine unanswered runs later, his ploy pays off. And while the bleacher fans sit glumly watching hits bang around the yard that aren't theirs, expletives begin to ring out. "Don't worry," I say to the sulking fat kid next to me, "they'll put in lights here someday and a guy named Sammy Sosa will light up the place, and you'll almost make the World Series in 2003, if not for an overzealous fan who shall not be named." His eyes just about pop out of his head, and as his family walks him out he starts telling his father everything I told him. "Don't talk to weirdos," I hear his dad say.

By the time Tug McGraw puts us away 1-2-3 in the 9th, I start to get anxious. Not because we'd dropped our 40th game of the year and are now 1-11 against Philadelphia, but because I don't know where to go now. If only each game went 16 or so innings, I would never have to leave my seat. I like sitting here in the late afternoon sun, lake gulls wheeling overhead and the sound of foot-popping soda cups echoing around the park.

And now I see a few security guards making their way through the empty stands. Please don't make me leave...

Game Two:

PHI 021 420 000 – 9 15 0

CHI 200 000 000 – 2 10 2

W-Brusstar L-Lamp HRS: Boone, Morales GWRBI-Bowa

American League through Sunday, June 15

Boston	36	24	.600	—
Kansas City	36	25	.590	0.5
New York	33	27	.550	3
Baltimore	32	28	.533	4
Texas	32	30	.516	5
Minnesota	27	34	.443	9.5
Chicago	25	34	.424	10.5
Cleveland	21	40	.344	15.5

National League through Sunday, June 15

St. Louis	36	25	.590	—
Pittsburgh	36	28	.563	1.5
Philadelphia	34	27	.557	2
Los Angeles	33	28	.541	3
Cincinnati	32	30	.516	4.5
Houston	29	33	.468	7.5
Montreal	24	34	.414	11
Chicago	21	40	.344	15.5

Bizarro Night at the Blue Swallow

June 17, 1977

TUCUMCARI, N.M.—I did always want to take Route 66, but never imagined I'd be cruising down it in an old Dodge Coronet with my psychiatrist and five-year-old version of myself in the back seat. We were heading out to California to track down Sherman Wayman, having ditched Lester after a week of dead ends, but it was getting late and it was 107 degrees with heat lightning at sunset and Little Me was starting to freak out.

So we holed up in the Blue Swallow Motel, where we met its nice owner Lillian Redman, who actually got the place as a wedding gift back in 1958. The air conditioner was noisy and trucks were going by off and on, so Little Me had a tough time sleeping and poked me awake around two in the morning.

"Mister? What happened to my Dad?"

I sat up, all groggy, peered over at Sheila in the next bed which he had just climbed out of and saw she had earplugs and a sleeping mask on.

"Well...if I knew that, buddy, I guess I would've told you by now, right?"

"Shouldn't we just go to another Red Sox game? Maybe he'll be there looking for me."

"Umm...we can't just yet, because they're traveling. Just like we are. But maybe we'll catch them somewhere in the midwest on our way back from California." We also needed to check in on poor Seamus Headley at some point, still recuperating back in Cleveland, but there was no point bringing that up. "Carlton? Was your dad...okay when he took you to that game? The one he left you at?"

Even in the dark I could see his little face screw up. "I don't think so...He said my bad grains were in his head."

"Bad grains?"

"Yeah. But they weren't mine."

"Oh—you mean migraines? Migraine headaches?"

"Uh-huh...He said he had my bad grains since Mom died. I'm going back to bed now. Goodnight, mister." And he did.

But now I couldn't.

Monday's game news from Sheila's SuperPhone:

PHILLIES 7-18-1, at CUBS 5-15-3 (13 innings) Schmidt leads off the game with his 12th homer and the Phils batter Reuschel for three runs, but Big Rick settles down from there, allowing the Cubs to tie the game and pull ahead on a 1-5 chance Gross homer in the 7th. It's 5-3 into the 9th, Sutter in for his third inning, and no one at Wrigley feels safe. With good reason. Schmidt leads off with his 13th homer. Murcer drops the next pitch for a two-base error. Luzinski and Sizemore whiff, but Hutton and Boone single to incredibly tie the game again. Four innings later off Willie Hernandez, Sizemore hits the go-ahead homer and the sweep is official. McGraw goes six relief innings for the win and will be out for a while.

EXPOS 8-10-2, at CARDS 7-7-4 Denny is sent running for cover and shower water after giving Montreal seven runs in the 2nd, but Rogers, giddy from actually having an offense behind him, lets St. Louis back in the game by giving them a five-run 6th. Kerrigan gets the sweaty save, but the game's almost-hero is Rawly Eastwick, who stops the Expos cold for six innings after their big outburst.

Tuesday's game news from Sheila's SuperPhone:

at CUBS 2-7-1, PIRATES 1-6-0 Inexplicable. The Bucs escape from the Astrodome to Wrigley Field with the wind blowing out. Facing the 1-10 Bill Bonham. With 9-3 Candelaria pitching for them. Bobby Murcer, Chicago's only home run threat, goes out with a 3-game injury in the 1st inning...And the Cubs beat them 2-1. I guess this must be baseball.

Game One: **REDS 8-14-0, at CARDS 2-9-1** Just like yesterday, a St. Louis starter gets hammered early —Urrea gives up eight—and a far worse pitcher comes in (Falcone) to shut down the opposition. And like yesterday, it's too late.

Game Two: **REDS 11-14-0, CARDS 2-12-3** Horrendous Cards pitching and fielding, along with Bad Base Hit Management 101 gives Cincy the sweep. It's so bad that Woodie Fryman gets a win, and to top off the day, Mumphrey,

Cruz and Hernandez all get hurt for the Cards.

PHILLIES 9-11-2, at ASTROS 7-13-4 By the time this ungodly slopfest is over, the Phillies find themselves in first place for the first time all year. Andujar has an off-night, Jim Kaat has a rare on-night, and Brusstar, the only pitcher in the Phillie pen without a dead arm, survives a 9th inning 'Stros rally by getting Puhl to bounce out with the bases loaded to end it.

at DODGERS 6-9-0, EXPOS 3-3-1 Happy Hooton throws a no-hitter through seven, Hough gives Perez a 3-run bomb in the 9th, but that's that. Twitchell's 1st inning: four walks, two wild pitches, two homers, and two outs before he's pulled like a rotten tooth.

at WHITE SOX 4-10-1, YANKEES 0-6-2 More of that piping hot bizarreness you ordered. All three White Sox catchers are injured, forcing Ralph Garr into a mask and shin guards. LaGrow and Dal Canton are both unavailable in the White Sox pen. The Yanks come off a day in Minnesota where they rack up 21 runs and 28 hits...and promptly get shutout by the 0-10 Steve Stone.

INDIANS 5-12-0, at ROYALS 0-5-1 Continuing the surreal theme, Wayne Garland blanks the Royals on their own Turf, the first time in nine tries the Tribe has beaten them.

ORIOLES 6-10-0, at TWINS 1-6-0 Birds get 13 walks off Minnesota "pitching" and win easy despite grounding into four DPs. That's weird enough.

RED SOX 12-15-0, at RANGERS 8-9-2 You might think this was a close game, but you'd be wrong. Going to the 8th, it's 12-1 Boston thanks to three taters off an acid-free Dock Ellis when Tiant gets bored and serves up three doubles and two homers to the Rangers before Willoughby comes on to give Harrah a 3-run homer in the 9th. Stupidly, Lynn and Yaz both get injured for three games toward the end of the blowout.

Real Chicks Dig Saves
June 18, 1977

KANSAS CITY–After watching my Cubs' miracle win against Pittsburgh yesterday, Lester here found out they had today off so I decided to bus my way down to Missouri and take in a game with my Royals and the Indians, who just staged their own miracle here with Wayne Garland's 5-0 shutout.

What I didn't know was that it was Halter Top Night at Royals Stadium. Not officially, of course, but the temperature was close to 100 at game time and swampy humid, and local lasses were wearing them all around me. When I watch Kansas City I keep an extra detailed scorebook, because there are many smart, number-specific fans and writers watching them, and I like to consider myself one, and having pretty girls close by can disrupt my thoughts about their on-base slugging coefficient. So I bought two Royals hats before the game and bent both bills straight down to form blinders. Play ball!

Game of the Day

It's Bibby against Andy Hassler, and K.C.'s fifth starter looks the best he has all year. Leadoff man Ron Pruitt gets on base three straight times off him with a single, double, and two-base Cowens error, but can't score. Meanwhile, a typically perfect run is created by the Royals in the 3rd on a Patek walk, stolen base, and two-out single by Cowens.

In the 6th they do it again. This time McRae gets hit and leaves with a slight bruise. Willie Wilson runs for him, steals second immediately, and scores on a gap double by Porter. Bibby then boots a dribbler by Otis, and Laxton comes on to face Mayberry. Heise pinch-hits and grounds out, before Kern comes on to get Patek and White to stop any more damage.

A skinny, tanned halter lady to my left polishes off her third beer—or at least the third one I count—and curses our team for not scoring more. I remind her how a 2-0 Royals lead has been a blueprint for victory about 86% percent of the time, but she just tells me in so many words to roll up my scorebook and insert it somewhere. Fascinating.

In the 8th, Pruitt gets on yet again on an error by Brett, and a Bochte single gets Pruitt to third. Hassler isn't tired at all, but Littell enters to force Buddy Bell to bat from his much weaker right side of the plate. Bell pops a fly deep enough to right to score the first Cleveland run, and they're back in the game, but with two outs in the home 8th, a single, walk and Patek single bring in some golden insurance.

Littell has been a handsome deposit in the bank since the season began, but his net worth suddenly takes a dive in the 9th. Grubb and Dade open with singles, and after Thornton whiffs, Norris pinch-hits a walk. The infield stays back for Kuiper, but Littell heaves one past Porter, scoring one run and putting Indians on second and third. Good Lady Halter groans, but is unable to hide her face in her shirt. The infield plays in for Kuiper. Little Duane fouls a couple off, then rifles a single past the drawn-in Frank White and two score! That Man Pruitt doubles Kuiper to third. Bochte flies out but Bell dumps a single into left for the fourth shocking run of the inning.

A Cowens triple and Brett single off Kern make it 5-4, but Wathan whiffs, Porter skies out, and the second straight incredible Cleveland win here in two days happens before our eyes. Good Lady Halter is too angry and sad and drunk to get home safely, asks me for a lift and I'm forced to inform her I came by bus. She gets me to hitch with her out of the lot, which is extremely easy due to her fetching wardrobe, and a guy with a Dodge truck drops us at her apartment building outside of an area called Budd Park.

She puts me up on her couch, and apologizes over and over for having a messy apartment with nine cats crawling everywhere. "I'm kind of crazy, you know" she says, which makes me feel so much better as she passes out on top of an old pizza box.

CLE 000 000 014 – 5 10 2
K.C. 001 001 011 – 4 8 2
    W-Kern L-Littell GWRBI-Kuiper

Nice to Be Sort of Home
June 19, 1977

LOS ANGELES—I'm what you call a private guy, which you'd probably find hard to believe if you'd spent even half of a seder around a table at the Wayman house. We would talk about everything but our stool problems, and sometimes even those too if Aunt Lolly was out of the room.

What I'm getting at is the three thousand bucks no one on the ward knew I stuffed in my Dr. Scholl's shoe the day I checked in there, just for emergencies like this. I was wandering around the middle of the country all last week thinking I was getting a blister, until I remembered I had the dough wrapped around a toe and bought myself a plane ride back out here. Hannah wasn't home and the curtains were shut and the place out in Reseda was all locked up, but I found a way to get inside anyway and will probably just live the bachelor life until she gets back.

The Pirates are out starting tomorrow for another big series, but we still had one left with the Expos so I revved up the old Buick in the garage and got on the 101 freeway around four so I'd have plenty of time to sit in traffic and not move on the way to the Ravine.

Game of the Day

Hard to believe Dodger Stadium is the oldest park in the league today after Wrigley. I can remember my first games there in '62 like it was a month ago. I'd skip Sunday Hebrew school with my friend Sidney and we'd take buses over from the valley and nab bleacher seats. They had a real exciting team that year, one of their best, and if it wasn't for the goddamn Giants we might've beaten the Yanks in the Series a year before we did. But whatever.

Now—I mean, in this strange version of '77—we've been winning again after a rough month, and the race is getting closer than the beef counter aisles at the Farmer's Market. Even the Reds are trying to sample the merchandise. Tommy John's on the hill again vs. Don Stanhouse, and Tommy's been a blessing, but ten minutes after the game starts it seems like he might be able to drag a rocker out there.

That's because Reggie Smith socks one into the bleachers after a Lopes walk. And Garvey creams one out after a Cey walk. And Baker follows that with a moon launcher. We're talking wham-bam-bam, thank you Stan.

Except Montreal is no bag of French fries. Tony Perez belts one after a Valentine single in the 2nd. Carter knocks one silly in the 3rd, and it's 5-3. John and Stanhouse both settle down from there, but in the last of the 6th Oates singles with two gone. John hits for himself and tattoos one in the gap, where Valentine does all kinds of sloppy business with it and by the time he looks up, Oates is chugging across home.

A double and three singles in the 7th make it 8-3 and finish off poor Stanhouse for the day. Other than me, never seen a guy with worse luck. At least he just pitched like an imbecile today, because usually he loses because his team doesn't hit. Andre Dawson wallops a solo one in the 8th, and—

Hold on a second...Is that Buzz Gip down in the walkway? With Dr Grossinger still? They actually hunted me down like a dog? This is an outrage! And who's that farshluggineh kid with them?

Okay, Lopes just homered to put this thing away, we're back in the race big time, and Ach! I gotta get the hell out of here—

MTL 021 000 010 – 4 8 2
L.A. 500 001 21x – 9 12 0

W-John L-Stanhouse HRS: Perez, Carter, Dawson, Smith, Garvey, Baker, Lopes GWRBI-Smith

Revenge of the Bucco Troopers
June 20, 1977

LOS ANGELES—I saw him. I know I did. And now we're stuck out here looking for that rat fink Sherman like he's a needle in a teased hairstack. Obviously he saw us too, because he was out the exit tunnel and across the parking lot with the other lame Dodger fans leaving early yesterday before I even had a chance to shout his name. The guy can move pretty quick for an old lunatic.

Luckily Sheila did have some good notes on him, so we narrowed his possible residence down to either Van Nuys or Reseda in the San Fernando Valley, which isn't what you'd call a small area. And I can't believe he'd be so dumb to just go home and sit around waiting for us. After my failed "surprise attack" plan, Dr. Sheila wanted to think out our next move a little more carefully, so she checked us into another motel, this one off the Sunset Strip with hookers on the sidewalks. I decided to get out and see another Dodger game, the first of the big weekend series with the Pirates, while she was doing her planning thing and reading Little Me bedtime stories. Besides, there was always a chance I'd see Sherman trying to sneak back into his seat. With the Bucs in town he wasn't going too far away.

Game of the Day

The last time the Bucs were here, they got swept, but since then the NL race has become a one big free-for-all pig pile death match between five teams separated by three games. Meaning anything can happen.

And it does with Doug Rau's first pitch, as Rennie Stennett grounds out, pulls a hammy and knocks himself out of action for six games. Pittsburgh almost scores in the first two innings anyway, but Rau gets out of both jams. It's left to Scrap Iron Garner to sock one into the bleachers leading off the 4th.

Then it's the Pirate Miracle Hour. Fernando Gonzalez, who takes over for Stennett at second base, rifles one out to lead the 5th, and after seldom-used Jerry Hairston (filling in for the injured Oliver) singles, Cobra Parker gets his teeth into a curve ball and hits it halfway up the right field bleachers. Two singles and a double finish off Rau in the 6th, and the Bucs take a 6-0 lead.

Jerry Reuss has been tough all game, but loses it in a hurry in the last of the 6th on a lead triple by Smith and singles by Cey and Garvey. Grant Jackson to the rescue! The lefty long man throws two scoreless innings to set things up for Tekulve, who runs into weird 8th inning trouble. Cey reaches on a dropped third strike by Dyer. Gets to second with two outs, and pinch-hitter Monday is walked to bring up Yeager. Steve doubles in two and it's suddenly 6-3.

The fans who haven't left yet to beat the traffic in their minds raise a loud ruckus, and Goose Gossage is hailed. Davalillo pinch-hits a walk, but Lopes pops out to end the mess. Jim Fregosi, who took over for Stennett, then gets injured himself but hits a sac fly in the process for more insurance. Bill Russell, who replaced injured Dodger shortstop Ted Martinez, leads the L.A. 9th with a single, but the Goose conjures up a Cey double play to end it. With the

Cards beating up the Phillies, these teams are now close enough to smell each other's bad breath.

PIT 000 132 001 – 7 15 1
L.A 000 001 020 – 3 10 1

W-Reuss L-Rau SV-Gossage HRS: Garner, Gonzalez, Parker GWRBI-Garner

Sam I Am Not
June 21, 1977

Friendly Fred back at ya, enduring some hot temps here in the Bronx while my Yanks are no doubt suffering worse in the midwest. Grandma woke up from her nap as I was all ready to watch game 2 of their big series out in K.C., and she looked like her wig was gonna melt off her head.

See, she had another nightmare about Son of Sam. "He was coming after me, George, clear as day!" she yelled, still thinking I was her Atlanta cousin, "Mr. Breslin put that letter of his in the paper a week ago and I don't think I've slept one minute!" I reminded her that the famous sick fool was mainly going after young couples, so not to worry, but all she did was stick the page of the *Daily News* in my face, all scrunched up from the 25 times she probably read it:

Hello from the gutters of N.Y.C. which are filled with dog manure, vomit, stale wine, urine and blood. Hello from the sewers of N.Y.C. which swallow up these delicacies when they are washed away by the sweeper trucks. Hello from the cracks in the sidewalks of N.Y.C. and from the ants that dwell in these cracks and feed in the dried blood of the dead that has settled into the cracks.

Well okay, the dude's got issues, but I was all over this thing back when it happened, and I don't—

Wait. Hold this crap one second. I know the mo-fo's name is David Bergstein or Boscowitz or something like that. I know he's got a few more people to kill and if I had my twenty pages of scribbled notes or a friggin' computer in this city that was smaller and faster than a washing machine I could find out exactly who them poor souls are! In other words, I can put this Sam-ass away a month early, save some victim's lives, become a hero and change who I am in the future!

Maybe. The Buzz-man did say about five times that he doesn't want us muckin' up things here in the way-back world, because who knows what other things it'll break? But how can I let a chance this righteous go?

Hmm...where's my beer and Grandma's remote? I can think about this between innings...

Game of the Day
KANSAS CITY—Damn! Why's it so hard for the Yanks to get some of that
big mo going? Even when they pull one out it's like a bad tooth, and today's
no different. Figueroa's got Royals on base every inning, and errors from his
lousy defense don't help. The Bombers open with three singles and a sac fly
by Reggie for a quick 2-0 lead, but a big old boot by Stanley comes before a
Poquette triple in the 4th and puts K.C. up 3-2.

We get two more and the lead back in the 5th and Alston rips a solo shot
off Colborn in the 8th, but Figueroa has to get bailed out of his sinking canoe
the last five innings. After he hits Poquette to start the 9th, Sparky comes on,
and Roy White gets in his business by dropping a one-out fly for a 2-base error. Lyle's been My Man big time lately, though, and gets McRae and Wathan
on miracle popups for the win.

Tomorrow we got a double dip, along with every other team but the Pirates and Dodgers, and we stand at 6-4 against the big bad Royals. I've also
heard some noise about Cliff Johnson comin' up from Houston soon to add
some serious right-handed sock, so I can't wait till they're back home and I
can get out of Grandma's place with its baked ham smells a few times.
NYY 200 020 010 – 5 9 3
K.C. 000 300 000 – 3 8 0
W-Figueroa L-Colborn SV-Lyle HR: Alston GWRBI-Reggie

Mixed Doubles
June 22, 1977

ST. LOUIS–That nutty girl in the halter top I met at Royals Stadium has followed me clear across Missouri. I don't mean like one of those stalkers—our
own Crazy Amy comes to mind—but Krystal doesn't seem to have a job or a
guy or a family from what I can tell, and when she asked if she could go along
with me to see my Cards play the suddenly first-place Phillies, what could I
say? She did put me up for a few days in her cat-covered apartment.

So we boarded our Greyhound, Krystal paying for her own bus ticket and
food. She only came into contact with me once when she nodded off somewhere near Boonville, and her head ended up on my left leg before I nudged
it away. Don't get me wrong, I do like Krystal, but she smells a little too much
like incense and has only just started asking me weird personal questions I

don't feel like answering, like why and how do I root for four teams at the same time?

When we got to St. Louis she used a pay phone outside the ballpark to call some friends, and we were joined by Dee Dee and Rufus a half hour into the game. They were even more bizarre than Krystal, and Rufus was more into discussing the crimes of Richard Nixon than watching the game, so I stopped talking altogether before long, and it was a good thing. Game one of the doubleheader tugged me inside its drama like no game has all year.

Game of the Day

Where did these Phillies come from? Weren't they in last place and under .500 for the first two months? Today Jim Kaat is mesmerizing us, giving up just three singles in the first eight innings while his teammates build a thin 2-0 lead on scattered hits and walks off John Denny.

But Buddy Schultz shuts them down through the 8th, Hrabosky through the 9th and then the Cards come up for the bottom half. With one out, Hernandez slices a single into left but Luzinski kicks it ten yards away for a 2-base error and Keith gets to third. Simmons rips a ball between Maddox and McBride for a triple, and it's 2-1. Brock fans, but with Cruz at the plate. Kaat unleashes a wild pitch and we're all tied up! Rufus almost notices this!

The Mad Hungarian stays on the hill into the 12th, when none other than Ted Sizemore golfs one over the fence to put Philly up 3-2. But my Redbirds have no quit. Reitz and Tyson single with one out, and Mike Anderson pinch-hits a walk. Tug McGraw, the only available arm in the Philly bullpen, finally relieves Kaat, and Templeton grounds one to Tom Hutton at first.

He boots it! We're tied again! Mumphrey then lines one toward center but Bowa leaps and nabs it. Hernandez grounds out and we keep on playing.

For another three scoreless innings that is, with Clay Carroll tossing eggs. Then Bob Boone leads the 16th with a double. Carroll gets Sizemore on a fly to right but Boone takes third. Eastwick comes on to face Hutton, the earlier goat, and the St. Louis infield moves up. Krystal and Dee Dee have gone off in search of beer and Rufus has dozed off, but I can hardly breathe. Hutton picks out a fastball and smacks it into right for the go-ahead single. Simmons leads the bottom of the 16th with a single, but a Brock DP ball kills the rally and essentially the game.

I'm determined to stay for Game Two, but I"ll be darned if I want my "friends" getting in my hair. So I climb over sleeping Rufus, take a ramp to the upper deck and find a nice half-empty section with a few sunbathers and pigeons to watch the nightcap from. I knew my friendship with Krystal was over when I said "I wish I had a cell phone" and she asked how long I was in prison for. Some things aren't meant to be.

Game One:

PHL 100 001 000 001 000 1 – 4 17 4

STL 000 000 002 001 000 0 – 3 9 0

W-McGraw L-Carroll GWRBI-Hutton

Game Two: **at CARDS 5-7-0, PHILLIES 3-10-1** Much more like it. The Phils are stuck with Dan Warthen and Randy Lerch on the mound, while the Cards get a great seven and a third innings from Butch Metzger to earn the split.

W-Metzger L-Warthen SV-Schultz GWRBI-Hernandez

American League through Sunday, June 22

Boston	40	27	.597	—
Kansas City	39	30	.565	2
New York	37	30	.552	3
Baltimore	36	31	.537	4
Texas	37	32	.536	4
Chicago	30	36	.455	9.5
Minnesota	28	40	.412	12.5
Cleveland	24	45	.348	17

National League through Sunday, June 22

Philadelphia	40	29	.580	—
Pittsburgh	40	29	.580	—
St. Louis	38	31	.551	2
Los Angeles	36	31	.537	3
Cincinnati	37	32	.536	3
Houston	31	38	.449	9
Montreal	28	38	.424	10.5
Chicago	23	45	.338	16.5

Sherman's Way

June 23, 1977

Our stakeout for Sherman Wayman began in late afternoon. Dr. Sheila had gone through enough of her notes to narrow his place down to an apartment complex in Reseda called the Luau Suites, one of those early 60s creations covered in cheesy stone work that haunt various L.A. neighborhoods. Little Me was getting cranky because we'd be in the car too long, and Sheila rejected every soul group I tried to play on the 8-track.

Then we saw Sherman, walking quickly up from the corner with a grocery bag and nervously looking over his shoulder. He unlocked the door to a first floor apartment, yelled "Hannah! I'm home!" and slipped inside. Sheila looked at me a second, then dug through her notes again.

"I swear his wife passed away in '76. That's when his downward spiral began."

"Well, maybe someone filled out the form wrong."

She stared at me hard. "No one fills out our forms wrong."

Just then Sherman reappeared, and went walking back up the street, like he had forgotten to buy something. As soon as he was around the corner, I motioned to Sheila and we hopped out. Hurried across the street, her holding Little Me's hand. I slid out some glass panes on a louvered window around the side, climbed inside.

The apartment had furniture, but every piece of it was covered in plastic except for a formica dining table down in the kitchen. "Anyone here?" I asked, and no one answered. I ran to the front door, let Sheila and Little Me in.

"She isn't here. The guy's nuts or something."

"This we know. What's that sound?" It was like a tinny broadcaster voice. We went to the kitchen. A portable radio next to the fridge had the Dodgers pre-game show on.

"I"m hungry!" Little Me said. The grocery bag had two steaks, two giant artichokes, and a box of rice. I opened a cabinet, found a package of Mallomars and handed the 5-year-old me one.

I suggested we hide in one of the back rooms but Sheila said it was better to confront a patient directly rather than shock him, so we sat at the formica table and waited.

He walked in five minutes later, holding a bottle of red wine. Took one look at us and almost dropped dead on the spot. I grabbed him before he could run again, though, Sheila took his other arm, and we sat him down at the table.

"Does Hannah know you're here?"

"You mean your dead wife?" I said.

"No, no. She must be dropping off the dry cleaning. I'm making London Broil for us because it's our anniversary tonight and it's her fave—"

"You need to stop the charade, Sherman," said Dr. Sheila in her calmest voice.

"Charade? You think I'm charading you? Forget me saving you a piece of steak. And who's this kid already?"

"Don't worry about him right now. There's time to explain. Right now you need to come with us to where Hannah really is." She put her hand on his shaking wrist. "Take us to where you know she is."

Sherman looked up at the ceiling, then the floor, then rubbed his face with both hands. A trickle of a tear leaked through two of his fingers.

"Okay...I'll take you to her. But first I need to eat something or I'll die, and that goes for listening to the Phillie-Dodger game too."

So that's what we did. And the game was as delicious as my first taste of London Broil.

Game of the Day

Have to admit that sitting around listening to Vin Scully call the game is almost as good as being there. Sort of. Sherman practically burns the meat and we have to open the back door to let the smoke out, making me miss a batter or two in the top of the 1st.

But it's just in time for Steve Carlton to take out his smoke, whiffing Lopes, Baker and Smith all in a row in the Dodger half of the 1st. Tommy John is shaky from the start, getting the side in order only once in his seven-plus innings, and if there was any justice in baseball, the Phillies would win this thing 6-0.

"Don't get me started on justice!" barks Sherman, halfway through his steak, and like me and Sheila, when she isn't downing her cabernet, we can't believe how the ball game turns out. Carlton gives up a Garvey solo blast in the 2nd, a Lopes walk and Baker blast in the 3rd, and retires everyone else.

With L.A. still up 3-2 in the 7th, Davey Johnson singles, Schmidt doubles, and Elias Sosa relieves John to face Luzinski. The Bull whiffs. The infield comes up and Maddox grounds to short to freeze the runners. McBride bats for Bowa and is walked to pitch to Boone, who grounds out. Then in the 9th against Charlie Hough, Hebner, Johnstone and Hutton all pinch-hit but the old knucklehead bails the Dodgers out.

"Fine!" announces Sherman after the last pitch, "now we can go find Hannah!" Of course Little Me is fast asleep by then, but we lay him out in the back seat and hit the road, heading east into the night.

PHL 000 001 100 – 2 8 0

L.A. 012 000 00X – 3 2 1

W-John L-Carlton SV-Hough HRS: Garvey, Cey GWRBI-Garvey

Good Thing the White Sox are Poopies
June 24, 1977

Hi. My name is Carlton Gip, and I'm five. I am also on a big long car trip to some mystery place. Uncle Buzz and Aunt Sheila are nice and buy me hamburgers and milk shakes a lot. Sometimes a toy. But I am not sure all the time if they know where they think they are going. Mostly they just stop at small hotels that have bad beds sometimes with bugs. And Uncle Buzz listens or watches ball games meaning I never get to watch Scooby or Superfriends.

Last night we had Grandpa Sherman with us, too, and he smelled funny and I don't think he's my grandpa at all. He didn't know where he was going either and we got lost and had to stop at another stupid little hotel in some desert. There was no TV just a little radio, and I was so mad I stole the radio when Uncle Buzz wasn't looking and took it in the bathroom and hid it in a closet behind toilet paper.

Fake Grandpa snored all night, and he is still asleep right now. Maybe after he wakes up I can get pancakes and we can try to figure out where he wants to go all over again. But I did hear Uncle Buzz say that the Red Sox beat up the White Sox again, which makes me happy. He likes them as much I like them. I can really tell he is my uncle.

I have to go potty now. Maybe I will pretend I found the radio. Bye.

Johnny Get Your Bat
June 26, 1977

SANDUSKY, OHIO—You won't believe old Crazy Amy here, but I snuck into the Cleveland hospital the other day where Seamus Headley's been since his head accident the first day of this month. The guy makes my blood freeze but I did kind of get used to him sweeping around my bed back in Squallpocket and was actually starting to worry about him. An intern told me he's still drugged up and at least a week from getting out, which is good, but I'm not sure I want to be the poor soul to come back and pick him up.

In case you've been wondering about me, I found a pretty nifty maintenance shack to live in underneath the Corkscrew roller coaster out at Cedar Point Amusement Park. It's a little hard to sleep sometimes, but I've eaten well with all the scraps left around on tables, and picked up a little cash from my part-time toilet cleaner job on the other end of the park before my idiot boss fired me when he caught me smelling Drano. So now I'm living under their dumb noses and doing fine.

I've also kept up on my two Ohio teams, but it wasn't hard to jump on one of their wagons. Seen the standings lately? The red-hot Reds have been scorching the league, or at least the Astros and Cubs and Dodgers, and I am so finished with Bill Plummer. I mean, he was cute, but Johnny Bench? He can hold seven balls in his hand! How can a girl not swoon over that?

They're home against the Expos starting tomorrow, so maybe I'll try and get down there for a game. I don't know. Found a little transistor radio in the shack here which has been doing me fine in between popcorn and fried dough runs.

Game of the Day

Marty Brennaman and Joe Nuxhall do the call from Wrigley on WLW, and it's another hot one. Seaver's going for his tenth win, which would be almost half of what the entire Cubs team has, and with Reuschel going for them, a pitcher duel threatens to break out.

But the wind is blowing out toward the other Great Lake, and it may as well be batting practice. Griffey triples with one out in the 1st, Foster whacks #27 and it's 2-0 Reds out of the gate. Tom ain't even close to being terrific, though. Greg Gross doubles, Biittner singles with two gone and Murcer pumps one into the bleachers and Chicago has the lead!

For a few minutes, anyway. Griffey singles in the 3rd, Foster whacks #28, and Cincy's back in front. A double and two-base error on the same play by Gross the next inning gives Geronimo a fake inside-the-parker, but Seaver can't get the batboy out in the last of the 4th, giving up three singles, a walk and hit batter before Reuschel finally hits into a 3-2-3 DP.

7-5 Cubbies into the 6th. Seaver fans to start the inning, before the Big Cubs trap door slides open. Morgan singles. Rose singles. Griffey walks. Foster walks for his fifth RBI. Johnny hits an infield single and Ontiveros kicks it for another error. Driessen misses a homer by inches and doubles home two more. Pete Broberg relieves the shellshocked Reuschel, but the carnage is done.

In the 8th, Johnny decides Foster's had too much fun and belts HIS 27th homer, and it's time for Marty and Nuxie to give us some numbers. Since June 8th they are 12-4. They now are tied with Boston with 102 team homers. They lead the league in runs with 406, thirty more than the Phillies. Joe Morgan is the Human Base-Clogger again. Griffey and Driessen are a perfect batting average and on-base pair with the powerful Foster and Johnny—who have 55 homers between them. The Reds have been scoring so much their shaky pitching hasn't even mattered.

I think I'm in love again.

CIN 202 105 020 – 12 15 0
CHI 300 310 000 – 7 10 3

W-Seaver L-Reuschel HRS: Foster-2, Johnny, Murcer GWRBI-Johnny

Thirsty for Water, Starved for Runs
June 27, 1977

Damn Sherman Wayman. Dragging me and Dr. Sheila and Little Me out to some wretched off-road spot in the desert that's practically in Blythe, California, just so he can show us where Hannah "disappeared and was never found" on their hiking trip in 1976. Yeah, right. Like why the hell would two old people from L.A. be wandering in the desert unless they were looking for a burning bush or something?

"Last place I saw her was right near that cave entrance, I think" he says, explaining how Hannah liked to collect precious rocks, and how her vanishing made him "all kinds of nervous and delusional" from then on. It's scorching hot already out here and it can't be later than nine in the morning, and our patience with him is evaporating. Sheila has her notebook out, crazily checking any background notes she still has on Sherman.

"Says here in a clipping that Hannah Wayman disappeared from a highway rest area near Indio. Sherman? What are we doing out here?"

Sherman has stopped. A touch of drool forms on his lower lip as he stares at the nearby cave entrance. "She loved those rocks. Sometimes it's all she would talk about. Sometimes for days. Sometimes for weeks. Sometime for days..."

'Hey, look at THIS funny rock!" says Little Me all of a sudden. He's just inside the cave, holding up a long white object he's yanked out of the dust. Sheila and me walk over. It has yellowed, been chewed on a bit by some wild animal. And there are others just like it at his feet.

"Get away from those!" yells Sheila, and Little Me scampers behind us. We kneel for a closer look, and the horror punches my gut like a hot fist.

"Oh my God..." I say, "They're bones!" Only a year or so old, one of them still wears shreds of a lime-colored blouse and gold bracelet. We slowly rise, turn to look at Sherman.

He's gone. Running back to our car with a crying, kicking Little Me under his arm. I tear after him. He stops when I'm five yards away, spins and whips a good-sized rock straight into my forehead. I drop in the dirt, stunned and bleeding. By the time Sheila has reached me, she's in a panic.

"Where are the car keys??"

"In the car!!" She tries to pick up the chase, but Sherman stuffs Little Me in the back seat, screeches away before she can get there.

"She didn't disappear at all," she says, as I stagger up to the empty, blistering two-lane road. "He either murdered her or left her out here to die! If that doesn't explain his paranoid schizophrenia and frequent guilt-ridden outbursts, then nothing does!"

"Hell with that crap. He's got Little Me with him! How do we get out of here?"

She takes a seat on the road until her butt starts to burn, then stands and paces instead. "We have to go get Seamus Headley in Cleveland. He's the one who sent us here, or at least those creeps he works for did...So maybe he has a plan how to reverse things. Chasing these patients around the country is a waste of time."

An idea scratches my brain. "If we can get over to Phoenix—and we can hitch there pretty easy—we can hop a bus or train to Texas and maybe borrow a truck."

Sheila rips off a patch of her blouse, sticks it to my head wound, then looks at me funny. "Borrow *whose* truck?"

Game of the Day
by Ed "Peachy" Calhoun
Jewett Babbler Sports Reporter

HOUSTON—You'd think with the Cards out in L.A. and the Phils and Bucs kicking off their 4-game Battle of the Keystone State, I could serve myself a better pennant plate by holing up in Jewett with my beer and TV.

Cubs and Astros in the Dome?? Yup, baseball sometimes just whips a surprise masterpiece your way to keep you awake.

Sure doesn't seem like one at first, just Bonham against J.R., and Richard whiffs the side in the top of the 1st on nine pitches. Cruz gets an Astro run home on a force, and we're up 1-zip for a half inning until two Cub singles, a hit by Trillo and sac fly by Mitterwald tie it up. Both throwers settle down from there, and it's still 1-1 in the 7th when Roger Metzger, the mighty mite only playing short because Julio Gonzalez can't field a ball, leads off with a line triple down the right field line. Richard gets him in all by his lonesome with a deep fly, and we're up 2-1.

Make that 3-1 in the 8th on a Cruz bleacher blast/scoreboard exploder, but J.R. can't close the deal in the 9th. Murcer and Buckner lead with singles, Mitterwald singles in one, and with two outs against Ken Forsch, Gross dumps one into left to tie the game!

Then the fun begins. Sutter takes the mound for the Cubs and goes seven relief innings. He 's knocked out of action for days now, but the Cubs manager could care less; he has got to win a game! Cruz triples his next time up in the 10th, but stays put on a Puhl infield single and ends up not scoring. The Cubs have people on all over the map against Forsch and then Sambito, but can't score.

Finally, in the top of the 18th, singles from Trillo, Gross and DeJesus put the Cubbies up 4-3. Willie Hernandez has been in there for Chicago three innings now, and Enos Cabell blisters one into the left field seats to tie the game again and keep us going! They stopped selling beers two hours ago and half the Dome has gone home, but Old Peachy's here for the duration.

Which finally happens three innings later. Sambito dribbles an infield hit toward Ontiveros at third, who throws it away. Ed Herrmann whiffs, but Cedeno rips a single up the middle to score the chugging Sambito and Houston wins two in a row the very, very hard way. It's the longest game of the season.

CHC 010 000 002 000 000 001 000 – 4 17 3
HOU 100 000 110 000 000 001 001 – 5 14 0
  W-Sambito L-Hernandez HR: Cruz GWRBI-Cedeno

The Indians Wanted the Bronx
June 28, 1977

When I woke up in this Cleveland hospital, the nurse asked me what my name was and it took me a good five days before I remembered it was Seamus Headley. I've had serious migraines for weeks, you see, and still have a crapload of pain in my lower back where I landed. Mostly I've just been laying here looking up at water spots on an asbestos ceiling, switching from soaps to local news to reruns of *Mannix* on the cheap-ass TV.

Those jackanapes at Timeco Incorporated never tested their 5-D dice before handing them over to me and Doc Sheila, and now I have no clue where she went or if she even hooked up with Gip and the other nutcakes. She certainly isn't a patient here. The other day I was half dozing and thought I saw Crazy Amy Gulliver staring into the room at me, but it could've just been a bad dream. I've had plenty of those since I got to '77. Still, if Amy was checking in on me that could mean the rest of them aren't far away, so I owe it to myself to eat my hospital slop and take my meds and get my behind out in the world soon as possible. I'm on a mission of my own doing, and wasting my time here isn't going to get it finished.

The orderlies here with their stupid bushy hairdos all seem to be Indians fans, and I hear them passing scores and player injury reports now and then. Today they were all stoked up because Cleveland was in New York giving the Yanks a rough time, like they actually have a chance of getting into the pennant race. My head hurts too much to even read a sports section, so I guess I can fill you in some details before I pass out again.

Game of the Day

NEW YORK—Boston has lost again, Gullett and his nine wins are on the hill for the home team, and Cliff Johnson has just been traded over from Houston for some added punch against lefties. What can possibly go wrong for the Yanks?

Um, everything? Reggie singles in the game's first run right away, they have Jim Bibby on the ropes, bases loaded and one out and Nettles at the plate. Nettles whiffs, Chambliss dribbles out and that's that. Then Dade singles and Gullett serves up a meatball to Johnny Grubb. Then Munson gets hit in the ribs and knocked our for this game and the next. Then after the usual double that gets past Mickey Rivers to open the third, Thornton and Dade single with two outs and Gullett serves up a triple to Johnny Grubb and the game is basically over.

Cliff Johnson makes his Yankee debut behind the plate, spelling Munson, and collects a walk and two singles in his three trips, but runners are left stranded in trees all over the yard before Gullett gets yanked in the 7th after giving up two more singles, a walk, and throwing a ball away. And Nettles will be benched against Ross Grimsley in the first game of tomorrow's doubleheader with Baltimore. Ghastly Graig is 0-for-his last 19 and seen his average drop to .192. Three days in a row now they've blown golden chances to catch Boston, and it's been a total team meltdown.

If it sounds like I'm mad about this, I am. I prefer five-team races to two-team ones, and it isn't as much fun without the Bombers bombing away. Of course I can't tell these orderlies that or they might spit in my soup or something. Go Tribe!

CLE 023 000 130 – 9 14 1
NYY 100 010 200 – 4 10 1
W-Bibby L-Gullett HRS: Grubb, Rivers GWRBI-Grubb

Strangeness on a Train

June 29, 1977

We hitched our way to Phoenix by sunset, and we were so hot and disgusting Dr. Sheila sprung for one of those sleeping berth rooms on the Sunset Limited just so we could shower and sleep on our way to Houston. The room had a pull-down and pull-out bed and was about as big as a walk-in closet, so with the swaying of the train the bathroom door kept popping open and I caught a glimpse of her maroon panties when she was undressing in there. Hopefully more on that later.

After I'd changed into shorts and an "Arizona is for Lovers" T-shirt I picked up at the train station gift shop, we found our way to the "dining" car to feast on roast beef sandwiches, chips and pickles. I saw that Dr. Sheila had her notepad along, and sure enough, the second we sat across from each other at a tiny table, she had it flipped open.

"Pretty strange to have your five-year-old self abducted in the desert, wasn't it?"

I gave her short answers, because I really just wanted to eat dinner and drink my Fresca and not get into any psychobaloney. And I had figured she was with me on this, because she had every chance to call the cops on Sherman and didn't because she was afraid of "scrambling" the future up. I have to say that in her orange Alvan Adams Phoenix Suns sweatshirt she looked awful cute, but she'd have no interest in a patient anyway, so why bother?

DR. GROSSINGER'S REPORT:

I've decided to soften my initial approach with Carlton. Perhaps it is from spending time with his young self over the last few weeks, but I'm shocked to discover that I now find the older Mr. Gip a pleasant companion. The constant travel and trying times we've been through have certainly created an odd, fascinating bond.

I can't believe the way Dr. Sheila eats her pickle, slicing it with a knife and fork like it's flank steak. What a freak. On the other hand, her question about Little Me getting abducted did make me feel strange. As I sat there chewing my sandwich I started flashing on a memory, one I'd forgotten about or blocked or something. An older guy was holding my hand and letting go, and it was super hot out and I had to go to the bathroom and started crying. Was it at Fenway Park, or somewhere else?...

Whatever. I smelled perfume in the train car just then and thought it was some lady at the table behind me but it wasn't. Sheila was wearing it. And she was looking at me more funny than usual.

Two train stewards walked by just now, talking about the Pittsburgh Pirates crushing the Phillies in a game I imagine they had wagered on, and for a brief moment I suddenly recalled looking at an album of old baseball cards with my mother on a rainy day in my childhood. Or perhaps it was my grandmother. A few names come to mind...Vaughn, Kiner, Law...Were those Pirates, I wonder?

Sheila took off her glasses to wipe her face with a napkin. I think she was sweating. "We need to...discuss this further, Carlton," she said. "Much further. In a more...private place." She stuck her glasses back on. 'This is quite difficult for me—"

I grabbed her wrist and a startled breath popped out of her.

Good Lord, he's taken my hand! Carlton has asserted himself, and I must admit my heart is racing. What should I do now?

She started to take off her glasses again, but I shook my head. "Uh-uh. Leave those on." She nodded, downed her cup of ice water and wiped her mouth with the napkin that was in her lap. Without looking at each other we got up the same time and went back down to the sleeper car, leaving our unfinished chip bags on the table.

American League through Sunday, June 29

Boston	43	31	.581	—
Kansas City	43	33	.566	1
Baltimore	41	33	.554	2
New York	39	35	.527	4
Texas	38	38	.500	6
Chicago	35	38	.479	7.5
Minnesota	32	42	.432	11
Cleveland	27	48	.360	16.5

National League through Sunday, June 29

Pittsburgh	44	32	.579	—
Cincinnati	43	33	.566	1
Philadelphia	43	33	.566	1
Los Angeles	40	33	.548	2.5
St. Louis	40	35	.533	3.5
Houston	35	40	.467	8.5
Montreal	30	43	.411	12.5
Chicago	24	50	.324	19

Meanwhile, in the Gladiator Pit

July 1, 1977

NEW YORK—Friendly Fred back at ya, with nothin' but baseball this time around. Boston's at the Stadium for three, peoples, and we got serious ground to be making up. Suppose I could have just watched the game at home, but I've been getting sick of Grandma lately, and it was no sure thing they'd have the Yanks and Sox on *ABC Monday Night Baseball.* Seems like they've mostly been showing Royals and Pirates games this year.

But don't think I forgot about this going-after-Son of Sam plan that I came up with. Still got a month or so before the next victims happen, you see, and I need to find something more real to do that could actually fetch me coin. Grandma's starting to wonder why I've been hanging around, and before she figures out who I really am I might have to locate my own pad.

Anyway, I had beers at Stan's Sports Bar before both games, copped upper deck seats over home plate and was in loud, nervous heaven. The double-header loss to Baltimore on Sunday was eight hours of hell, and if the dang Sox make us bite the pillow now Stan's might end up being my new address.

Games of the Days

Monday. Crazy-ass business right from the start. Jim Rice puts a Figueroa pitch in the left field seats with Carbo on, and it's 2-0 chowderfaces. But Tiant's much worse, and the Yanks greet him with a Zeber homer then a walk and three straight hits with one out before Nettles wakes up from his coma and bombs one. Rivers pops a ball in the seats the next inning and we're up 7-2, but not one of the 50,000 plus of us are cozy with it. Boston gets one in the 3rd, back-to-back blasts from Fisk and Yazamatazz in the 5th, and it's 7-5 just like that. Meanwhile Tiante mellows out until Nettles gets his third hit, an RBI single in the 7th. Spaceman Lee replaces him and gets Randolph to rap into a trippy 6-2-3 DP to end our scoring. All that's left is a Yazzarino triple and Nettles two-base error in the 9th to give us our 23rd heart attack, before Hobson and Lynn ground out to end it. We're just three games out of first again!

BOS 201 020 001 – 6 9 0
NYY 610 000 10x – 8 15 1

W-Figueroa L-Tiant HRS: Rice, Fisk, Yaz, Zeber, Nettles, Rivers GWRBI-Alston

Tuesday. The Stadium crowd is louder, rowdier. And Rice shuts them up again with another two-run homer in the 1st, this time off Torrez. And we get the fools right back again! Zeber and Rivers with singles, Munson with his incredible tenth triple of the year to tie it. Torrez is no Figueroa though. He ain't even Dick Tidrow. Carbo walks to lead the Boston 3rd. Fisk doubles down the line. After Yazzoli grounds into a home force out, Rice doubles. Hobson punishes a 3-run homer. Oh, we try to give some payback off Aase, but it's never enough, and our bad-range fielders are at it again, and Torrez serves Denny Doyle of all people an upper deck cookie, and Bernie Carbo must've sprinkled wacky weed on his Wheaties because he checks in with a double, two homers and a walk in five trips. Know that fancy-ass new OPS stat Lester's always squeakin' about? Well Carbo's is now a stupid 1.080. We're four games out of first again and drop to 3-7 against these New England fools. Least we got Louisiana Lightnin' vs. Reggie Cleveland tomorrow in the big rubber. See ya on the flip side!

BOS 204 001 030 – 10 13 0
NYY 200 200 130 – 8 13 2

W-Aase L-Torrez SV-Campbell HRS: Rice, Hobson, Carbo-2, Doyle, Chambliss GWRBI-Rice

By the Time We Left Phoenix, Got to Houston, and Kept Going

July 2, 1977

Both Texas teams had hit the road, and here I was with Sheila after two incredible days getting to know her in a doctorless way. It would have been less than two days but the train stopped for many hours for no special reason somewhere in New Mexico, and neither of us minded one bit. The window in our dinky train compartment got wicked steamy, and I was surprised how warm her skin was under her usually cold personality. The fact she kept her glasses on didn't even make a difference, but when those got foggy too she finally ditched them.

Anyway, we got ahold of Ed Peachy Calhoun up in Jewett, made up a good story about our situation and he drove down to pick us up. He had no interest in lending us his pickup like I thought he wouldn't, but when we said he could go with us to get Seamus Headley up in Cleveland he honked like a goose and just about went off the road. I got the feeling old Peachy hadn't been out of Texas in maybe his whole life.

The cool thing is we had radio ball games all the way up the center of the country, when thunderheads weren't making the stations crackle. We caught some of the Astros out in L.A., some of the Rangers in Minnesota, a taste of the Royals at Comiskey and even Steve Carlton taking on the Reds. Sheila held my hand for 80% of the drive, and admitted she had this secret liking for the Pirates she couldn't really explain or understand, so she was kind of rooting for the Reds to lose now that they've climbed to a sniff away from first.

All I can say is that cozied up next to her in the truck with the windows open and a humid night breeze whipping through and Peachy whistling and Denny Matthews describing George Brett's swing and lightning flashes blessing the sky from a hundred miles away, I felt like I was in heaven. Certainly one I'd never been allowed to visit.

Games of the Day

at EXPOS 8-11-0, PIRATES 6-11-0 PIRATES 5-10-1, at EXPOS 1-9-0 Ah yes. Remember twi-night doubleheaders? Rooker takes a 6-2 lead to the 8th in the first game but Montreal gets all kind of rolls, cut the lead to 6-4 to bring on Grant Jackson—and Andre Dawson celebrates his future Hall of Fame induction with a game-winning grand slam. In the nightcap, Larry Demery is pressed into service because Forster isn't rested, and with nearly everything going Pittsburgh's way of late, the Demster mows down the 'Spos on 1 run and 7 hits before getting pulled for Tekulve in the 7th. Three out of four for the resurgent Bucs, who now head to a sold-out Riverfront Stadium for three with the Reds, including a July 4th doubleheader. Duck!

at YANKEES 3-8-3, RED SOX 2-6-3 (12 innings) Sloppiest thriller of the year, and the Yanks take their first series vs. Boston. Guidry gives up two Sox runs in the 4th, Cleveland does the same in the 7th. Two late errors for defensive subs Dent and Blair give Boston excellent scoring chances but Guidry gets out of every jam. Willie Randolph then sends Friendly Fred and the rest of the 50,000 home happy with a 1-6 HR roll off Bill Lee in the last of the 12th.

Pirate Plunge into a Red Abyss
July 3, 1977

Noticed a whole bunch of folks wearing Reds hats walking around the last few days here at Cedar Point Park, what with their ball club storming the National League bastille and all. And with Cincy home for three with first place Pittsburgh, including a Fourth of July double-dipper tomorrow, there was no way Crazy Amy was missing that action.

I tried to fall asleep earlier in my maintenance shack so I could get up at the crack of dawn, but somebody was snooping around it in the middle of the night and I had trouble falling back asleep. It wasn't any night watch-man either because he didn't have a flashlight, and there was a creepy deep breathing I'd never heard before.

So I was plenty spooked when I creaked the door open this morning and peeked out. Got my behind out of the park and onto a bus for Cincinnati, my Egg McMuffin shaking in my hand while I ate it.

Boy, was Riverfront Stadium ever packed! It was one of those matinee games with camp groups making a racket, and business dudes in their shirt-sleeves skipping work, and I'd never seen so many killer sideburns in one place in my life. My hopes of seeing Bill Plummer play weren't in the cards, especially the way Bench has been hitting, but I didn't care. The pennant race tension was more than entertaining.

Game of the Day

It's a battle of lefties, Reuss and Capilla, neither guy doing squat lately. Ca-pilla sets the Bucs down on three ground balls in the first, while Reuss gives up a Griffey single but gets Rose to rap into a DP. Not-so-gorgeous George Foster then leads off the Reds 2nd with a laser beam of a homer into the up-per deck, his 34th of the year (on pace for 65, by the way), and the stadium goes mental.

Reuss bears down right away and gets the next six hitters on ground outs, but loses it all over again in the 4th. Griffey and Rose open with line singles, and Foster works a walk. Bench whiffs even though I'm up on my seat screaming for him, but Driessen walks in a run, Concepcion singles in a second one, Geronimo walks in a third, and pitcher Capilla slices a single into left for two more! It's 6-0, strangers are hugging, and I barely notice when someone comes up behind me and puts their hand on my shoulder. I spin around—

"What happened to your friends, Miss Gulliver?" says a tall guy with mir-rored shades and a bandage on his head. I'm standing there looking right at Seamus Headley, in all his creepy glory. The bastard must have spotted me when I checked in on him at the Cleveland hospital, and since then snooped around my shack and followed me down here!

"I have no clue where they are, so get lost." He grabs my arm, sits me down and takes the empty seat beside me.

"Don't get excited," he says, "All I want to do is find Buzz Gip."

"And not Dr. Sheila? Didn't you guys time-travel here together?"

"Let's just say...we don't see eye to eye. The Pirates aren't out of this thing yet. Finish enjoying the game and then we'll find a place to talk."

There isn't much left to enjoy. Pittsburgh opens the 7th with two singles and

Sarmiento comes on to retire pinch-hitter Pops Stargell, give up an RBI single to Stennett but escapes with just one run scored. Fryman and Hume pitch the 9th, the crowd explodes, and our Reds are a mere half game out of first!

"Didn't know you were a baseball fan," I say to Seamus as he escorts me out, a bit too roughly for my tastes.

"I was once," he says, "Damn strikes ruined the sport for me, along with other things… What say we go find a cozy nook?"

We followed a mob up the street into an area with bars and restaurants. One little opening, that's all I needed. One chance to put a knee in his crotch and lose him in the crowd.

Except I guess it wouldn't hurt to hear his story. Come to think of it, until today I didn't know he could even talk.

PIT 000 000 100 – 1 9 0
CIN 010 500 00x – 6 9 1
W-Capilla L-Reuss HR: Foster GWRBI-Foster

The Bullpens Bursting in Air
July 4, 1977

In honor of Independence Day, 1977, and the season's non-official halfway point, I thought I'd let our diverse cast of characters report in from their scattered doubleheader locations. Take it away, peoples!

DODGERS 9-14-0, at CUBS 3-11-1 DODGERS 14-20-0, at CUBS 2-7-1 *by Sherman Wayman:* Drove Gip's rent-a-car all the way to Chicago here, his little kid who looks just like him whining the whole way, and thank God I had money to buy him hamburgers and shut him up. Anyway, it's been worth it because my Dodgers took double advantage of the wind blowing out of Wrigley by wiping the field with the Cubs like brown mustard on a kaiser roll. Reggie Smith socked three out of the park, Hooton and Rhoden got the wins and here's what the two Cubbie starters did for the day:
Renko—one and two-thirds IP, 9 hits, 2 homers knocked out trailing 7-0
Lamp—one and two-thirds IP, 8 hits, 2 homers knocked out trailing 7-0
Nine straight Dodger wins makes it a big party for me, but then Gip's kid had to go play hooky on me halfway through the second game, and now I gotta go find the little noodnik in the city of Chicago. Oy…

at REDS 5-11-0, PIRATES 0-4-2 at REDS 2-7-0, PIRATES 0-3-2 *by Crazy Amy Gulliver:* I did like I said would, kneed old Seamus in the nutcakes and left him somewhere near Fountain Square last night. I'm sure he was back at Riverfront here looking for me, but I bought a Reds sweatshirt and goofy hat and found some shade to sit in and keep my eye out for him. Meanwhile Seaver and Soto undress the Bucs like they're a team of Charlie Browns, and Cincy takes over first place without hitting one homer! I love these guys, Plummer or no Plummer.

at PHILLIES 9-9-1, EXPOS 1-4-0 at PHILLIES 7-6-0, EXPOS 6-14-0 *by Mikey Spano (1982-2010-1977):* Yeah I know, I'm supposed to be dead and all, and I guess I am because I fell into the Royals Stadium fountain and drowned a month and a half ago, but with my Phils playing this good I'm gonna watch the goddamn games if I have to hover over the outfield every day. Which is what I did for the Fourth. Expos lead the opener 1-0, before Schmitty and the Bull go yard in the 6th, Johnstone hits a bomb the next inning that just misses me and then six more score in the 8th. We're down 3-0 in Game 2 thanks to Randy Doofus Lerch, but Ozark has the good sense to yank him for Brusstar, and we take the lead on a Davey Johnson salami off Schatzeder in the 5th. Carter then bombs a 3-run shot in the 8th, but the Bull does it again, winning both ends of the twinbill with a 2-run shot off Kerrigan. Devo-stating! What's that? Shit, gotta drift away again...

ASTROS 6-9-0, at CARDS 4-11-4 at CARDS 5-14-1, ASTROS 4-4-2 (10 innings) *by Lester:* I am beginning to enjoy my aimless midwest drifting, following whichever one of my teams I want. Did you know I have a 31.25% chance of seeing one of my favorite clubs each day? Well, today I had two at once, always a bit confusing, and the Astros and Cards are 5-5 with each other and always seem to play close games. As they do here at Busch. Game 1 is neck-and-neck, filled with sloppy St. Louis fielding and many unforseeable events. Like Gene Pentz outpitching Bob Forsch. Like Tony Scott returning from a very long injury and going out for three more games in his first at bat. Like Roger Freed taking right field for him and cracking a triple and homer. Like Jose Cruz finally winning it with a two-run shot in the 8th. Bannister and Falcone are their usual awful selves in the nightcap, but the Cards have to squeak out the win in extras on a Templeton single, despite outhitting Houston 14-4.

RED SOX 11-9-1, at INDIANS 3-6-0 at INDIANS 4-10-0, RED SOX 1-2-0 *by Buzz Gip:* So Peachy drops us at the Cleveland hospital yesterday, where we find out that Seamus flew the coop. Hello Motel 6, along with a Boston-Tribe doubleheader to pass the time while we think of yet another next move. Sheila sits in the packed grandstand with me, but I can't tell if she's distracted about Seamus' disappearance or her Pirates being blanked twice in Cincinnati. Anyway, the first game is your basic Boston bombing mission, with Rice, Lynn and Yaz going deep off Bibby and Buskey. None other than Al Fitzmorris stifles the Sox later, with Grubb homering in the 1st off Paxton and driving in three.

TWINS 13-18-0, at WHITE SOX 2-7-3 at WHITE SOX 3-8-0, TWINS 2-7-0 *Carlton Gip (age 5):* I ran away from Fake Grandpa at the Cubs baseball game and got lost in the street. A cab driver put me in his car and when I said what happened he took me to a different baseball game with different teams in the same city. I liked this one better because they had a real shower going out in the sunny seats and I put my head under a lot of times and it was fun. The people out there booed for the whole first game and cheered in the second one. A player named Caroo kept getting good hits and I heard his hitting number is .425 now. Bye.

RANGERS 6-16-0, at ROYALS 4-12-1 at ROYALS 10-12-0, RANGERS 7-15-0 *by Ed "Peachy" Calhoun:* Never did like sister-kissers, but what the heck, two out of three in this scorching turf pit is pretty darn good. Dock Ellis runs into two bad innings but gets us home free after we beat up Colborn in the opener, Willie Horton driving in the winner in the 7th. Devine's been pretty solid in spot starts all year, but he throws like a crippled squirrel in Game 2, coughing up a 2-0 lead, then giving Cowens a grand slam to kick off a seven-run 4th. Doug Bird is left in the whole game for them and survives after losing most of his feathers.

YANKEES 11-12-1, at ORIOLES 6-12-1 YANKEES 7-12-1, at ORIOLES 1-7-1 *by Friendly Fred:* Now THAT's what I'm talkin' about! Yanks with the gloves, Yanks with the bats, Yanks with the balls to get them two games out of first! My Man Reggie with the game-winners in both games, Piniella with six hits, El Figueroa and Tidrow with the big-ass hurls. Look out, K.C. and you Beaneaters, 'cause the bombin' Yanks are finally over your 'hood!

Dearest Goose
July 5, 1977

While Carlton and I drove the roughly 350 miles to Philadelphia for the two Pirates games there before the All-Star rest, I had a sudden urge to stop in the hills of McKeesport, just south of Pittsburgh. It was one of my many childhood homes, and the old man who lived there in 1977 didn't remember meeting me or anyone in the Grossinger family, but he did save a shoebox full of old, unmailed letters he found in the cellar once.

They were written by mother Sophie, an obsessed Pirates fan, and they were love letters to Bill Mazeroski, Dale Long, Ralph Kiner and other team luminaries of the 50s and 60s. I was ashamed to even show them to Carlton, but he was fascinated and read some aloud while I drove for an hour or two. I suddenly realized why I had this buried affection for the Pirates, and why I felt compelled to see them play in Philadelphia after their horrific visit to Cincinnati. I actually cared about them.

The game we saw today was deeply satisfying, and if my mother were alive she might have dashed off the following letter while sitting in the baking stands...

Dearest Goose:

How do you do what you do? Even with Candelaria on our hill we were in a queasy state throughout this game. A double by Robinson and two-run triple from Parker staked us to an early 3-0 lead, but John wasn't fooling the Phils one bit and it was a blessed miracle we weren't behind by the middle innings.

Mike Schmidt and that dastardly mustache of his was the culprit, alright. After Candy hit him in the 1st, he singled in their first run and homered in their second to cut our lead to 4-2 in the 7th. Two singles and a walk followed, but Tim McCarver bounced into that double play to let us escape with our lives. I saw you warming up out there right before Sizemore doubled to begin the Phillie 8th, and when you emerged from the bullpen cart, as formidable as you've ever looked, I have to say my heart soared.

And then you went to work, fanning Johnstone. Hebner walked, before you poured untouchable gas past the evil Schmidt for the second out. Luzinski managed to dribble a single but McBride lined out to Stennett and all was well. The 9th was simple by comparison. I adored the way you whiffed Downtown Ollie Brown after Hutton hit a pinch two-out single.

I do pray you are able to pitch more often, because our pennant hopes may depend on you. And if you ever pass through McKeesport, I am hoping you will ring me up so I can show you the local sights.

Yours always, Sophie Grossinger

PIT 012 001 000 – 4 10 0

PHL 000 100 100 – 2 10 0

W-Candelaria L-Kaat SV-Dearest Goose HR: Schmidt GWRBI-Gonzalez

Break Time!

July 6, 1977

ST. LOUIS—Lester doesn't like it when his Cards lose, and Lester's been very unhappy lately because the darn Dodgers have owned us since the season began to the tune of ten out of twelve, and we have to beat them today at Busch to prove we belong in this pack of pennant chasers.

It doesn't look good for us at first, because L.A. goes up 2-0 right away on two singles, two walks, and an error by pitcher Underwood. But Tommy John and his 10-4 record are having an off day, and Keith Hernandez clears the bases with a 3rd inning triple. Simmons follows with an upper deck shot, and we take the lead 5-2!

Why does it have to be Underwood pitching, though? Lacy walks, Yeager triples, and lesser Tom is booted for Butch Metzger with nobody out in the 4th. Butch whiffs two guys but walks two others, and Penguin Cey wafts a fly deep to left that drops just over the wall for a grand slam. Any air that's left in the Busch pit is sucked out, and I can feel my hair curling up from the heat radiating off the Astroturf. Another cheap homer by Yeager follows a two-base Templeton error the next inning, and every roll of Mr. Fate's dice is going the Dodger way.

The wait at the ice cream and lemonade stands lasts a good two innings, but no one cares. And guess who I bump into, but Sherman and some little kid named Carlton who Sherman says is his grandson. Carlton looks miserable, but Sherman buys him a giant-size lemonade AND a snow cone to perk him up a bit. I follow them to a shaded part of the grandstand, where lots of Cards fans who are still around have sought refuge.

A vendor selling ice cream sandwiches with a wet towel over his head keeps coming over and pestering us to buy one, but Sherman keeps shooing him away. I have to admit I've missed the crazy old buzzard.

"Get a hit, Garvey, you woman!" he yells. The Biggest Dodger Fan in the Land is thrilled with the result so far, of course, but can't ride his first baseman enough. Eastwick and Hrabosky do the mopping up, with Baker smacking a solo shot for good measure, but by the time John finishes off his tidy little 16-hit complete game, we're 2-11 against these guys and six games out of the first place we were actually in a few weeks ago.

Sherman says he has a car, and I talk him into giving me a lift to wherever he's going for the All-Star break. He says either a big lake or Canada, because the Dodgers start play again up in Montreal on Thursday. I offer to drive because I know how old he is and how tired he can get, and he says sure after grumbling for twenty seconds and hands me the keys.

Except as we get to his car, the weird, annoying ice cream vendor corners us again. I get aggravated, rip the towel off his head—

—and see Seamus Headley standing there, head bandaged and standing a little wobbly, pointing a .38 at my stomach. "Hello Lester...and Sherman...and—"

He stares at little Carlton a long time, blinks, and then his legs give out and he collapses right in the parking lot! What the heck? A couple concerned fans run over, lift him and help him into Sherman's back seat. I get behind the wheel, hide the gun under my seat, and we're off. Hopefully when he comes to, we'll all get some answers. I'm sure Buzz and Fred and Amy and Dr. Sheila will spend the next three days doing the same.

L.A. 200 520 011 – 11 10 1

STL 005 001 001 – 7 16 2

W-John L-Metzger HRS: Cey, Yeager, Baker, Simmons GWRBI-Cey

American League through Sunday, July 6

Kansas City	49	35	.583	—
Boston	47	34	.580	0.5
New York	45	37	.549	3
Texas	44	39	.530	4.5
Baltimore	41	40	.506	6.5
Chicago	36	45	.444	11.5
Minnesota	34	47	.420	13.5
Cleveland	31	50	.383	16.5

National League through Sunday, July 6

Los Angeles	48	33	.593	—
Cincinnati	48	36	.571	1.5
Philadelphia	48	36	.571	1.5
Pittsburgh	48	37	.565	2
St. Louis	42	39	.519	6
Houston	38	45	.458	11
Montreal	33	49	.402	15.5
Chicago	26	56	.317	22.5

Previously, in "Ball Nuts"...

July 10, 1977

Carlton "Buzz" Gip is just an ordinary divorced father, living out his early middle age watching baseball games in his Maine trailer—until he discovers he is actually a mental patient at Squallpocket State Hospital. He swears that two strange men in black visited him with a mission to replay the 1977 season using a set of custom time-transporting Strat-O-Matic dice, but was it all in his head?

Sharing the possible delusion are his equally odd ward-mates, all followers of teams other than Buzz's beloved Red Sox, and rolling rights to the "special dice" are soon debated. In a nasty, multi-patient wrestling match over the dice one day, all five patients are accidentally zapped back to 1977, leaving Dr. Sheila Grossinger and Seamus Headley, a mysterious hired spook posing as the hospital sweeper, to join forces, transport themselves back to '77 using newer, more powerful dice, and retrieve the patients.

Our odd gang enjoys an eventful month or two beaming around to various ball games and even taking in the premiere of Star Wars. *Surly Phillies phanatic Mikey Spano accidentally drowns in the Royals Stadium fountain, creating some tension, but for the most part they all stay as sane as possible, and even befriend a semi-retired Texas sportswriter to help them get around.*

When "Dr. Sheila" and the Sweeper appear outside the Indians' ballpark, though, the patients panic, flee in all directions. While Seamus recovers from a severe concussion in a Cleveland hospital, Buzz and the doctor hit the road to track the others down. They scoop up the five-year-old Buzz from the bowels of Fenway Park, where he was apparently abandoned back in '77, and take the unaware boy west in search of Dodger fanatic Sherman Wayman.

As we return to our tale, Buzz and Dr. Sheila have lost Sherman and Little Buzz along with their used car, but have found romance on an Amtrak sleeper; Friendly Fred is waiting around on the east coast for his chance to capture Son of Sam; Crazy Amy Gulliver is living under a roller coaster at an Ohio amusement park; and wandering schizophrenic Lester has suddenly found himself driving north with Sherman, Little Buzz and a woozy, recently armed Seamus in the back seat...

* * *

"So what if customs asks for IDs?" It's the third time Sherman has asked me that since we crossed into Pennsylvania.

"What did I tell you? Canadians are all nice, even the customs people. They'll believe whatever we make up."

"How do you know, junior? You've never even been there."

"Neither have YOU!"

The argument gets the boy whining, and Seamus pops awake. Sees his wrists tied together with about fifty yards of dental floss.

"Where are we?..." he growls.

"Heading up to Montreal," I say. "Sherman might die on us if he misses one stupid Dodger series."

"At least they're in first!" Sherman barks, "Where's your lousy Cardinals and Cubs and White Sox and Royals and Twins these days, huh?"

"The Royals are in first."

"Oh....right. But that league doesn't count."

Seamus tries to rip his hands free but the floss digs into his skin. "You guys don't know what's going on here, trust me."

"We should trust you? Pulling a gun on us? How come you fainted before when you saw the kid?"

Sherman's question freezes him. He glances out the window at passing trees. Little Buzz stares at him the same empty way he did down in the Busch Stadium parking lot. Like he might even recognize him.

"It doesn't matter..."

"So what does??" I yell, turning north toward Erie and Buffalo, "Who the frick are you, and what the frack is going on??"

Seamus sighs. "I talked myself into a contracting job for Timeco Incorporated a long time ago, just so I could keep tabs on Buzz. But now I'm in too deep. And you all could be in danger."

"I'm in danger of crapping my shorts if we don't find a rest area soon!" says Sherman, "Spit it out, son."

"Yeah, why do you even care about Buzz?"

Seamus sits up the best he can, leans forward and plops his chin on the seat, right next to my shoulder.

"Because he's my nephew, you lunatic."

Sherman and I share a stunned glance in the rear view mirror. Little Buzz suddenly whirls around in the passenger seat, stares at our bound companion.

"Uncle Seamus?"

Game of the Day
WHITE SOX 16-19-3, at RED SOX 7-16-0

Not exactly the way the Bostonians want to open the second half. The scary thing is that the butchering comes with Don Aase on the hill, and his team is down 10-1 when he leaves after three and two-third innings. Seven Chicago homers clear the boards, as they have to be thrilled to just play in a hitter's park. Steve Stone and the usual swiss cheese White Sox defense do their best to let Boston back in the game when Fisk caps a 3-run 8th with a homer, but Dal Canton comes on to strand the bases full and mercifully end it.

How We Spent Our All-Star Vacation
July 11, 1977

It's hard to believe I had never made it to Cooperstown, living on the east coast my whole life, but the three-day All-Star break and a bunch of free time with Sheila finally made it possible. Forgot to mention last time that we had just enough money left to buy a used VW van from some hippies outside of Cleveland, which is how we putt-putted our way to Philly for those Pirates games.

But now we wanted a little alone time to just enjoy the country roads, and what better place to do that than the Hall of Fame? Ernie Banks and Al Lopez are getting inducted next month, along with a couple of Negro Leaguers Pop Lloyd and Martin Dihigo, and it would be nice to be back for that, but that weekend would also be extra crowded.

What nobody tells you about Cooperstown is how incredibly beautiful the lake and little village are. We ended up sleeping in back of the van on a futon, not being able to afford the fancy inn we were parked in the lot of, but definitely had our fill of the local sights. Best of all was Doubleday Field, a gorgeous little ballpark where some high school kids were playing. Looking at the trees and a church steeple and houses right outside the fence, we felt like we were back in the late 1800s or something.

Sheila was starting to get restless, though. She was itching to find out how her Pirates were doing, and wasn't getting good reception on her Super-Phone. Then she learned in a bar that the Cubs had beaten them in extra innings, putting her in a sour mood the whole night.

So today we kept moving, and ended up over in the even more gorgeous Berkshires to see the Boston Pops play at the Tanglewood Music Festival. Or I guess I should say *hear* them play, because that's where the grooviest adults put picnics together and sit on the huge lawn for the show. We camped out next to two couples who swore they had even seen The Who perform *Tommy* there seven years ago. One of the guys said he would kill to see the Beatles do a reunion show at Tanglewood sometime. "They got about two years to pull that off," I said, and Sheila poked me in the ribs to shut me up.

Sheila and me shared a bottle of Mateus and some take-out fried clams, and I have to say it was pretty nice even though I couldn't tell you Arthur Fiedler from Cecil Fielder. The cool thing was that the lawn was littered with a half dozen or so Red Sox fans, following their game with Chicago on transistor radio earphones. I only made three bathroom trips but still caught a lot of the scoring details by checking in with the same fans.

Then the Sox were behind again, and I was suddenly the one bummed out. I told Sheila it was time to get serious tomorrow about rounding up the nutty troops, or at least tracking Seamus down, because he seemed to be the key to getting us out of this weird decade.

"Are you sure Carlton?" she asked, gazing at me through the amber, heart-shaped sunglasses she had found in back of our van. "I suspect I'm beginning to...I don't know...dig the scene here."

I stared at her for one second, then took a second bathroom break.

Game of the Day
at PHILLIES 8-9-0, ASTROS 7-12-2
The Astros need to undergo deep hypnosis to convince themselves they're in the Astrodome at all times, because they sure can't win anywhere else. This time their Cruz and Watson homers are topped by Luzinski and McBride homers, and they're down 6-2 when they go into orbit for five runs off Lonborg and Garber in the 8th. Only to have Forsch boot a grounder with one gone in the Phillie 8th and Schmidt pop another homer for yet another dramatic late win.

Perfect Place for a Coma

July 12, 1977

MONTREAL—Olympic Stadium is two-thirds full for the series finale with the first-place Dodgers, but the team's lackluster play since April has drained most of the spirit out of their home.

I am all right with that, because ever since Seamus announced he was Little Buzz's long lost uncle, we've all been in a bit of a coma, and an Expos game in its ethereal suburban wasteland facility provides the matching hypnotic atmosphere. Sherman is oblivious, of course, because he's too focused on his team's league-leading action, but I'm too distracted to even score it. "Lester?" asks the boy, "How many whiffers does Twitchell have now?" He loves to use the word whiffer and say the name Twitchell, and after the third time he asks the same question I just make up a number that will satisfy him.

Seamus, Buzz's dad's younger brother, apparently knew all about that Fenway game back in real '77 where Buzz was abandoned, and had found ways to watch over Buzz ever since. His contracting work with Timeco Inc. and job at the hospital were all part of the plan. Like Buzz, he had no clue what happened to his brother, whose name was Trevor Gip, only that Buzz's mom had died and Trevor was an emotional mess at the time. Seamus hinted that something else traumatic had happened between him and Buzz a long time ago, but he wouldn't talk about it. Which maybe explains why Buzz never recognized Seamus or even remembered his name since then...

CRACK! Reggie Smith powers a Twitchell fastball out of the park in the 1st, Sherman hoots and pounds my back, and the game is on. Russell boots a Cash DP ball in the 2nd to help Montreal tie it up off Rau with a Cromartie double, and then we sleepwalk through five scoreless innings.

The smoked meat sandwich Seamus got for Little Buzz is declared "yucky," and while I'm up buying him a tub of stale popcorn instead, I miss the start of a Dodger rally in the 8th. Lopes and Russell single, chasing Twitchell for Schatzeder, but he walks Smith to load the bases. Dues comes on for the tough righties but Baker walks in one run, and after a 5-2-3 Garvey DP, Cash boots Cey's grounder for a 2-run L.A. lead.

Carter starts the Expo 9th with a clean double, his fourth straight hit off Rau (though his lefty-mashing buddy Valentine goes 0-for-4), and after Perez and Cash single, Hough relieves. Cromartie rolls one out to Russell, who kicks it for the tie game! Everyone but Sherman cheers, and we're not even Expo fans, just underdog and good pennant race rooters.

Relief ace Joe Kerrigan takes over for the 10th. Smith singles. Baker goes down swinging but Garvey works a very rare walk. "Is that the Penguin Man?" Little Buzz asks, as Cey steps to the plate. "You bet," I say, "and he gets more clutch hits than any—"

WHACK! The first pitch is planted deep in the left field bleachers before I can even finish my sentence. Shades of the Rick Monday playoff homer coming here in four years, the Big O crowd goes mute. Except for annoying Sherman, of course.

"That's a pennant winner, you noodniks, that's a pennant winner!"

And with that, we pile back into our car to schlep back over the border. We got smart on the way up and bought little Canadian flags to ease our entry, but going back we might need to get more adventurous.

Meanwhile, the Dodgers head to Philadelphia for the biggest showdown of the year so far. I hate to admit it, but I wish Mikey was still around to put Sherman in his place.

L.A. 100 000 020 3 – 6 7 2

MTL 010 000 002 0 – 3 10 1

W-Hough L-Kerrigan HRS: Smith, Cey GWRBI-Cey

Teke Experience

July 13, 1977

My plan was for us to get to Philly as soon as possible, because I had a good hunch Sherman, Little Me, and our former, faster car would be there for the big showdown with his Dodgers, but Sheila had other ideas. She's suddenly become a nervous nellie about the Pirates, realizing they had some meaning in her buried past, and taking in their Sunday doubleheader with the Cards was her way of "facing her fears" or some junk. So go ahead, babe, knock yourself out...

DR. GROSSINGER'S GAME REPORT:

Perhaps it is due to recent failure against Ray Burris and the win-challenged Cubs, but the Pirates and their attentive throng of fans appear less confident today than is often reported. I will have to pay special attention to this.

1:18 p.m. Second baseman Stennett twists ankle running out grounder, will be in recovery for eight days. All fears realized.

1:37 p.m. John Urrea, St. Louis right-thrower who has defeated them twice already this season, faces James Rooker in first game, takes early advantage with 2-run Templeton single and 3-run parabola of a home run by Hernandez. 5-0 Cardinals top of 3rd.

1:45 p.m. David Parker, he of the "Cobra" moniker, re-galvanizes locals with his own 3-run missle. 5-3 Cardinals, after three.

2:33 p.m. Oliver produces solitary 4-bagger leading off 6th, 5-4 Cardinals and crowd decibel level rising.

3:11 p.m. Reitz double, Tyson (reaching base fourth straight time) single add insurance digit in 9th, sink gathering into further depression. Beer sales increase. 6-4 Cardinals.

3:21 p.m. Urrea vanquishes Taveras and Parker with two subjects aboard to complete contest. I locate cold 16-ounce cup of Rolling Rock for further study.

* * *

3:45 p.m. Second game commences. Pitching duties assigned to notable mediocrities Dierker and Forster. Dierker issues home run to Stennett replacement Fregosi to begin Pirate 1st. Scoring ground out produces 2-0 lead for them. Elation.

4:16 p.m. In succession, Cruz triple, Brock double, Reitz and Tyson singles tie game up in 3rd, Templeton single puts Forster behind 3-2. Shock and dismay.

4:32 p.m. Doubles by Moreno, Parker and Oliver and 2-base gaffe by Reitz put Pirates back up 5-3. Guarded joy.

4:40 p.m. Consecutive home runs from Hernandez and Simmons begin the 4th, tie game 5-5. Widespread anger and guttural language, some panic.

4:47 p.m. Omar Moreno solo home run puts Pirates back ahead. Just plain shock.

5:10 p.m. Forster expunged from mound in flurry of walks, doubles and Oliver field mistake. Grant Jackson takes over but it is 9-6 Cardinals when wreckage cleared.

5:22 p.m. Parker single and Oliver homer off new pitcher Metzger tighten gap to 9-8. I locate another cold cup of beer for more intensive study.

6:17 p.m. Following two remarkably scoreless innings, Robinson single and Ott home run put Pirates in front 10-9 after seven. Success!

6:40 p.m. Jackson replaced by Gossage after one-out single in top of 8th. Goose inexplicably awful, throws wild pitch, allows two singles and Brock double and Cardinals go back up 11-10. YOU SUC—excuse me, what I mean is that misery is rampant.

6:48 p.m. Three straight fly outs to Cruz comprise Pirate 8th. Tekulve slinks up to pitching hill for us.

7:14 p.m. After "Teke" throws scoreless top of 9th, Robinson turns about Metzger fastball and blasts it into upper deck for tie game. BOH-YEAH!!!!

7:35 p.m. Humiliation, ghastly and unexpected, pervades the emptying stadium. Teke walks two, gives Reitz a single and Reitz a 3-run home run in the top of the 10th. Schultz finishes us off, and it is incomprehensible that five different Pirates swatting homers cannot produce victory. All feels lost, and I dread facing my peers. I gather that good sleep and ample coffee tomorrow will be my only remedy.

—S.H.G.

STL 005 000 001 – 6 7 1

PIT 003 001 000 – 4 7 1

W-Urrea L-Rooker, HRS: Hernandez, Parker, Oliver GWRBI-Templeton

STL 032 400 020 4 -15 17 1

PIT 231 200 201 0 – 11 17 1

W-Schultz L-Tekulve HRS: Hernandez, Simmons, Reitz, Fregosi, Moreno, Oliver, Ott, Robinson GWRBI-Brock

American League through Sunday, July 13

Boston	49	37	.570	—
New York	49	38	.563	0.5
Kansas City	50	39	.562	0.5
Texas	46	42	.523	4
Baltimore	44	42	.512	5
Chicago	38	48	.442	12
Minnesota	36	50	.419	13
Cleveland	35	51	.410	14

National League through Sunday, July 13

Philadelphia	52	36	.591	—
Los Angeles	50	35	.588	0.5
Cincinnati	50	39	.562	2.5
Pittsburgh	50	40	.556	3
St. Louis	45	41	.523	6
Houston	40	48	.455	12
Montreal	34	53	.391	17.5
Chicago	29	58	.333	22.5

Escape from New York

Friendly Fred back at ya, hitch-hikin' my butt out of the Big Dark Apple. Here I was for the last month, fixin' on catching this Son of Sam clown and I forgot the whole damn city was losing its power last night. There was serious looting all over my grandma's neighborhood, and I got stuck in a crowd that was trashing a Sam Goody's, and then fires broke out and I SWEAR I had nothing to do with any of it but then the riot cops were there throwing us into wagons and I had to knock one down with a tape deck just to get away.

The real bummer is that the Yanks just got to half a game out yesterday, have one more game with the White Sox tonight, and I'll be damned if I'm going to the Stadium with the place ringed by nasty-ass cats in uniforms and helmets. Screw that. I'm going down to Philly instead for the end of that righteous Dodgers series. See ya on the flip side tomorrow...

Seamus Headley and the Ticking Clock

July 14, 1977

PHILADELPHIA—First, the ball game. If ever a team has their Thang going, it's the Phillies. With Schmidt, McBride and Boone all injured and having to face Don Sutton with the awful Christenson going for them, winning is still no problem.

McCarver fills in for Boone and babbles a 3-run homer out of the park in the 1st. The Dodgers take five innings to tie it up, before Christenson triples, Johnstone singles, Maddux singles, steals second, Luzinski doubles and that's that. L.A. strands 12 runners, including the bases filled against McGraw in the 9th, and drops a game and a half out again.

* * *

Then there's the company we keep. Sheila did recover from her double Pirates disaster to drive to Veterans Stadium with me, and we're delighted and shocked to not only find Sherman, but Lester, Friendly Fred, Little Me, and even that Texas sportswriter Peachy Calhoun in the same box seat section. With everyone in the same great spirits. Seamus is also there, having somehow been given the tickets at the last minute. Sheila asks him what's going on and he says, "Later, Doc. When Timeco Incorporated buys everyone dinner at the best place in town."

And what a place it is: Le Bec-Fin on Walnut Street, gourmet French food for Bastille Day. Crabcrake green beans, prime petit filet Armagnac, Jerusalem artichoke, pecan sour cream coffee cake for dessert and we're thinking, when did we die and go to heaven?

The first thing Seamus does after he stands with his glass of pinot is apologize. For keeping us all in the dark, especially me, and I have to say I hardly remember him being my uncle. Timeco Incorporated, the shady corporation who first gave me the 4-D dice and contracted Seamus to keep an eye on me, has apparently been trying to develop a technology called VISTT, or Virtual Internal Sports Time Travel, where fans can pick their favorite team from any major sport and go back in time to "be there" for their greatest moments. If the technology flies it can be a virtual gold mine. This 1977 replay I've been enlisted to do? A slimy ruse to get a "beta tester" for the project.

Except now that the other hospital inmates have been trapped in the past with me, Timeco Incorporated has expanded their research and changed their agenda. "They've been in touch with me since my concussion," says Seamus, "through an audio microchip they planted in my head six months ago. Anyway, after we nab Amy Gulliver at the Dodgers game in Cincinnati tomorrow, if we can just stay together for the rest of the season all our needs will be provided, and we'll travel from one baseball park to another on a special space-warping bus called the Ball Nut Express."

"So what's the catch?" I ask. Seamus pours himself another glass of wine before continuing. "We're all rooting for different teams here. Timeco believes…that whichever club wins the '77 replay, also has the fans with the strongest rooting interest. Meaning…the member of our group whose team goes all the way will serve as the VISTT model, be allowed to go back to the present and be released from Squallpocket Hospital."

Stunned silence fills our private dining room. "So what about the rest of us?" Sherman blurts out, "We all go poof or something?" Seamus lets out a deep sigh, and we already know the awful answer.

"TSE, they're calling it. Time Segment Evaporation. It ain't pretty. But I'm still negotiating with them, I promise."

I grab my salad fork, rush up and hold it to his neck. "You better negotiate, buddy boy..."

"And Lester roots for five teams at once!" yells Fred, "We got a better chance of winning at an Attica poker table!"

"The Phillies might even win the World Series," exclaims Sheila, "and then what? Poor Michael Spano isn't even here anymore!"

Seamus shares a dry smile. "Timeco can do just about anything with their time travel technology. And they've already provided for that. Excuse me..." He swings open a back door and Mikey Spano, still in the dripping wet clothes he drowned in back in the Royals Stadium fountain two months ago, stands there with a goofy expression.

"What's up, meatheads? How 'bout them Phils today?"

L.A. 002 010 001 – 4 14 0
PHI 300 030 00x – 6 10 1
W-Christenson L-Sutton SV-McGraw HRS: Yeager, McCarver

Beware the Ides of July
July 15, 1977

CINCINNATI—They're after me, I know it. I can see all my inmate room-mates filing into that great box seat section here at Riverfront before to-night's game with the Dodgers, and am I ever pissed.

First of all, I was convinced I'd seen the last of that creep Seamus after he tried to put the moves on me a few weeks ago and I put my shoe in his nut-cakes, but I also had to take three different buses to get down here from Cedar Point today and almost missed batting practice.

The good news is I'm in a seat way down the right field line next to the Reds bullpen, with a perfect angle on Bill Plummer's sweet behind. I already told you all how he's my second favorite backup catcher hunk, and now, if only Seaver could get in trouble for a change, I might get an inning or two of seri-ous squat viewing while he warms a reliever.

Just my luck, the ball game turns into a Tom-Tom club, with John and Seav-er both dealing. Reggie Smith cracks out a solo shot right past me in the 1st, but the pitchers take over from there. Actually it's Seaver who does the taking over, because the Reds lineup abuses John all kinds of ways without scoring a run. Four out of the first five innings they put two guys on base, then get two more singles with two gone in the 6th before Griffey finally ties it with another single.

Then that skinny, weird-looking Foster does it again, mashing homer number 37 leading off the 7th and the stadium goes nuclear. I borrow binoculars from a lady next to me and can make out Seamus half up in his seat, scoping the stands with his binocs and paying no attention to the game. Bench and Concepcion single after the Foster bomb to finally drive John out of the game, and you'd think because we're outhitting them 13-3 we'd have a huge lead, but then Geronimo bounces into a 4-6-3 on Sosa's first pitch to prove why we don't.

Lasorda puts Hough out there for the 8th, and he's as bad as Tommy John, handing out three walks and a 2-run Bench single to put them away. Smith hits another homer in the 9th, though, and could it be? Is Seaver losing it? C'mon, Sparky, c'mon. They didn't call you Captain Hook for nothing.

Yes! Sarmiento's taking off his jacket. And there's my boy Bill donning his mask, grabbing his glove! I love you, Bill Plummer, I love—

Item in CINCINNATI ENQUIRER, July 16th...

Amy F. Gulliver, a female Reds fan, was arrested last night at Riverfront Stadium during an assault attempt on reserve catcher Bill Plummer in the home bullpen during the 9th inning. No charges were filed, and Miss Gulliver's $500 bail was quickly paid by a couple of alleged friends of the assailant.

L.A. 100 000 001 – 2 4 0
CIN 000 001 12X – 4 14 0
W-Seaver L-John HRS: Smith-2, Foster GWRBI-Foster

Where Have you Gone, Dave Rosello?
July 17, 1977

Little Me snuggled up to my shoulder minutes before the Ball Nut Express zapped us back to Vet Stadium for the Cubs-Phillies game. He was kind of excited because Sheila had given him the Orioles to root for so he wouldn't be without a team, but he was also kind of worried about his future—with good reason.

"Is evaporating the same as going to heaven?"

"Well, buddy...Can't say because none of us have ever done it. But it might be. Uncle Seamus isn't even sure himself. Tell you what, just think good thoughts about your Orioles and maybe they'll win the pennant."

"But Lester told me they don't have a chance because they have the worst team OPS and a super-thin bullpen!"

"Lester doesn't know everything. He just thinks he does. The Royals bull-pen is actually thinner and look how close they are."

Mikey was up in a front seat making barking sounds, already stoked about his Phillies probably about to kick Cubbie butt, even though I pointed out that something very different might happen if that was where the bus was dropping us off. Little Me sighed and tried to close his eyes.

"I don't like Mikey. He's a poopie-head, and I wish he really drowned that time."

I leaned into his little face. "Don't say that about anybody, buddy. Ever. Someone gave him a second chance for a reason..." I looked out the bus window, at Philly's Center City beginning to take shape. "And I guess that's true about all of us."

Game of the Day

PHILADELPHIA—The best vs. the worst, record-wise at least. The Cubs nearly squeaked out a win yesterday with Reuschel, and now put Bonham up against the assassin Carlton. Mikey is back in obnoxious form, up and down in his seat, yelling at the field with food in his hand, refusing to believe his drowning was anything more than a two-month coma.

His team sure isn't in a coma, putting two guys on in the first two innings, but Bonham squirrels out of each jam. With Trillo still out another day or two, Chicago has their young Puerto Rican bench player Dave Rosello in the 2-hole against Carlton, because he hits lefties a bit better. Dave comes through in the 3rd, knocking a sac fly to put the Cubs up 1-zip.

The lead lasts about 15 seconds. Schmidt begins the Philly 3rd with a single. McBride gets hit and knocked out (again!) for two games. Luzinski bounces a sure DP ball out to Rosello, but the ball plays him and scoots up his arm for a huge error. Bonham's rattled, as Hebner and McCarver draw bases-loaded walks. Maddox fans but Bowa pops a sac fly and it's 3-1 Phillies for no reason.

But this game has weirdness written all over it. After Buckner singles to start the Cub 5th, Steve Swisher shows his son Nick who won't be born for three years how to do it, whacking a Carlton fastball over the wall to tie the game!

Bull Luzinski bounces another ball out to Rosello to start the Phillie 5th. He boots this one, too. Hebner then launches a drive to deep right. Murcer races back, leaps and snags the ball before it leaves the park. Lester giggles with glee and Mikey threatens to give him an ass-hat. McCarver lines into a DP to kill the inning.

And Murcer does it again two innings later, robbing Johnstone of a homer! Bonham and Carlton have both settled down, and both guys pitch into extras. But when Johnstone singles to begin the Phillie 10th, Sutter is hailed into the game, and told to pitch until his arm falls off. He strikes out the side for starters.

Can the Cubbies win it for him? Doesn't look that way. Murcer doubles with two outs in the 12th, but guess who gets nailed at the plate by Maddox? Yup, Dave Rosello. Top of the 14th, though, Swisher doubles, is balked to third with two gone, and Dashing Dave does it! Lines a double into the gap to put Chicago ahead! Lester gets the remnants of Mikey's hoagie in his face for cheering, but doesn't care.

Naturally, Bowa singles to start the Phillie 14th, gets over to third on ground outs, and Schmidt grounds a single past—yup, Dave Rosello—to tie the game! Mikey hoots, gives Lester his napkins. The damn bus might leave without us. Brusstar finally takes over for Carlton, who was pulled for a pinch-hitter, and Murcer and DeJesus greet him with singles. Buckner then dumps one into center, Biitner pinch-hits another one off McGraw, and the Cubs are ahead 6-4!

That's what we think. Sutter still in there, his arm almost in a sling, Luzinski singles. McCarver singles him to third with one out. The Bull scores on a force. Maddox tries to get a lead at first but can't, Bowa grounds into a force, and it's over! The mighty Cubs win their 30th, and improve to 2-14 against the Phillies!

CHC 001 020 000 000 012 – 6 19 2
PHL 003 000 000 000 011 – 5 11 1
  W-Sutter L-Brusstar HR: Swisher GWRBI-Buckner

Raging Royals
July 18-19, 1977

We spent two nights in the funky Bronx because the Royals were in town for three games with the Yanks, and Friendly Fred bet a top sirloin steak dinner with Lester over the outcome. Fred's been in a weird place all year, but with the blackout riots and three straight horrible games by his Bombers before finally winning yesterday, he's become a prime candidate to ditch this coop and screw the chances of any of us getting back to the present. Meaning we had to humor him.

One thing nobody expected, though, was the games being more flat-out insane than Friendly Fred. In the style of the great old boxing matches, here for your nostalgic pleasure is...

Friday Night at the Fights!

We got Kid Splittorff in one corner, Gorgeous Don Gullett in the other, the Yanks with an 8-4 edge so far this year. The joint is packed, but Gullett's on the ropes early. Cowens and Brett and Mayberry and Patek and Otis and Brett again and McRae and Mayberry again all get on the bases, and guess what, folks? Not a one of 'em score, I'm talking eight left on base in the first three rounds by the K.C. boys. You couldn't dial up a worse omen by calling Transylvania.

Clouds of cigar smoke roll over the grandstand as the bell rings for Inning 4, still scoreless, and surprise, surprise, the raging Royals go to work. Patek opens with a line double uppercutted into the gap. Otis floats a ball deep to left, Pineilla on his heels, jumps at the wall but it's off his glove and over for as cheap a shot as this reporter's ever seen. One out later Brett gets a free pass and McRae jabs a single. Wathan puts a left hook around the foul pole for three more runs. Porter and Mayberry rip single shots and Gorgeous Don is out of the ring for Ken Clay.

The Clay Man fares no better, folks. Joe Lahoud pinch-hits a single, Patek singles, Otis walks, Cowens skies a ball out to Blair in center who drops it for two more runs. Kenny the Hebrew Holtzman jogs in for the shell-shocked Clay, and Brett pounds him with a right, a 3-run smash to the upper deck and it's 12-0 Royals as the bell ends the inning. A tragedy, people, a disgrace.

Except this Kid Splittorff hasn't thrown a good one since he was in diapers, and no one bets a dime on him tonight. Good thing. Randolph doubles in a 5th inning run. Reggie homers in two more in the 6th. Cliff Johnson and Blair both with 3-run right hooks after K.C. scores three in the 7th and it's 15-10 for the blue hat boys. Tidy Dick Tidrow's taken the ring for the Yanks and makes a mess of things, letting Mayberry sock him for another 3-run homer and it's 18-10 in the 8th.

Three Yank singles and another 3-run belt from "Palooka" Johnson makes it 18-14 and Mingori hits the action before Kid Splittorff is skinned alive. A walk and two singles later it's a 2-run game, and I'll tell ya there hasn't been a bout like this in the Bronx since Joey Maxim battled Sugar Ray Robinson in 1952!

K.C. gets two more aboard in the 9th, gunning for 20, but two fly outs end the threat. Mingori's got three tough customers to take care of in Rivers, Piniella and Johnson, but it's 1...2...3...and it's over! 34 runs and 38 hits later, the Royals are your Friday night champions!

K.C. 000 (12)00 330 – 18 20 1
NYY 000 0 1 2 760 – 16 18 3
   W-Splittorff L-Gullett SV-Mingori HRS: Otis, Wathan, Brett, Mayberry,

Jackson, Johnson-2 GWRBI-Otis

And Saturday Afternoon...

Revenge is a dish best served after a cold slap in the face. Four K.C. runs on five hits and two walks against Figueroa kick off the next contest, but Every-so-often Eddie gives them nothing but a single and double the rest of the way. The Yanks? Two in the 1st, two in the 2nd, two in the 3rd, two in the 5th, two in the 6th, and Jm Colborn is laying on the Stadium grass like a splattered hunk of road kill.

K.C. 400 000 000 – 4 7 1
NYY 222 022 00X – 10 12 0

W-Figueroa L-Colborn HR: Poqyette

Oliver!

July 20, 1977

Riding this joke of a bus every day isn't the best thing for my *tuches*, but I have to keep the kvetching down because we're off to Three Rivers today for the rubber game between my Dodgers and Dr. Sheila's adopted Pirates, and the last thing I need is her analyzing me for the whole damn game. What's she trying to prove anyway, telling us she's been a Bucs fan her whole life but "forgot about it"? You root for the team you grew up with, and anyone who can forget about that's already got one foot in the shock treatment room.

Actually, the old girl's been pretty nice about me driving off with the kid and not telling the truth about what happened to Hannah, but that's what happens when you end up in an even bigger mess. I'm not the bragging type or anything, but my Dodger rotation's got everyone else's beat, meaning I got a good shot at beating this evaporation nonsense. If I don't? Feh, I'm old and half-dead anyway.

Anyway, the Phillies have skunked two in a row to the Cards, so it's time we got off our heinies and nabbed some of that ground back. You don't win a pennant by sitting around like yesterday's matzah balls.

Game of the Day

PITTSBURGH—We definitely got the edge in this one, with Douggie Rau throwing against Odell Jones. but this game wasn't invented to do what it's supposed to. Sure enough, doubles by Taveras, Robinson and Gonzalez and singles by Fregosi and Oliver put the Pirates up 3-0 and gets Dr. Sheila braying in my ear. Rau looks awful, giving up eight hits in the first three innings, but the Dodger pen has been worked a lot and Lasorda really doesn't want to use it.

We get back in the swing of things in the 4th. Dusty bombs one with two outs, Garvey, Monday and Oates follow with singles, and it's 3-2. Jones stinks up the place with two outs again in the 5th, as Smith singles, Cey walks, and Baker ties the game with another single. Forster comes on to get rid of Garvey, then throws a scoreless 6th.

With Stennett still out a few days, Taveras leads the Pirate 6th with his fourth straight hit, a hell of a double. Parker singles him in with two outs (again), they're up 4-3, and I have to tell Dr. Sheila to wipe that smirk off her face.

Tekulve's on for the 7th, but we wreck him with—you guessed right—two outs, as Smith singles, Cey and Baker double and it's 5-4 Blue Boys. Make it 6-4, as Rau bats for himself and singles in Monday.

Dr. Sheila hides in the ladies room for the top of the 9th, then crawls back to her seat when Robinson leads the Buc 9th with a walk. Gonzalez singles him to second but Fregosi whiffs on a great curve. Here's Al Oliver again, who I think they call Scoop but it's hard to remember when I can barely remember my birthday. Scoop can't hit lefties much, and Rau can be tough against—

He did it. Oliver did it. He ruined my day, my night, and my week. A friggin' three-run homer on a 1-2 roll?? (10% chance). A travesty of an outrage! You should die, Doug Rau! You get out of every stupid jam the entire game and do THIS to me in the last of the 9th?? Ach. Give me a glass of Bromo and let me sleep.

L.A. 000 210 210 – 6 12 1

PIT 003 001 003 – 7 17 0

W-Demery (!) L-Rau HRS: Baker, Oliver GWRBI-Oliver

American League through Sunday, July 20

Boston	55	38	.591	—
New York	52	42	.553	3.5
Kansas City	53	43	.552	3.5
Texas	50	45	.526	6
Baltimore	47	46	.511	8
Chicago	41	53	.436	14.5
Cleveland	40	54	.426	15.5
Minnesota	38	55	.409	17

National League through Sunday, July 20

Philadelphia	56	39	.589	—
Cincinnati	55	42	.567	2
Los Angeles	52	40	.565	2.5
Pittsburgh	54	42	.563	2.5
St. Louis	50	42	.543	4.5
Houston	43	53	.448	13.5
Montreal	37	57	.394	18.5
Chicago	31	63	.330	24.5

About Those Visigoths...

July 22, 1977

KANSAS CITY—Lester wouldn't talk to me for three days while my Red Sox were busy spanking his Twins, but now that we have to face Dennis Leonard and his Royals, he's getting geek-cocky all over again.

"Think you'll still have isolated power in Royals Stadium?" he says, raising a middle finger he's been jabbing his calculator with, "Isolate this." Actually, he's got nothing to brag about. Since K.C.'s hot 16-4 start, they've been playing a game under .500, and Leonard's been the only guy in their rotation who hasn't been shaky lately.

I take that back. He almost blew a big lead his last time out in Fenway, and Boston's peppering his butt in the early going today. I think I called them the Visigoths after their latest hacking of the Twins, but in this more spacious arena, a pack of wild dingos comes to mind.

Leonard is in trouble practically every inning. Yaz walks and Rice singles with two outs in the 1st but Evans whiffs. Lynn and Hobson walk in the 2nd, and with two outs Carbo bombs his 22nd homer for a 3-0 Sox lead. Rice doubles to start the 3rd, but Leonard gets Evans, Lynn and Hobson.

Meanwhile Don Aase gets the first nine Royals he faces, before Poquette starts the K.C. 4th with a line single. Team MVP so far Al Cowens then rips a triple into the gap for their first run, and after Brett bounces out, Mayberry singles to make it 3-2.

Back come the barbarians, as Yaz, Rice and Evans all single to begin the 5th, but Leonard holds the fort, getting Lynn on a force at home and whiffing Hobson and Burleson. Bottom of the 5th, Cowens singles in the tying run with one out, Brett and Mayberry follow with scoring doubles, and the Royals are up 5-3. Lester is an inch away from me pouring my cold soda down his back.

Leonard continues to fool nobody, though. Yaz singles to start the 7th but a whiff and DP follow. A Lynn walk, Burleson single and botched grounder by Patek fill the bases in the 8th, but Carbo fans and Fisk flies out. Same story in the 9th. With two gone Evans singles and this time Brett kicks a ball away. Burleson creams a pitch toward left field but Patek snags it for the win!

Thirteen freaking runners left on base by Boston, and only five for them. The only thing I like about my team losing is I can get through another night on the Ball Nut Express without everyone hating me. Even Mikey, who stayed on the bus to watch the Phillies game on TV so he didn't have to look at the dreaded Royals Stadium fountain again, had nothing but a big grin for me.

They don't need to worry yet. Between the widespread streakiness and the way these two races are packed, it seems more and more like our fates won't be decided until the final week.

BOS 030 000 000 – 3 11 0
K.C. 000 230 00x – 5 9 2
W-Leonard L-Aase HR: Carbo GWRBI-Brett

My Funky Valentine
July 23, 1977

ST. LOUIS—Seamus reporting in. Decided to cave to peer pressure after all and take on a team to root for the rest of the way. Since I've always been a believer in lost causes I tried to pick Cleveland when I was recovering in the hospital there, but Crazy Amy took over the whole state of Ohio on me so now I'm opting for the Expos. Why the hell not? They wear classic goofy hats and have three all-star boppers and Steve Rogers and a great closer in Joe Kerrigan and the best beer in baseball at their park. And at least they're better than Lester's poor Cubs.

Today we get another shot at Lester's not-as-poor Cards. Dawson clubbed Rasmussen over the head in their 9th inning dark alley yesterday, and today they're all over Tom Underwood, one of the worst excuses for a starter in either league. Of course it doesn't help that he's a lefty, a species of pitcher the Expos tend to obliterate. A 2-run Dawson homer and two-out Valentine single in the 3rd give them three runs, and a double, single, and two walks give them another in the 4th before soiled Underwood is dropped down the laundry chute. Righty Eastwick is hailed, but Parrish stays in there and reams him for a double anyway and a 6-0 lead.

But these damn Cardinals...With Simmons, Scott and Mumphrey all injured, they storm back against Steve Rogers anyway, mashing four doubles, the daily Garry Templeton triple, and tie the score with three runs in the 5th and three in the 8th. Dues and Kerrigan shut them down from there, but Eastwick has been busy blanking the Montrealers since he gave up the big Parrish double.

But this is the National League, people, meaning necessary pinch-hitters, so bye bye Rawly, hello Butch Metzger. He throws a scoreless 10th and 11th, but a Dawson walk and Dave Cash single start the 12th. A DP bouncer to Templeton gets heaved past Hernandez at first to put the Expos ahead, and righty-suffocater Clay Carroll comes on to face Valentine with the bases stuffed.

Stuff this, Clay. Ellis lines it over the wall in 3.2 seconds for a shocking grand slam, and Montreal makes it two in a row and improves to 4-13 against their No. 1 tormenters.

MON 003 300 000 005 – 11 11 2
STL 000 030 030 001 – 7 12 2
W-Kerrigan L-Metzger HRS: Dawson, Valentine

Getting Wicked Crowded in Here
July 24, 1977

Spending over two months in a bus with the same nine people ain't easy. I mean, I have best friends I wouldn't want to drive three hours in a car with. On top of that we got pennant race lives at stake, everyone thinking they deserve to win, and on some days, like this one where we go nowhere because Seamus has to fix some kind of transport sensor in the engine, the whole operation starts to feel like some bean-brained sitcom...

INT. BACK OF BUS – DAY
Fred exits rest room, chewing on a toothpick. Sees the bus TV tuned to the Boston at K.C. game and visibly freaks.
FRED: What the hell? Change that shit!
BUZZ: Forget it, man. Two contenders in a game beats one.
LESTER: 67 percent to 50, to be exact.
FRED: Shut your geek hole, Lesterine, and put the damn Yanks on. Figueroa's goin'!
On the TV, Fred Lynn smacks one out against Colborn to but Boston ahead 3-1 in the 4th. Fred GROANS.
FRED: Uh-uh. No way. I ain't watchin' this—

He grabs the remote off a seat and switches to Minnesota, where the Yankees have just scored six runs in the top of the 1st. Fred lets out a WAR CRY that wakes Little Buzz from his nap and gets Amy out of her celebrity trash magazine.

AMY: Keep it down, wackos! And what's the Cleveland score?

FRED: Nobody cares about the crummy Indians, or those right-wing Reds of yours, so keep outta this—

Amy's soda can ring hits his eye and he HOWLS, drops the remote. Lester grabs it, switches back to the Royals game. Rick Wise is falling apart, gives up a Mayberry double to cap a 3-run rally and put K.C. ahead 4-3.

LESTER: I sense broom activity here, boys.

BUZZ: It's the 5th inning, Lester. And it's also Jim Colborn.

LESTER: And it's also Rick Wise.

Sheila appears with a cup of yogurt, grabs the remote from Lester and puts the Pirates game in Houston on. For all of three seconds.

SHEILA: Huh?? I didn't even see the score.

BUZZ: Bucs are ahead, so relax. Thursday is American League Day in these parts.

SHEILA: Says who?

BUZZ: Says me. And three-fifths of Lester.

SHERMAN (O.S.): Dodgers on yet?

FRED: Go back to sleep, fool!

On screen in K.C., a rested Littell relieves Colborn in the 5th, after two singles, two walks and two more Boston runs and it's 5-4 Red Sox.

DISSOLVE TO:

INT. BACK OF BUS – TEN MINUTES LATER

Five straight Royals have reached to start their 5th, Stanley is in, and the Royals are back up 8-5. Fred rocks back and forth on the seat, talking to himself, flashing Buzz and Lester dirty looks. Lester nudges Buzz, who SIGHS and puts the Yankee game back on. What used to be an 8-1 New York lead has been cut to 9-6.

FRED: Damn!! You jinxed it! Give me that thing—

He grabs the remote, tosses it out the bus window.

SHEILA: Fred? That was not acceptable! Lucky for you we're not moving...

She hurries down the aisle and out the door to retrieve it. Fred suffers as Cliff Johnson leads an inning with a double...and doesn't score. Nettles leads the 8th with a double...and doesn't score. Blair triples with one out in the 9th...and gets stuck there. But Figueroa sets the Twins down in the last of the 9th for the complete game, and the seventh straight loss by Minnesota.

FRED: Thanks, brothers. Couldn't have done it without you.

Shaking, he retreats to his spread-out sleeping bag way in the back and curls up in a fetal position.

Back in Kansas City, Mingori comes on for the final four outs, and the standings onscreen show all three teams a mere half game apart again. Buzz gives Lester's hand a freak shake.

BUZZ: Nice sweep, man. But don't forget us New Englanders like to get even.

Lester doesn't respond. He already has his trademark glassy-eyed stare back, his mind in another ball park.

LESTER: Did I tell you Ted Simmons is back today?

FADE TO BLACK

BOS 101 120 110 – 7 13 0
K.C. 100 340 00x – 8 8 0
W-Littell L-Wise SV-Mingori HRS: Lynn, Brett GWRBI-Otis
NYY 601 110 000 – 9 13 1
MIN 010 112 100 – 7 11 3
W-Figueroa L-Zahn HRS: Zeber, Cubbage, Carew GWRBI-Zeber

Like...Wow
July 25, 1977

LOS ANGELES—Me and Sheila played hooky from the Phillies-Dodgers game because we knew listening to Mikey and Sherman squawk at each other for nine innings would've been unbearable. Instead we hopped a real bus and got up to a part of the Sunset Strip still populated by hippie burnouts and had a late dinner at a fun little outdoor sandwich place called the Psych-o-Deli. Being on that damn Ball Nut Express day and night hasn't given us much alone time, and with the pennant races way more stressful than they were before, it's important we get away once in a while.

Not that we're alone now. There's freaky guys with hair down to their waists and skanky girls in monster afros and go-go boots and Jackson Browne playing on a stereo system and the couple right behind us is sharing a giant doo-bie with the smoke billowing over our corned beef and alfalfa sprout platters.

"If my Pirates and your Red Sox meet in the World Series," Sheila asks, grabbing my hand, "how will we ever deal with it?" I tell her it's too early to even talk about something like that, but as we keep eating and get more and more of a contact high from the Maui Wowee smoke, that all changes.

"Look, you would have Candelaria for three of the games, and the best I could throw against him would be Don Aase. Bill Robinson would absolutely tattoo Fenway Park. So if anyone needs to worry it's me, but see I'm not, because if there's real genuine love between us...and feelings...then even if I lose and evaporate we'll still be together, man...in some cosmic ballpark somewhere...and you'll still be a psychiatrist and I'll still be your patient of love."

She just nods with a dreamy smile, and the check comes and we decide we don't need to pay it and just float out of there and up the street to Book Soup and then maybe up to the Whisky to catch a set of Blondie and maybe we'll meet everyone back at Dodger Stadium later or maybe we just don't want those people cramping our style, right?

Dang That Polish Fellah!
July 26, 1977

ARLINGTON, TX—I knew he was gonna crush that ball. Top of the 1st, Carl Whateverski coming off a game-ending fly out last night that put them Yanks in first, and here's Doyle Alexander floating in a lazy curve thinking he's gonna keep that Boston boy's head messed up. Sure, Doyle, tell me another one. Yazzer hit it into the right field bleachers without one sweat bead, even though it was 103 in Arlington Stadium today and old Peachy here needed two lemonades before the players even warmed up.

Now Alexander sometimes pitches good and sometimes looks like a leaky rowboat in the Gulf of Mexico and this was one of those days. Two doubles made it 2-0 Red Sox in the 2nd, Bernie's Carbo latest bomb made it 4-zip in the 4th and a Dewey Evans two-run blast the next inning sent him right to the glue factory.

Meantime Fergie Jenkins was doing his thing, walking nobody and getting out of danger all day, and when Wills, Sundberg and Harrah started our 8th with singles, Soup Campbell took over and closed the kitchen. After getting out of that first jam (and another RBI single from the Polish guy) he whiffed Harrah with two outs and the tying runs at the plate in the 9th for his 17th save.

What really blew my gasket is we would've been two everlovin' games out if we'd won this thing. Instead it's back to four, because the Yanks lost too. Least we got Blyleven and Devine going tomorrow in the Sunday double-dater, against Aase and that hippie freak of theirs Bill Lee. Gotta say I like my chances.

BOS 110 220 001 – 7 12 0
TEX 000 100 030 – 4 10 0
  W-Jenkins L-Alexander HRS: Yaz, Carbo, Evans GWRBI-Yaz

Happy Birthday to Lester
July 27, 1977

To celebrate Lester's 25th birthday (He arrived this day in 1985, but who says we can't celebrate eight years early?) Seamus reprogrammed the bus coordinates to take us to all five of his teams' ballparks. Don't need to tell you we were on edge, because there was a chance he'd be emotionally pulled in five different directions and could absolutely lose it before the day was over. But Seamus had a special white jacket all ready, and Sheila was on hand with her special observation notebook. And wearing those hot glasses I like...

DR. GROSSINGER'S REPORT:
CHICAGO—Patient Lester, who suffers from acute schizo-rooting due to be-ing shuttled between divorced parents throughout the midwest for his entire childhood, appears to be at his happiest in sunny Wrigley Field. His spirits are apparently buoyed by his Cubs' last two wins against the muscular Reds, but events go sour quickly, as 16 Chicago hits only produce four runs in the first of two games, while Cincinnati scores five in the 1st and wins going away. The Cubs then manage 11 runs in Game Two, but it is unfortunate that the Reds score 17 on 23 hits, with potent athletic specimen George Foster swatting three home runs. Coupled with one in the first game, he has now struck 44. Patient Lester takes the two losses with good humor, and it is on to...

ST. LOUIS—Where humor leaves him, to be replaced by a quiet depression. Leading 3-0 with their Pirate-slayer John Urrea pitching, Lester's Cardinals are beaten about the head with Stargell and Ott home runs, then a 2-run Oliver home run in a 3-run Pittsburgh 8th that decides the first game. Tekulve survives a brutal 8th to only allow one St. Louis run, and Jackson saves it in the 9th. Lester is kept away from alcoholic beverages between games, and it is the proper decision, for one Larry Dierker starts Game Two and allows another Stargell homer and two by the diminutive Garner in the first four innings. Terry Forster throws miserably for the Pirates, but thankfully–I mean, oddly enough, St. Louis can only score one run at a time, and Pittsburgh completes the sweep to become the first team to reach 60 wins. Lester refuses to leave the stadium lavatory for a full hour, and Mr. Headley is forced to retrieve him and get us off to...

MINNESOTA—Where Lester seems refreshed by the cooler high plains air, and the sight of marginally talented Paul Thormodsgard rendering the Orioles impotent. Flanagan is also sterling for them, but a 7th inning single from Wynegar is all the scoring in Game One and color returns to Lester's face. By the end of Game Two he is beaming, as McGregor gives up 15 Twins hits in less than five innings and the shocking four-game sweep is complete. (Poor little Carlton Gip is most distraught after his Orioles drop two games below .500, but I have scheduled an imminent session at a Toy Barn as treatment.)

KANSAS CITY—Lester's mood brightens further, as Paul Splittorff is dazzling again, snuffing the Indians 7-0 in the first game with the help of a bases-clearing Cowens double. Cowens homers to begin the second affair and the Royals go up 3-0. They lead 4-2 in the 5th when everything that can possible go awry for Doug Bird and Steve Mingori does. Six runs later, the Clevelanders are ahead to stay. Lester is notably surly at this juncture, and blames everyone in the traveling party for the loss...Mr. Headley expedites us to our final destination, which is...

CHICAGO—And Comiskey Park this time, for one game with the Yankees. This contest turns out to be a case study in the New Yorkers' erratic fortunes, for after surrendering three hits and one run to the first three White Sox batters, Catfish Hunter retires the next 13, and 19 out of 20. Paul Blair hits a 3-run home run off Steve Stone, but as they often do, the Yankees waste countless opportunities to add to their advantage. An Essian solitaire blast makes it 3-2 for the visitors, but after a Bannister single begins the 8th, Sparky Lyle is summoned. The Chicago manager leaves his lefties in to face him, because as Lester explains, he knows how hideous Lyle's outings under pressure have been. A single, double and single produce the tying and winning runs, as Lester is not only elated but his thesis proven correct.

"We will take a 4-5 record any day," he says, bedding down at the rear of the bus by approximately 11:16 p.m. Serious incidents were averted, and it is apparent that a very full day of sunshine and ballpark activity has been rewarding therapy for him—even though I still find him crazier than a neutered squirrel.—S.H.G.

American League through Sunday, July 27

Boston	57	43	.570	—
New York	56	44	.560	1
Kansas City	57	46	.553	1.5
Texas	54	48	.529	4
Baltimore	49	51	.490	8
Chicago	44	56	.440	13
Cleveland	44	57	.436	13.5
Minnesota	42	58	.420	15

National League through Sunday, July 27

Philadelphia	59	41	.590	—
Pittsburgh	60	43	.583	0.5
Cincinnati	59	45	.567	2
Los Angeles	54	44	.551	4
St. Louis	51	48	.515	7.5
Houston	45	58	.437	15.5
Montreal	42	59	.416	17.5
Chicago	34	66	.340	25

It Ain't Always This Sunny in Philadelphia
July 28-29, 1977

By Mikey Spano

So you haven't heard much from me lately. Kind of what happens when you fall into a ballpark fountain and drown, and the clowns who zapped you back in time in the first place do some kind of sci-fi CPR and bada bingo—you're alive again! Don't you hate that?

Before I get to the latest Phillie disasters, I thought I'd tell everyone how I ended up with so much attitude. See, with my team winning in '08 and looking damn nuclear this year before we hit the '77 road, I should probably be more like Lester, one of those sprout and cucumber eaters who just rolls with everything. But that ain't my makeup.

My dad Marty—may he rest in peace with his Alka-Seltzer—grew up in the 1950s and rooted for Richie Ashburn, who was awesome, but also Bobby Del Greco and Don Ferrarese, and the Gene Mauch team that lost 23 straight in '61, and the Gene Mauch team that crashed like a tray of beer glasses in '64. So by the time he lost his truck hauling job when I was three or four in the mid-'70s when the Phils were good but kept losing playoffs to the Dodgers, he had already started smacking me around the apartment.

But this drowning thing's woken my ass up a bit, and me the Phils are both getting a second chance here. Actually if you count me getting put away for beating up those two high school teachers and Sister Katherine at reform school, it's my third chance.

In other words, when Bull Luzinski grounded into those two horrible DPs yesterday in L.A., the first off Tommy John and the second off Hough when they were down 3-2 in the 8th with runners on the corners to kill our team for the day, all I did was turn and shake Sherman's hand. And when Bull hit into another one tonight in St. Louis with the bases loaded in the 8th and Buddy Schultz on the mound, all I did was buy Lester a 16-ounce cup of Bud.

Nope, it ain't always sunny in Philadelphia, but I'm through with the booing and the bashing. It's really no fun being a jerk all the time, and you might not believe it but I got soft spots in here. Doesn't everyone? Even that Mussolini guy was on his mama's boob once.

PHL 000 000 020 – 2 8 1
L.A. 100 001 10x – 3 8 0
   W-John L-Christenson SV-Hough HR: Yeager GWRBI-Garvey
PHL 000 100 000 – 1 8 0
STL 113 010 10x – 7 12 0
   W-Underwood L-Kaat HR: Cruz GWRBI-Hernandez

Why We Play the Games
July 30, 1977

LOS ANGELES—Is there anything worse than having a drippy cold in sunny L.A.? Little Buzz came down with one while we were in St. Louis, so now everyone on the bus including me has Niagara Mucus Falls going. Sometimes I just hate myself.

What this means is we get to follow the Pirates-Dodgers battle from the crowded comfort of the Ball Nut Express, Row 17, while parked in the lot of Tito's Tacos. At least the game keeps us awake.

Game of the Day
Burt Hooton vs. Odell Jones. Damn. May as well be Bob Gibson vs. Dooley Womack. Except this is 1977, where anything can, most likely, and usually does happen. Steve the Garv tries to reverse that notion early, lofting a high fly into the Dodger bullpen with two aboard for a 3-0 1st inning lead. But it's Hero/Goat Appreciation Day in the Ravine, as Steve-O kicks away a Bill Robinson squibbler to open the 2nd. Ed Ott picks out a Hooton ball and deposits it in the RF bleachers and it's 3-2 in a flashbeat.

Make that tied at three in the 3rd, when Oliver triples and Pops Stargell doubles down the line with two gone. Then it's Odell Time, as Jones wipes the field with 15 of the next Dodgers he faces. Yup, L.A.'s offense has been that bad. Luckily, Hooton matches him until the 9th, when Stargell leads with a walk, Moreno runs, and tears around to third on a two-out Garner double. Skinny Frank Taveras, back at short for the Pirates after a brief injury, rips one up the middle that gets past a diving Lopes for a 5-3 Pittsburgh lead!

With an overused Gossage in the pen, Odell is allowed to start the last of the 9th, but loses it quick. Smith leads with a single, is wild pitched to second, and after Garvey grounds out, Baker and Cey work him for walks.

The Goose jogs in anyway, but he's more tired than we thought he was. Monday lines a single for one run, and Oates walks in another. Vic Davalillo pinch-hits for Hooton, and bounces a possible DP ball out to recent Buc hero Taveras—

CLANK. Ballgame. And Sheila, sitting a foot away from a cheering Sherman in the stuffy bus, sneezes in his direction.

PIT 021 000 002 – 5 8 1
L.A. 300 000 003 – 6 7 1
W-Hooton L-Jones HRS: Ott, Garvey

Veeck—as in Drenched

July 31, 1977

CHICAGO—We found ourselves at 35th and Shields this morning, in humidity so thick you could peel it off your skin and use it for pizza dough. Since I was the only one recovered from our two-day cold epidemic, I volunteered to take in the Indians-White Sox game, and was glad I did. Not only was it a businessman's special, but it was Shower with Harry Caray Day!

Yup, the fearless broadcasting legend was doing the game with Jimmy Piersall from centerfield, and on the urging of owner Bill Veeck had vowed to douse himself under the fans' bleacher shower between at least three of the innings! Needless to say, I went for a nearby seat.

It was nice to pay a little attention to the Chisox, too, who as usual haven't been getting the attention the Cubs do, even with the north siders in the middle of an atrocious year. And lately, these guys have been playing as well as they did in April. Their main starters Barrios and Stone have both cranked it up a notch, and they've been hitting enough to compensate for their swiss cheese defense.

It's just a rowdy, fun atmosphere in old Comiskey anyway, even on a day when you can hardly breathe. Jorge Orta bangs a deep triple off the wall right below me to start the Sox second, then scores on a Soderholm fly. Eckersley's going for Cleveland, and I can see his long hair whipping around from over 400 feet away. Lefties just eat him for breakfast, though, and Oscar Gamble swallows a fastball and belts it high into the upper deck in right with Garr aboard in the 3rd. "HOLY COW" I hear Harry bellow from his makeshift bleacher booth, and with the home boys up 3-zip after three, here he comes down to the shower, wearing a Hawaiian shirt and polka dot swim trunks. We cheer as he douses himself with a mighty bellow, slicks back his white hair and returns to his seat.

The Tribe's also been playing great all month, and even with four of their hitters out, they bounce right back. Dade singles, Thornton triples and Lowenstein singles off Stoney to begin the 4th. Ron Pruitt then bombs one between Garr and Lemon, but Chet grabs the ball, whirls and throws a perfect relay to Bannister, who cuts Lowenstein down at the plate to ice the rally! Just seeing the White Sox make any kind of great play is a rare event, judging by the exploding cherry bombs around me.

A Garr single and steal, Lemon double and Zisk sac fly in the 5th put Chicago up again 5-2. Harry stumbles back down to the shower after the 6th, no doubt after a couple of drafts, and this time a handful of fans jump in with him. Gamble blasts another shot off Eck in the 7th, his 25th of the year, and the lead is big enough so when Stone does his typical 3-run meltdown in the 8th Dal Canton and LaGrow can come on for the combo save.

Eckersley finally loses his mind in the last of the 8th, Soderholm, Spencer, Bannister and Garr plastering the park with four straight hits and getting all three runs right back. The White Sox may not be winning anything this season, but damn do they ever play some fun games. Right Harry?

"Absho...tively!"

CLE 000 200 030 – 5 10 0
CHI 012 020 13x – 9 14 0
    W-Stone L-Eckersley HRS: Gamble-2 GWRBI-Soderholm

Poor Mr. Flanagan

August 1, 1977

KANSAS CITY—Hi again, it's Carlton. I'm glad I got a baseball team to root for, but I wish it wasn't the Orioles because they don't hit enough and I like to watch hitting, which is why I rooted for the Red Sox before Uncle Buzz said they were his. I don't care how much he looks like me, sometimes Uncle Buzz just isn't nice. At least Aunt Sheila buys me toys when she isn't asking me weird questions.

I sure had fun with Uncle Lester at the Orioles and Royals game tonight, though. This is the place with the big fountains, and it was real hot out again but they told me I couldn't go swimming in it which I thought was stupid.

At least the Orioles looked good for a while this time. Mr. Bumbry got a walk and Mr. Kelly hit a home run off the big pole in right field, and this happened against Mr. Leonard, who is a real good pitcher. Uncle Lester got me the biggest blue cotton candy I ever had, and I was so busy eating it I missed that nothing happened in the game for four innings. Mr. Flanagan, who seems to have the worstest luck of anybody on the Orioles, was making every Royals batter look dumb. What was bad was that Mr. Leonard stopped giving up anything after the 1st inning, so the Orioles couldn't make the score get bigger.

Then it was the 6th inning, which was when Uncle Lester got me a pop-corn box that was so delicious it didn't even need butter on top. It was also when the sleepy Royals got up from their nap. Mr. Cowens and Mr. Brett got loud singles, and Mr. McRae walked. This brought up their extra catcher Mr. Wathan, who Lester told me had a batting number of .376 and had 48 runs which he batted over the plate in only 197 times that he hit, which I think is pretty good. Just like I thought he would, he hit the ball super far over Mr. Bumbry's head for a big triple and now the dumb Orioles were losing.

Uncle Lester tired to make me feel better by getting me a big soda but I just was kind of sick then and thought maybe I would even go pukie. But then the baseball came to the rescue like it does a lot. A Mr. Dauer double and Mr. Kiko Garcia single started the 8th inning, and Mr. Bumbry hit a far enough fly ball to tie the game 3-3.

The Royals REALLY wanted to win, though, because the Red Sox were win-ning against the White Sox, and Mr. McRae took care of that with a scary triple with two outs. The little Orioles manager with grey hair whose name I always forget then walked Mr. Wathan on purpose to let Mr. Joe Zdeb hit, but Mr. Flanagan must have pooped in his pants because he bounced a pitch past the catcher right then and the winning run scored.

I don't think I want to see any more Orioles games until they're winning more. I don't even care how much snacks or toys I get. Somebody is going to have to stay on the bus with me. Bye.

BAL 200 000 010 – 3 7 0
K.C. 000 003 01x – 4 8 0
    W-Leonard L-Flanagan SV-Littell HR: Kelly

The Cage Match
August 2, 1977

It was bound to happen. Rooting for your team in a tight pennant race can be stressful enough, but when the penalty for losing is instant evaporation, it kind of puts you a little more on edge. Well today at Wrigley, one of us flat-out snapped. Here's some of what I heard as Lester's Cubs were skunking Dr. Sheila's Bucs for a second straight inexplicable day:

LESTER: I just can't believe this. A DeJesus double to lead off our 1st and four consecutive singles from Morales, Murcer, Gross and Trillo? Do you know what the mathematical chances of that are?

SHEILA: No Lester, I do not. Will you sit back down please?

LESTER: I mean, I realize the hits came off Jerry Reuss, who has been nothing short of craptastic lately. (reaches in his satchel) Did I show you his UZ-CRP rating for July yet?

SHEILA: I have no interest, Lester. If we're going to keep working together, I need you to not pull out your number. Have you seen the beer vendor lately?

LESTER: Gee, Dr. Sheila, the game's just started, We have eight more innings and Bill Bonham's pitching, which almost guarantees success for you. Actually— (opens satchel again and Sheila kicks it into the nearest aisle)

We move to the 5th. Oliver doubles and Parker singles to get one back in the Pittsburgh 4th...

SHEILA: Good! A single for Taveras. I must admit he owes us one. Come on, Reuss, a nice little bunt now to set the run up for Stennett.

LESTER: Reuss is actually not the best bunter—

SHEILA: Quiet, please. (Reuss pops into a DP to end inning) Gahhh-kdfdgrz!!!

LESTER: See? If you had known the stat, you wouldn't be so shocked and disturbed.

SHEILA: I am not the one disturbed, Lester. You are. You're my patient, remember? I get to ask you questions, and I get to call you disturbed. (swallows too much of her draft beer and chokes for at least a minute)

We move to the 7th, Bonham incredibly with a 3-hitter. Robinson singles with one out and Ott singles him to third...

SHEILA: Yes!! Your team is about to fail miserably, Lester! Do you hear me? Fail miserably!! (Garner bounces into an easy 6-4-3 double play. Sheila's face hardens into some kind of clinical voodoo mask.)

LESTER: With DeJesus and Trillo playing back, Garner's DPLF was a worse than average 49— (Old Style draft beer is suddenly dripping down his hair and into his short sleeve shirt pocket.)

A Morales single and Murcer homer off Tekulve in the 8th finishes off the Pirates for good. Robinson grounds into yet another double play to end the game in the 9th, but by that point Sheila is pulling me down the exit ramp. Shaking, in tears. I tell her she's still in first place, in a better place than anyone in our group except me, and she suddenly tugs me into the shadows and throws her arms around my waist.

"Let's get married," she blurts out with beery breath, her glasses fogged up.

"Are you crazy? Won't that screw up the future when we get back?"

"I need something stable in my life to get me through this, Buzz. And who says we're both getting back?"

I stare at her. She might have a point. Except that in the future...I'm already married.

PIT 000 100 000 – 1 6 0
CHI 300 000 02x – 5 9 0
W-Bonham L-Reuss HR: Murcer GWRBI-Morales

Nothing to Be Grouchy About
August 3, 1977

LOS ANGELES—What a marvelous day this was. What a privilege.

Buzz and his doctor girlfriend were too busy smooching outside Dodger Stadium to notice, so I detoured and went for this club level ticket some idiot movie industry guy was selling dirt cheap.

Turns out the seat was right next to the private boxes, and in the very first inning Del Unser fouled a Hooton fastball straight back at our neighborhood. It bounced out of the hands of this old guy in the first box, bonked off a railing and landed right in my lap! I felt bad for the man, so got the attention of a nurse who was in the box with him, and tossed it to her to give to him.

The next thing I knew I was being ushered into the guy's box. Sitting there in a wheelchair, hooked up to fluids and drugs, but still wearing his beret and smoking a cigar was none other than one of my lifelong heroes, Groucho Marx!

"Thanks for the ball, fellah," he said in a scratchier version of his smooth sarcastic voice, "You're a stand-up guy. I'd stand up myself but O'Malley probably doesn't want another lawsuit. Pull up a chair and enjoy the game. I hear we're having Vegas showgirls between innings and they brought their own wieners."

I was given a chair beside him. From what I remembered, Groucho had a couple more weeks to live, but he'd always been a Dodger fan and probably wanted to see one more game so was let out of Cedars Sinai for the afternoon. I sure wasn't going to be the one to break his actual departure date to him.

"This Hooton's a good thrower, but if I were him I'd change my name. Sounds like either a horned owl or a horny teenager. What did you say your name was?"

"I didn't. It's Sherman. Sherman Wayman."

"I was wrong. *You* sound like a horny teenager. Does your mother know you're sitting with an old pervert? What's the score, anyway?"

"None yet. Don Stanhouse is walking people again. It's amazing the way the Expos never hit for him."

"Probably because they don't like his demeanor. It rubs off, you know. Sometimes you have to go to Woolworth's and buy a gruffy demeanor stain remover. Hey—we got a run!"

Ron Cey had just singled in Reggie Smith for a 1-0 Dodger lead in the 3rd. I was told I could order anything I wanted, so got myself a jumbo kosher dog and a giant bag of peanuts. I offered a handful to Groucho.

"No, son. Keep the change. Besides, I already drank my lunch through these handy tubes. You should try them sometime. Uh-oh, it's that guy they call the Hawk. He scares me, and believe me, nothing scares me these days except doctor bills and reruns of *F Troop*."

"Dawson's good. He might make the Hall of Fame sometime."

"That or a police lineup. It's a fine line, you know."

The Hawk rifled one at that moment, high and deep and into the bleachers for a 2-1 Montreal lead. Groucho made a guttural noise and shook his head.

"That's what I get for betting on a teenage owl. Well, we can still win this thing with a field goal."

Cey singled in a second run soon after to tie the score, and then we went scoreless for the next four innings. It was a hot day and Groucho fell asleep, cigar ash and a bit of drool dripping on his shirt. Boos woke him up when Carter blasted a solo shot with one out in the 10th.

"What happened? Am I dead yet? Hope not, because I forgot to pick up my dry cleaning."

I told him we were losing 3-2 but not to worry because there was a special reason I was at this game. A reason I couldn't really talk about.

"Don't keep secrets from people. You'll regret it. It'll also make your life a helluva lot easier."

Like he's done twelve other times this season, Stanhouse blew the lead, giving up a walk and booting Baker's grounder, before Manny Mota tied the game with a double. Groucho cheered as loudly as he could.

"Manny Mota! Sounds like a lost Marx brother, or one of those idiot Stooges. Moe and Larry sure never hit like that!"

Kerrigan came on to get Yeager and the game dragged to the 12th. Groucho was fading, but didn't want to leave. Finally, a Garvey walk, Cey's third single, and a winning pinch single by professional bench man John Hale brought in the winner.

"Thank god. Now I can go back to my hospital room and still catch *Bonan-*

za. Oh wait—Hoss died five years ago. Thanks for the ball, son, but now it's yours," He tossed it weakly back to me, J. H. MARX scrawled on it between two of the seams. "Let's do this again sometime and say we didn't."

I hesitated a long second, then told him I would sure try. What more could I say?

MTL 000 020 000 100 – 3 10 2

L.A. 001 010 000 101 – 4 9 0

W-Hooton L-Kerrigan HRS: Dawson, Carter GWRBI-Hale

American League through Sunday, August 3

Boston	61	45	.575	—
Kansas City	61	48	.560	1.5
New York	59	48	.551	2.5
Texas	58	51	.532	4.5
Baltimore	52	55	.486	9.5
Chicago	48	59	.449	13.5
Cleveland	48	60	.444	14
Minnesota	43	64	.402	18.5

National League through Sunday, August 3

Philadelphia	62	45	.579	—
Pittsburgh	63	46	.578	—
Cincinnati	62	48	.564	1.5
Los Angeles	58	47	.552	3
St. Louis	56	50	.528	5.5
Houston	46	62	.426	16.5
Montreal	44	62	.415	17.5
Chicago	37	68	.352	24

Left-Wingers Diatribe

August 4-5, 1977

PITTSBURGH—Mikey's Phils are tied with Dr. Sheila's Bucs for first place, and all we get is a lousy one-game series? Who made this crazy schedule? The Pirates hold the season edge so far, 9-4, with nine more still to play, but at least we get Big Lefty Carlton (14-6, 2.94) facing off against the Candy Man (17-5, 1.85) in a bonus battle between the league's best pitchers. Take it away, Pennsylvania!

Game of the Day

Jerry Martin rips a Candy curve down the left field line with one gone in the 1st, and one out later Michael Schmidt jacks one off the facing of the upper deck for a 2-0 Philly lead to spring Mikey out of his seat. "Diagnose that one, Doc!" he yells at Sheila, who merely makes a note in her scorebook. Candelaria puts runners on the next three innings but escapes each jam, while Carlton has the Pirate hitters all out of whack.

Singles by Sizemore, Martin and Davey Johnson start the 5th, before Luzinski beats out an infield hit and Maddox pops a sac fly. 4-0 Philly, and Mikey produces a solid minute of farting sounds. Sheila nudges my arm, flashes me her new scorebook notation:

Michael showing no signs of the calm optimism he professes to be adopting. Am fast approaching a crossroads concerning the proper treatment for this ingrate.

And then the Cobra uncoils. He leads the home 6th with a line drive missle of a homer. Smashes another solo shot with one out in the 8th. Carlton bears down, smokes Robinson and Gonzalez on called strike threes, and Martin gets his second big hit in the 9th, a one-out homer off Tekulve to make it 5-2.

But the battling Bucs are never out of a game. Oliver doubles into the gap to lead the last of the 9th. Taveras grounds out but Duffy Dyer doubles and it's 5-3! The elder Jerry Hairston pinch-hits and whiffs, but Jim Fregosi, who filled in for Stennett after Rennie's latest injury in the 7th, draws a walk. Garber comes in to face Garner, but there's a stirring in the Pittsburgh dugout.

"Here comes Popsy!" yells Sheila, and by the time I correct her, Willie Stargell has already taken a called strike. Everyone in Three Rivers is standing, even barely interested Sherman. Stargell does his windmill warm-up swings, Garber goes into the stretch, throws—

and Pops cracks it deep to right. Back goes Johnstone, to the warning track, to the fence...and catches it to end the game and put the Phils back in first.

"GARBIE DOLL!!" yells Mikey, pounding Sheila on the back. "What a game!!"

Sheila is too upset to react, so I turn and tell Mikey to keep his claws off her if he doesn't want to be wearing his ass for a hat.

"No problem, Buzz," he says with a big grin, "See you in the World Series."

It's a little too early for that.

PHI 200 020 001 – 5 13 0

PIT 000 001 011 – 3 9 1

W-Carlton L-Candelaria HRS: Schmidt, Martin, Parker-2 GWRBI-Schmidt

Crazy Amy Has Left the Building

August 6-7, 1977

CLEVELAND—Let's get to the ball games first, and why everyone hates me even more. The Eck mowed down my Red Sox on Tuesday, but on Wednesday and Thursday the boys pull out their voodoo dice and resume scoring in their sleep like they've done all year. In between the FIVE homers they hit off Wayne Garland, they get four 8-rolls (40% chance) and two 7s (35%) to keep every rally going. The Tribe manage three taters , two off Wise and one off Soup Campbell, but it isn't enough.

Then it's Pick on Jim Bibby Day. To the tune of four runs in the 1st, thanks to the Bib walking Carbo, Fisk and Yaz to start the game and igniting the rally. Jenkins actually pitches worse, but as usual, makes the right pitches at the right time and ups his record to an amazing 13-3.

Hate to say it, but with the erratic way the Yankees and K.C. are playing, if New York doesn't sweep the upcoming three games from Boston before the Sox get back home, this league could be a runaway.

But I can't let the bozos on our bus read those words, because I'd like to survive to see what really happens. Lester and Peachy have been slipping me some trash talk lately, and I even caught Little Buzz sticking out his tongue at myself.

Everyone's on edge, even Seamus, who we count on being our sort of calm navigator. After the game in Pittsburgh Lester saw a Pennsylvania map on the dashboard, and suggested we make a detour to Shanksville to warn some farmers that a plane might be dropping out of the sky there in 24 years. Well, Seamus went nuts, saying that kind of thing was off limits and could "jeopardize everything in the future."

Today Lester brought it up again, and it got everybody out of their seats and yelling. "Isn't 9/11 something we should be jeopardizing?" I asked. "Hell," yelled Friendly Fred, "I would've caught that Son of Sam punk myself if there wasn't a blackout up there!" "And I got to watch a Dodger game with Groucho Marx," said Sherman, "It didn't change a thing, I mean he's still going to die on the 19th, three days after Elvis, but I'm sure it eased his kishkas for his last few days, right?"

Seamus just grumbled, and punched in our next day's location. "This discussion's over. Take your seats and buckle in please." We hesitated a long time, then headed back down the aisle.

But something was wrong. The back window was open, and I could hear footsteps running across the Municipal Stadium asphalt. I looked outside, but couldn't see anything.

"What's wrong?" asked Sheila. I spun around, checked all the faces gaping at me.

"Where's Amy?"

"You mean the goofy girl?" piped up Little Buzz, "She climbed out the window."

Seamus hopped off the bus in a panic, scanned the crowded parking lot. I leaned into the boy's little face. "Did she say why? Was it because her Indians lost twice?" Little Me had no clue, but Sheila's eyes suddenly popped with an idea. She ran to her satchel, thumbed through patient folders until she found Amy Gulliver's.

"If I remember correctly...Aha! 'Patient Gulliver's mother had a fatal stroke on the day Elvis Presley died in 1977. This most likely was the cause of her daughter's unnatural obsession with Presley and his music.' "

Seamus jumped back on board at that moment, winded and irritated. "Well that's just great..." He rummaged through a basket of maps behind his seat that had been dumped out. "She even took one of my maps!"

"Tennessee?" asked Sheila.

"Yeah...at least the two I had for the south. What the hell is she doing?"

Sheila bit her lip, afraid to say the obvious. But then she said it.

"I think she went to save Elvis."

(8/6)

BOS 300 120 101 – 8 13 0

CLE 010 100 202 – 6 10 2

W-Wise L-Garland SV-Campbell HRS: Evans, Lynn, Carbo, Rice-2, Thornton, Blanks, Fosse GWRBI-Evans

(8/7)

BOS 400 000 010 – 5 9 0

CLE 000 110 000 – 2 7 0

W-Jenkins L-Bibby HR: Lowenstein GWRBI-Evans

Strictly Busch League

August 8, 1977

ST. LOUIS–Everyone was in a big nutty tizzy because Crazy Amy bolted on us yesterday. Buzz and Dr. Sheila are positive she's headed for Memphis to keep Elvis Presley from killing himself, but Seamus is afraid to make any detours that would get us off track with the pennant race-watching. Meanwhile, the Cubs and Cardinals fans in me just wanted to get to Busch to see more of our great rivalry, and also to see if St. Louis could keep up their red-hot ways. Good thing Seamus was driving the bus.

* * *

You would think Steve Renko vs. Bob Forsch is an easy Cards win, but the Cubs haven't been playing like themselves lately—meaning they've been winning a few. When Greg Gross rockets a double to open the game and DeJesus singles to make it 1-0 Chicago, I'm already half smiling.

But Renko isn't exactly Three-Finger Brown out there. Templeton singles, Mumphrey and Hernandez walk, Simmons singles, and the Cubs are behind already. I bet myself a jumbo hot dog that the Cards will hang on, but I'm not taking any of that action. And after two great starts in a row, Forsch falls apart in the 3rd. Mitterwald singles, Gross doubles again with one out, DeJesus singles in two, Ontiveros walks and Biitner singles in another and it's suddenly 4-2 Cubbies!

"Take that, Lester!" I yell, jumping out of my seat.

"Sit down and shut up, Lester!" I yell back.

Everyone in our section turns to stare at me at that moment, so I imagine they're enjoying our good-hearted banter. But then Mike Tyson fists out a solo homer in the 4th and it's 4-3. A Simmons double, Freed single and Reitz double in the 6th ties it up and finishes off Renko.

And then it's six innings of nervous time, meaning six innings of stranded base runners and no scoring. Newly acquired lefty Dave Roberts throws two and two-thirds of shutout ball, Sutter three more before Willie Hernandez takes over.

But it's glovework that decides this thing, or lack of it. Mumphrey, who took over for Freed in right, drops an easy fly in the 13th (naturally), and after one out, Buckner slaps a single the other way for the go-ahead run. Per usual, Hernandez almost gives it back, as Simmons singles and Brock doubles to start the last of the 13th. I'm ready to strangle myself. But Willie bears down and gets Scott on a grounder, Reitz on a pop, and Tyson on a weak fly to snap the latest Cardinal win streak. The Cub in me doesn't have long to live, so every win is a small blessing.

CHC 103 000 000 000 1 – 5 13 3
STL 200 101 000 000 0 – 4 13 3
W-Hernandez L-Metzger HR: Tyson GWRBI-Buckner

Last Train Out of Riverfront
August 9, 1977

SOUTH OF CINCINNATI—I'm really not a complicated girl. I mean, I got issues just like your annoying sister-in-law or seventh grade gym teacher, and yeah I tend to stick on a guy and follow him around until I get arrested, but it's part of the simple rules I got growing up. Meaning figure out what you want and go after it like a rabid dog, else you won't go nowhere in life.

So when Sherman accidentally reminded me that Elvis only had a little over a week to live, you bet your bunion I was going to try and save him this time around. My mom keeled over and croaked when she heard the news on the TV back in real '77. I found out later she was at the counter making sweet potatoes, and I was in my room with my Etch-a-Sketch and was wondering why she went to sleep on the floor. I started having troubles after that and one thing led to another, but I did end up with all her Elvis albums and 45s and memorized lyrics for almost every one.

Anyway, I hitchhiked down to Cincinnati yesterday, and hid out in Riverfront to watch my Reds stink against the Phils and make plans for how I was going to pull Operation Elvis off. The problem was that Bill Plummer, my official hear-throb for the season, was starting for injured Johnny Bench, and watching him squat all game was way too distracting for me to think about Memphis.

Game of the Day

Today it's even worse, because Plummer is catching Tom Seaver, the best pitcher in the universe, and like Bill he's just a hunk-a-hunk of burning love. The Reds only give him one run for six innings, on a two-out Driessen single in the 1st, but Tommy is ON. Through six he gives up singles to Hebner and Hutton and nothing else.

Rose starts out 6th with a base knock off Lonborg, Griffey and Driessen single with one gone to make it 2-0, and a double by Geronimo sub Mike Lum brings in two more. Luzinski tags a solo shot in the 7th, but this girl's far from worried. Even after Johnstone smacks one to start the 9th it's just 4-1, and Seaver mows down McBride and Luzinski to put Philly on the gallows trap door.

Except Schmidt, that guy with the white man curls and real scuzzy mous-tache, walks. Hebner singles. Just get Bob Boone, Tom, come on!!

Nope. Boone ropes a ball between Lum and Foster for a game-tying two-run triple! Bastard! Seaver gets Bowa to end it, but what a disaster. The Reds then start the last of the 9th with a Concepcion single and walk to pinch-hit-ter Armbrister. Here's my boy Plummer, and I'm screaming, and screaming...

...and he whiffs. And despite a Morgan bloop single to load the bases after that, Rose grounds into a force to send us into extras.

With Manny Sarmiento on the hill. This is is usually a great or awful thing. Well, Randy Lerch singles to start the 10th, if that gives you a clue. Johnstone singles with one out, and one out later, Luzinski powers a ball off the fac-ing of the upper deck, his second homer of the game. Schmidt, Hebner, and

Boone follow with doubles, and Sparky leaves Manny out there to rot.

Danny Ozark likes that idea, and leaves Lerch out to rot because he knows the undermanned Reds don't stand a chance of coming back. Smart guy. Even after three singles, a double and wild pitch to start the last of the 10th, Armbrister, Plummer and Rick Auerbach all go down on strikes and I'm outta this funeral parlor.

I find a local train yard and hop into a slow-rolling boxcar moving south. Munching on a fast-food burger I have time to think about all this.

Elvis was still touring early in the summer, and now he's down in Memphis getting ready to go off on another one. I know he's in awful shape and popping all sorts of drugs and he probably has security up the yin-yang but I don't care a fartin' fig. 'Cause I'm going to Graceland...Graceland...Memphis, Tennessee I'm goin' to Graceland.

PHI 000 000 103 5 – 9 14 0
CIN 100 003 000 3 – 7 13 0
W-Lerch L-Sarmiento HRS: Luzinski-2, Johnstone GWRBI-Luzinski

Back in the Hood, Inside my Hood
August 10, 1977

NEW YORK—Friendly Fred in yo face again, first time in town since the lights went out and the Bronx burned. Nice of my man Seamus to zap us to the last Yank showdown with the Boston Chowderasses, 'cause I know there's a bigger piece of business on his mind. Yeah yeah, that crazy-ass Amy girl split the scene to stake out Elvis Presley's crib, but damn, we still got pennant races to watch, and why should I care about some fat, bling-wearin', soon-to-be-wormfood white dude who made millions robbing the black man's music? Tutti frutti *this*, sucker!

Game of the Day
Can't find sweeter weather in the Bronx, that's for damn sure. Place almost looks like one of those French extortionism paintings. Catfish is goin' against Reggie Candyass Cleveland, and I don't care how weak we've played lately, if the Bombers can't bomb him we got serious problems.

Well, we got serious problems for the first three innings, but My Man Catfish is up for the fight, giving up a Dwight Evans double through three and nothing else. Then Jimmy Rice and Evans spank his behind for two straight doubles in the 4th and we're down 1-0. This ain't good. Except Cleveland's just a big fool and shows his fool-ass colors in the 5th, kickin' away a Zeber grounder in the 5th with one out. Thurman singles him to third and the better Reggie gets him in with a deep fly.

That pain-in-the-butt Polish chump puts one in the upper deck with one gone in the 6th, and Catfish's next pitch hits Rice-a-Roni in the wrist. He whips his bat away, looks out at Catfish and yells something that makes Dr. Sheila's face go all red. The ump throws his ass out right there, even though the bruised wrist would've knocked him out anyway.

Bottom of the 7th now, still down 2-1, a Zeber single and Munson double chase Cleveland and bring in Willoughby. Jackson walks. Rivers pops a weak fly, deep enough to score Zeber, but Nettles hits one right to the wall, just missing a righteous slam, and the tying run's in!

Then the bottom of our lineup goes to town in the 8th. White lines a double, Stanley singles in the go-ahead, Alston doubles him in and Campbell is on. Zeber singles in another and it's 5-2 in a Bronx minute.

But the Sox ain't in first place 'cause they bribed the man. They've been stakin' a CLAIM. Tidrow takes the hill and Evans hits his first pitch 450 feet to dead left. Sparky takes the ball, and Freddy Lynn hits it 420 feet to deep right. Two pitches, two taters, and it's 5-4. Hobson gets smoked, but Burleson and Doyle both single, and my hood's over my head. Just can't watch this shit. Buzz tells me that Carbo grounded to Dent. I peek out, see Fisk heading for the plate, and duck inside my hood again. I hear the crack of the ball, the crowd noise risin', look out and see White snatch the ball near the foul line to end our latest root canal.

Somehow we're just two and a half out again. The Birds fly in next, while the Sox go home to Cleveland, but damn—what I wouldn't give for an easy win one of these years!

BOS 000 101 002 – 4 9 1

NYY 000 010 13x – 5 16 0

W-Hunter L-Willoughby SV-Lyle HRS: Yaz, Evans, Lynn GWRBI-Stanley

American League through Sunday, August 10

Boston	64	48	.571	—
Kansas City	64	51	.557	1.5
New York	62	51	.549	2.5
Texas	62	52	.544	3
Baltimore	56	57	.496	8.5
Chicago	50	63	.442	14.
Cleveland	50	64	.439	15
Minnesota	45	67	.402	19

National League through Sunday, August 10

Philadelphia	65	46	.586	—
Pittsburgh	65	49	.570	1.5
Cincinnati	65	50	.565	2
Los Angeles	61	50	.550	4
St. Louis	61	52	.541	5
Houston	48	66	.420	18.5
Montreal	46	66	.411	19.5
Chicago	40	72	.357	25.5

Texas Two-Step of Terror

August 11, 1977

By Ed "Peachy" Calhoun
Sports Reporter Jewett Babbler

Been a fair amount of time since I had reason to talk to you folks, but as long as I'm along for this crazy ride with the crazies, might as well fill y'all in on the two games in my home state, both which we managed to get to. Good old Seamus Headley, see, he got some special news yesterday from his employers up in 2010, that my Rangers are going to the World Series! Well if that ain't a two-headed hen, 'cause I never thought I'd see that day.

Anyway, before we make a loony detour to Tennessee to see about some big Elvis "rescue" my new nutcake buddies think is in the works, our bus whooshed us to a day game at the Dome, and a night one in Arlington, so let's go see how my two teams of boys made out...

Games of the Day

HOUSTON—It's been a rough bunch of months for the Astros. J. R. and Niekro are the only starters able to win lately, and with our best lefty-masher Cliff Johnson off to them Yankees and Cedeno not amounting to a hill of pep-percorns, we got a fight on our hands every time out.

Shaky Lemongello's on the hill today, but lucky for us the worst Dodger pitcher Doug Rau has the other ball. After Garvey singles in the first run to put us behind we come right back with two leadoff walks, but Cabell hits into a double dipper. The next inning we get three singles to load the sacks, but Lemongello does the same dang thing.

Then the Big Lemon kicks away a Dusty Baker dribbler to start the 5th.

Monday doubles him to third with one out, a balk brings in one run and a Lopes single another and we're behind 3-0. Old Sherman's sittin' two seats away just about gigglin', and all I wanna do is kick his senile bee-hind to the curb.

But the Astros get him back for me. Cruz walks to begin our 7th and Gonzalez doubles. Knuckleballin' Hough relieves, and all he does is step in something dark and smelly. That would be a pinch Ferguson single, a Cedeno walk, a plunked Terry Puhl, a walk to Cabell, a sac fly to Watson and we got a 4-3 lead before an out's even made.

Sambito comes on, gets Smith, Garvey and Cey without a burp in the 8th. Cedeno doubles in a piece of insurance and it's 5-3 and all looks safe. But then the scary 9th begins, when Sambito has a knack for screwin' the pooch. Yup, there he goes again. Baker singles, Yeager walks, Mota walks to load 'em with one out. Lopes doinks a single to make it 5-4. Glenn Burke bats for Russell, lines a 2-run single and poof, we're behind again. Joe realizes what he just went and did and whiffs Smith and Garvey, but the pigs are out of the pen and we don't even make a peep our last time up. I'm tellin ya, if I had a nickel for every close, late-inning disaster Houston had this season I could retire in Corpus Christi with a lifetime supply of Lone Stars and a 26-inch color TV.

L.A. 100 020 003 – 6 9 0
HOU 000 000 410 – 5 10 1
W-Hough L-Sambito SV-Sosa GWRBI-Burke

ARLINGTON—What a matchup we got in this one, Leonard against Blyleven, my Rangers fresh off an 11-0 pounding of the Twins and just three games out of first again. Arlington Stadium's packed, and with my binocs I can even see a few folks on the Six Flags Over Texas roller coasters next door pausing on the hills to take in a pitch.

Except no one told us the Royals were here to sauce us up and put us on a spit, because that's what they do. Four singles, a walk and a Hargrove error give 'em three runs in the 3rd. A two-out Harrah muff and Darrell Porter bleacher shot gives 'em two more in the the 5th. Two singles, a walk and double, again with two outs, this time in the 7th, plus four runs off reliever Steve Hargan in the 9th and our nightmare in the mirror is over. Recognize this score? Sometimes baseball just works in strange and punishin' ways.

K.C. 003 020 204 – 11 15 0
TEX 000 000 000 – 0 6 2
W-Leonard L-Blyleven HR: Porter GWRBI-White

It's Now or Never

August 12, 1977

MEMPHIS—Well, I finally got here. Only took two buses, some hitching and the last train to Clarksville. Had supper in a pretty yummy barbeque place, then walked the last mile down Elvis Presley Boulevard to Graceland.

I was right about the security. Don't stand a chance of sneaking in this place. There's a big old gate with music notes on it and kind of a low wall around the yard, but I've seen less guards outside the White House.

Can't believe Elvis is still alive and actually in there. How can I do this? There's only four days until he buys it. I got a little bit of spending money left that Seamus gave me, but no sense blowing it on one of the tacky motels around here.

Then it starts pouring like a son-of-a-bitch, so I find a storm drain with some dry spots under the road to spend the night in. I did see a bus shelter across the street from the mansion, so maybe if I spend a day sitting there and making mental notes about the guard routines, I can figure out how and when I can get on the property. Yeah, I like that plan. Maybe I'll even get a cheap transistor radio so I can listen to a ball game or two while I do it. Believe me, if the Reds were playing tonight I'd have bought the damn radio already.

Hang in there, King. I'll see ya soon.

Night of the American League Dead

August 13, 1977

BOSTON—Seamus was afraid to re-route the bus to Memphis to keep Amy from messing up Elvis history, so today he showed me the controls, jumped ship and rented a car to drive down there himself. Personally, I don't know what the big deal is if the King survives. Worse comes to worse he plays a few hundred more gigs in Vegas and probably gets a reality show at some point. It ain't like the Clash and U2 aren't gonna happen.

The thing that I'm scared of is this ghastly day of American League play by the front-runners. Like foul inhabitants of second division Hades, their vastly inferior tormentors crawled from their red clay tombs, sweat oozing from pores, razor-sharp hits spilling off their bats. Horrified fans fled to the exits as the clocks struck midnight, still shaking and shivering, feeble words of comfort echoing from their mouths…"It's only a ball game…only a ball game…"
INDIANS 13-22-0, at RED SOX 5-11-0

Anyway, I take us to Beantown for the second Indians game, and what a travesty of a disgrace of an abomination! Eckersley is throwing the way he usually does, meaning seven strikeouts, no walks and five homers, but the Tribe absolutely tattooes Tiant, Paxton and Willoughby for 22 hits and their second straight win. Boston can mash taters until the cows and whaling ships come home, but if they keep getting non-Jenkins starting pitching like this they're not winning crap.

Saving Graceland
August 14-15, 1977

MEMPHIS—So I slipped over the Graceland wall late last night after spending a day watching security guards. Made myself a nice hiding place under a bed of leaves and fallen branches and waited to get closer. Spent part of the day listening to the Cards blow one in Chicago on my cheap transistor radio and earphone because the Reds had another day off, but that was okay; this savior business took concentrating.

There were big cars coming and going, friends and family members no doubt, and I caught a glimpse of Ginger at one point, his current girlfriend. Wasn't sorry to see her take off tonight. I brought a whole bunch of crackers I nabbed from that local diner, but had to keep the munching down because guards were walking by lots of the time, their walkie-talkies barking at each other like electric cocker spaniels.

I don't know when I fell asleep but then a new sound woke me up, like a loud golf cart or something, and I stuck my head out of the leaves. It looked like one of the guards, a fatter one wearing a weird jogging suit, was tooling down on the curved driveway on this 3-wheeler thing. He was driving it kind of wobbly, came pretty close to me and made a hard U-turn to head back to the house, but lost his balance and the thing went off the driveway and headed right at a tree next to me! I jumped out of the leaves, all instinct, reached out—

—and Elvis Presley fell in my arms.

"Whoaa!!" he blurted out, "Where'd YOU come from?"

I told him I'd run away from home, because for reasons I just couldn't explain, something was drawing me to Graceland. "That could make a groovy song, know that?" he said, his face all puffy and his eyes bloodshot, and we helped each other to our feet. He took a look at the tree he almost hit, brushed some leaves out of my ratty hair.

"I think you're some kind of angel, honey." Security guards had heard him fall and were running over from all directions. He put up a hand when they arrived.

"Everything's cool," he told them, "This here's..."

"Amy."

"Right...Angel Amy. Feel like a late-night lemonade, Angel Amy?"

Well...duh.

And that's how I got into Graceland. The house was incredible, not as tacky as I thought it would be, and we went up to his private rooms where he showed me his massive teddy bear collection and gold records and stuff. I kept saying I didn't have much time, which he didn't seem to understand, so I had to get more real.

"You ain't gonna make it, Elvis."

"Make what?"

"You gotta stop all the drug-taking right now. Otherwise they're gonna find you dead in your bathroom in like 24 hours."

He heard that one. Looked down at the floor a long time, then back at me.

"That's crazy. I'll be in Portland, Maine in two days, back on tour. So I ain't gonna let that happen."

"Well...I know the future, see? I'm one of those psychic people."

He stared at me with his druggy eyes, moved a little closer on the couch. "You are? Who's gonna be the next president then? And don't tell me Jimmy Carter again."

"Uh-uh...Try Ronald Reagan."

"The movie actor?" He chuckled. "I think you're the one who's high, lady. Anyway, I know I got a little overweight problem now and take too many kinds of pills, but the Lord's gonna do what He's gonna do, right?"

"That's a cop out, Elvis. You can control what happens to you. Trust me."

He smiled, kissed the top of my head. "Thanks for them words. Take you up on that in the mornin'." He curled up and nodded out with his head on my shoulder.

Sometime before morning a guard burst in the room, waking us up. "Sorry Elvis. Ma'm. But there's some guy downstairs, says he's this girl's dad and came to take her home."

Seamus! That bastard!

"Whaddya talkin' about?" said Elvis, "She can't go! She's my angel!"

"I really don't think you want the authorities here, sir." The guard grabbed my arm, hauled me out. Elvis looked stricken. I didn't even have a chance to say goodbye. Seamus shoved me into his rent-a-car a minute later and my big mission was over.

"I don't want to hear about it," is all Seamus said after I got through yelling at him. "Screw up one piece of history and we might all be screwed." I turned in my seat and watched Graceland disappear in the morning fog. Damn. Was Elvis ever going to be depressed later.

Don't Be Cruel, Baseball Gods
August 16, 1977

PHILADELPHIA—They're discovering Elvis' body right around now, so I guess you could call me a trifle upset. Seamus did understand, a big leap for him, and zapped me up to an absolutely incredible game here at the Vet for some serious distraction.

Unfortunately, the game was as devastating as anything that happened down in Memphis. Seems like less than a month ago my Reds were hotter than a jalapeño and bashing everyone in sight. Now, even with most of their injured regulars back, the baseball dice gods are still kicking their butts for the sheer hell of it. If you ask me I'm getting punished for going AWOL, so don't expect me to leave the damn bus again until I win the pennant or evaporate.

Game of the Day

Geronimo's the only guy still out, meaning we put Knight in left and Foster in center, but with the crappy Christenson going for Mikey's Phils, we still got a helluva shot. Right on schedule, Morgan and Rose walk to start, Griffey singles, Foster walks, Driessen hits a scoring grounder and we're up 2-zip. Fred Norman then says "Match that!" and the Phillies do. Sizemore leads with a walk, Maddux triples, Johnson hits a sac fly and we're tied 2-2.

With two outs, nobody on in the 5th, Morgan singles and steals, Rose doubles, Griffey walks, Foster singles, Bench is intentionally walked, Driessen walks, we got three runs and lead 5-2. Fred Norman then says, "Match that!" and the Phillies do again. Christenson singles, Sizemore and Maddox hit back-to-back smacks and we're tied 5-5.

McBride homers in the 6th to put us behind but a rare Boone error, Foster double and Bench single put us back up 7-6.

Then it's Sarmiento time, not for the faint of heart or stomach. He starts by giving Hutton a pinch walk. Gets out Schmidt and Luzinski but balks Hutton to second. Bowa dribbles one near the mound but Manny can't make the play and it's first and third. Boone lines a single over Concepcion and we're tied 7-7.

From here, against Christenson, Garber and Brusstar, the Reds are 1-hit for the next NINE innings, while the Phillies blow chance after chance to put the game away. Finally, in the last of the 16th against the less cursed but equally erratic Pedro Borbon, Bowa singles with one out, steals second on Bench—their fourth rob of the game—and Boone rips another single for the winner.

With the win, Cincy would have closed to within two games of first, but when you blow a lead three times, don't count on egg in your beer.

CIN 200 030 200 000 000 0 – 7 8 1
PHL 200 031 100 000 000 1 – 8 18 2

W-Brusstar L-Borbon HRS: Sizemore, Maddox, McBride GWRBI-Boone

Leave the Gun. Take the Hot Dog.
August 17, 1977

BOSTON—Friendly Fred was going to write the game report today, but he was so stupidly happy about the result his words sounded like hailstones on a roof, so I'll fill in. Better yet, here's Mikey Spano, straight from the Cinema of Little Italy...

* * *

"So Johnny, did you take care of that thing for me?"

"Sure did, boss. Every last one of 'em. Startin' with Looie the Fat Cuban."

"Oh yeah? Humor me, why don't ya?"

"The Yanks had themselves a splatter party, that's what. Reggie and Nettles went back-to-back off Tiant right away, Nettles doubled in two more in the 2nd and them Sox were stumblin' around not lookin' too good."

"Then what happened?"

"What happened with what?"

"With the game, you moron!"

"Oh yeah. So Little Mickey tripled to start the 3rd, On-Base Roy doubled, Even Littler Willie singled and that was it for the Cuban. You won't see him no more. Anyways from there it got kinda bad."

"I do hope you mean bad for them."

"Hey, I ain't exactly cryin' here. The only time we didn't score was the 4th, and if anybody in the league had a way to get Carl the Hall of Fame Polack out—he got three more hits and another homer—we might've shut out these creeps. As it is they put that long-haired, pot-smokin pitcher in after we already had eleven runs, whatshisname...the Space Clown!"

"You mean Bill Lee?"

"Yeah, whatever. The screwball with the screwball. I told the boys to work 'em over and they just about choked him with his own jock. Chambliss with a 3-run smash in the 8th, then a single, a walk, Reggie and Nettles back to back for the second time in the game in the 9th, and we shoved eight more runs right in his hippie puss. Thirty-two hits, boss, they moided 'em!!"

"Nice piece of job, Johnny. Now do me a big favor. After the Yanks get shut out on three hits by Jim Colborn and the Royals at the Stadium Tuesday, break their freakin' legs."

NYY 322 022 382 -24 32 3
BOS 100 100 011 – 4 9 0

W-Torrez (CG!) L-Tiant HRS: Jackson-2, Nettles-2, Chambliss, Piniella, Yaz, Evans GWRBI-Jackson

American League through Sunday, August 17

Boston	66	52	.559	—
Kansas City	67	55	.549	1
Texas	66	55	.545	1.5
New York	64	55	.538	2.5
Baltimore	62	59	.512	5.5
Cleveland	54	68	.443	14
Chicago	52	68	.433	15
Minnesota	50	69	.420	16.5

National League through Sunday, August 17

Philadelphia	69	49	.585	—
Pittsburgh	70	51	.579	0.5
Los Angeles	65	53	.551	4
Cincinnati	65	55	.542	5
St. Louis	63	57	.525	7
Houston	53	68	.438	17.5
Montreal	50	69	.420	19.5
Chicago	43	76	.361	26.5

Freddie's Not Dead, but He's Killing Me

August 19, 1977

NEW YORK—Lester here again. It isn't easy to get through a day when your very existence depends on the skills of Jim Colborn and Freddie Patek. The Yanks are 11-6 against my Royals so far, and with the whacking the Bombers just gave the Bosox in Boston, I know it's going to be tough for us in the

Bronx, but come on boys! You and the Cards are the only teams I have with a spitter's chance in this thing!

It looks rosy at first, because Stanley boots a ball in the 2nd and Mayberry puts a Catfish gopher ball in the upper deck for a 2-0 lead. Just as I figure, the Yankees struggle with the bats one game after racking up 32 hits, though Paul Blair, playing center for Rivers, robs Otis and Porter of homers in the first four innings. When Nettles finally touches Colborn for a 2-run shot of his own in the 4th, the game is tied.

Then Little Freddie Patek goes to work. (I realize it must have been a burden for him to be called "Little Freddie Patek" his entire career, but that's the way the peanut brittles; the guy was 5-foot-4.) He doubled after Mayberry's homer earlier, and this time pops one down the left field line that lands in the stands over Roy White's glove! 3-2 K.C.!

The Yanks then do what they usually do best: blow scoring chances. Lead-off singles by White and Stanley in the 5th and 6th go for naught. Colborn kicks away a grounder right back to him in the 7th, Rivers slaps a double, but Piniella and Zeber can't get the run in.

Meanwhile DPs off the bats of Mayberry and McRae kill two Royals chances in the 7th and 8th, and it's still 3-2 us going to the bottom half. Stanley leads with another single, his third of the game. Reggie works a walk. Munson bounces a silver platter DP grounder to Little Freddie—

—and it bounces off his chin for an error. Bases loaded, nobody out. This isn't shocking, because Freddie has had X-chart disease all season, but Colborn is ready to kill the mighty mite, and me to stuff him in a potato sack. Lefty Mingori comes on to face Nettles, who walks in the tying run. Lefty-murderer Cliff Johnson strolls up to hit for Chambliss. Here comes Littell to face him. Here comes Alston to hit for Johnson. And he walks in the go-ahead run. Littell bears down to get White, Rivers and Piniella, but Sparky's on, this one's history, and as the Royals drop below the Rangers for the first time all year, another piece of me begins to ache.

K.C. 020 010 000 – 3 6 2
NYY 000 200 02x – 4 7 2
   W-Hunter L-Colborn SV-Lyle HRS: Mayberry, Patek, Nettles GWRBI-Alston

New Sheriffs in Town
August 20, 1977

BALTIMORE—The Rangers have a chance to snag first place tonight, but I don't exactly trust our trusty Texas friend Mr. Calhoun to be impartial about it if it happens, so Buzz here will be doing the reporting. Compound that with Little Me still teary-eyed over last night's Oriole loss, and there's a good chance we'll be doing some post-game toy and ice cream damage control tonight.

It's Alexander vs. Grimsley, and both guys are spot on through the first six innings, Doyle with a 2-hit shutout and Ross with a 1-hitter. Little Me whines about "Uncle Peachy" growling too much, even though they're sitting five seats apart, but Peachy isn't the only one. This is a very tense ballgame and every one of us is feeling it.

Then Texas puts the first chink in the polished marble. Harrah walks to begin the 7th and Horton singles him to third. With the infield up, Ellis raps into a DeCinces-to-Skaggs force at home. Bevacqua singles, though, Harrah scores and it's 1-0 Rangers. Tippy Martinez is on to hit Keith Smith in the back and load the bases, but he retires Beniquez on another force home, Wills on an easy roller, and further blood is avoided.

Skaggs and Maddox single in the last of the 7th but Alexander strands them. On the scoreboard, the Twins are pounding away in Boston, and the unthinkable is getting more possible.

Then things get wicked strange. Kelly walks and steals with one out in the Baltimore 8th, even with Sundberg replacing Ellis behind the dish. DeCinces singles him to third and Len Barker is hailed. Singleton dumps in a namesake for the tie game, and after Murray whiffs, Skaggs rips one in the gap for a 2-1 Birds lead!

Little Me is on his second cotton candy and jumping around in his seat. Peachy is on his fourth beer and third crabcake sandwich. If the Orioles can just hang on, Boston remains on top.

So here's backup defensive outfielder Ken Henderson to face Tippy with two gone in the Texas 9th. Not much of a stickman at all, Henderson's been getting miraculous hits all season, and whacks one deep to left. Kelly races back to the track, leaps, and IT'S GONE! Tie game! Unnerved, Skaggs orders a knockdown and Tippy throws the next pitch at Keith Smith's noggin. Smith whips the bat away, says something uncurtly to Skaggs and they're punching away at each other on home plate.

Minutes later, order restored and both players suspended for three games, Beniquez rolls out to end the inning. Barker keeps the Orioles quiet in the bottom half before Texas ignites in the 10th. Wills singles, Hargrove walks, Harrah singles in the go-ahead after one out before Horton greets Dennis Martinez with a bases-clearing double. While Peachy whoops it up, Sheila takes the sobbing Little Me into the tunnel and they miss Barker getting the final three Birds on ground outs to put the Rangers on top for the first time all year.

As Peachy might say, can't say I saw this coming but I didn't so I won't.

TEX 000 000 101 3 – 5 7 0
BAL 000 000 020 0 – 2 7 0

W-Barker L-T. Martinez HR-Henderson GWRBI-Harrah

Play-by-Play, Session 122
August 21, 1977

PITTSBURGH—With the Dodgers opening their final three games at Three Rivers, I knew Sherman and Sheila would be at each other's throats, so I made sure they sat at opposite ends of the aisle. Little did we know the Hooton-Candelaria "pitcher's duel" would morph into a crazy, back-and-forth bash-fest. Afterwards, I was able to nab their heavily-annotated game scorecards and weave them together for all of you to follow along:

Top of 1ST (Sherman Wayman) Lopes grounds to Taveras. Martinez pops to Stennett. Smith walks. Cey whiffs, like you're surprised?

Bottom of 1ST (Dr. Grossinger) Oliver retires himself on a ground ball. Garner is struck four inches below the left sternum and given a three-day leave of absence to mend his wound. (Fregosi takes his place on the running path.) Parker is out on strikes. Stargell draws four balls. Robinson singles sharply, accurately placed between the left and center fielders, scoring Garner. Stennett grounds into a force out play. 1-0 PIRATES.

Top of 2ND Baker hits the crap out of one but right to Fregosi. Garvey flies to Parker. Lacy, Yeager and Hooton all get themselves doinky singles, but what the hell, Lacy scores and we're tied, right? Lopes bounces out to Candelaria. Schmuck.

Bottom of 2ND Dyer singles cleanly. Taveras is fanned. Candelaria flies out. Oliver lines out.

Top of 3RD Martinez counts his lucky stars when he's safe on rare Stennett error. Smith, Cey and Baker all fly out because they're all trying to put the damn team on their backs.

Bottom of 3RD Fregosi is out on a lackluster, dribbling grounder to the catcher. Parker flies out. Stargell propels the ball to the farthest region of the upper deck in right field. Robinson grounds out. 2-1 PIRATES.

Top of 4TH Garvey lifts his skirt and pops to Taveras. Lacy rips a double down the line. Yeager bounces one to Taveras, who kicks it every which way but up and we got first and third. Hooton singles again, scoring Lacy. Candelaria doesn't have it today, I'm tellin' ya. Lopes whiffs. Schmendrick. Martinez singles to load 'em. Smith walks again, scoring Yeager. Cey grounds to Taveras but we're back in front! 3-2 DODGERS.

Bottom of 4TH Stennett strikes out. Dyer grounds out. Taveras singles. Candelaria strikes out. Seven pitches, less than a minute to complete the inning.

Top of 5TH Baker and Garvey fly out. Lacy with another single! Why doesn't Tommy start this guy every day? Yeager grounds to Taveras.

Bottom of 5TH Oliver decisively singles. Fregosi labors, but produces a walk. Cobra BELTS ONE. It's high, it's deep, IT'S GONE!!!!! WOO-HOO!!! (my apologies) Stargell flies to right. Robinson strikes out. Stennett rolls out. 5-3 PIRATES.

Top of 6TH Mota hits for Hooton, reaches on Fregosi error. Lopes the Schmuck whiffs again. Martinez singles, but Smith whiffs and Cey flies to Oliver. I don't need any more of this crap, I really don't.

Bottom of 6TH With Garman the new pitcher for Los Angeles, Dyer singles. Taveras forces himself on a grounder, then steals the second base bag, no doubt the result of childhood feelings of want. Hough replaces Garman, and retires Candelaria and Oliver with impressive dexterity.

Top of 7TH Baker and Garvey? I've had it up to here with the two of 'em. After they both fly out they're 0-for-stinking-8 on the game. Lacy doubles, making him 4-for-4 in a wasteland. Yeager lines to Taveras to prove what I'm talking about.

Bottom of 7TH Garner walks. Parker walks. Stargell obliterates the rally with a 3-6-3 double play. Robinson is out on strikes.

Top of 8TH Burke hits for Hough and flies to Robinson. Lopes just about gives me a heart attack by walking. Martinez singles him to third and Smith hits a sac fly. Now we're cookin'! Cey doubles, knocking Candy Butt out of the game, maybe his worst all year. That skinny schlemiel Tekulve takes over, and we smack him around too, Baker and Garvey ripping singles for three runs out of nowhere! 6-5 DODGERS.

Bottom of 8TH With my prognosis for this game hopelessly skewed, Stan Wall is now pitching. Stennett grounds out. Dyer doubles for his third safety! Taveras rolls out and Gonzalez bats for Tekulve and fans.

Top of 9TH That overfed Goose is in, meaning Yeager, Wall and Lopes go 1-2-3, but I still got a chance to see us win if my liver doesn't give out.

Bottom of 9TH Oliver leads off and BASHES ONE OUT OF THE PARK. Tie game! Fregosi singles. Parker singles. Al Downing comes on to face Stargell, who takes a called third strike. Robinson walks, loading the bases. Here's Stennett, and he singles up the middle past the diving, unstable, non-confident Lopes for the winning run! The Pirates return to first place!!

Patient Wayman has regrettably entered a manic-depressive state, as his Dodgers are now losers of five in a row. I will be monitoring his condition daily, though plan to hold back any aggressive study until his team departs from Pittsburgh.

L.A. 010 200 030 – 6 13 0

PIT 101 030 002 – 7 12 3

W-Gossage L-Downing HRS: Stargell, Parker, Oliver GWRBI-Stennett

To Have and Have Not a Bullpen
August 22, 1977

Far from the distant sounds of organ music and crunched peanut shells, I held Sheila in my arms. The horrors of Bill Campbell had subsided for the time being, but my body was still bruised, my brain spent. Sheila, having endured no such pain with her Pirates on the triumphant end of another massacre, sympathized but could not share my grief.

"What will become of us darling?" she asked, "If your team is eliminated before mine?"

"Oh, must we talk of this again? I'll evaporate, like a pussy willow before a child's breath, and will be heard of no more."

"Then I want the Bucs to be eliminated first, or at least on the same day!"

"I'm afraid baseball isn't like that, my love. It has been proven since time immemorial, that when it comes to predicting or affecting the game's outcomes, no one knows diddly crap."

"Tell me that isn't true, Carlton! Tell me there's a season to everything, and a time to every purpose under Heaven."

"Where the hell'd you hear that?"

"Never mind. Just put today's game behind you. There's still the whole month of September coming. You can get hot again. I know it!"

"I need at least ten minutes for that. And I'm awful sorry, sweetheart, but today's game was a demoralizing puddle of vomit. A 7-2 lead on K.C. going to the 9th with Soup Campbell pitching and they score five runs on a bunch of bleeders and walks? Followed by six more of the same in the 11th topped by a pinch-hit 3-run homer by Joe Zdeb? YOU tell me how to recover from that! Go ahead, tell me!"

"Oh Carlton, I hate it so when you lose your emotional equilibrium."

"Well, then I suppose you should get used to it. Because right now with our hitting cooled off, our rotation is pitching us off a cliff!"

Her dry but tender fingers came up from below the sheets and rubbed the back of my neck, for the moment easing my mental scars.

"Forgive me, darling...for kicking the Dodgers' butts again on one of your worst days. I hope you realize it had nothing to do with us."

Suddenly Friendly Fred popped up from the bus row in front of us, wearing his star-shaped sleeping sunglasses.

"Hey yo! Romeo and Jive-Lady! Shut the hell up!"

K.C. 000 200 005 06 – 13 16 1

BOS 010 330 000 00 – 7 14 1

W-Littell L-Campbell HRS: Mayberry, Zdeb GWRBI-Mayberry

Tiant in his last three starts: 16 IP, 32 H, 21 ER

The Rabid Dog Days of August
August 23, 1977

The fourth 100-degree day in a row blew two gaskets in the bus' engine, so while I worked on the thing I got us a bunch of motel rooms somewhere in Jersey, wired the TVs into our Ball Nut Express satellite feed and everyone got to see their teams in action at some point.

Big mistake. Right now Buzz and Friendly Fred are off smoking or popping something in the nearest alley, Mikey has remembered how to curse all over again, and even Dr. Sheila took an extra migraine pill. I really don't know why everyone's so scared about evaporating when there's a better chance they'll all kill each other or themselves first.

Seamus out.

We Bozos are Off This Bus
August 24, 1977

CLEVELAND—The last pitch thrown by Mark Littell to Larvell Blanks was probably an hour ago, and me and Friendly Fred have already hitched halfway to Buffalo. By now they must know we've split. Jetted. Vamooshed. Gone from that crazy bus faster than a college calculus class for spring break.

Sorry, Seamus, Lester, Sherman, Amy, Little Me and even you Sheila, but YOU'RE the ones who are crazy, following these horror movie pennant races around to their deadly ends. Right, Fred?

"Damn straight and a half, fool!"

I mean, when the Timeco creeps showed up at my trailer or cot or wherever the hell it was back in February, I felt like I had a chance to do some-

thing special. You know, like perform community baseball service or something.

But not anymore. Nope. We're not gonna be the ones to bend over and get
time warped for these greedy techno-bolts. Me and Fred? We like it here in
'77 and we are gonna hide out where no one from Squallpocket is ever gonna
find us.

"Damn straight and a half 'n' half, fool!"

Fred's already said I can stay with him at his grandma's in Harlem, but far
as I'm concerned, it's wide open. Camping in the Maine woods sounds like a
possible plan. Maybe I'll even go look up Pam again in Norwalk, CT, that girl
I'm slated to marry, if Fred can help me get up the nerve. Hell, we can actually get real 1977 jobs, like working in a record store or starting our own weekly
newspaper. Just long enough to hang in here until New Year's, because I'm
dying to find out what happens when the clock hits '78.

"Watch it, brother. Don't you be usin' that nasty-ass word."

Fred's right. Not even the thought of dying or evaporating or even bad vibes
here. Just keep us away from the sports pages and we'll be fine. Just fine. And
the baseball scores on TV, can't forget those. And walking by newsstands.

And to think Seamus and Sheila and all them probably think our ball teams
going in the crapper has something to do with this. Can't figure out where
they'd ever get an idea like that.

TEX 70[10] 000 031 – 21 24 0
BOS 00 0 100 000 – 1 4 0

W-Alexander L-Wise HRS: Harrah (grand slam), Hargrove, Bevacqua GWR-
BI-Bevacqua

TEX 140 000 120 – 8 16 0
BOS 012 000 100 – 4 11 0

W-Devine (CG) L-Paxton HR-Evans GWRBI-Bevacqua

American League through Sunday, August 24

Kansas City	72	57	.558	—
Texas	71	57	.555	0.5
New York	66	59	.528	4
Boston	66	59	.528	4
Baltimore	64	63	.504	7
Cleveland	58	70	.453	13.5
Minnesota	55	70	.440	15
Chicago	54	71	.432	16

National League through Sunday, August 24

Pittsburgh	74	54	.578	—
Philadelphia	70	54	.565	2
Los Angeles	67	57	.540	5
Cincinnati	68	58	.540	5
St. Louis	68	59	.535	5.5
Houston	56	70	.444	17
Montreal	52	73	.416	20.5
Chicago	48	78	.381	25

Rebirth of the Cool Blue?

August 25-26, 1977

PHILADELPHIA—You know my Dodgers must've got back whatever they lost if Sutton wins us a game. Seriously, the guy's been a garbage disposal in the middle of the rotation for months now, and even after this one still has our worst starting ERA at 5.22.

Maybe it's a mental thing, who knows, but ever since they hired this psychic voodoo lineups expert with his stats ouija board back in Pittsburgh, they haven't lost a game. Yesterday Hooton got his 18th win and we pounded Christenson for TEN doubles in a 9-4 win, and getting them kick-started again today is the guy I was recently calling a schmuck, Davey Lopes. Jim Kaat's first pitch is clubbed over the wall in left, Martinez singles, Cey doubles, Smith singles both of them in with another single and the Blue Boys are up 3-zip.

Kaat settles down until the 5th, when he gives Martinez a double with one out, fields a Cey roller with his other left foot for an error and gives Smith another single before Ozark sticks McGraw in. The Tugger has no better luck, as Baker walks, the Garv singles and Yeager walks and it's 6-0!

Sutton naturally tries his best to crap it away, but Philly strands nine guys in the first five innings, finally getting on the board with a 2-run Maddox smash in the 7th. Bring on Sosa for three shutout innings, and can you believe it? We sweep the Phils and have won four straight! Poor Mikey Spano isn't exactly doing jumping jacks about it, but you don't see HIM smoking drugs and running away like a girl, either.

Which reminds me, everyone on the bus is bent out of shape because that meshugener and his schvarze sidekick flew the roost two days ago, and they're scared that Seamus is gonna risk our behinds by going off to look for them. Whatever. I don't have a lot of time left in the living room either way. As long as I can go out with my Dodgers wrestling at the top of this race again, I'll be one happy Sherman.

L.A. 103 002 021 – 9 14 0
PHI 010 030 000 – 4 13 2
   W-Hooton L- Christenson SV-Hough HRS: Lopes, Hebner GWRBI-Lopes
L.A. 300 030 010 – 7 13 0
PHI 000 000 200 – 2 10 1
   W-Sutton L-Kaat SV-Sosa HRS: Lopes, Maddox GWRBI-Lopes

Does a Bear Die in the Woods?
August 27, 1977

PITTSBURGH—Not the Cubbie ones. Mine do it in classic humiliating fashion before 30,000 screaming Bucs nuts.

Their tragic elimination number down to one, Seamus gets me to Three Rivers so one fifth of me can evaporate with them live and in person. I suppose he's showing me a little support by doing this, but I think I'd rather be in Cincinnati with my Cards, or Baltimore with my Royals, or Cleveland with my Twins or Boston with my White—no, I'll pass on that one.

Regardless, Krukow is facing Rooker, and there's a fierce determination in the Cubs players' faces; I can see it from our seats behind first base. Morales gets us a run home in the 1st with a double play ball, and Swisher makes it 2-0 with a sacrifice fly in the 2nd. Garner ties it fairly quickly with a 2-run poke, but Swisher singles in Trillo his next time up and we're back on top again. Ott ties it rather immediately with a solo shot, but Morales homers, Taveras boots a grounder with Murcer on third and we're back on top again 5-3.

Hernandez takes over for the shaky Krukow, but nothing about this game feels right. The Pirates have been coming back late all season. Sure enough, it's 5-4 after Gonzalez hits a scoring double play ball, it's 5-5 when Bill Robinson scores on a two-out wild pitch from Sutter in the 8th, and then Tekulve throws his third shutout relief inning in the 9th.

"Aw quit with the mopin!" yells Mikey to me at that point, "You got four other teams to root for."

"Right, but two are the White Sox and Twins."

He has no comeback for that. And I have the dreadful feeling the Cubs' minutes are numbered.

Jim Fregosi hits for Tekulve, hoping just to draw one of his typical walks and get a rally started. Instead, he picks out a Sutter split-finger fastball and rifles it toward the left field fence. I can't look. The crowd rises and roars all around me. I stay in my seat as Morales races to the warning track. Grit my teeth and peek through the fingers of my right hand. The explosion of noise tells me it's gone, that my Cubs are gone from the race, and—

And my right hand is no longer there.

CHC 110 120 000 – 5 10 1

PGH 020 101 011 – 6 11 1

W-Tekeulve L-Sutter HRS: Morales, Garner, Ott, Fregosi GWRBI-Fregosi

The Bitches are Back

August 28-29, 1977

UNIONDALE, NY—Me and Friendly Fred just got out of an Elton John concert in that hockey arena where the Islanders play. Now Elton isn't exactly Fred's cup of funk, but I'll tell ya, after yesterday afternoon's Orioles-Yankees game, he would've been ready to see the Partridge Family.

See, we've really bonded in the last 48 hours since we split from the Ball Nut Express. Just proves that if two people are in the same dire straits, even if one's a Red Sox fan and the other pulls for the Yankees, they can find a way to get along. I just promise not to talk about David Oritz if he never brings up Bucky Dent and all's just fine.

We hitched our way into the Apple early Thursday, had a late breakfast at his senile grandma's in Harlem (who thought Fred had never even left), and made it to the Stadium for the matinee. Grimsley was facing Gullett, and has been the case all year after the Yanks enjoy a big blowout win, they can't hit the side of a prison for the next three days. A Johnson walk and singles by Rivers and Piniella load their bases in the 2nd and get Fred all stoked, but Munson raps into a 6-2-3 DP, Blair dribbles out and so much for that.

Top of the 5th, this bench-warming nobody named Tom Shopay, who Weaver starts in left because he has some serious power against lefties and nothing else, rips one into the bleachers for a 1-zip Baltimore lead. Now Gullett can be pretty dicey against lefty hitters, and proves it again with meatball #2 to Shopay in the 7th for a 2-0 Baltimore lead.

Cliff Johnson finally does something useful with a bomb into the LF bullpen in the last of the 7th, but Gullett loses it again in the top of the 9th. Singleton walks, Mora walks, and here's that man Shopay again.

"Put him on, Billy!!" yells Fred, eyes bulging out, popcorn flakes falling off his shirt, "I don't care if it's Tom Chump-face Shopay, PUT THE SUCKER ON!!" Billy doesn't listen, but Sparky Lyle is unavailable anyway, so Gullett pitches to him. And Shopay puts it 450 feet into the upper deck.

It's another classic Yankee disaster in a never-ending series of them. Nine whiffs for Gullett, only four hits allowed, but three of them are Tom Shopay home runs.

Which is why we took in the Elton John concert tonight on the Yankee off-day. The thing that shocked me, besides Elton's outfit, was that Fred knew every lyric to "Goodbye Yellow Brick Road." It seemed fitting.

BAL 000 010 103 – 5 4 0
NYY 000 000 101 – 2 7 0

W-Grimsley L-Gullett HRS: Shopay-3, C. Johnson, Rivers GWRBI-Shopay

We Interrupt This Replay...

August 30, 1977

...to allow the proprietor to go a little batshit.

Once a year, I will play a Strat game that is so baseball-realistic—meaning so incomprehensibly torturous—that it deserves more detailed reportage in my own voice. The sole purpose, of course, is to purge the anger and deadly, baffling poison of the event from my system, but if you're entertained along the way, then all the better. So here goes...

LOS ANGELES—Home from their long eastern swing after some pretty hot play, the Dodgers welcome in the just-eliminated Cubbies for some likely ground-gaining. That's what she said.

Sutton gets the ball for L.A., possessor of maybe one quality start in his last ten, and falls behind early again on a Larry Biitner scoring triple (yes, a Larry Biitner triple) and George Mitterwald 2-run homer. (As I believe I mentioned, the Cubs are eliminated.)

Baker gets one back with a solo shot off Reuschel in the 5th, then powers a three-run smash in the 6th to put L.A. on top. Even Monday gets in the act with a solo whack in the 7th. Elias Sosa takes over for old pubic-head in the 7th to snuff a potential Cubs rally, and then Charlie Hough comes on for two innings of knuckle duty.

Now Charlie was personally responsible for a recent Dodger debacle in Montreal after taking a 6-0 lead, but seems to have it back here after escaping a minor jam in the 8th. Then why does he inspire about as much confidence in me as Lady Gaga in a bullfight arena?

Because of the following 9th: Jerry Morales rips a double. Trillo singles him in and it's 5-4. Mitterwald gets his fourth straight hit, a single to get Trillo to

third. Buckner pinch hits a ridiculous 1-3 (15% chance) single to score the tying tun and push Mitts to second. Fifty-thousand pretend Dodger fans pelt
Hough with their empty suntan lotion tubes. It's ugly, but Charlie fans Clines
and DeJesus and gets Ontiveros on a fly.

What follows, against Willie Hernandez, Bruce Sutter, and Paul Reuschel,
are nine consecutive innings of completely impotent Dodger offense, despite
the Cubs making three errors to try and help them score. Hough gets out of
a bases loaded, nobody out jam in the 11th, Stan Wall and Mike Garman gets
L.A. out of three more jams, before Garman finally falls apart in the top of
the 17th, with the help of Boulderus, the all-seeing, all-infuriating Baseball
Dice God. Boulderus already gave Bill Buckner a little karma gift in the 9th
with his 1-3 single roll, and now bestows the same reward two more times on
Biitner and Morales to help Chicago get its rally going. Trillo and Mitterwald
also follow with singles (George's SIXTH hit of the day, a feat even beyond
the capability of most baseball deities and warlocks), three runs are home
and the Cubs take the lead.

All that's left is for the final straw, the icing on the melting cake, the coup
de garbage. And who better to provide that than the biggest Dodger disap-
pointment of the year, ex-MVP Steve Garvey. Okay, he's had a few timely
homers, but his 105 RBIs are mainly due to Lopes and Smith being on base
ahead of him, he has a whopping 24 walks all season and has failed to come
through repeatedly in clutch situations.

Today the Garv is 0-for-6. So Russell singles, Smith works a walk, the Perfect Ballplayer steps up...and grounds into a 5-4-3 DP to end the game. Calm-
ly and methodically, I lift his card, rip it into four pieces and let it drop back on
the table, to let the crows of dust and stray dog hair have at its frayed edges,
never to darken my dark wood veneer field again.

It's a lie, of course; I've already Scotch taped the bastard back together.
But man oh man oh man, what do you have to do with these guys? It's only
a game, I keep saying, and they do have two dozen left. I guess all in all, this
was an improvement over the 1924 Batshit Classic I rolled last year.

CHC 120 000 002 000 000 03 – 8 22 3
L.A. 000 013 100 000 000 00 – 5 13 0

W-P. Reuschel L-Garman HRS: Mitterwald, Baker-2, Monday GWRBI-Mit-
terwald

Mission Implausible
August 31, 1977

HARLEM—Friendly Fred stared at me so long I thought his Egg McMuffin was going to freeze in his hand.

"Say what?"

"You heard me."

"Wish to hell I didn't. Say it again."

"We are going to save John Lennon."

He gulped down his orange juice. Stared at me again.

"You crazier than Amy, fool."

He was right, of course. But seeing Lennon pop out on stage at the Elton John concert the other night to do "Whatever Gets You Through the Night" with him put the idea in my head, and I knew right away it was bigger than tripping down to Memphis to keep some fat, washed up 50s rocker from overdosing.

"He's a Beatle, brother. Who doesn't like the Beatles?"

'Beatles ain't Sly."

"Aw c'mon. We're talking worldwide impact here. If John survives he might even come to his senses and do a Beatles reunion! Can you imagine them on *The Daily Show*? Or on iTunes??"

Fred said nothing.

"Anyway, he moved into the Dakota Apartments four years ago. and there's like three more to go until that turd assassinates him. Meanwhile we're sitting around here in '77 following two slacker teams—"

"Maybe yours is, fool. My Man Reggie hasn't even lit the stove yet."

"Yeah, probably because Your Man Mickey and Your Man Sparky keep blowing the stupid fire out. Anyway, instead of stressin' about getting eliminated, why not do something good for humankind before we leave? I figured out the dates in my head and next week is the 30th anniversary of Lennon getting shot up in the real world. If we can't find a way to warn his Liverpool ass before then, what good are we?"

Fred just scratched his head, so I knew my idea was swimming around inside it. He sighed, then snapped a finger at the *New York Post* sitting on the table.

"Gimme the damn sports page. Wanna see how Candy Man did against Philly."

Game of the Day

PITTSBURGH—Seamus reporting in, Candelaria with a chance to be the first 20-game winner and my designated rooting team Expos on the brink of liquidation out in Cincinnati. But I'm not worried. I got connections with Timeco Incorporated, see? They'd be out of their skulls to let ME evaporate. Who else is gonna watch these nuts?

But Candy Man's the nervous one at Three Rivers, hitting Boone in the back to start the 3rd and then giving up a McBride single, Ron Reed sac bunt, Sizemore single and Maddox double, good for two quick runs. Forgot to mention that Luzinski's out for a game, but Schmidt is back from his injury and the Phils look pretty scary after taking yesterday's whitewash.

Except for the fact that no one tells the Pirates what to do. Not no one. Not no how. Oliver doubles to start their 4th. Parker singles with one out, Stargell doubles, Robinson singles, Ott singles with two outs and it's 3-2 Bucs just like that.

On the out-of-town board, the Reds have a 3-0 lead on my Expos after two. One loss or Pirate win finishes them off. So when Sizemore homers in the 5th to tie it here, Mikey Spano isn't the only one of us to cheer.

Oliver, though. A freaking clutch force all season. He bashes a Reed curve over the wall in the 5th, and after the Phils ties it again on a Bowa single, he homers again to put Pittsburgh ahead. Robinson singles for an insurance run, Ott homers for another in the 8th, and it's a good thing, because Candy Man is melting.

Taveras boots a Hutton grounder to start the 9th, and after Sizemore whiffs, Maddox lines a homer to left center and it's 7-6! Out goes Candy, in comes Goose. Johnstone pinch-hits a weak grounder for the second out. It's up to Mike Schmidt for Candy's 20th win and the Death of Les Expos. Again, I'm not concerned.

Then my inner cellular transmitter vibrates, and the voice of Barnstable Cox, head of Timeco, fills my ear.

"It has been our pleasure to have known and employed you, Mr. Headley."

"Wait-what?"

Goose winds, throws, Schmidt grounds one out to short...

"Farewell."

"NOOOOOO!!!"

Taveras fires the ball into Robinson's mitt and

DR. GROSSINGER'S REPORT

4:03 P.M. Any elated feelings I may have had for the Pirate victory were dulled considerably by the regrettable evaporation of Seamus Headley. With two of our patients now in a foolish wayward phase of their self-treatment (one whose name I can barely mention), who will be transporting our bus to each baseball engagement?

4:19 P.M. My earlier question has been answered, and not favorably. Along with Mr. Headley, our bus has disappeared.

PHI 002 011 002 – 6 9 0

PIT 000 310 21X – 7 11 1

W-Candelaria L-Reed SV-Gossage HRS: Sizemore, Maddox, Oliver-2, Ott GWRBI-Oliver

American League through Sunday, August 31

Kansas City	74	59	.556	—
Texas	73	59	.553	0.5
New York	70	61	.534	3
Boston	68	61	.527	4
Baltimore	67	66	.504	7
Cleveland	60	72	.455	13.5
Minnesota	58	74	.439	15.5
Chicago	57	75	.432	16.5

National League through Sunday, August 31

Pittsburgh	77	56	.579	—
Philadelphia	72	58	.554	3.5
Los Angeles	72	59	.550	4
Cincinnati	72	60	.545	4.5
St. Louis	70	62	.530	6.5
Houston	61	71	.462	15.5
Montreal	53	80	.398	24
Chicago	50	81	.382	26

Twisted Sister-Kissers

September 1, 1977

WHEELING, WEST VIRGINIA—We grabbed a normal bus from Pittsburgh to here, and now Dr. Sheila is off looking for another vehicle we can rent. She's real upset about Seamus and the Funkyland bus disappearing, she's upset that those cowards Buzz and Fred ran off to probably do nothing important, she's upset she has to look out for Little Carlton every second—Heck, she's just upset.

Meanwhile, while I stand in this roadhouse bar getting the scores of today's eight double-headers from local Wheeling TV, five out of the eight being "sister-kissers", I'm anything but upset. See, even though my eliminated Cubs eliminated one of my hands, another of my five teams still has a darn good shot at winning this thing...

Game of the Day

KANSAS CITY—Two pitchers hotter than flapjacks have at each other, Barrios and Leonard, but it's the Royals who can't keep the skillet warm. After singles by LaCock, Cowens and Brett in the 3rd they score on a wild pitch with Porter at the plate, then ground into DPs and strand runners all over the place the rest of the day.

Gamble homers for the 34th time leading off the 4th to tie things, but after a two-out single Leonard no-hits the Chisox for the next six and two-third innings. LaGrow relieves a tired Barrios in the 10th, but Poquette pops out with the bases juiced to end the threat. Two outs, top of the 11th, no one aboard, Chicago pecks Leonard to death. Orta walks, Downing, Spencer, Soderholm, Kessinger and Garr all single in a row, four runs are in, and K.C. looks doomed.

But LaGrow has had his share of 11th hour disasters. Mayberry leads with a walk and Patek homers. White hustles out a double. LaCock, Cowens and Brett string together singles to tie the game. McRae, a bust in all six of his at bats, pops out, but Wathan rips one past a drawn-in Orta and the miracle win is complete!

Doug Bird starts the nightcap, has only one inning in which he craps the bed, and it's enough to sink the Royals and relegate them to a split. Luck stays on their shoulder, though, due to the Rangers dumping two down in Arlington...

CHI 000 100 000 04 – 5 8 0
K.C. 001 000 000 05 – 6 16 0
  W-Leonard L-LaGrow HRS: Gamble, Patek, GWRBI-Wathan
CHI 004 002 000 – 6 9 1
K.C. 010 010 011 – 4 8 0
  W-Knapp L-Bird HRS: Spencer, McRae GWRBI-Garr

Imagine It Never Happened
September 3, 1977

NEW YORK—The air conditioner repairman outfits me and Fred stole from the truck over on 73rd did the trick. Our idea was still crazy, but we had to try something, especially after spending a day and a half on the Dakota Apartments' sidewalk sweating our butts and brains off. Didn't see John or Yoko come out of the building once, and the one limo we did see had the same rich Jewish lady getting in and out.

We already learned from a UPS guy what floor Lennon lived on, so then it was just a matter of fooling the doorman and getting in the building, which on a 106-degree day with 98% humidity, wasn't too tough.

We were ready for anything when we knocked on the penthouse door— Lennon in his robe or birthday suit, Yoko with her hair in curlers, maybe even another seven-day peace vigil happening in their bed.

What we didn't expect was a toddler boy swinging open the door who couldn't have been two and a half. "Dada!!" he cried after taking one look at us, before John appeared in a T-shirt and jeans and scooped him up. He had a cigarette in his free hand and a stretched out telephone in his ear.

"Apparently we are far from an agreement then," he said into the phone in his perfect King's English, waving us inside. There were empty chinese food cartons on a counter, along with a forest of empty beer bottles. John had his shoulder-length hair back in a rubber band and looked pale and pretty hungover. I didn't care. Seeing him in front of me was enough to freeze my feet to the floor, and Fred had to poke me from behind to get me moving.

"Fine. Then I will talk to good lady Melissa. Cheers." He hung up, shook his nose into his son's hair until the boy giggled, lowered him back to the floor. "Bloody money people. Sometimes you just want to holler. So which conditioner needs mending, lads?"

I was tongue-tied. Fred sensed it and scurried across a big open living room. "I'll check over here!"

"Sorry for the messiness," said John, "the world unravels a bit when Sean's mum is out of town, you know?"

"Uhh...right. We need to tell you—"

"I mean, the boy has no problem opening a door for strangers, but when we took him to the circus recently, he was damn near terri—"

"We're not air conditioner men, Mr. Lennon."

He stared up at me through his round, tinted glasses.

"You're not a pair of slags are you? You know, autograph seekers? What about the CIA or FBI? They bloody despise me."

"Maybe we should sit down a second."

"Maybe I should ring up security then—"

He reached for the phone and I grabbed his wrist. "We're here to save you, man!"

He paused, looking amused and frightened at the same time. I let go and backed away.

"Listen. I know this is gonna sound weird, but we have good reason to believe—a very good reason—that this crazy guy is going to fire shots at you on the sidewalk in front of this building. When you come back from a recording session."

"Oh really. And when is this ungodly event supposed to happen?"

"Well...in three years."

Now John looked utterly baffled. I leaned closer.

"See, we're from a new private agency called the um, CVP. Celebrity...Violence Prevention." (Fred stood in the living room, rolling his eyes.) "We have many deep sources, and have learned that there's an obsessed fan who is plotting to kill you."

"In three years?

"In three years."

John stared at me for a long time, then dropped the rest of his cigarette in a beer bottle. "Perhaps we should sit down. But not here. There's a fine pub down the street where no one bothers me. This might require an imbibement or two, wouldn't you say?"

"Yo Beatle!" yelled Fred, "They got a TV there so I can watch the Yanks?"

"Er, American cricket is not one of my passions, I'm afraid. But yes, I imagine they do. Let me just ring our nanny up, and we'll be off."

* * *

John was right. No one bothered us, and we were hammered on Watneys Red Barrel beer before long. Lennon asked all sorts of questions about the CVP, forcing me to make up all sorts of answers, while Fred spent a lot of time at a jukebox in the corner, punching in one classic soul song after another with the pile of quarters John gave him.

"Another round, lovely!" John yelled to the annoyed waitress, lighting another cigarette and leaning back in the booth. he seemed elated to have someone to drink with.

"What did you think of *Walls and Bridges*, guv'nor?" he asked. I told him I liked it, especially the song "Watching the Wheels," and he gave me this dumbfounded look. Damn! I had jumped the gun a little. But then, in the drunken state we were in, I figured it was as good a time as any to fill him in.

"Look John, my partner and I ...are really from the year 2010. See, the hospital—I mean, office—sent us back in time to follow and correct a bunch of bad historical things. Mostly baseball things from this year, but also...you being shot."

His face went blank, mind trying to focus. Then he broke into a fit of hysterical laughing. "To quote an old song from an ex-songwriting partner, this is just getting better all the time!" he shouted, and laughed some more. "Tell me, son, did we start another Vietnam War?"

"Umm, yeah actually. In Iraq. Twice." This really got him going, until he sighed and ran out of laughs. "Just don't tell me Peter Frampton becomes bigger than we ever were, okay?" He polished off his beer, tossed a wad of cash on the table and wobbily stood up. "Don't want to spoil the party, lads, but I need to relieve the old nanny. Best of luck luck with further preventions!"

He started for the exit. "Mr. Lennon? You remember what I said, right? Three years and a few months from now?" He winked back at me and stumbled out the door. I made my way to the bar to join Fred, who was already cursing out Guidry for walking the park in the 1st inning at Cleveland. I had no idea if Lennon believed a word I said, if he'd even remember it, or if any huge cultural thing in the future would change, but I had to get back into the ball games, because if my team can't pull this title out I might not be around to find out.

The Scrappy and Crappy Show
September 4, 1977

CINCINNATI—I wasn't going to do it. I wasn't going to let my Reds suck me back in. Figured after I pissed off Seamus with my Save the Elvis mission I would just hang at the back of our supersonic bus, drink cheap beers and wait for the end to come. But then Seamus left us, took the bus with him, and after ditching the rental car idea and riding here on a smelly Greyhound last night, complete with snoring old-timers and whiny kids, I heard that Capilla—Doug Capilla!—shut out the Bucs on two hits. Our record against them jumped to 11-5 and dang if we didn't have a chance after all.

So I here I am to report the latest sorry-ass news: after Seaver and sometimes Norman and Capilla once in a red moon, the Reds are pitching themselves right down the crapper.

Today it's Jack Billingham's turn to be handed his posterior for Christmas. Against Kison, another guy who looks either great or awful, Rose puts us up 1-0 with a pop fly homer to right in the 1st, and Doc Sheila at the end of our row looks more quiet and intense than she usually does.

Then the 3rd inning begins. Omar Moreno, playing the outfield in place of Bill Robinson, rips a double with one out. Kison belts one over the fence for the Pirate lead. Oliver singles. Taveras walks. Parker singles. Stargell walks. Stennett singles. Scrap Iron Garner, who I intend to stuff into a wastebasket if I ever run across him in the players' parking lot, bashes a grand slam for the eighth straight Buc to reach base and an 8-1 Pittsburgh lead. Mr. Billingham? It's been real nice, honey.

Make that score 10-1 after a Parker single, Stargell double and 2-run Garner single the next inning, giving Mr. Scrappy six for the game. The Reds then decide to wake up, Geronimo doubling in a run in the last of the 4th. With the lack of a useful bench, Sparky sends up pitcher Tom Hume to bat for Dale Murray and come in the game. BAM! Three-run homer and it's 10-5. 10-6 after doubles by Driessen and Concepcion in the 6th.

Now the Bucs have been playing on eggshells all season with the super brittle Stennett and Stargell, and when Pops whiffs to end the 6th, he windmill-swings himself into a pretzel, tears a muscle in his rib cage and knocks himself out of the lineup for 15 games. Nothing seems to get this team down, though, and singles by Garner (again), Duffy Dyer and Kison (again, his fourth hit in five trips), add two more runs as Bruce mows down the last ten Reds he faces.

Still, we got five more chances at these guys late this month, including the last three games of the year. If Stennett joins Pops on the DL in that time, we just might take 'em, but I wouldn't bet my non-evaporating life on it. Pittsburgh, you see, is the first team to win 80 games. —Amy G.

PIT 008 200 200 – 12 16 0
CIN 100 401 000 – 6 8 0
W-Kison L-Billingham HRS: Kison, Garner, Hume GWRBI-Kison

Midwest Shrinkage Day
September 5-6, 1977

CHICAGO—One-armed Lester here, after another awful bus ride to the Windy City for some double crosstown action. At Wrigley it's the Cubs spoiling the Dodgers' sofa again in typical excruciating fashion, while over at Comiskey, the White Sox need a win against the first-place Royals and 18-game winner Leonard to stay mathematically alive. And with the weird Indian summer weather they're having, they have to do it with their shorts on. Crazy Amy's been waiting all season for a bare-legged Chisox game, and now that we got one she's slipped into a box seat behind their on-deck circle for some closer looks. That girl is just plain strange.

K.C., who wiped out Texas on Thursday and Minnesota on Friday, jumps all over Wilbur Wood with four runs in the 3rd, helped by a Cowens run-scoring double and singles from Brett, Wathan, and Patek. Willie Wilson, filling in for Otis today against Dal Canton in the 6th, triples in White, then gets singled in himself by Brett to make it 7-2, Leonard retires eleven in a row heading to the last of the 9th, and Chicago is three outs away from death and I'm wondering which limb of mine is next to go.

But Zisk singles, Orta rips a double, Essian singles home two and Littell is summoned. Patek boots a grounder, Spencer singles the bases filled and when Joe Zdeb drops a Kessinger pop to left, two more runs are home and it's suddenly 7-6! Second and third, nobody out! Nothing comes easy for Littell, but he's used to this. Garr skies out to Wilson, Spencer too slow to score. Lemon whiffs. Oscar Gamble is due up but Herzog puts him on to face Zisk, already with a double and single.

Zisk grounds to short to end it, and the White Sox are gone from the race. They gave it their all and played in many thrillers, but leaky pitching and a waterfall of horrible defense did them in.

Meantime, with my left leg now missing, Mikey and Dr. Sheila have to help me out of the park. It's a two block walk to the el train, but suddenly Amy is waving us over to a hidden subway stairwell we hadn't noticed on our way in. A weird glow can be seen at the bottom of a humming escalator.

"What the hell's this?" asks Sherman, "I thought we catch the elevated train!"

"Screw it," says Amy, and she hurries down the escalator. The rest of us follow, even though no one else on the street seems to be using the entrance.

We reach the subway platform and stop. A shiny, customized two-car train is waiting for us, Ball Nut Zipline painted on the side. Its doors wide open. Delirious, we step in. It's everything we hoped the Ball Nut bus would be, and much, much more: reclining leather seats that fold out into beds, air conditioning, a 60-inch hi-def screen tuned to extra innings of the Rangers game in Minnesota, fully stocked refrigerator and food cabinets, jacuzzi tub in the roman-sized bathroom.

The doors close, we find seats and a pleasant male voice comes over the speaker, a voice that sounds a bit familiar. "Next stop...Houston..."

"What??" Sherman blurts. "Since when is there a subway from Chicago to Houston??" The train hums, vibrates slightly, and shoots into the dark tunnel at warp speed. We're pinned to our seats a few seconds before the pressure evens out. And then we notice a glowing white light coming from the front car.

"Whoa!" says Amy, "I gotta see who's driving this thing". She stands, takes one step to the forward door and it slides open. For a moment we're blinded by the light, and when we regain our vision, see an old friend standing there, mirrored sunglasses still on, but now with chalk-colored hair and a dazzling white leisure suit with giant lapels.

"Seamus?" I cry.

"No," he says, "Seamus has been..shall we say...reimagined. Call me Seamus the White."

K.C. 104 002 000 – 7 10 3
CHI 100 100 004 – 6 7 1

The Buena Vista Bosox Club

September 7, 1977

BOSTON—A short Amtrak journey up here, and me and Fred get two days of relaxing slugfests at Fenway between the Indians and Bosox, two teams going nowhere. Yesterday's 11-10 Tribe win had me cracking up all day, and today we get Looie Tiant, ringmaster of Boston's daily nine-inning circus.

The stats for this guy are beyond bizarre. 195 innings pitched, 275 hits given up, 36 of those homers, yet with only 60 walks for the year and a winning record at 12-11. He draws Rick Waits, another hot and cold specialist, but it's Looie who kicks off the extra base buffet, dishing out taters to Thornton and Carty to begin the 2nd. After a Grubb triple and Duffy double it's 3-0 Tribe, and we all lean back for another long afternoon.

The teams trade runs a few innings later, before Montgomery nets a solo shot to make it 4-2 them. Tiant escapes big jams his next four innings, and we all know what that means. Yup, Scott walks to start the Boston 6th. Hobson singles with one out. Dewey Evans hits for Helms and pounds a 3-run homer. Miller doubles and here comes Al Fitzmorris with Kern unavailable. Burleson and Fisk single, four runs are across and it's 6-4.

Anyone who think this lead will last clearly hasn't been paying attention. Carty and Fred Kendall single to start the 7th. Campbell enters, terminating Tiant for the day (6 IP, 15 H, standard for him), and Grubb greets Soup with a single. Two walks later it's 7-6 Cleveland. An Evans sac fly ties it 7-7 after seven. Fisk singles with one out in the 8th and Laxton is in just for Yaz. Yaz smashes a double. Pat Dobson tries his luck with Rice and whiffs him. But Bernie Carbo, who pinch-hit a double to start the last Boston rally, cracks one over the bullpens this time, his second 3-run shot in two days, 31st of the year, Boston's 200th, and they're up for good 10-7, actually picking up a game for a change!

Meanwhile, Fred can't even look at me on the way out because the Orioles have beaten his Yanks for a second straight day. As we exit Fenway I side up to him.

"Cheer up, man, the Sox need a miracle, too."

"Don't butter me up with that jive-ass sugar, bro. I'm in pain here!"

"I know you're in pain. I'm saying that I'm here for you. Actually I think it's cool that a Red Sox fan and a Yankee fan can—"

WHAM! He body slams me, knocks me to the Kenmore Square sidewalk and drops on my chest. His eyes are crazed.

"You ain't no soul-friend, fool. You want my team to die just like I want yours to, so don't you go talkin' no Amos & Andy Starsky & Hutch Kirk & Spock Brokeback bullshit all of a sudden, hear me?"

It's hard to answer somebody when they're on your chest, but I don't have to, because at that moment the pavement shakes, the wall next to us opens like a brick flower and an escalator appears, leading down into a hidden subway station.

"Express Ball Nut Zipline now boarding" says a voice over a speaker that sounds awful familiar.

"Damn!" says Fred, "and my tab of windowpane hasn't even kicked in yet!" I push him off me, start down the escalator. Turn and wave him through the opening, which the people on the sidewalk obviously can't see.

See you soon...from wherever.

CLE 030 100 300 – 7 17 2

BOS 001 104 13X -10 15 0

W-Campbell L-Fitzmorris HRS: Thornton, Carty, Montgomery, Carbo GWRBI-Carbo

American League through Sunday, September 7

Kansas City	78	62	.557	—
Texas	77	62	.554	0.5
New York	73	65	.529	4
Boston	71	65	.522	5
Baltimore	72	68	.514	6
Cleveland	63	76	.453	14.5
Minnesota	61	79	.436	17
Chicago	60	78	.435	17

National League through Sunday, September 7

Pittsburgh	81	59	.579	—
Philadelphia	76	61	.555	3.5
Los Angeles	76	62	.551	4
Cincinnati	75	63	.543	5
St. Louis	73	66	.525	7.5
Houston	64	74	.464	16
Montreal	55	84	.396	25.5
Chicago	53	84	.387	26.5

Fast Train to Somewhere

September 9, 1977

Here we were, the Squallpocket Nine reunited again, shooting our way west under the earth at 700 miles an hour. Seamus, who everyone assumed had evaporated, was actually spared and revitalized to lead us to season's end, and Fred and me had everything to do with it.

Seems that Barnstable Cox, the CEO of Timeco Incorporated, was also a monster John Lennon fan, and because our day spent with the ex-Beatle last week apparently enabled him to survive into the future, Timeco's reward was a brand new luxury mode of ballpark transportation for us. In addition to being a creepy millionaire entrepreneur, Cox also had a crapload of stock in the Rand Corporation, which was developing an eerily similar high-speed tube train project during the 70s.

"Don't think for a second, though, that evaporation still won't happen," said Seamus as we dined on roast capon and fresh greens in the Zipline's dining car. As he said this he stared right at Amy, whose Indians half of her Ohio rooting interest were next on the endangered list.

"Yeah, but YOU sure didn't!" she barked. "How come?"

"We've been over that, Amy. Employee perks. Besides I was just following the Expos, not fanatically obsessed with them."

Sheila wasn't all that thrilled to see me again after I ditched the group, but she obviously still had feelings. As the train rose and lurched somewhere under the Appalachians, she slid closer to me on one of our leather couches.

"I know this sounds weird..." she muttered, "but I do hope our teams get to play each other in the World Series." I told her not to get her hopes up the way Boston's pitching staff was going, and she reached for my hand and squeezed it.

"There's still a few weeks left, Carlton. If we believe in ourselves, give 110%, never say die, don't say till it's over till the fat lady says it's over, win one for the Gipper, humm baby and pound some Budweiser, it just might happen."

"Yeah, maybe. Except Reggie Cleveland sucks."

Game of the Day

ARLINGTON, TX—As Fred's Yanks take the field against Peachy's Rangers for the first of their final two against each other (barring a one-game playoff), things have tightened even more. K.C. has already been pecked to death by the Orioles, while Boston has gopher-balled another one away at Comiskey. If Texas wins here they're back in first.

Ellis gets the ball against Figueroa, and they're scoreless through three until Zeber walks, Rivers gaps a double and Reggie crushes one way out to Beniquez for a sac fly and 1-0 lead. Figueroa isn't wetting himself for a change; it's the New York bats that aren't giving him help. White and Chambliss rap into DPs to kill rallies, and the Rangers knot it in the 6th on a Keith Smith double and two-out Beniquez single.

You can usually set your watch for a late-inning Yankee meltdown, and it starts in the 7th. Wills pops a solo shot leading off. Rivers butchers his umpteenth fly of the year for a double and error, Harrah sac flies Sundberg home and just like that it's 3-1 for Dock.

But Ellis has had his fill of late-inning misery, too. Stanley and Alston open with singles to get him tired. Enter Roger Moret, and Zeber greets him with a double to make it 3-2. Rivers whiffs, but Reggie gets ahold of one and rams it into the left center bleachers for a 5-3 lead! (Fred just jumped on my back.) The Blair-Randolph-Dent defense team comes in, Lyle takes over for Figueroa...and Beniquez hits Sparky's first pitch over the fence. If I had a dime for every time Lyle gives up an extra-base hit to the first guy he sees, I'd be eating filet mignon at Del Frisco's right now.

This time, though, he recovers. Campaneris singles with two outs, but Alomar grounds out. Then in the 9th, Sparky gets Ellis, Harrah and Hargrove with ease, the Yanks are just three out again (two in the loss column), and their upcoming final two at Royals Stadium are looking huge.

NYY 000 100 040 – 5 10 2
TEX 000 001 210 – 4 9 0
W-Figueroa L-Moret SV-Lyle HRS: Jackson, Wills, GWRBI-Jackson

Murderer's Rau

September 11, 1977

LOS ANGELES—So what are you telling me? That I should have faith in my Dodgers despite the half dozen conniption fits they've given me lately? That I should take them being two out in the loss column with Pittsburgh coming in next week as a serious thing? That I shouldn't expect to give a reading of my will soon? Well...for you? Okay.

Game of the Days

Sutton beat these Expos in the first game, making us 14-6 against them. I've seen worse. The problem is we got John and Rau going the last two, both lefties, and Montreal turns most lefties into Canadian chopped liver. Good thing they got Bahnsen, because he's no good, and even after Dawson and Parrish hit solo shots early, Dusty B. pops one in the bleachers with two aboard and we're up 3-2. Both Lopes and Yeager are out with bug bites, those malingerers, and Lasorda gets creative and sticks Manny Mota in left leading off, Smith in center and Baker in right. Mota gets two singles in his first three trips, only messes up one flyball into a triple, while Jerry Grote catches and gets a double and triple.

Carter gets a single, double and homer off John, and after he gets the first out in the 7th up 5-3, Sosa takes over and it's lights out in Elysian Park. The first seven he faces go down, but with two gone in the top of the 9th, Unser pinch-hits a walk. Jose Morales pinch-hits a single. Here comes Dawson again, hotter than scorpion piss since July, and rifles a triple over Monday's head in center to tie the game for cryin' out loud. That bum Hough isn't even responsible!

Anyway, against their relief ace Kerrigan, Sosa bats for himself and starts the last of the 9th with a single. Monday lines out but Russell doubles down the line, Sosa to third! Smith fouls out with the infield up, and then it gets real funny. Baker is given four wide ones to load the bases with two gone and pitch to Garvey, who gets about as many clutch hits as I got sperm cells. Garvey stands there for what seems like forever, and with only 26 bases on balls the whole season, works a walk from Kerrigan to end the game!

MTL 101 010 002 – 5 10 1
L.A. 003 200 001 – 6 10 1

W-Sosa L-Kerrigan HRS: Dawson, Parrish, Carter, Smith GWRBI-Garvey

I'm not done yet. There was another one this afternoon, and this time Dougie Rau gave up three solo shots but walked nobody and won his fifth straight because the Blue Boys were all over Steve Rogers, giving him his sixth loss in a row and seven of eight. That's 16-6 for us over the Expos on the year, our best mark against anyone. We got the Phillies coming to town next, a half a game up on them now, followed by the Buccos. Guess you can say it's take care of business time or fold it the hell up. —*Sherman*

MTL 010 100 010 – 3 5 1
L.A. 004 120 00X – 7 9 0
   W-Rau L-Rogers HRS: Perez-2, Dawson, Smith, Baker, GWRBI-Russell

Deep in the Heart of the Cotswolds
September 12, 1977

   The Ball Nut Zipline made an unscheduled stop underneath Peachy Calhoun's house in Jewett, Texas, because even with two huge games in K.C. and L.A. today, his Astro and Ranger affairs had the edge in thrills and bizarreness. Before Peachy takes it away, though, I have to warn you. Because he's an actual resident of 1977, he isn't subject to the same sad fate as the rest of us, and the Timeco Incorporated evaporation system malfunctioned when Houston got eliminated. In other words, Peachy is now one half good ol' Texas boy and one half English butler.

   HOUSTON—I must say, this indoor pitch lends itself to some scintillating ball play. With Messers Twitchell and McLaughlin having at it, the Montrealers rush to the forefront with three tallies in the 3rd, on two single hits, a walk and one two-bag blow by Ellis Valentine. Dang it all!
   Not that I give a coyote's butt what happens to the 'Stros anymore, but they've playing crazy good the last few weeks and still got an outside chance at hitting the .500 mark. Bo ain't wowin' them this time, though, and after singles by Garrett, Speier and Twitchell with two gone in the 6th, he's yanked for Tom Dixon. Splendid.
   The seldom-utilized Mr. Dixon responds rather well, embarrassing David Cash with a strikeout and making Dawson, Carter and Valentine redundant in the 7th. Meanwhile, as if the expulsion of their mound ruler had awoken them, Houston brings two runs of their own across right away and forces the Expos overseer to fetch William Atkinson from the pitching reserve. Yee-ha, we're still in this thing!
   Ken Forsch takes care of the French guys in the 8th and 9th, getting Valentine on a DP with the bases loaded that Enos Cabell starts. It's a damn good omen, and even though Kerrigan gets the ball for the last of the 9th, I dare admit that I am not at all quivering with dread.

The reason? Edward Herrmann pinch-strikes a single. Joseph Ferguson does the same. Cesar Cedeno follows suit admirably. Robert Watson minds the gap by sending a loud two-sacker into it to knot the contest. And it's Jose Cruuuuuz, with a laser single into center that almost takes Speier's noggin' off, and we win it with five straight hits off Kerrigan without making an out!

Hot bloody damn, is all I can say.

MTL 003 001 000 – 4 11 0
HOU 000 002 003 – 5 12 0
W-Forsch L-Kerrigan GWRBI-Cruuuuz

ARLINGTON—What can one possibly say about birds of prey? Orange and black are their feathers, demon red their eyes, determined to finish with honor in this championship campaign. And yet...and yet...Here are Messers Singleton and Murray, the former notorious for his game-deciding exploits, the latter a pale visage of his allegedly superlative self. The Rangers left-fielder makes a foolhardy play to begin things, batter Kelly reaching second base, and one out later Mr. Singleton launches Doyle Alexander's first offering on a monstrous parabola, over 30,000 Texas hearts sinking, for the ball sails—

Okay, shut your Shepherd's pie hole. Singleton hits three homers, knocking in five, and Murray also hits three homers, knocking in six. And I got nothing more to say about it except that when I get back on the train, I'm gettin' stupid drunk.

BAL 350 100 301 – 13 10 0
TEX 000 001 001 – 2 9 3
W-Flanagan L-Alexander HRS: Singleton-3, Murray-3 GWRBI-Singleton (16th!)

Code Yellow and Black
September 13-14, 1977

We camped out in Peachy's living room for a few days. After getting crushed yesterday in St. Louis, the Bucs were heading into the Dome for a Sunday double-dip en route to their big showdown in L.A., and it seemed a lot more fun than following my depressing Red Sox around. Peachy is actually more stoked about the Rangers' three games in K.C. on the final weekend, and by then there might only be three of us left to watch it.

Sheila really wanted to do the reporting today but I talked her out of it because she gets too distracted and anal and whatever and big pennant games need the objective focus I can supply. Just as soon as I finish this beer.

Games of the Days

HOUSTON—The Pirates have been cold, the Astros piping hot, making this a spoiler's paradise. Stargell isn't due back until the second to last game of the year, and after this doubleheader, the Bucs' have just two with the Dodgers and five with the Reds, who they're a paltry 6-11 against.

Meaning it's Cobra Time. Big Dave Parker is an MVP shoo-in if Pittsburgh takes the pennant, and in his all-yellow duds today he looks like a freakin' school bus. Despite "negative clutch" ratings on his Strat card, he is hitting in the high .360s with over 125 RBIs, and just seems to come through whenever needed. The 21-8 Candelaria tries to do away with pesky Houston, who's been giving everyone grief lately, but it's Art Howe who gets things going with a line shot solo homer off Candy Man in the 2nd.

Lemongello keeps it 1-0 Astros for five innings, getting out of a flood of jams. He hits Parker on his second at bat, and on the third, leading off the 6th, Cobra uncoils a missle launch into the right field seats to tie the game, his 30th of the year. He singles Garner to third his next time up, but Dixon comes on to whiff Robinson. Top of the 8th, though, still 1-1, Oliver leads off with a gap double. Forsch comes on for Ott, who singles in Oliver. Moreno, already with a surprising double, hits a shocking triple and it's 3-1 Pirates. Parker singles in Garner in the 9th for added insurance, Candy Man mops up his 3-hitter for win #22, and the first one's in the books.

PGH 000 001 021 -4 13 0
HOU 010 000 000 – 1 3 0

W-Candelaria L-Dixon HRS: Parker, Howe GWRBI-Ott

A battle of mediocre lefties is on tap for Game 2, Forster vs. Bannister. The Bucs score twice in the 1st on a sac fly and wild pitch, but the 'Stros storm right back with two on a Cabell single and Ed Hermann triple. The clubs trade zero eggs for the next three innings, until Forster leads the 5th with a walk. Bannister fans Stennett and gets Garner on a fly, but here's Parker again.

And THERE IT GOES. Homer #31 just past the foul pole and a 4-2 lead! Forster gets into a couple of jams the rest of the way but bails himself out each time, Houston fatally stricken by now with Cobra poison. Parker goes 5-for-8 on the day, gets on base seven times, ups his RBI total to 131, and Pittsburgh ends up 15-7 against Houston on the year.

"Win in L.A. and I'm here to stay," says Sheila after the game, thinking she's Emily Dickinson all of a sudden. I'm about to remind her that the Reds won't exactly be pushovers, but stop myself. It's always beter to have your doctor in a good mood.

PGH 200 021 000 – 5 8 0
HOU 200 000 000 – 2 7 0

W-Forster L-Bannister HR: Parker, GWRBI-Parker

American League through Sunday, September 14

Kansas City	81	65	.555	—
Texas	78	66	.542	2
New York	77	66	.538	2.5
Boston	74	69	.517	5.5
Baltimore	74	70	.514	6
Cleveland	67	79	.459	14
Chicago	64	80	.444	16
Minnesota	63	83	.432	18

National League through Sunday, September 14

Pittsburgh	85	62	.578	—
Los Angeles	82	62	.569	1.5
Philadelphia	78	65	.545	5
Cincinnati	78	65	.545	5
St. Louis	76	69	.524	8
Houston	67	78	.462	17
Chicago	56	87	.392	27
Montreal	56	90	.384	28.5

To Die and Live in L.A.

September 15-16, 1977

On the eve of the first of two Pirate-Dodger showdown games in Los Angeles, I overheard this conversation in the rear salon car of the Ball Nut Zipline...

DR. GROSSINGER: In our last session, I believe we were talking about your feelings of sports-rooting inadequacy.

SHERMAN: You were talking. I was ignoring.

DR. GROSSINGER: Yes, but you did admit that the passing of your wife produced a general helplessness before the start of every Dodger game. For instance, tonight's critical match against Jim Rooker. Wouldn't you agree that your chances against the rugged, unflappable Pirates are slim at best?

SHERMAN: Speak for yourself, Doc. Pops Stargell isn't back until Game 153, and after the Candy Man, who thank God we're missing this time around, your staff ain't exactly Maddux and Glavine out there.

DR. GROSSINGER: We are discussing you today, Sherman. Not me—

SHERMAN: Yeah, yeah, but enough already. I'm on my last wheels here. What I wanna know is when did you become such a Pirate lackey?

DR. GROSSINGER: Lackey? Certainly an odd choice of word...Regardless, I suppose you can say there was a rooting interest in my family. Which I had... forgotten about. But that really isn't germane to—

SHERMAN: The hell it isn't! You got a two-game lead on me because my bums fell sleep against Paul Moskau last night, but guess what? We're just one back in the loss column! How's our next "session" gonna go after you crawl home to face nothing but Cincinnati, who's rolled you like pizza dough all year?

(long pause)

DR. GROSSINGER: Oh my, will you look at that. Six p.m. already! Time we headed for the ballpark, right?

Game of the Days

LOS ANGELES—Sherman was right. The final Dodger game with the Reds last night was a disaster, as Rau had nothing, Moskau everything, and stupid errors by Cey and Russell helped the Reds build a 5-0 lead before Lopes tried to make things interesting with a futile 2-run shot in the 8th.

But tonight the air is radioactive. Standing room only, which we actually have to spring for, though it does make it easier to keep Sheila and Sherman separated. Anyway, Cey opens the scoring with a redemption smash off Rooker, high into the bleachers, the place goes ape, and it's 1-0 Blue Guys. Hooton walks Robinson and Oliver to start the 2nd, but Ott and Moreno go out. Taveras singles too hard for Robinson to score, and Rooker whiffs with the bases juiced.

Big waste, because Baker walks to lead the Dodger 2nd and none other than Steve Garvey rips one into the Dodger bullpen and it's 3-0! Holy crap. And they're not done. A walk and two singles load the Dodger bases in the 3rd with no one out. Reggie Smith lines one right at Garner who steps on third and nearly turns a triple play. Baker grounds out and that's that.

Hooton is tantalizing, giving up a single here, a plunked Stennett there, but no Buc can swing to the rescue all night. Dave Parker never even gets the ball out of the infield. A Lee Lacy walk and Cey triple in the 5th make it 4-0 and finish the scoring, the Penguin going 4-for-4 and a double away from the cycle. Tekulve and Grant Jackson get Pittsburgh out of a few late jams, but the game's out of reach by then. Hooton's shutout makes him a bona fide Cy Young threat to Candelaria, sharing his 22-8 record.

Sherman treats us to midnight egg creams at Canter's Deli later (Sheila opts for a cottage cheese salad and sits in her own booth), and all the place is talking about around us is the Dodgers—now even in the loss column and one game back.

Reuss and Sutton, a pair of underachievers this year, will get the balls for the finale, and hopefully will pack some of their own.

PIT 000 000 000 – 0 5 1
L.A. 120 010 00x – 4 8 0
W-Hooton L-Rooker HRS: Cey, Garvey GWRBI-Garvey

Shenanigans I Could Do Without
September 17-19, 1977

Did I ever tell you how my wife used to make the telephone ring? First she'd go in the bathroom with a relaxing cup of tea. Then she'd pour herself a warm bath, maybe even drop in bubble stuff or some of that lady oil. She'd be wearing that pretty kimono I got her in Japan on our honeymoon, and she'd take that off, climb in and lean back, lots of times with a romance paperback...and presto! The goddamn telephone would ring.

See, in my book, the world runs on three things: karma, mishegas, and shenanigans. Some people—and I'm talking very few of them—drive through life weaving around those things like they're not even in the road. Wayne Gretzky, Michael Jordan and that Billy Gates guy come to mind. The rest of us? We're screwed. If something's out there to go wrong, it'll find us.

And my Dodgers just smashed into a shenanigans brick wall. How else can you explain this? We're tearing up the league for two weeks like we still got Snider and Campanella, the Bucs are stumbling, and lose Stargell until the second to last game. Hooton smokes them out in the first game to put us even in the loss column, they got their big oaf loser Jerry Reuss going in the finale, with us being much more dangerous against lefties—

—and we get beat by a 9th inning pop home run by Ed Ott and scoring double by Ken Macha? What happened?

Then this happened the next day:
PIRATES 4-11-1, at DODGERS 3-7-0 Sutton had it going from the 2nd in-

ning till the 8th, and Penguin gave us a 3-2 lead with his 29th dinger in the 5th, but you still have to play the 9th, and the Bucs have been absolute poison at the end of almost every close game. At least Hough didn't blow this one.

And then there's this new garbage that happens today, in two stadiums no less...

Games of the Days

PITTSBURGH—The first of five games between the Bucs and Reds stretched over nine days, thanks to the crackpot who made this schedule. Maybe it was God, because He throws the Reds right off a cliff. Buzz showed me the dice rolls in his notebook afterwards and it's enough to make you weep. Or at least me.

Doug Capilla's billed against Odell Jones. Every game for the Reds is huge but with Billingham facing Candelaria next, this is the one they HAVE to win. Too bad their first baseman turns out to be a schlemiel. Bottom of the 1st, Stennett rolls an infield hit toward Driessen and he chucks it in the stands for an added 2-base error. Garner knocks a single two seconds later and it's 1-zip Pirates.

Bench clubs an upper deck shot with Rose aboard in the 3rd, but a Garner walk, Parker grounder and Gonzalez single ties it 2-2. Then Rose homers, Griffey doubles and Bench singles him in and it's 4-2 Reds in the 5th. I'm excited now. Then Capilla can get nobody out in the 6th, walks Oliver, hits Ott, walks Taveras, and Grant Jackson makes it 4-3 with a sac fly. Stennett bloops a single and we're tied.

All this time the Reds have been rolling the dice like they got some weird Egyptian plague. Foster misses a 1-9 homer shot (45%), Morgan a 1-14 homer shot (70%), and Geronimo and Griffey miss 75% and 85% single chances that would have scored more insurance runs.

Manny Sarimento, one of the more luckless relief bastards around, though it's usually his own fault, starts the bottom of the 8th. Parker rolls another infield single out toward Driessen, and sure, why not? Throw the thing into the seats again, you imbecile! (For those following along, his first 2-base botch was an error roll of three 1s, and the second one a roll of three 6s. Remarkable.) Anyway, Robinson doesn't wait too long to bring the pain, lining the first pitch into left for the go-ahead run. Goose relieves after Jackson's three and a third 1-hit innings, mows down Griffey, Foster and Bench like they're pussy willows, and my death is just a little bit closer.

CIN 002 020 000 – 4 7 2

PIT 101 002 10x – 5 8 0

W-Jackson L-Sarmiento SV-Gossage HRS: Bench, Rose GWRBI-Robinson

ST. LOUIS—After this one I'm just speechless, and I hope Lester's happy for ruining my life. Our record against the eliminated Cards before game time? How about 12-4. We got John going for his 20th win. Unfortunately they got Bob Forsch, pitching his brains out lately. We put a guy on each of the first four innings and can't score. (Dice nonsense: Forsch has a 70% HR shot on his card for hitters with normal power. Bill Russell, the only guy in our lineup with weak power, manages to hit it twice and ends up with singles.) Lopes walks to lead the 5th, 31-4 on the base paths—and gets picked off (on a 75% chance to get back). Naturally Russell follows with his second single, Smith walks, and Baker and Garvey do nothing.

John gets out of two late jams after one-out Simmons doubles, each time by walking Tony Scott to face Reitz, but the upcoming malarkey is written all over the Busch Stadium wall. Bottom of the 11th, John still in there, the Dodgers with just four crappy singles off Forsch, Hernandez walks. So does Simmons. And death comes off the bat of Heity Cruz, household name in some Puerto Rican town, who smashes Tommy's first pitch off the left center wall.

We may be still alive math-wise, but I'm done. Buzz can tell you what happens the rest of the way. I need to go write my 100-page apology letter to God for whatever the hell I did to Hannah.

L.A. 000 000 000 00 – 0 4 0
STL 000 000 000 01 – 1 7 0
  W-Forsch L-John GWRBI-Cruz

REMAINING SCHEDULE:
Pirates: *Reds (1), at Reds (3)* **Dodgers**: *at Cards (2), Astros (1), Cards (3)*

The End is Near and Just About Here
September 20, 1977

Okay, let's regroup the group. Sheila and her Pirates are flying high after their last huge comeback win in L.A., and Sherman has officially checked out. Amy and Mikey have been drinking a lot of beer, with their Reds and Phillies evaporating. In the American League camp, Friendly Fred is so high he barely knows his Yankees are in trouble. Meanwhile my Red Sox are three losses or Royal wins away from extinction, and Little Me's Orioles only one. I bought him a Slinky to play with on the train and distract him.

But I'm calm, and not all that shocked. Gotta say I've never seen a team go from unstoppable to unmentionable in such a short time more than this Boston bunch, but the real team that year didn't win either, and in fact finished as far behind New York as they are now, so there's that.

Seamus the White keeps telling us that evaporation is painless. I suppose, but I'd still like to see Pam and Timmy before I leave. In case you don't remember, they were the rest of my family before I ended up in the Squallpocket loony bin.

"Give it up, Buzz," says Seamus. "Just a week left in the season, and we got some Royals and Rangers action to pay attention to."

"C'mon man, this train can take us anywhere."

"Yeah but it makes no sense. Pam is in grade school and Timmy isn't even a notion."

"So I'll find Pam at school. You gotta let me do this, Seamus."

He grumbled, eased the Zipline's controls as we glided to a stop underneath Arlington Stadium.

"We'll talk after the game."

Game of the Day

ARLINGTON, TX—The Rangers have played the Royals tough, 9-8 against them on the year, and with them just two back in the loss column, it's time they got tougher.

Too bad no one told Doyle Alexander. BOOM! First pitch of the game to Pete LaCock is into the bleachers on this warm Saturday afternoon. First pitch of the 2nd inning and BOOM! Further into the bleachers by Darrell Porter.

Claudell Washington leads the last of the 2nd with the third leadoff homer in two innings, but Doyle isn't fooling anyone but Freddie Patek. Whiffs him to end the 2nd, whiffs him to end the Royal 4th after two walks and a single load the bases. A two-out triple by Beniquez ties the game minutes later, getting Peachy all amped and Lester hot and bothered.

Then there's the top of the 5th, and hell is unleashed. White leads with a clean double. LaCock singles him to third. Al Cowens, the K.C. MVP by any standard, cranks one over 420 feet and the Royals are up 5-2. Alexander then walks Brett. Throws away an infield single hit to his left. A doinky single in front of Campaneris is heaved into the seats for an additional two bases. Mayberry hits a sac fly and six runs are across just like that.

But Campy isn't done. He bobbles a LaCock grounder in the 6th, and with two outs Brett pounds one out of sight to make it 10-2. Alexander is finally put out of his misery for Mike Marshall, Sundberg calls for a very inside pitch on McRae and Marshall hits him in the head. McRae staggers back up, jumps on top of Sundberg and starts punching him Nolan Ryan style! Yeah, baby! McRae and Sundberg are both tossed for three games, Campaneris makes his third error in two innings, but Otis grounds out to end the mess.

Texas anger is stoked though, like mesquite coals with a blowtorch. Dennis Leonard, shooting for his 20th win, has already given up seven hits himself, five for extra bases. Washington starts the last of the 6th with a single. May forces him, but Beniquez, Campy, Ken Henderson and Wills all single in a row. A wild pitch is followed by a John Ellis single, filling in for the jettisoned Sundberg. Herzog out to the mound, but with the usual thin bullpen behind Leonard and Dennis not officially "tired", he stays in. A Harrah walk, Hargrove double and Washington single later, it's 10-9!

Leonard just yawns, settles back down and retires the next ten Rangers he faces. And the Royals are back in business in the 9th. A walk and single with two gone brings Moret in for Barker. It don't work. Wilson bats for LaCock and walks. The Amazing Mr. Cowens clears the bases with a triple, giving him six RBIs on the day. Brett doubles and it's 14-9.

It's about this time I check the out-of-town scoreboard. The Yanks won again, and the Orioles pulled off a clutch win against swan-diving Boston, but I remember that a Texas loss here will finish off the Birds. Oh geez, and little Carlton doesn't even know, sitting next to me and dropping popcorn kernels through his Slinky. Let's go Rangers!!

Washington and May go out, but Leonard fumbles a grounder by Beniquez, the sixth error of the game. Campaneris, still hearing the boos for his three glove cramps, bashes one into the seats and it's 14-11! Henderson walks, and if Wills can reach the tying run comes to the plate!

Mingori finally takes the ball from Leonard, but here's Willie Horton, the big Texas lefty-masher. I can't watch, but I have to. Willie skies one deep to center, Otis runs to the track, draws a bead on it and—

Lester here. Otis caught it. But Buzz is gone. Just plain gone. And Carlton too. Which makes sense because he's Buzz as a child. All that's left is his Slinky. I can't believe this. Dr. Sheila is crying. The hell with my team winning and dropping their magic number to four with six to play, not to mention Leonard's 20th win. We're devastated here.

K.C. 110 062 004 – 14 14 2
TEX 010 107 002 – 11 16 4
W-Leonard L-Alexander SV-Mingori HRS: LaCock, Porter, Cowens, Brett, Washington, Campaneris GWRBI-Cowens

REMAINING SCHEDULES:
Royals: at Rangers (1), at Twins (2) Rangers (3) **Rangers**: Royals (1), at White
Sox (3), at Royals (3) Yankees: Indians (1), at Red Sox (3), at Indians (3)

Raise the Funky Jolly Roger!
September 21, 1977

Ever since Ed Ott silenced the Dodger Stadium throng with a game-tying,
9th inning blast off Don Sutton, everything has been sailing the Pirates' way.
Need the Dodgers to stay shell-shocked in St. Louis? No problem. Need for
the Phillies and Reds to self-destruct? You got it. All this with Stargell being
on the DL, too.

Lester here, after a very quiet Zipline ride up from Texas. I asked Dr. Sheila
if she wanted to report the possible pennant-clincher for her Bucs, but she
was too distraught over losing Buzz and Little Buzz to even talk, let alone
write. She did say she'd follow the Dodger and Phillie games on the out-of-
town scoreboard, so at least that's something...

Game of the Day
PITTSBURGH—Crazy Amy isn't exactly full of mirth either, with her Reds
having to beat 22-game winner Candelaria to stay alive another day. And the
horrible Jack Billingham goes for her side, with as short a leash as possible
around his neck.

Griffey and Rose manage one-out singles, though, in the 1st, and after Foster's expected whiff, Bench works a walk. Driessen leaves them loaded with a
roller to 1st, and that's that. But Rennie Stenett, first man up for the Pirates,
gets hurt for the rest of the regular season! Good for them they have a small
cushion. Oliver, Ott and Taveras string their own singles together in the last
of the 2nd, it's 1-0 Bucs, and the Steel City is rocking anyway.

But here come the Reds in the 3rd. Morgan leads with a walk. Griffey and
Rose single for the tying run. Foster manages a sac fly to put Cincy ahead and
Bench bombs one into the second deck. 4-1 Reds!

DR. GROSSINGER: *At first scoreboard glance, MON is dominating PHI by a
3-1 margin after three innings, but LAD has just tied STL 1-1 in the 2nd inning. I
have doubts regarding both contests.*

Billingham throws a 1-2-3 3rd, but when Robinson singles and Oliver walks
to start the home 4th, Sparky Anderson doesn't muck around and pulls him
for Pedro Borbon, who gives up a Moreno single for one run but nothing else.

Neither team scores for the next two innings, and the Candy Man gets the

Reds out with just a single in the 7th. Dr. Sheila? It's stretch time!

Yes, I'm sorry. Oh my, STL scored three runs in the 3rd, but now LAD has gone ahead 5-4 in the 5th. As I diagnosed, this is a highly problematic event. MON is still ahead of PHI, though 4-1 now after six.

Bottom of the 7th at Three Rivers. Borbon still in there but Taveras rips a single. Moreno gets another single and Candelaria bunts them over. Up steps super sub Jim Fregosi, filling in for Stennett but with two weak groundouts on the day.

And Fregosi CLUBS it! Deep to left, Foster to the track and it's OUTTA HERE!! 5-4 Pirates and the place is up for grabs and—

Yahooooo!!! Screw the other games! We got the lead!!

Calm down, Doc. We still have two innings to play. And here's Rose starting the 8th with his third hit, a double into the corner. Foster flies out and Bench whiffs, and it's Driessen's turn. Driessen singles past Taveras, Rose scores and we're tied 5-5!

Yeah? Well guess what, smarty Lester! STL just scored twice in the bottom of the 8th against LAD. Isn't Hooton pitching that one?

She looks over at Sherman, who just rocks back and forth saying a Hebrew blessing, an empty popcorn bag over his head. Meanwhile Sarmiento pitches the 8th for the Reds and does a decent job, giving up an Oliver single and nothing else.

And then the seldom used Gary Nolan, a lefty killer who is incapable of getting righties out, starts the last of the 9th against the 2-for-3 Moreno. This time Omar walks. And Omar steals second. Candelaria bats for himself from the left side and grounds one to first to move Omar to third. Soto, a righty killer who can't get lefties out, comes on to face Fregosi and Garner. Infield in. Everyone's standing.

STL beat LAD for a sweep, honey! And MON held off PHI 5-4! This is it!!

She's right. If Moreno scores, the National League race is over. But Fregosi swings and misses for the second out. And it's up to Phil Garner or we're going extras. Scrap Iron's clutch, but no one's walking him to face the Cobra, even with Parker 0-for-4.

Soto looks in...throws...and Garner whacks it into the left-center gap! Foster and Geronimo give chase but can't reach it and here comes Moreno and the PIRATES WIN THE FUNKY PENNANT! THE PIRATES WIN THE FUNKY PENNANT!

Dr. Sheila jumps in my arm. Sherman and Mikey evaporate before our eyes, an empty popcorn bag and half-drunk cup of Rolling Rock left on their seats. Peachy Calhoun and Friendly Fred are still here, but that's it, folks. Just the four of us.

Except for Seamus waiting on the Zipline, of course. Destination: American League cities.

CIN 004 000 010 – 5 8 0
PIT 010 100 301 – 6 10 0
W-Candelaria L-Nolan HR: Bench GWRBI-Garner

The Lester Line
at CARDS 6-8-0, DODGERS 5-7-1 The Pirates were clutch all year, but L.A. has no one to blame but themselves. In the last month, I counted ten times that they blew games late. Are you ready?

8/17 vs. HOU: Cedeno 3-run HR off Hough in 9th, lose 6-5

8/19 at CIN: Concepcion single bottom of 8th, lose 2-1

8/20 at CIN: Lose 6-5 bottom of 15th

8/21 at PIT: Lose 7-6 on two Pirate runs bottom of 9th

8/28 at MON: Blow 6-0 lead, Hough loses lead in 9th, then game 8-7 in 10th

8/30 vs. CHC: Hough gives up two in 9th to tie, Dodgers lose 8-5 in 17th

9/3 at STL: Hooton blows 6-0 lead, Hough gives up two in 9th to lose 7-6

9/6 at CHC: Dodgers battle back from 8-3 to tie in 8th, Hough gives up run in 10th to lose 9-8

9/17 vs. PIT: Sutton blows 3-2 lead in 9th, loses 4-3

And finally, this travesty today: Two-run Smith homer puts L.A. up 5-4 in the 5th, but with two outs, nobody on in the 8th, 22-game winner Hooton gives up a Simmons double, Brock and Scott walks, and when Sosa relieves him, Reitz rips a ball past no-range Lopes at second for two runs and the final, fatal meltdown. Sorry, Sherman.

at RANGERS 6-13-0, ROYALS 2-6-1 Now for the real good stuff. Completely unaware he's going into the Hall of Fame in 34 years, Big Game Bert Blyleven throws a masterful CG, whiffing nine Royals and keeping the AL pennant race going at least a few more days. Major goat from yesterday Campaneris gets Texas on the board with a big double in the 2nd, and Bevacqua and Ellis add homers off Splittorff to put the Rangers just two back in the loss column again. K.C. now heads for Minnesota, who have unfortunately lost six in a row, while the Rangers go to Chicago.

American League through Sunday, September 21

Kansas City	83	66	.557	—
Texas	80	68	.541	2.5
New York	80	68	.541	2.5
Boston	77	71	.520	5.5
Baltimore	77	73	.513	6.5
Chicago	69	80	.463	14
Cleveland	67	83	.447	16.5
Minnesota	63	87	.420	20.5

National League through Sunday, September 21

x-Pittsburgh	88	63	.583	—
Los Angeles	83	67	.553	4.5
Cincinnati	81	67	.547	5.5
Philadelphia	81	67	.547	5.5
St. Louis	79	70	.530	8
Houston	69	81	.460	18.5
Montreal	60	91	.397	28
Chicago	57	92	.383	30

Watching the Defectives

September 23, 1977

Seamus reporting in, because it is my job once in a while. But I got a fun one for you today. Being we're down to the wire in the American League, even though no team except one really seems to be wanting this pennant, I thought I'd give us all a treat and rig up a special day of scoreboard watching. Most players and managers say they don't start watching the out-of-town business until September, but I don't buy that. It sure isn't true for me. I'm watching the scoreboard from the first inning on Opening Day, a) because it's fun and b) because it fills those boring gaps between innings.

So what I did was soup up the Ball Nut Zipline by welding a special turbo time splitter into the engine, y'know, like in one of those Back to the Hogwarts movies? Christ, why be at one ball game when you can pull off three at once?

Anyway, before I get into the play-by-plays from Fenway, Comiskey and Metropolitan Stadium, let's set the standings. The Royals magic number is four, up by two in the loss column over the Yanks and Rangers, with the Red Sox having to win and KC lose to stay alive.

Got it? Good. Now scroll down nice and slow on these slugfests. You can always skip to the final scores if you have no patience. I won't be insulted, but what fun is that? In my baseball experience, suspense is everything.

at BOSTON (Gullett vs. Tiant; Evans, Doyle injured)

NYY 1st: Rivers whiffs...Randolph dribbles out...Munson dribbles out

BOS 1st: Burleson singles...Fisk grounds out...Scott singles..Rice sac fly...Hobson grounds out. **1-0 Red Sox**

NYY 2nd: Jackson singles...Nettles HOMERS...Piniella HOMERS, Chambliss grounds out...White flies out...Stanley grounds out. **3-1 Yankees**

BOS 2nd: Yastrzemski HOMERS...Montgomery walks...Lynn triples...Dillard sac fly...Burleson walks...Fisk walks...Scott singles...Rice sac fly...Hobson walks...Yaz flies out. **5-3 Red Sox**

NYY 3rd: Rivers HOMERS...Randolph singles...Munson doubles, Randolph out at home (on %80 chance)...Jackson fans...Nettles flies out. 5-4 Red Sox

BOS 3rd: Montgomery walks...Lynn fans...Dillard fans...Burleson walks...Fisk doubles...Scott walks...Rice flies out. **7-4 Red Sox**

at CHICAGO (Ellis vs. Barrios; Sundberg suspended)

TEX 1st: Wills flies out...Harrah flies out...Hargrove grounds out.

CHI 1st: Downing flies out...Lemon fans...Gamble walks...Zisk walks, Zisk grounds out.

TEX 2nd: Bevacqua fans...Washington doubles...May walks...Beniquez hits into DP.

CHI 2nd: Orta grounds out...Essian grounds out...Soderholm HOMERS...Bannister singles...Spencer grounds out. **1-0 White Sox**

TEX 3rd: Campaneris grounds out...Fahey singles, Wills hits into DP

CHI 3rd: Downing fans...Lemon fans...Gamble lines out

at MINNESOTA (Colborn vs. Goltz; McRae suspended)

KC 1st: Poquette flies out...Cowens grounds out...Brett doubles...Wathan grounds out

MIN 1st: Bostock singles, goes to second on balk...Wynegar singles...Carew walks...Hisle flies out...Adams grounds out...Cubbage grounds out. **1-0 Twins**

KC 2nd: Porter walks...Otis walks...Mayberry HOMERS...Patek singles...
White sac bunt...Poquette singles...Cowens hits into DP. 4-1 Royals
   MIN 2nd: Chiles flies out...Wilfong grounds out...Smalley fans
   KC 3rd: Brett HOMERS...Wathan grounds out...Porter grounds out...Otis
fans. **5-1 Royals**
   MIN 3rd: Bostock grounds out...Wynegar grounds out...Carew singles...
Hisle singles...Adams flies out

at BOSTON

   NYY 4th: Piniella fans...Chambliss doubles...White flies out...Stanley flies
out. **7-4 Red Sox**
   BOS 4th: Hobson grounds out...Yaz whiffs...Montgomery dribbles out
   NYY 5th: Rivers grounds out...Randolph grounds out...Munson HOMERS...
Jackson singles...Nettles doubles...Piniella doubles (Willoughby replaces
Tiant)...Chambliss fans. **Yankees 7, Red Sox 7**
   BOS 5th: Lynn grounds out...Dillard flies out...Burleson fans
   NYY 6th: White walks...Stanley flies out...Rivers safe on Scott error...Ran-
dolph walks (B. Stanley replaces Willoughby)...Munson hits into 6-4-3 DP
   BOS 6th: Fisk doubles...Scott fans...Rice triples...Hobson singles...Yaz
doubles...Montgomery sac fly...Lynn HBP...Dillard pops out. **10-7 Red Sox**

at CHICAGO

   TEX 4th: Harrah fans...Hargrove walks...Bevacqua walks...Washington hits
into DP. **1-0 White Sox**
   CHI 4th: Zisk fans...Orta singles...Essian grounds out...Soderholm walks...
Bannister grounds out
   TEX 5th: May singles...Beniquez sac bunt...Campaneris grounds out...Fa-
hey grounds out
   CHI 5th: Spencer triples...Downing singles...Lemon singles...Gamble dou-
bles...Zisk whiffs...Orta triples (Devine replaces Ellis)...Essian grounds out...
Soderholm HOMERS...Bannister flies out. **7-0 White Sox**
   TEX 6th: Wills doubles...Harrah doubles...Hargrove flies out...Bevacqua
HOMERS...Washington singles...May whiffs...Beniquez singles...Cam-
paneris singles...Fahey safe on Spencer error...Wills singles...Harrah grounds
out. **7-6 White Sox**
   CHI 6th: Spencer grounds out...Downing flies out...Lemon walks...Gamble
grounds out

at MINNESOTA

KC 4th: Mayberry singles...Patek fans...White singles...Poquette HOMERS (Serum replaces Goltz)...Cowens grounds out...Brett grounds out. **8-1 Royals**

MIN 4th: Cubbage grounds out...Chiles grounds out...Wilfong singles... Smalley flies out

KC 5th: Watahn grounds out...Porter fouls out...Otis singles...Mayberry flies out

MIN 5th: Bostock singles...Wynegar walks...Carew walks...Hisle singles... Adams singles...Cubbage, Chiles and Wilfong all ground out. **8-5 Royals**

KC 6th: Patek flies out...White walks...Poquette walks...Cowens grounds out (Butler replaces Serum)...Brett singles (T. Johnson replaces Butler)...Wathan pops out. **9-5 Royals**

MIN 6th: Smalley, Bostock and Wynegar all ground out

at BOSTON

NYY 7th: Jackson flies out...Nettles lines out...Pinella singles...Chambliss pops out. **10-7 Red Sox**

BOS 7th: Burleson grounds out...Fisk flies out...Scott singles...Rice singles...Hobson whiffs

NYY 8th: White grounds out...Stanley flies out...Rivers singles...Randolph singles...Munson singles (Campbell replaces B. Stanley)...Jackson lines out **10-8 Red Sox**

BOS 8th: (Lyle replaces Gullett) Yaz, Montgomery, Lynn all ground out

NYY 9th: Nettles safe at second on Rice error...Piniella singles...Chambliss sac fly...Zeber bats for White and singles...Stanley ties game with single but gets hurt...Rivers dribbles out...Randolph pops out. **Yankees 10, Red Sox 10**

BOS 9th: Dent at short, Blair in left. Dillard flies out...Burleson singles... Fisk singles...Scott walks...Rice walks to win game.

at CHICAGO

TEX 7th: Hargrove walks...Bevacqua fans...Washington walks...May flies out...Beniquez grounds out. **7-6 White Sox**

CHI 7th: Zisk singles...Orta singles...Essian hits into DP...Soderholm singles...Bannister doubles...Spencer singles...Downing singles (Marshall replaces Devine)...Lemon flies out. **10-6 White Sox**

TEX 8th: Campaneris fans...Fahey grounds out...Wills singles...Harrah doubles (Hamilton replaces Barrios)...Hargrove whiffs

CHI 8th: Gamble doubles...Zisk doubles...Orta flies out...Essian doubles... Soderholm doubles (Umbarger replaces Marshall)...Bannister grounds out... Spencer doubles...Downing flies out. **14-6 White Sox**

TEX 9th: Bevacqua, Washington and May all ground out.

EIGHT straight wins for Chicago!

at MINNESOTA

KC 7th: Porter triples...Otis HOMERS...Mayberry singles...Patek fans... White walks...Poquette grounds out after wild pitch...Cowens safe on Cubbage error (Holly replaces T. Johnson)...Brett lines out. **12-5 Royals**

MIN 7th: Carew singles...Hisle singles...Adams singles (Mingori replaces Colborn)...Kusick bats for Cubbage and fans...Ford bats for Chiles and singles...Borgmann bats for Wilfong and hits GRAND SLAM HOMER (Littell replaces Mingori)...Smalley walks...Bostock hits into DP. **12-10 Royals**

KC 8th: Wathan singles...Porter HOMERS...Otis fans...Mayberry flies out... Patek doubles...White triples (D. Johnson replaces Holly)...Zdeb bats for Poquette and singles...Cowens walks...Brett whiffs. **16-10 Royals**

MIN 8th: Wynegar and Carew whiff...Hisle grounds out

KC 9th: Gomez at second, Randall at third. Wathan doubles...Porter singles...Otis sac fly...Mayberry pops out...Patek safe on Smalley error...White singles...Zdeb grounds out. **18-10 Royals**

MIN 9th: Adams singles...Randall grounds out...Ford flies out...

And back at Fenway, the whole team and half the fans out on the field watching the scoreboard, the fate of Boston's season lies in the pinch hitting bat of Willie Norwood. Littell throws, and Norwood belts it to deep left... Zdeb to the track hauls it in and the misery is over. Sorry Buzz, wherever the hell you are.

NYY 031 030 012 - 10 18 0
BOS 142 003 001 - 11 14 2

TEX 000 006 000 – 6 12 0
CHX 010 060 34x – 14 20 1

K.C. 041 301 342 – 18 21 0
MIN 100 040 500 – 10 14 2

Three teams left in the hunt now, and the KC magic number is down to two.

The Only Dang Game in Town
September 25, 1977

By Ed "Peachy" Calhoun
Jewett Babbler Sports Columnist

Sheeeeyit. Never thought I'd say it, but I miss every one of those nice folks that rooted for the wrong teams and got evaporated. Not as much fun being on a supersonic luxury high-speed train under the earth if you're only sharing it with a stuck-up lady doctor, a Nebraska farm boy in a wheelchair with one limb left, and a creepy guy in shades and white clothes who almost never comes out of the driving compartment.

On the other hand, it's nice to help myself to the fancy beers and roast beef bar and baseball DVD collection we got stocked with. Even saw *Major League* for the 16th time last night.

Anyway, sure gotta hand it to my Ranger boys for hanging in this long. We took that last game against the Royals because Dutchman Blyleven stepped up, and now he has another chance to keep us alive when he gets rematched against Denny Leonard in KC tomorrow. It's gonna be one epic hoedown.

The hero for today, though was good ol' Doyle Alexander. He'd lost four straight, pitching all kinds of cruddy, then went into Comiskey having to win or we'd be dead and shut them White Sox DOWN! Meanwhile Willie Horton singled one in to get us going in the 3rd, Hargrove took Kravec into the upper deck for a 3-run pie, we left 16 idiots on the bases but damn, that was still so easy!

You can bet tomorrow night won't be, but hell, we are 10-9 against them Royals so far, so don't count us out yet. All we gotta do is sweep all three games and take a one-game playoff. And by the way, Seamus says because I ain't from the future I won't be doing any evaporatin'. Got my nice easy chair back in Jewett waitin' on me.

TEX 002 320 000 – 7 13 2
CHI 000 000 001 – 1 7 1
W-Alexander L-Kravec HR-Hargrove GWRBI-Horton

And not like I forgot yesterday...
RANGERS 6-15-0, at WHITE SOX 3-9-1 Gaylord was almost as good as

Doyle was, and Texas destroys Steve Stone, kicking the game off with a Bump Wills pop homer off the foul pole, followed by six singles in the 2nd. Chicago's 8-game win streak ended here.

ROYALS 6-11-1, at TWINS 2-6-1 And this one eliminates the Yankees once and for all. Guess who the most clutch KC pitcher has been. Would you believe Andy "No" Hassler? Another CG win , and he keeps Carew hitless for all four at bats. Frank White with a huge three-run smash in the 6th off Thormodsgard to put the game away.

Uh-Oh...
September 26, 1977

KANSAS CITY—I would prefer to not even imagine the unthinkable. But here I am in the quickly emptying Royals Stadium, having just watched Bert Blyleven mow down my Royals like he's some kind of Hall of Fame pitcher. And for the second time in two weekends. Hmm.

Leonard matched him pretty well, giving up a Harrah walk and Hargrove and Washington singles to start the 4th and pretty much put us away, but after kicking the skunk out of the Twins for two days we couldn't have hit that big Dutch curveball with a snow shovel.

So now what? Ellis against Splittorff, followed by Perry against Colborn. We have two more days to win one from Peachy's boys or it's a one-game playoff on Monday, which from my calculations would be Doyle Alexander against Marty Pattin. Let us pray it doesn't come to that.

TEX 000 200 001 – 3 7 0
K.C. 000 000 000 – 0 4 0
W-Blyleven L-Leonard GWRBI-Washington

The Crowning Touch
September 28, 1977

KANSAS CITY—Geez Louise. What a game, and what a finish.

Seemed pretty ordinary at first. Splittorff giving up two-out singles to Harrah and Horton in the 1st but escaping without blood. And Dock Ellis mowing us down in the 1st, yet another Royals scoreless inning.

But then some dormant KC magic bubbles to the surface. Wathan, filling in for the injured Porter, rips a single to begin our 2nd. Otis walks and Mayberry beats out an infield dribbler to load the bases, no one out. Patek works a walk for an actual run. Frank White drops a perfect squeeze down the third base line, Harrah can't field it and it's a base hit! Royals Stadium is rocking and Peachy's cursing. With the infield up, Cowens shocks the park by grounding into a 6-2-3 DP, but Poquette doubles in the gap for two more, and it's 4-0! Is this the day?

Maybe, says Texas, and maybe the hell not. Singles by Hargrove, Harrah and Horton give the Rangers a quick run right back, and then the Docktor goes to work. After Poquette's double, Ellis puts away the next thirteen K.C. hitters in a row.

In the top of the 5th, though Texas opens their barbeque. Hargrove leads with another single. A wild pitch moves him up. Alomar singles him to third. Harrah singles. Horton doubles. Washington grounds out but Ellis singles past a drawn-in infield. Herzog gets Mingori and Littell up, his only halfway decent relievers, but it's way too early to bring them in. Splittorff hits Keith Smith to load the bases but Campaneris pops out, Beniquez grounds to Patek and the Rangers settle for four runs and the lead.

Splittorff regains his pitching sense after that, and it's still 5-4 Texas in the last of the 7th. Mayberry starts it with a walk. Patek lines a single into center, Mayberry "motoring" to third. White whiffs but Cowens walks. With Ellis fatigued, in comes lefty Roger Moret to face Poquette. Up comes pinch-hitter Willie Wilson. The infield is up. I'm standing with 40,000 others going nuts. Willie picks out a fastball and rips it into left! Two runs score and we have the lead back! And here's Brett with a base hit, 7-5 Royals! Len Barker's in to face McRae, and Hal singles, too! Buck Martinez at the plate, who came in when Wathan went out with a sprain, whiffs, but with Otis at the plate, Barker loses it. Throws two straight wild pitches before Otis singles for the sixth run of the inning! I can't believe it!

The excitement's apparently too much for Splittorff, because he goes off the tracks in the 8th, walking Campaneris, getting a DP ball out of Beniquez, but then walking Hargrove. Littell comes in, gives pinch-hitter Wills a single, then a cheap hit to Harrah to load the sacks. Man alive, will this craziness ever end? Big bad Horton pops to Patek on a hittable pitch, and the 8th inning does.

Darold Knowles comes in to get Brett with two aboard to end the K.C. 8th, and then Peachy becomes the good sport I knew he was. With three outs left in his Rangers' season, he shakes my hand, gives Dr. Sheila a big hug, and wishes us luck in the World Series as he backpedals toward the exit ramp, no doubt to catch a series of buses back to his home in Jewett. So he isn't around when Washington flies to Zdeb in left...when Sundberg strikes out... and when Bevacqua flies to Zdeb to put this American League pennant in my pocket. YES!!

TEX 001 040 000 – 5 15 0
K.C. 040 000 60x – 10 12 0
   W-Splittorff L-Ellis SV-Littell GWRBI-Wilson (1st of the year!)

American League FINAL Standings

x-Kansas City	87	67	.565	—
Texas	83	71	.539	4
Boston	82	72	.532	5
New York	81	73	.526	6
Baltimore	79	75	.513	8
Chicago	72	82	.468	15
Cleveland	69	85	.448	18
Minnesota	63	91	.409	24

National League FINAL Standings

x-Pittsburgh	89	65	.578	—
Los Angeles	86	68	.558	3
Cincinnati	85	69	.552	4
Philadelphia	84	70	.545	5
St. Louis	80	74	.519	9
Houston	72	82	.468	17
Montreal	61	93	.396	28
Chicago	59	95	.383	30

A Tale of Two Small Markets

Once upon a time, in a baseball galaxy far, far away...

PITTSBURGH—*Seamus here. The three of us are settled into adjoining rooms at the William Penn Hotel, the Steel City primed for Game One later today. The way these two teams battled all year, I'd be amazed if this thing didn't go six or seven games. Then again, that's why we roll the dice.*

Here's Lester and Dr. Sheila with breakdowns of their teams, followed by my swing votes. Keep it civil, you two.

FIRST BASE (Royals) John Mayberry. Great fielder, decent power, and could pop a few out to right at Three Rivers.

(Pirates) Willie Stargell, Bill Robinson. Mr. Stargell was hurt for much of the season, but recovered triumphantly on every occasion. The large individual they call "Pops" batted .280 with 24 home runs, 72 RBIs and a .988 OPS in just 296 at bats. Robinson, who plays first against left-handed pitching, finished at .300, with 27 home runs and 113 RBIs.

ADVANTAGE PITTSBURGH

SECOND BASE (Royals) Frank White. Not much of a hitter but a superb fielder and base runner, and can bail K.C. pitchers out of many innings.

(Pirates) Rennie Stennett. A .303 hitter and like Mr. Stargell, very clutchy when not sidelined. Nearly as good a fielder as White.

ADVANTAGE PITTSBURGH

SHORTSTOP (Royals) Freddie Patek. One of those scrappy, gritty, lunch pail kind of guys who plays the game the right way. Also steals lots of bases, has a small amount of pop in his bat and can turn double plays with White when he isn't making errors.

(Pirates) Frank Taveras. Also steals bases, occasionally hits, but fields ground balls like he's fighting off bees.

ADVANTAGE KANSAS CITY

THIRD BASE (Royals) George Brett. Fourth in the MVP voting at .330, with 21 homers, 103 RBIs and a .927 OPS. A bit sketchy around the bag, but does absolutely everything else.

(Pirates) Phil Garner. The individual they coin "Scrap Iron" struck 22 home runs and had the pennant-winning hit, is a fine base runner and better-than-average fielder. And I admire his fat rodent of a moustache.

ADVANTAGE KANSAS CITY

LEFT FIELD (Royals) Tom Poquette, Joe Zdeb. A workmanlike platoon arrangement. Both had some big hits, both fielded well enough to be out there.

(Pirates) Bill Robinson, Fernando Gonzalez. Another platoon, with frightening gloves but much more power.

—DRAW—

CENTER FIELD (Royals) Amos Otis. Best defender on either team. Amos batted just .246, but with 15 homers, great speed, and countless runs saved in the outfield.

(Pirates) Al Oliver. Far weaker with his glove, but .304, 24 home runs, 76 RBIs and a .852 OPS make him a decided threat.

—DRAW—

RIGHT FIELD (Royals) Al Cowens. The runner-up MVP. Slightly worse hitting stats than Brett (.323, 22 homers, 103 RBIs, .881 OPS) but incredibly clutch and a faultless outfielder with the same killer arm as Otis.

(Pirates) Dave Parker. My hero. .365, 32 homers, 133 RBIs, 1.021 OPS. Incredible arm, great base runner. Mr. Headley has to bring me a cool drink whenever he bats.

ADVANTAGE PITTSBURGH

CATCHER (Royals) Darrell Porter, John Wathan. Both hit equally well against righties and lefties, with Porter having the far better arm. Like Mayberry, Porter could be a power force in Pittsburgh.

(Pirates) Ed Ott, Duffy Dyer. Less of everything than the KC catchers possess, but just as many productive, timely hits.

ADVANTAGE KANSAS CITY

DESIGNATED HITTER (Royals) Hal McRae. Fearsome DH. A .308 average with 44 doubles, 17 homers, 97 RBIs and .874 OPS. Flattens left-handed pitching, which the Pirates have much of.

(Pirates) At press time, I have yet to be notified of any designated hitter plans for the middle three games, so I will refrain from offering any—COUGH COUGH Fregosi COUGH—suggestions.

ADVANTAGE KANSAS CITY

BENCH

(Royals) Cookie Rojas, Bob Heise, Pete LaCock, Dave Nelson, Joe Lahoud, Willie Wilson, Buck Martinez. LaCock and Lahoud offer a bit of batting average and power, and Wilson is the best pinch-runner on either team.

(Pirates) Jim Fregosi, Ken Macha, Omar Moreno, Jerry Hairston, Miguel Dilone, Bobby Tolan and yes it's true, Mario Mendoza. Fregosi is a walking machine, Moreno a late-inning defense fill-in, and Macha had a fine collection of meaningful hits toward the end. The rest of the specimens can be incinerated.

—DRAW—

STARTING PITCHING (Royals) Leonard, Splittorff, Colborn. One ace, two unpredictables.

(Pirates) Candelaria, Rooker, Kison. One ace, two unpredictables. Reuss could have been the third hurler but lost 16 games, had a grotesque WHIP of 1.56 and McRae really needs to face at least one right-hander.

—DRAW—

MIDDLE RELIEF

(Royals) Pattin, Hassler, Bird, Gura. Pattin and Hassler are good enough to start, and should bring much-needed depth to the Royal pen. Bird and Gura are bad enough to just watch.

(Pirates) Grant Jackson, Terry Forster, Odell Jones, Larry Demery. Mr. Jackson is perhaps the only reliable entry here, though Mr. Reuss can also be used in a desperate pinch.

ADVANTAGE KANSAS CITY

CLOSERS

(Royals) Steve Mingori, Mark Littell. Mingori is generally putrid (1.69 WHIP) but Littell is a nerve-wracking beast.

(Pirates) Kent Tekulve, Goose Gossage. One is a string bean, one a handlebarred specimen able to unleash utter fear.

ADVANTAGE PITTSBURGH

You guys done? Okay. I count a 5-4 advantage for the Royals, with four draws, which of course, probably won't mean squat. But I can hardly wait to find out.

Little Mac Attack

October 1, 1977

DR. GROSSINGER'S PRE-GAME

Has the concluding destination at the end of this long, long pennant road really arrived? It's a stunning October day in western Pennsylvania, a region I know rather well, and I feel more than confident that Mr. Candy Man Candelaria will stifle the Royal bats. Mr. Leonard will start for the visitors, a wonderful pitcher in his own right, but I know he is hittable...

PITTSBURGH—Lester reporting, and Dr. Sheila is right. It feels like early summer, and I'm thankful my grandstand seat is under a concrete overhang.

Whitey Herzog took a chance by putting Hal McRae out in left with his scary 4e17 rating, but against Pirate lefties it was a darn good risk.

And Hal rewards Whitey right out of the gate. After a leadoff Otis walk he smashes one over Oliver's head in left center and off the wall for a triple, scoring Amos with the first run of the Series. But that's nothing. After Otis strokes a two-out, two-run single off Candy Man in the 2nd, McRae bombs one over the boards in the 3rd and it's 4-0 K.C.!

The crowd might as well be at a wake in a library. The 23-8 Candelaria is getting racked. A Porter solo shot in the 6th ups the score to 5-zip. Meanwhile Leonard is solid smoke, throwing a 2-hit gem through seven innings. Fregosi crushes a pinch-hit homer to get the Bucs on the board in the 8th, but Mingori and Littell squirm us out of a bases loaded jam after the Fregosi shot, and with two on and two out in the 9th and a run in, thanks to a Patek boot, Littell gets the lethal Oliver on a fly to Zdeb to end the last threat and the game.

So Game One is a one-sided affair, but the late Pirate uprisings have me worried, and the very smashable Splittorff is on tap for Game Two.

Game 1
ROYALS 121 001 001 – 6 9 1
PIRATES 000 000 011 – 2 5 0
W-Leonard L-Candelaria HRS: McRae, Porter, Cowens, Fregosi GWRBI-McRae

Deja Blue All Over Again

October 2, 1977

DR. GROSSINGER'S PRE-GAME

I have a headache and chills that won't go away. The headache is called McRae, the chills are called Otis, and I did not like my ace pitcher being batted about in his own home. I did not like it not one little bit. Mr. Rooker needs to earn us a split before we go back on the road, and Seamus needs to warm my soup from the hotel kitchen before bringing it up to me...

PITTSBURGH–Should I be gloating? My Royals beat Candelaria in his own yard, rather easily, and after this one it's easy to believe we were facing tougher competition all year and weren't even realizing it.

But the Pirates are the ones doing themselves in. Against Splittorff, a guy who gives out hits like kandy korns on Halloween, Pittsburgh gets singles in the 1st from Stennett, Parker and Robinson, but Fernando Gonzalez raps into a quick White-Patek-Mayberry DP, to set the tone for the afternoon.

And that little man McRae is at it again. He singles in the 2nd, then hits a sac fly to put us ahead in the 3rd after Cowens bashes a long gap double to score Otis. Rooker bails himself out of that one with only two K.C. runs in, but completely loses it in the 4th. Patek and White open with doubles, and after Rooker whiffs, Otis smacks another double! Jackson is summoned and immediately hits Cowens, McRae singles in another with two gone and it's 5-1 us in a Pittsburgh minute.

It's hard rooting for the Royals surrounded here by black and yellow, and my cheers basically come out like chirps. And since when did Splittorff decide to start pitching? He scatters six singles and one measly run through the first six innings, before Oliver doubles, Dyer singles him in and Taveras grounds into the expected 4-6-4 DP to kill the 7th.

Tekulve tries his luck and does pretty well in the 7th, but when Gossage takes the ball to a) get some work and b) pitch to McRae, Hal the Barbarian cranks one over the wall with his damn eyes closed. Through two games now, McRae has two homers, five RBIs, and triple slash totals of .883/1.000/2.167, for an OPS of 3.167. And the Pirates haven't hit one fielding chart ball in his direction.

Anyway, Marty Pattin throws an inning and a third of hitless relief after the Bucs get a leadoff Stennett single in the 8th and third DP of the game, this one off Garner's bat, before Stargell flies out with two aboard to end the game, the second day in a row the Pirates strand the tying run in the on-deck circle.

A change of venue can only help them—and a new handful of dice.

Game 2
ROYALS 100 300 010 – 6 13 0
PIRATES 000 000 100 – 2 10 0
W-Splittorff L-Rooker SV-Pattin HR: McRae GWRBI-McRae

Goose Loose in K.C. Masterpiece
October 4, 1977

DR. GROSSINGER'S PRE-GAME
The Hotel Raphael is nice, though it looks very much like my room at the William Penn. Mr. Headley has been coming to my bedside quite often now with a thermometer and World Series updates, and I have an odd feeling that my Pirates are going to rebound. Like they did that one magical year for my mother. Hopefully I'll be well enough to join Lester at one of the games soon…

KANSAS CITY–It's a crisp October day here in western Missouri, and all 40+ thousand of us are ready to continue this World Series party. Bruce Kison was nothing short of dreadful in his last two starts of the year, and come to think of it, the Pirates have been outscored 36-11 in their last four games.

So that's why I'm not worried when Parker hits a solo rope over the fence with two outs in the 1st. My team has that same thang going that helped them start out the season 16-4. Sure enough, Porter rips a double off Kison in the 2nd, Mayberry puts one airborne, and we're up 2-1 in a flash. Make that 4-1 on a Poquette single, Cowens single, Brett double and McRae (him again) sac fly in the 3rd.

Kison gets out of two straight gnarly jams following that, but Colborn has the Pirates' number. He puts down twelve of them in a row until Fregosi dunks a single into center in the 7th. But it just never feels like the Royals are in trouble.

But they are, Sheila. They are. It starts so innocent-like, with a Garner triple and Taveras sac fly beginning the 8th. But then Patek, who's had fielding issues since April, boots a Stennett roller to bring up Al Oliver. Oliver scoops Colborn's first pitch deep into the bleachers and we are tied 4-4!

No one can believe it, not even the Pirates, who take no chances by bring Goose Gossage in with one gone in the 8th. After they go out in order in the top of the 9th, Taveras starts the 10th with a deep double to right center. A grounder gets him to third, and after Mingori comes on to face the three tough lefties, Oliver walks. Cobra fans, though, Stargell lines to White who makes a lunging grab, and we're out of the 10th.

Meantime Gossage is pumping out his goose eggs. Gives up a single and walk last of the 11th but then gets White and Poquette. And whiffs Brett and McRae to end the 12th.

Then it's the 13th. Why is it always the 13th? Oliver leads with a walk. Stargell singles him to third with one out and Littell comes on...to walk Robinson and load the bases. Fregosi then pops a fly out to Poquette, Oliver tags and scores and the Bucs are up 5-4!

Gossage isn't through making us all crazy, though. Working in his fifth inning (there's no way he can pitch tomorrow, and may not pitch in Game 5), Porter leads with a single, Wilson runs and gets bunted over, and Mayberry walks. But Goose bears down, honks out Patek and pinch-hitter Lahoud and that gosh damned jolly roger is finally raised.

Tomorrow it's a re-match of aces, Candelaria and Leonard, Pittsburgh trying to notch this spectacle at two games apiece, and standing room only seats are already on sale.

Game 3
PIRATES 100 000 030 000 1 – 5 8 0
ROYALS 022 000 000 000 0 – 4 9 1
W-Gossage L-Mingori HRS: Parker, Oliver, Mayberry GWRBI-Fregosi

Awed, then Shocked
October 5, 1977

DR. GROSSINGER'S PRE-GAME
I had a morning free of headaches, so Mr. Headley got me out of bed and dressed and out into the sweet October air. It was good to be going back to a baseball park, and it made me think Pittsburgh winning that thrilling Game 3 boosted my health along with my spirits...

KANSAS CITY–John Candelaria simply has to pitch better today; he could not have performed worse than he did in the Series opener. And here's Oliver with a slicing one-out double to get my men off the map in the 1st. Parker singles him home and just like that my club is ahead. How could I have entombed myself in those hotel beds, wallowing in self-pity when we won 89 games this season against grueling opposition? Sometimes I believe I have no business being a psychiatrist.

Otis singles to start the first Royals inning, but Candelaria takes over from there, setting down the next eleven batters. In the 4th, a Parker walk, Robinson single and scoring force in front of the plate by Fregosi makes it 2-0, and the sun shining on my grandstanded face feels all the warmer.

Then a cloud passes overhead, and Hal McRae strikes a homer up on the grassy embankment that resembles a golf ball leaving a 3-iron. But my Pirates answer back in the 5th, when Taveras gets hit on the shoulder, steals second, advances on Wathan's throwing error and scores on a sacrifice fly by Stennett.

Once again, Candelaria is the lord and master, giving up just two walks in the 7th and nothing else until the 9th. Those that believe in omens, however, truly find their calling card in the 8th. Oliver and Parker open with singles to put Pirates at the corners. But Leonard strikes out Willie Stargell for the fourth straight time. Clearly, Mr Stargell is suffering from acute overswinging, and I will text him later to suggest a long pre-game batting cage treatment tomorrow—assuming he knows what a text is. Regardless, Robinson also fans, Fregosi weakly grounds out and a chance to increase the advantage has been self-jettisoned.

On to the last of the 9th now, Candelaria still with a 2-hitter, the proper defensive alignment in place for Pittsburgh. Royals fans are silent around me, with Lester quieter than all of them.

And Otis leads with a line single. Now I have not been one to show panic, but I must confess to an odd glandular change in my underarms here. Cowens then singles Otis to third. I am suddenly numb. George Brett strolls to the plate, and all I can think about is his obvious handicap in having to fact the toughest lefty in the National League.

Except Brett then hits the ball so hard and so far to left-center that the crack of the bat makes me jump. Oliver and Moreno give chase but the ball hits the top of the fence, bounds away and seconds later Brett is on third and the game is tied! Tekulve is sent in to face Hal McRae, but I am again drowning in despair. Even after Mr. McRae lines to shortstop, because here is Darrell Porter to bat for Wathan, and there goes the first pitch out to Moreno. He backpedals a step, snags it and fires plateward, but Brett beats the ball by inches and the stands explode around me.

I need to go. Mr Headley? Seamus! Back to the hotel...NOW please...
LESTER'S POST-GAME ANALYSIS
Royals up 3-1 with a chance to win it at home tomorrow! Woo-hoo!!

Game 4
PIRATES 100 110 000 – 3 7 0
ROYALS 000 100 003 – 4 4 1
   W-Leonard L-Candelaria HR: McRae GWRBI-Porter

A Dreamy Fall

October 6, 1977

DR. GROSSINGER'S PRE-GAME

After yesterday's devastating loss, I have taken to my hotel bed again. Mr. Headley has no choice but to wait on me, for all I can do is lie here and dream of past Pirate heroics. My long departed mother has filled my head with all of the ones I was too young to remember. See, when my father died in World War II, and she re-married and changed her name from Spanelli to Grossinger, that was when she started putting those scrapbooks together...

KANSAS CITY—Lester here, and this is it, friends. Can't expect to win every game we play back at Three Rivers right? Splittorff was just fine in his first start, but today he's in trouble right away, thanks to a Patek error in the 1st, a Parker single and sac fly by Robinson. Followed by an Oliver single, Taveras double and Duffy Dyer single in the 2nd to put us down 2-0.

Little Freddie makes quick and serious amends, though, lining one into the left field bleachers with two aboard in the last of the 2nd and hey! We're on top 3-2!

Little did I think that's the last we'd be heard from, while the Pirates just tear Splittorff, Gura, and Pattin apart for a total of 16 hits. Rooker's the one with all the stuff, scattering just three hits through seven and a third after Patek's blast. The true low comes in the 4th, when Mayberry leads with a single and takes second on a Garner boot. With one gone, White hits one out to center but John forgets there's only one out, strays off second base and gets himself tagged out.

I know Dr. Sheila's almost comatose again, but after this depressing, no-drama fifth game I could slip into that bed right beside her. Well, you know what I mean.

So it's back to Pittsburgh on the Ball Nut Zipline, to put an end to this season once and for all. Can't say I'm all that worried, but the Pirates are no strangers to coming back from 3-1 deficits. Try 1971. Or two years from now.

Game 5
PIRATES 112 001 101 – 7 16 1
ROYALS 030 000 000 – 3 9 2
   W-Rooker L-Splittorff SV-Tekulve HR: Patek GWRBI-Dyer

Reuss-o-Rooter!
October 8, 1977

DR. GROSSINGER'S PRE-GAME
They had the sixth game on in the hotel today, and I sat in the William Penn lobby with the other guests to watch. Needless to say, I was transported. Mr. Headley wants me back at Three Rivers with him tomorrow, and says there will be no discussing the matter. I'm weakening slowly, but suppose I can handle another few hours of fresh air. Mr. Headley really has turned out to be a gentleman of his word...

KANSAS CITY–Jerry Reuss? Are you kidding me? I guess any mediocre pitcher's capable of a great game; even Ray Burris won three times this year. It was a shrewd move by Chuck Tanner to dump Bruce Kison for him, but a smart one. Three Rivers helps the lefty power and Kison gives up practically nothing to lefties but power. Still, though...

Patek boots the first ball the Pirates hit in the bottom of the 1st for another error, his fourth of the Series, it turns into a Stargell sac fly and it's all downhill from there.

Even though the Royals had runners falling out of the trees. A leadoff triple by McRae in the 2nd and they don't score. Singles by Cowens and Brett to open the 4th and they don't score. Two Taveras errors in the 8th and they do nothing with them, before a hit batter and walk in the 9th are left out to dry.

Meanwhile, Colborn gets raked in the 3rd for two singles, a double and Garner triple when McRae mistakes the rising liner for a badminton birdie and it shoots over his head in left to score two runs. Garner, who by the way is a crappy 2-for-22 when the game begins, crushes an Andy Hassler pitch for a solo jack in the 6th to pretty much entomb all Kansas City hope.

Reuss goes the distance until he hits Mayberry to start the 9th, gets a monstrous ovation from the over 50,000 here, but Tekulve gives Gossage his third straight day off after the Goose's five-inning stint in Game 3. Kent whiffs

Patek, gets Poquette on a foul out, and after walking Joe Lahoud, retires Otis on a lazy fly to tie this sucker up at three games apiece.

Game 6
ROYALS 000 000 000 – 0 5 1
PIRATES 103 001 00x – 5 10 3
  W-Reuss L-Colborn HR: Garner GWRBI-Stargell

All Good Things Must...
October 9, 1977

PITTSBURGH—Seamus reporting, because Lester is off drinking pints of Dunkelweizen at Max's Allegheny Tavern with both of the other Royals fans who showed up at Three Rivers, while I'm here by Doc Sheila's bed watching the poor girl vanish into the sheets.

It was a pretty anti-climactic seventh game, as far as seventh games go, but because it WAS a seventh game in the first place, I think I'll just shut up and let Red Barber call every inch of the action. Got this right off his broadcast on the Olde Tyme Radio Network today and wrote it down as fast as I could. If there's one thing I learned in my years with the CIA it's shorthand...

KC LINEUP: Otis CF, Cowens RF, Brett 3B, McRae LF, Porter C, Wathan 1B, Patek SS, White 2B, Leonard P

PIT LINEUP: Stennett 2B, Oliver CF, Parker RF, Stargell 1B, Robinson LF, Ott C, Garner 3B, Taveras SS, Candelaria P

Howdy folks, this is Red Barber, speaking to you from a packed-as-punch Three Rivers Stadium, for Game 7 of the Ball Nuts World Series...One more time it'll be Leonard for the Kansas Citians, and Candelaria for the Pittsburghers. Will the third time be the charm for the Candy Man?

A big change in the Royals lineup finds John Wathan for some extra batting average against the lefty Candelaria...John Mayberry's a paltry 4-for-23 so far, and can always go in for defense later on...Every reliever is available to go...

Pretty amazing that after 157 games for each team, it can all come down to this one big simmering pot roast...

Anyway, here's Amos Otis stepping into the box...Candelaria winds and gets him on strikes! That was sure quick...Cowens now...flies out to Parker in right, two gone...George Brett up there, only at .259 but with some big hits...

And he SINGLES! And here's Hal McRae, 7-for-21 with all kinds of production...Candy Man had no answer for him in Game 1...and there's a HIGH FLY BALL—deep to left...Robinson back and it is GONE for a HOME RUN! Hooboy, right out of the starting gate and it's 2-0 Royals! Porter flies out to right to end the top of the 1st but this black and yellow nest is a-buzzing...

Leonard against Stennett to lead off the Pirate half of the 1st and there's strike three!...Oliver sails one out to McRae, looking a bit wobbly again...but this time he makes the catch for the second out. Herzog knows he's taking a risk with McRae out there, but oh that offense of his...Parker now, a ferocious 12-for-25 in the Series...grounds to Patek and that's the first inning, with the score **KC 2-2-0, PIT 0-0-0**

Here's John Wathan, the second game he's started...the other at catcher... and he grounds to short, one away...Patek fouls to Mr. Ott...White is gone on strikes and we go to the bottom of the 2nd.

Willie Stargell...had a fine Game 6 with a sac fly and double, but he is out on swinging strike three!...Roninson with a hard liner—but right to Brett at third...Ott SINGLES sharply up the middle for the first Pirate hit...Here's Garner, also with a fine Game 6...triple and homer...hits one out to Otis here, who puts it away. After two innings, folks, it's **KC 2-2-0, PIT 0-1-0**

Leonard starts the 3rd...with an easy little pop to Taveras...Otis grounds it back to Candy, out number two...Cowens grounds to short for a 1-2-3.

Taveras rips a SINGLE to right to open the last of the 2nd...Pirate fans try to get it going...clapping in rhythm to some soul music number...Candelaria bats, a very decent hitter and a lefty to boot...But he grounds one to Patek, who flips to White and on to first for a double play...That sure hurt...And Stennett flies out to end the inning. After three now, it's **KC 2-2-0, PIT 0-2-0**

Brett leads off the 4th, singled his first time...Grounds one to Taveras for out number one...And here's that little big man McRae! Starting to boo him more now...sign of respect...but McRae answers back with a LINE SHOT to deep right-center, bounding around out there—and McRae into third with a sizzle of a TRIPLE! I'll tell ya, he is putting on a Clemente-esque performance in this Series. 9-for-23 now...And Porter strokes a SINGLE into right, 3-0 Kansas City as McRae SCORES!...Bullpen's up for the Pirates early...Wathan grounds one through into left for another SINGLE, Porter hustling and gets to third...Pitching coach Larry Sherry is out...Patek due at the plate...Candy throws to Freddie and Patek BOMBS it deep to left, off the wall for a double as Porter SCORES! 4-0 Royals!

Four straight hits and that is going to be it for Candelaria. Tanner not messing around and is bringing in Goose Gossage...Big man hasn't pitched since Game 3 and with Leonard out there, the Bucs certainly can't afford to slide down the laundry chute any further...Infield comes up for White, who grounds to short and the runners hold at second and third...Leonard at the plate... but there's a WILD PITCH—right past Ott and here comes Wathan with run number five! Leonard bounces to third but this was one upside down disaster cake! 5-0 Kansas City as we go to the last of the 4th...

Oliver to lead off for Pittsburgh here, after getting hit with a pretty large mallet...Al's at .440 for the series but I'm sure he doesn't care a crumb.... Grounds out to first and there's one gone...Parker lines a SINGLE into center...Stargell again, whiffed against Leonard his last five times...And he does it again, strike three! Boy o boychick...Robinson SINGLES, though, Parker over to third base...Here's Ed Ott...grounds one to Patek, who KICKS IT AWAY! Parker SCORES and the Buccos are on the board the cheap way! Error number 5 on Patek for the Series...Garner stands in...Crowd's getting all hot and loud again...but Phil grounds to Patek who steps on the bag to end the inning...After four innings now, it's **KC 5-6-1, PIT 1-4-0**

Gossage blows away Otis on strikes to begin the 5th...Cowens is gone in the same fashion...Brett SINGLES though with two away, and guess who's up...Harold Abraham McRae of Avon, Florida...32 years young...personally owned Candelaria in this Series but now he faces the Goose...and it doesn't matter as he WHACKS one down the left field line, pulls into second with a DOUBLE, as Brett SCORES all the way from first...and McRae is one measly single away from the cycle, folks! More important, it's 6-1 Royals now...Porter pops to Stennett, for the inning.

Taveras grounds to White...Pinch-hitter for Gossage here, gotta get something going...and it's Ken Macha, utility fella...and he lines to third...Stennett bounces to first, Leonard covers, and after five innings, it's now **KC 6-8-1, PIT 1-4-0**

Tekulve the new hurler for Pittsburgh...Which means Mayberry will bat for Wathan, and will surely go afield...flies to Parker for the first out of the 6th... Patek nearly homered last time...grounds to short this time...White with a broken bat SINGLE into left...Leonard fans and that's that.

Oliver takes a leadoff WALK in the last of the 6th...Pirates down by a big five...Parker at the plate, and there's a WILD PITCH by Leonard...Oliver up to second...and here's ANOTHER WILD PITCH, Oliver to third! Dennis just shaking his curly top out there...Parker LINES A SHOT—deep in the right field gap for a clean DOUBLE and it's 6-2! Boy that Cobra can sting. 14-for-28 now, an even .500...Look out, here's Stargell...and would you believe he's out on strikes again?? Seven straight times to Mr. Leonard! Robinson grounds to short...Ott flies to right. After six it's **KC 6-9-1, PIT 2-5-0**, but it probably should be closer.

Seventh inning now, and they're getting as nervous as squirrels in autumn around here. Four runs off Leonard in three innings won't be the easiest thing to pull off, y'know…Amos Otis with a LINE SHOT into left center, skipping it's merry way to the wall! He's around second, into third with another Royal TRIPLE! Infield's all the way up for Cowens, who's been quiet lately…Tekulve delivers, and it's strike three called!…One away to George Brett, 2-for-3…and Brett BLASTS ONE, last seen heading for the upper deck in three seconds for a long HOME RUN and 8-2 Kansas City lead! Good gracious golly…won't see Brett hit a ball that hard until he faces Goose Gossage three years from now…McRae up there, needing just a single for a cycle…he grounds to second and the crowd boos him. Well, that figures…Porter with a fly to center to end the top of the 7th.

Tell ya what, that moon-skipper by Brett just about took the starch out of this crowd…Garner with an easy grounder to third, one away…Taveras gets HIT BY A PITCH…Wouldn't be surprised if he just stuck his rib cage out there…Fregosi now to hit for Tekulve…But Jim grounds to second, Taveras advancing…Stennett lines to third and that's the 7th, folks. **KC 8-11-1, PIT 2-5-0**

Mayberry starts the 8th, and fouls out to third…Patek with a SINGLE, hit no. 12 for the Royals…and Freddie ROBS second base without a throw! Oooh boy, stealing a base up by six? Not advised…White pops to short…and here's Leonard, getting a big hand by the enemy fans…Ain't that nice? He grounds out to short, and gets an even bigger hand. 8-2 Royals to the last of the 8th.

Six outs left for the Pirates to come alive. Mark Littell waiting in the wings if needed…Oliver's first, 0-for-2 officially…and he dribbles one out in front of Porter, who fires to first…Dave Parker now, 2-for-3, and he looks at called strike three! And here's Willie! Leonard has punched his clock seven times in a row between this contest and the fourth one…AND DOES IT AGAIN on a windmill swing! Two yellow and black sombreros for Mr. Stargell in this Series…After eight innings, folks, it's looking grim in Steeltown, **KC 8-12-1, PIT 2-5-0**

Top of nine…the witching hour around here…and Otis with a line SINGLE off new pitcher Grant Jackson…Cowens whiffs again, his third…And here's Brett with another SMASH down the right field line! Cowens around third, Brett into second with a DOUBLE and it's 9-2!

Brett 4-for-5 in his climactic game…Jackson won't mess with McRae at all, as he throws four wide ones to put him on…He'll face Porter instead… But Porter SINGLES up the middle! Brett scores and they're in double digits, folks!…Mayberry with a little foul pop for the second out…Patek WALKS, taking all four pitches under his little chin, and they're loaded up…Bruce Kison will come on to face Frank White...Kison got bumped from yesterday's start for Reuss, and I guess that was a good thing...and he gets White on a pop to center. Here we go to the last of the 9th!

Dennis Leonard going for a complete game here, and why the heck not? Got himself an 8-run lead...He'll face Robinson, Ott, and Garner....Here's Robinson...the crowd standing, for the lack of anything better to do at this point...and Robinson SINGLES, a bullet into left!...Well, that gets the home folks jumping a bit...These Pirates came from behind to win 36 times, second in the league to Philly's 44...Got a long hike up a rocky ravine here, though...Ed Ott, 1-for-3 on the day...and Leonard strikes him out! That's no. 7 for Dennis, 4 of them Pops...Garner to the plate now...zero-for-3 after that big Game 6...and he skies one out to left, where Hal McRae, left out there for his heroics, no doubt...makes the catch for out number two. And the Ball Nuts baseball season is one out away from crowning a champ...Batter will be Frank Taveras...

Leonard shakes off a sign or two...glances over at Robinson on first...Third base coach Alex Monchak claps his hands at Taveras...hoping to get some more business down there..and here's Leonard's pitch...

Hit on a line out to left...McRae races back five yards, snags the ball and the KANSAS CITY ROYALS ARE YOUR '77 BALL NUTS WORLD CHAMPIONS!!

They're all out on the field now, mobbing Leonard...Couple of young Royal fans are out of the stands, pounding Brett on the back, shaking Porter's hand...As Walt Whitman may have said, they came to play this sunny day and made some hay! And Leonard beats the Candy Man all three times they meet...Not only that, but cleanup Pirate Wilver Stargell goes a combined 1-12 against Leonard with nine big whiffs...

But how about that Hal McRae? 10-for-25, with 1 double, 3 triples, 4 homers, 10 RBIs, and a 1.679 OPS, whatever in tarnation that thing is...Looks like he and Leonard will be the co-MVPs of this classic....

Anyway, thanks for following along, folks! This is Red Barber, saying goodnight, and have a nice, short rest of your winter!

Game 7
ROYALS 200 310 202 – 10 15 1
PIRATES 000 101 000 – 2 6 0
W-Leonard L-Candelaria HRS: McRae, Brett GWRBI-McRae (third of the series)

Season Finale
October 11, 1977

LOCAL LADY LEAVES LIT LEGACY
By Maggie Finch
Squallpocket Honker Lifestyles Editor

Sheila Grossinger was never one to go quietly. The 86-year-old former psychologist and Maine native, bedridden with acute dementia for nearly twenty years at the Squallpocket Acres Nursing Home, passed away Wednesday but left behind a most rare gift for her family.

"It's a literary find, is what it is," says Carlton "Buzzgip" Grossinger, one of her two surviving sons.

While cleaning Ms. Grossinger's Squallpocket room after she departed, a young orderly named Fred Washington found an ornate, leather-bound book wedged under the mattress and fished it out. Inside were over 200 handwritten pages, documenting a fictitious cross-country "time travel journey" in which Ms. Grossinger and a host of others followed the 1977 baseball season. Needless to say, Washington quickly drove it over to a grateful Carlton at the local trailer park where the local stereo salesman lives with his wife and son.

"Sheila was a model resident," says Seamus M. Headley, Director of Operations for the nursing home, "Chirpy, polite, participated in the group activities the best she could. Who would have thought she had so much imagination inside her?"

Ms. Grossinger, who spent most of her teenage years in McKeesport, Pennsylvania, was not only a noted "dream psychologist" in her time, but a diehard Pittsburgh Pirates fan. According to Headley, her dementia was diagnosed in 1992, following an especially traumatic Pirate playoff loss to Atlanta, and from then on required special care.

Ms. Grossinger's love of baseball apparently ran in the family. Her natural father, Vincenzo Spanelli, was an avid Phillies fan, and even served as the club's batboy for part of 1924. When Spanelli lost his life at Salerno during World War II's Italian campaign, his daughter took up the sport in a big way.

"You could tell she was into it," says Amy Gulliver, Squallpocket's chief nurse, "She wouldn't say much when games were on in the common room, but she would just stare at that screen like it was the King James Bible."

"I bet with her on games all the time," says Sherman Wayman, another elderly resident, "and I always lost. Hope to hell she didn't put that in her journal thing."

Carlton Grossinger says he has no immediate plans to try and have the journal published, but wouldn't rule it out. Ms. Grossinger's other surviving son, Lester Grossinger of Davenport, IA, was in Las Vegas attending the John Lennon and the Fab Experience concert, and could not be reached for comment.

"We'll certainly miss her around here," Headley continues, "but more than anything, we're glad she was able to finish out her 'season' before she left us, and has left her two boys something to cherish." Carlton, who admits to having only a passing interest in the sport, says he might even take up a dice simulation game to replay 1977 for himself sometime soon.

"It's hard to explain why," he tells me, "but I feel like I need to keep this going."

The End

ABOUT THE AUTHOR

JEFF POLMAN is a journalist, screenwriter, and baseball blogger. He has written for the *Boston Phoenix, Huffington Post, Baseball Prospectus, Hardball Times, Seamheads, ChicagoSide Sports,* ESPN's *SweetSpot Network,* and other Web sites. *Ball Nuts* was adapted from *Play That Funky Baseball,* the second of his five fictional replay blogs, which also include *1924 and You Are There!, The Bragging Rights League, Mysteryball '58* and his latest, *Dear Hank.* He is a lifelong Red Sox fan and resides with his wife and son in Culver City, CA.